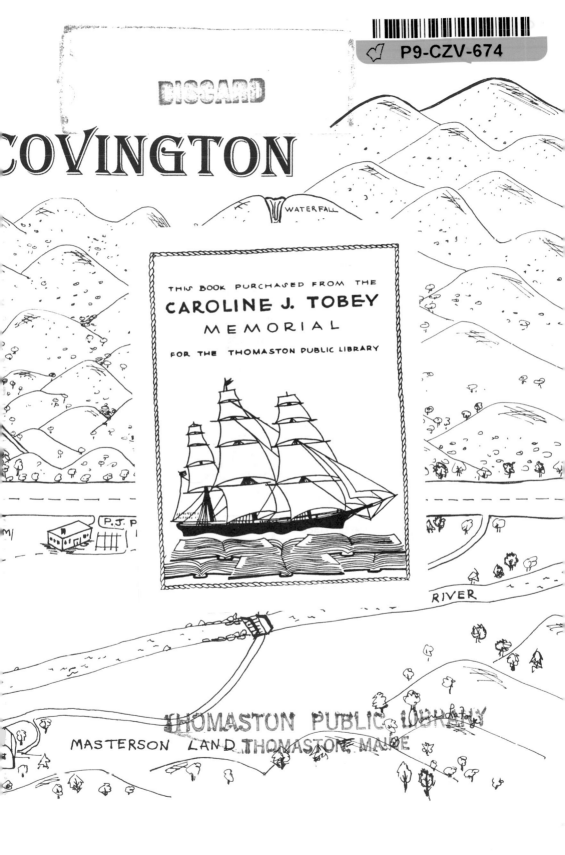

COVINGTON

WATERFALL

THIS BOOK PURCHASED FROM THE
CAROLINE J. TOBEY
MEMORIAL
FOR THE THOMASTON PUBLIC LIBRARY

RIVER

DISCARD

P9-CZV-674

THOMASTON PUBLIC LIBRARY
THOMASTON, MAINE

MASTERSON LAND

From the Heart of

Covington

THOMASTON PUBLIC LIBRARY
THOMASTON, MAINE

Also by Joan Medlicott

The Gardens of Covington
The Ladies of Covington Send Their Love

From the Heart
of
Covington

Joan Medlicott

Thomas Dunne Books
St. Martin's Press ≈ *New York*

*Fic
Med*

55751

THOMAS DUNNE BOOKS.
An imprint of St. Martin's Press.

FROM THE HEART OF COVINGTON. Copyright © 2002 by Joan Medlicott.
All rights reserved. Printed in the United States of America. No part of this
book may be used or reproduced in any manner whatsoever without written
permission except in the case of brief quotations embodied in critical
articles or reviews. For information, address St. Martin's Press,
175 Fifth Avenue, New York, N.Y. 10010.

www.stmartins.com

Illustrations copyright © 2002 by Dianne LaForge

Library of Congress Cataloging-in-Publication Data

Medlicott, Joan A. (Joan Avna)
    From the heart of Covington / Joan Medlicott.—1st ed.
        p. cm.
    ISBN 0-312-28555-8
    1. Aged women—Fiction. 2. Female friendship—Fiction. 3. North
Carolina—Fiction. 4. Boardinghouses—Fiction. 5. Retirees—Fiction.
I. Title.

PS3563.E246 F73 2002
813'.54—dc21

                                                        2001058487

First Edition: May 2002

10 9 8 7 6 5 4 3 2 1

To my husband, C. Eben, and children,
Damon and Karen, David and Sharon, Paula, Polly, Eben and Sandi

9-02 B&T $24.95

From the Heart of

Covington

1

In the Blink of an Eye

Butterflies drank deeply from the faces of red salvia and purple verbena in Hannah's garden. Along the edges of the stream, vibrant orange daylilies bobbed and waved in a brisk summer breeze. Across the road from the ladies' farmhouse, open fields were dappled with George Maxwell's dairy cows. With a light heart and an all's-wells-with-the-world feeling, Grace noted all this as she drove slowly down Cove Road and turned into the driveway of the home she shared with Hannah and Amelia. Immediately her mood changed.

"What's wrong, Hannah?" Grace asked, as she hurried from her car toward the front porch of their farmhouse where Hannah Parrish sat in her white wicker rocking chair staring into space. "You look distraught."

Tears trailed down Hannah's face. She lifted her hand to wipe them away and dropped it back into her lap. "It's my daughter Laura. She's been badly hurt."

Grace was beside her in a moment, kneeling, her hands on Hannah's knees, and looking up into her friend's anguished face. "Laura's been hurt? How? Where? Tell me." She shook Hannah's leg. "Talk to me, Hannah. Tell me what's happened."

For a long moment Hannah sat without speaking, then she turned stricken eyes to Grace. "A Dr. Romano called from Puerto

1

Rico. He said there'd been a hurricane, and Captain Marvin's boat . . . his ketch . . . dashed to bits on a reef. Laura's been injured." Hannah, reliably cool and collected, stoic, and not given to tears or drama, lowered her head and cupped her chin to stop its quivering. After a moment, she rallied and looked at Grace. "They never found Captain Marvin." Hannah buried her face in her hands. Her shoulders shook.

Getting up off her knees, Grace's arms circled Hannah's broad shoulders. Her fingers brushed Hannah's thick salt-and-pepper hair. "I'm so sorry." She had a million questions. What had happened? Why were they on a boat in a hurricane? How badly was Laura hurt? "Where's Laura now?"

"Hospital in Puerto Rico. Broken leg, all banged up, stitches. They had to remove her spleen."

"Have you spoken to her?"

"Not yet. Been sitting here waiting for you or Amelia to come home." Then Hannah turned troubled eyes to Grace. "That boat was Laura's home. She's lost everything. She's got no place to go from the hospital but here."

"Of course, but how will she get here?"

"By ambulance plane. Seems people in the Caribbean buy ambulance plane insurance."

"Ambulance plane." Grace sat heavily in her rocker alongside Hannah. "When can she travel, did they say?"

Hannah dug in a pocket of her slacks and pulled out a small slip of paper. "She's being discharged in five days." Hannah sounded exhausted. She muttered something Grace did not catch, shifted her hips in the rocker, and heaved a deep sigh. Several moments passed in silence. "That cold I had, more like a flu, has left me feeling emotionally as well as physically weak. I need time to digest this whole thing. Never been close to Laura. Haven't seen her in years. She was pretty, you know, prettier than her sister, Miranda, but hard to handle, rebellious. We seemed to grate on each other's nerves."

"That's in the past. Laura needs you now." Softly, Grace stroked Hannah's arm. "She needs you." Wisteria flowers hung like clusters

2

of lavender grapes from vines firmly established along the fretwork of the porch. Several papery petals fell into Hannah's lap. She lifted one, rubbed it between two fingers, then let it fall to the floor.

"I know." Her blue eyes sought Grace's. "It's been so many years. We're strangers. Don't know my own child. What will I say to her?" She rubbed her forehead with her hand. "Hope I'm up to the challenge. I'm not like you, Grace. I've never been good at taking care of sick people."

"I'm here for you, for Laura, and I'm sure Amelia will be too."

It was summer, glorious green and glowing summer, a trifle warm, but night temperatures were cool, in the low sixties, and comfortable. The ladies' farmhouse sat well back from Cove Road, beyond a long stretch of grassy lawn. In beds on either side of the gravel driveway, red roses had put on a striking display in May, while in June a stunning show of purple irises and mustard-yellow Stella d'Ore daylilies were followed by exquisitely formed tubular, purple Coventry bells rearing their heads behind the salvia, verbena, and white geraniums that filled the flower beds that ran the length of the porch on either side of the front steps.

Hannah's news weighted the lightness Grace had felt earlier. Summer was passing too fast. The Fourth of July celebration was now a pleasant memory. As usual, the fireworks in the small, family-filled park twenty-minutes away in Barnardsville had been intimate, spectacular, and fun. Sitting there watching the sky explode into bursts of color, Grace had thought how well things were going for all of them and how happy she was. Now she shook her head, feeling the uneasiness that lies at the heart of any transition. A blink of an eye, that's all it took for a pleasant, easygoing life to tumble like a shirt in a clothes dryer. Poor Laura. Grace had never met her. Neither had their housemate, Amelia, but if Laura needed to come home to her mother to recover, so be it. Grace would support Hannah in every way she could.

"It'll be all right, Hannah. We have the extra bedroom upstairs. If Laura needs to be downstairs, we'll convert the dining room for her, like we did when you had your hip replacement surgery."

"Seems so long ago, over two years," Hannah said. "You took such good care of me." Hannah gave Grace a grateful look. "I can always count on you, can't I, my friend?"

"Yes, you can." Grace squeezed Hannah's arm. "Three Musketeers. You said that once, when we were deciding to come down here to see the farmhouse, remember?"

"I remember," Hannah said. She looked deep into Grace's gentle brown eyes. "Oh, Grace, thank God we're not still living at Olive Pruitt's boarding house. Thank God Amelia inherited this farmhouse, and we had the guts to move from Pennsylvania down to North Carolina."

"And bless Amelia for so generously putting the deed into our three names," Grace said.

"Indeed. Now, I have a home my child can come to."

When Amelia returned from her photo shoot, her reaction was the same as Grace's. "*Mais oui*, Laura must come here." Her splendid sapphire eyes filled with concern.

"It won't be easy. Laura'll be on crutches for many weeks," Hannah said.

"So? We'll convert the dining room into a bedroom for her, like we did when you had surgery," Amelia said.

"Can't let you do that. We entertain a lot, and Grace loves to cook."

Grace waved a hand. "I can still cook, and if we have anyone over we'll set out a picnic right here on the porch. Who do we have over, anyhow? Mostly friends. They'll understand."

"It's settled, then," Amelia said. "Don't worry about anything, Hannah. Grace and I will see about having our dining room furniture stored."

Hannah nodded. It was hard for her to ask for or even to accept help, but she was learning. "Dr. Romano, Laura's doctor, said Laura's injuries are severe but not life threatening. She's bruised inside and out, stitches down her left arm, and a nasty gash and stitches across her cheek. He said she had the best plastic surgeon on the island, and she won't have visible scars."

4

Amelia's hand moved to her neck, where her burn scars were carefully concealed beneath one of her fine silk scarves.

Hannah's brow wrinkled. "When they told her about Captain Marvin being lost at sea, they say she screamed and screamed. They had to sedate her."

Amelia's eyes clouded, and her lips tightened. "I know how your daughter feels. Because of my burns, they didn't tell me for a long time that my Thomas had been killed when that car crashed into ours, and when they did, I went berserk." Amelia brought her hands to her throat. "*Mon Dieu*, I wanted to die. I tried to force open a window in the hospital to jump out. They had to restrain me. Imagine poor Laura, unable to get out of bed. What could she do but scream?" Tears banked in Amelia's eyes, and she looked away.

It was very quiet. No cars drove by on Cove Road. The wind had died down, and birds had ceased singing as if they too mourned Laura's losses.

"Laura's lucky to have you, Hannah, and someplace to go." Amelia looked at them with pain filled-eyes, and when she spoke, her voice was a mere whisper. "After they released me from the hospital, I had no one to go to, no place to go, no one to talk to, nothing." Pulling back her shoulders, Amelia tossed her head in a familiar gesture. "Well, *mes amies*, I'm going upstairs to shower. Mike and I are going to Asheville for dinner. He'll be picking me up soon. Anything I can do for Laura, let me know."

"Thanks, Amelia." But as Amelia closed the front door behind her, Hannah speculated that of the three of them, Amelia was the least likely to spend time with someone as sick and as miserable as Laura was bound to be. For many moments, Grace and Hannah sat silent. Then Hannah said, "Since Amelia's fling with that scoundrel Lance Lundquist ended, she's been consumed with her photography. Doubt she'll have the interest or time for Laura."

"Or," Grace replied, "perhaps she identifies with what Laura's going through."

Hannah's eyes clouded. "Can't believe this whole thing is happening. All those years Laura and Captain Marvin lived on that boat in Maine. Why did they pick up and move to the Caribbean? Why

5

a hurricane so early in the season? Storm Watch, on the weather channel, keeps saying that August and September, not July, are the worst months for hurricanes." Abruptly Hannah stopped the motion of her rocker. "How am I going to handle this, Grace? I'm a wreck already."

"Moment by moment, I imagine. You always handle things, Hannah. You'll see."

2

Coming to Covington

The ambulance attendants rolled the gurney into the dining room/bedroom the women had prepared for Laura. Sedated for her flight from Puerto Rico, Laura had no awareness of where she was. When she opened her eyes, it took many moments to take in the decor of the strange room with a chandelier hanging from its ceiling and walls covered with rose-colored toile wallpaper. Surprise followed, and confusion, at seeing the sad-looking woman sitting in a chair near her bed. So many years had passed since she had seen Hannah that, for a moment, Laura did not recognize her mother. "Mother?" she whispered. Shakily, Laura raised herself on her elbows. Her back, her side, everything hurt. Laura sank back on the pillows.

"Yes, Laura," was all Hannah could say.

Her mother's eyes were sad, her mouth grim with anxiety. Laura lay quiet and sought to orient herself. Could she have seen her own compressed eyelids, her lips clamped tight in the effort to shut off words, her anguished face, Laura would not have recognized herself. Had she been able to look into a mirror, she would have hastily turned away, for her smooth, clear skin had been chafed and blistered by sun and wind, and a scar, red and angry, ran across her lower cheek. Black-and-blue marks marred her forehead, and her wide-set blue eyes, which had gleamed with humor and curiosity, were dull now, without sparkle, and her full mouth—that Marvin called sensual and loved to kiss—drooped.

Laura felt a deep sense of helplessness, and a memory of being six years old and waking up from a nightmare all tangled in her sheet and screaming for her mother flooded her mind. "Mother," Laura said again.

"I'm here." Hannah choked back tears.

"My leg's broken." She felt like a child.

"Tibia, long bone below your knee. In a couple of weeks, the cast will be off. Remember the cast on your arm when you were ten?"

Laura nodded. She remembered the weight of the cast, the itching, her irritability, her relief when the doctor had sawed it off, her incredibly stiff arm, and the exercises she hated but had to do in order to regain mobility. It was déjà vu, to be tolerated. She remembered more. After a few days in the cast, her arm had not hurt. But her leg was different. It continued to hurt. Perhaps the cast was too tight. Laura clasped her chin to still its quivering. Pain shot down the length of her arm as the stitches pulled.

Silence filled the room. Words between them had been stingy and limited, always. Laura looked at her mother. The stern mouth that she remembered had softened and quivered slightly as if Hannah, too, struggled not to weep. The blue eyes, so like her own, had always seemed forbidding. The caring and worry in them now were obvious. The wide, hard hand, so often raised either to slap her or placed firmly across her teenage mouth to silence yet another smart aleck retort or arrogant argument, felt warm now and gentle as it held hers.

Laura closed her eyes. Marvin used to say, when she complained about Hannah, "Time, Laura. Time and understanding change things. Think what it must have been like for your mother dealing with a drunken husband staggering in at night, knocking over chairs, cursing. Why wouldn't your mother have been edgy, shrill, and angry? One day you must talk to her, find out who she really is, let her get to know you."

But now, talking to her mother was the last thing Laura wanted

8

to do. Memories of Marvin flooded her mind. Sitting with him on the deck of the *Maribow* at sunset, snorkeling the underwater trail around the coral reef at Truck Bay in St. John, and afterward, a native boy scampering up a coconut tree. The coconut water they drank that day from a hole the boy cut at one end of the coconut had been cool and tangy, and dribbled down their chins. The boy had laughed at them. The memory sundered her heart. How would she go on living without Marvin? Laura moaned.

"Can I do anything to make you more comfortable?" Hannah asked.

Touched by the attention and obvious concern, Laura replied, "No. Thanks. I'm fine." But, dispossessed of hope, an opaque pit of despair within her deepened, threatening to engulf her. Laura moaned again and closed her eyes.

Laura slept, for how long she did not know, but when she awakened, it was dark outside, and kitchen sounds—silverware clinking, dishes being stacked, a chair pushed back—were clearly audible. She needed to use the bathroom. "Mother," she called.

Immediately, Hannah appeared in the doorway. And when, leaning heavily on Hannah, Laura made it to the small powder room under the stairs, she found that the door must remain open nearly a foot to accommodate the stretch of her leg. Then, aided by her mother, she returned, exhausted, to her bed only to endure the ordeal of meeting her mother's housemates.

"I'm Grace Singleton. Just as soon as you're able, we've got a nice new wicker rocker out on the porch for you, with a hassock for your legs. The sunsets are wonderful." Grace fingered a bandanna tucked into the waistband of her skirt. She waved an arm about the room. "I hope you'll be comfortable. We thought it would be easier than having to go up and down stairs."

Laura could not recall her mother ever having had women friends, and yet here was this sweet-faced, slightly plump, soft-spoken little woman going on and on about how glad she was to see Laura and welcoming her with a gentle hug.

9

Laura looked around her more carefully then: big bed, night tables, good lights, mirror, dresser, a maroon recliner—she hated maroon—and those awful, sweet, lace curtains on the window. Laura nodded and wished that Grace, kind as she was, would go away, which moments later she did.

Grace's departure was followed by the entry of a pretty woman with magnificent sapphire eyes and a blue silk scarf wound about her neck who introduced herself as Amelia Declose. "*Bonjour,* Laura. I hope you'll be comfortable. Anything I can do for you, just ask." And then Amelia was off with a man named Mike who called to her from the porch.

"Mike was Amelia's photography instructor, and they've become good friends. He's like a member of our family," Hannah explained once they were gone. "Amelia's published a book of her photographs. It's lovely." Hannah pointed to a copy of Amelia's book *Memories and Mists: Mornings on the Blue Ridge* that lay on a table near Laura's bed.

Laura shrugged. Amelia struck Laura as flighty and somewhat affected, and what did Laura care who Mike was. She wanted to yell, "You want to do something for me, all of you? Bring back Marvin."

After years of living, working, sleeping in snug, small spaces on the *Maribow,* the room they had prepared for her seemed cavernous. Laura wanted to pull the walls closer, so she could reach out a hand and touch them. "Mother, do you think you could help me shove this bed closer to the wall?" she asked. "I'll try to get up."

"Try no such thing. I'll get Grace. Do it in a jiffy."

Moments later the two women removed one of the night tables and pushed the bed within a foot of the wall. "This close enough?" Grace asked.

Grace's voice was soft, warm, and mellifluous, and for a moment it soothed and comforted Laura. "Yes, it is, thank you."

✻

After dinner that night, and after Laura had taken a pill for pain and sleep, Grace joined Hannah in Hannah's bedroom. It was a cheerful room, painted a soft shade of green, and cozy with potted plants. "I'm worried about Laura," Hannah said. "So much to recover from, injuries, the loss of her home and all her belongings, Marvin."

"It'll take time," Grace said. "It always takes time. Caring people help. We'll all help her. Maybe in a few weeks I can introduce her to Emily. She's starting a new life here with Russell and Tyler."

"That's a good idea, Grace. But do you think that'll work, Emily just married and Laura having sustained such a loss?"

"I don't know. Maybe not, maybe in a few months."

"So how is Emily doing?" Hannah asked. "I've hardly seen them since their wedding in June."

"She's busy with a new house, new job, husband and stepson, as well as Bob, and me. But she's always bright-eyed and welcoming. I like her, Hannah. I'm glad Russell found a strong yet gentle woman like Emily."

"Will Laura like Emily, I wonder."

"I'm sure she will," Grace assured Hannah. She rose from the chair by the window. "I'm off to bed. Stop worrying now and get some sleep."

"I hope Amelia comes in quietly and doesn't disturb Laura."

"There you go worrying again. I'm the worrier in this household, remember. You're supposed to be the cool-headed one." With those words, Grace hugged Hannah and opened the door into the upstairs hall. She moved to the top of the stairs and peered down. A light shone from under the door to the dining room. Music from a small radio they had placed on Laura's night table drifted up to her. Regardless of how she assured Hannah, Grace knew that both Laura and Hannah could anticipate many worrisome and sleepless nights to come.

3

Harold Tate Falls Ill

Early one morning, several days after Laura's arrival, Grace was in the kitchen and grabbed the phone when it rang.

"Grace, is that you?" A woman's voice, familiar yet distorted by what, crying?

"Brenda? What's wrong?" Grace felt her heart beat faster. Why was Brenda weeping like this? Was someone hurt or sick? Brenda's mother, Millie, lived down in South Carolina. Had something happened to her? Or to one of Brenda's young grandsons? Grace's hand rested on her heart. Somehow, she knew that whatever Brenda would tell her would pain her. "Please," Grace said, "Brenda, take a breath and tell me what's the matter."

Brenda stifled her gasps. "It's Harold. He's been coughing a lot lately. I insisted that he go to the doctor." She stopped, blew her nose, then blurted out, "Lord, Grace, he's got cancer in his right lung."

Cancer. The dread word. "Oh, my God, no." Grace's hand fell from her chest and slid around her middle. She clenched her fist. The house was very still. Out on Cove Road, Grace watched a blue pickup zip past a black one on the narrow country road. Young drivers, she thought. Always in a hurry. For them, time can't go fast enough. She thought of her husband, Ted, his cancer, his surgery, debilitating chemotherapy. Less than a year later, he was gone. That was four, or was it five years ago?

"They're operating on Harold on Thursday." Brenda collected herself, the way she did when, as principal of Caster Elementary School, she addressed an assembly. "Harold said he'd promised to take you and Hannah over to Joyce Kilmer Wilderness. I wanted to let you know, he won't be . . . sorry, Grace. Harold always seemed so strong, so invincible." She was crying openly now.

Grace wanted to cry along with Brenda. She knew what lay ahead for the family, and she empathized. Grace waited for Brenda to grow calmer, then she said, "Brenda, that trip to Joyce Kilmer doesn't matter. It's Harold I care about. I am so sorry. Thursday, you said?"

"Yes. Hardly time to think. I'm scared, Grace."

"I'm sure you are. Is there anything I can do for you or Harold?"

"My mother's coming up from Greenville, and I have Molly here. You know how crazy she is about her dad. She's going to take some time off from teaching when he comes home from the hospital."

"Still, if there's anything, anything at all I can do, or Hannah, any of us."

"You all have your hands full with Hannah's daughter. How's she doing?"

"Well as could be expected. These things take time. Please let us know how Harold is, and when we can visit, and Brenda, we'll be praying for him."

"Thanks. He's in God's hands. Gotta go now, Grace."

Grace set the phone back on its cradle and stood for a moment watching wisps of steam sputter from the mouth of the kettle, knowing that any moment it would whistle, unaware that Hannah had come in, and Amelia, and behind them, Laura balancing on her crutches. They were all staring at her.

"You look as if you've seen a ghost," Amelia said.

Frowning, Grace turned to face them. "It's Harold. Very bad news. He's been diagnosed with lung cancer." She could see their faces tighten, their eyes fill with concern, then shift to an incipient fear.

"Harold, of all people, so fit looking," Amelia said.

"He's only fifty-seven," Grace said,

"That all?" Amelia asked. "He looks older."

"What do you expect, all those years as a farmer, the sun, wind," Hannah said brusquely.

"Who's Harold?" Laura hobbled into the kitchen and eased into a chair Hannah pulled out for her.

"Harold was my cousin Arthur Furrier's friend," Amelia said.

Grace said, "Arthur's the cousin Amelia inherited this place from. Harold was our first friend in Covington. He opened this house for us, and when we decided to repair it, he recommended reliable workmen. Covington's named for his family. They were the original settlers here back in the 1880s."

Amelia poured cornflakes into a bowl from a box Grace placed on the table and offered Laura the same. Laura shook her head but accepted a steaming cup of coffee from Grace.

"Harold says that years after the Civil War ended, it was so bad with marauders and carpetbaggers that his ancestor, Patrick Arless Covington, packed up his family and walked all the way from somewhere east of Raleigh until they arrived in this valley. He named the area Covington. In time most of their family migrated south to Georgia and Alabama, where it was warmer, to grow cotton. Harold's grandfather, Arless James, worked at timbering for a time and the family raised sheep, cattle, and later tobacco."

It was clear from the glazed look in Laura's eyes that this was more than she cared to know.

"Anyway," Amelia said, adding milk to her cereal, "I just hope he'll be okay."

"Chemo's tough. Ted was horribly sick," Grace said. "My husband," she explained to Laura, "passed away from cancer."

"I saw on TV that they've got new, less virulent drugs now." Amelia dipped her spoon into the bowl.

Laura pushed back her chair, stood, and with a grimace slipped her arms under the crutches. "I think I'll go lie down," she said and hobbled from the room.

"She's pretty unsteady on those things," Amelia said.

"Takes time to get used to crutches." Grace looked pensive. "I think I upset Laura, talking about Ted dying."

Hannah set Laura's cup in the sink. "Life must got on," she said.

Grace and Amelia finished breakfast in silence before Grace said, "Hannah, you look totally frazzled."

Hannah moved to the table, leaned across it, and lowered her voice. "Whatever I try to do for Laura, offer her a cup of tea, ask if she'd like the light off or on, she rebuffs me, politely of course."

They all lowered their voices. *"Mais oui.* She's depressed, and why not after all she's been through."

Hannah nodded. "Know how that feels."

"Depression's visited us all at one time or another." Grace's brows drew together over grave eyes. "And it takes so long to come out of it, you think you never will."

"Work. Staying busy is what always helped me," Hannah said.

"After my little girl, Caroline, died, and then Thomas died, I was immobilized, impossible for me to even decide what I would wear each day, much less go out and do anything. Without my breaking down, getting therapy, I would never have recovered," Amelia said.

"Good friends helped me when Ted was sick. They stayed with Ted, while others dragged me with them to the dry cleaner, to the bakery, to pick up their kids after school. And when he passed away," Grace said, "they hovered around me for months. They prodded me to get dressed, made me eat, took me to the movies."

"Lucky you, knowing all those people. We are the 'they' in this case, and we'll have to try to figure out what Laura needs," Amelia said.

Hannah looked from one to the other. Her eyes misted. "I appreciate everything you're doing, being so kind to Laura."

"What have I done?" Amelia shrugged. "I drop into her room from time to time to say hello, bring her a book, a few flowers."

For a time no one spoke, and then Hannah looked from one to the other. "I called Brenda yesterday. She gave me the name of an orthopedist in Asheville, a Dr. Harvey Gedlow. Laura's asked me to make an appointment for her with him. Would one of you go with us? I need another set of ears. Doctors make me nervous. I'm never sure what they've said."

"I'll go with you," Grace said.

"What's the problem?" Amelia asked.

Hannah frowned. "Incessant pain in her leg. Maybe the cast is too tight."

A horn tooted outside. "Oh, there's Mike. I'm off," Amelia said.

Grace turned to Hannah. "I feel that I ought to go down to the Tates'. "

"Let me change my clothes, and I'll walk down with you," Hannah said.

✳

A crisp breeze whipped Grace's skirt about her legs. Overhead gray clouds played hide-and-seek with the sun as she and Hannah walked down the road. At Cove Road Church, they stopped. Pastor Johnson stood by the entry door, his hand on the knob, seemingly undecided whether to enter or not.

"Going to the Tates'?" he asked. Bending slightly forward, his shoulders appeared more humped than stooped. Straggles of white hair fell over his forehead. "Terrible news, just terrible."

They nodded and waited, thinking that he might join them. "And how are you, Pastor?" Grace asked.

"Kind of you to inquire. Been fighting a cold. I've not had one that hung on this long. Ten days now."

"Hannah had a cold that sent her to her bed recently."

"You recovered all right?"

"I did," Hannah replied.

"You've decided me, then," he said, stepping closer to the church door. "When a man's facing surgery he doesn't need exposure to whatever it is I've got. I'll wait a few more days. Tell Harold, will you, that I'm praying for him."

"Be glad to do that," Hannah replied, moving off with Grace following.

✳

17

Harold and Brenda pressed close together on their porch swing. Harold's feet, in a quick kicking motion, propelled the swing back and forth; Brenda's shoes hung suspended a bit off the unpainted wooden porch floor. The severity of her shoulder-length auburn hair, pulled back and clipped with a large green barrette, accentuated the tightness and pain in her face. She clutched her husband's hand in hers and with the other waved the women toward them. "Come on up."

"How you feeling, Harold?" Hannah slipped into one of the ladder-back wooden rocking chairs that lined their porch.

"Bit of a shock, the news. Feelin' a trifle muddled in the head." Harold gave the swing a good shove, causing Brenda to jerk forward and back.

"More than muddled." Brenda adjusted herself in the swing. "You know men. They can't just come out and say they're scared out of their minds."

"Got to take what life dishes out," Harold said.

Grace relayed Pastor Johnson's message and that he was recovering from a cold.

They sat without speaking for a time. Cars passed. They all waved. "Who'd a thought it'd be me gettin' the cancer?" Harold muttered, rolling his head toward his cousin Frank Craine's car. "He smokes three packs a day, more than I ever did."

"Doctor says Harold will have to have chemotherapy and maybe radiation. But he's going to be just fine." Brenda reached up and kissed her husband's check. "I know you will be, darling."

Grace knew someone who had recovered fully after losing a lung, and she told Harold that. "So will you," she said.

"Your mouth to God's ears." Harold smiled sadly.

Later when they said good-bye, Brenda reached for their hands and squeezed hard. "Bless you for stopping by. It helps to know people care. Y'all come back."

🍂

As they walked briskly home, Grace turned to Hannah. "I wonder if the troubles people have in this life are purposeful or just a throw of the dice. It would sure be easier if we knew for certain that there was some larger plan, something important to be learned from our experiences. What do you think, Hannah?"

"I don't waste time thinking about things to which there are no answer."

"But maybe we're supposed to question things and try to figure out the meaning of our lives."

"I'll leave that to you, then." Hannah took Grace's arm and steered her around a fallen limb, then bent, grasped the end of the limb, and dragged it to the grass on the roadside. "This wasn't here when we came down."

Grace paid no attention to the limb. Her mind was elsewhere, pondering chaos and order and meanings.

4

Diagnosis and Denial

Slipping off her bathrobe, Grace climbed into bed. The mattress, the sheets, her pillows, three of them, all down and soft, usually welcomed her, and sleep generally came easily. In all her life no bed had been this comfortable, this cozy, a source of such comfort, and she could count her beds on the fingers of one hand: the single bed of her childhood, the bed she had shared with Ted, her too-soft bed at Olive's Pruitt's boarding house. But this bed, this absolutely wonderful pillow-top, queen-size bed. Selecting this mattress had been serious business, three stores, many mattresses, and when she tested this one, she knew.

But tonight, both comfort and sleep eluded Grace. Tossing and turning, first on her right side, then her left, then on her back, she rehashed her doctor's words. "Your blood sugar is one hundred and seventy, which means that you have what we call type two or adult onset diabetes."

Her mind had simply gone blank.

He continued. "You can control it without medication if you take off twenty or twenty-five pounds and begin a regular exercise program."

The doctor must be wrong. Diabetes did not run in her family. Her blood sugar that day simply reflected too many sugar cookies the day before. She would stay off sweets for a day or two, and he'd see. Her blood sugar would be normal. But then she remembered why she had gone to him in the first place, the tiredness, excessive thirst, running to the bathroom every few hours all night long. Sitting on his high table half dressed, feeling dumpy and inadequate, all she wanted at that moment was to quit his office.

That was six months ago. She and Bob were still running the tearoom, which of course was why she was tired. So why even bother to mention this diabetes thing to Bob, or to Hannah and Amelia? But a follow-up visit in June, just before Russell and Emily's wedding, reconfirmed the high sugar level in her blood and led to her doctor's suggestion that she attend a class on diabetes downstairs in the building where his office was located.

How boring all that talk had been, about how cells can no longer properly use the sugar (or glucose) obtained from food, and how in people with diabetes, the pancreas, a small organ behind the stomach—they had shown the whole anatomy of the thing on a big chart, which Grace had glanced at briefly and looked beyond, out of the window—no longer produced enough insulin to process the sugars in foods, and the process goes awry. She was absolutely not like the other people in that class listening so raptly to the young nurse educator.

The diagnosis was a mistake, she was sure. Since selling the tearoom she was less tired, and she had none of the other symptoms the doctor had run off: blurred vision, slow wound healing, genital itching. So how could she have diabetes?

On her third visit, her doctor had emphasized, again, that the preferred way to control type two diabetes was by weight loss and exercise. He was thin as a rail. What did he know about how hard it was to lose weight? Grace decided then to cut down on portions and eat half the amount of sweets. That would be hard enough to do. But today, six months after her first visit, the nurse had called with a number of two hundred and five and an admonition to come in to the office to talk with the doctor. Yet, after tossing and turning, and hours of rationalizing that the blood results were a fluke, Grace ambled down to the kitchen for sugar cookies dunked in a good, strong cup of tea.

After a time, she opened a cookbook from a shelf in the kitchen and perused it, turning the pages slowly. She would make a special dinner tomorrow for Bob and his family. It would be their first family dinner at Bob's apartment since Emily and Russell and Tyler moved into their new home in Mars Hill.

The next morning, Grace phoned and made an appointment with her doctor for two weeks hence. She shopped, then went to Bob's apartment and turned her attention to preparing a dinner that culminated in the wonderful odor of baked duck and plum sauce that soon filled the apartment. A casserole of potatoes au gratin bubbled in the oven, and candied carrots needed only to be heated on the stove. Bob had spent the day picking up newspapers and magazines, returning books to shelves, sweeping the patio, and vacuuming carpets that showed no sign of dirt or wear. Now he came into the kitchen, put his arms about Grace, and kissed her neck. She stepped back, pushing against his chest.

"I'm all hot and sweaty. Goodness, it's late. They'll be here in ten minutes." She untied her apron. "Have I time for a quick shower?"

"Go shower. Take all the time you need." Grace fled the kitchen. Sauntering out onto his porch, Bob leaned against the railing. After last night's rain, every fold of every hill was clearly differentiated one from the other. It was the kind of day one wished would last into eternity. Bob's eyes scanned the heavens, aglow with golden spin-off from the setting sun. He was not a religious man. Other than for the wedding of his son, Russell, to Emily, he had not been to a church service in years. Yet suddenly Bob found himself thinking of the Bible, and Genesis, and God's stated satisfaction at the end of each day's creation, *He saw that it was good*. It warmed his heart remembering his grandmother sitting in her rocking chair near the fireplace, reading the words aloud and smiling reassuringly at him, as if she'd had a hand in conceiving and creating the world. The words moved him now, and Bob studied the majestic dome of sky, his eyes roaming the spill of hills. As if he were engaged in a personal chat with the Creator, he whispered, "It is still good."

"And who, may I ask, are you talking to?"

Turning, Bob drew Grace close to him. "God. Just letting Him know that the world He created is still good." He laughed. "Look." He pointed to the patio of a condo farther down the hillside. A man and woman waved up at them. They waved back.

"Do you know them?" Grace asked.

"Not really. See him on the golf course occasionally."

"Do you think they're lonely moving to a rural area like Covington?"

He shrugged off the question.

She looked up at him, feeling feminine and very safe as she always did with Bob. "What amazes me is that a man like you, so well traveled, and with thirty years of army life behind you, can be so content and settled here."

"There's this woman," he said, chuckling. "I'm in love with her, you see, and even though she refuses to marry me . . ." His bushy eyebrows drew together. He raised both hands in a gesture of resignation. "I'm crazy committed to her."

Grace poked his arm. He joked about her refusal to marry or live with him, but she knew that Bob never stopped hoping she'd change her mind.

The doorbell rang, and moments later Tyler slid in ahead of his father and stepmother and threw his arms about Grace's middle. "Granny Grace. I miss you so much. Please come work at my new school, so I can see you every single day." He craned his neck back, and his dark eyes pleaded. "Please. Please."

He was eleven and small for his age. Grace hugged him, feeling his skinny body, and loving him, grateful that he loved her. Then he scooted off to throw his arms about his grandfather, and Grace embraced Emily and reached up to kiss Russell's cheek. "You're glowing," she said to Emily. "Marriage agrees with you."

Emily exchanged a shy glance with Russell.

"Blooming, like a rose, is what she is." Bob waved them all into the living room, and moments later Tyler passed the glasses of wine his grandfather had poured for them. "Me too?" Tyler asked, hopefully holding out a glass.

"Grape juice for you," his grandfather said, patting the boy's red hair.

Dinner was relaxed and casual. Emily seemed more comfortable with her new family than she did at her own mother's table. Meals at Ginger and Martin Hammer's household, Grace recalled, were stiff and strained. The tension and verbal sparring between Emily's parents embittered the food and knotted one's stomach.

As they ate, Russell tried explaining to his father, a computer dummy, about computer viruses and a new antivirus program popular with his clients. Emily told Grace she was tired from shopping for furniture, finding new doctors, even a new hairdresser who cut her hair the way she liked it. "What I like best are the times Tyler and I spend together," Emily said, smiling down at the boy. Tyler beamed. Having finished his dinner, he turned his attention to a handheld computer game.

"Do you like the law practice you joined?" Grace asked.

"It's different and interesting," Emily said. "Ray Hotchkiss is definitely a good old boy, born in Laurel, been practicing here for thirty-five years."

"How come he invited in a Yankee woman?" Bob teased.

Emily smiled. "With all the newcomers in Madison County, I guess he figured he needed a good old Yankee gal." She hesitated a moment, then said, "Ray said something to me the other day that really surprised me. He asked me if I realized that the South is the only section of this country on whose soil a war was fought and lost."

"It stuns me, just hearing you say that," Bob said. "I certainly never thought about that."

"You're fixated on World War Two, Dad. I bet you never think about the Civil War." Russell poured sauce liberally over his duck.

Bob scratched his head. "I'm ashamed to say you're right."

"Ray says it's reflected in Southern literature, in the way they see the world, in everything. He says that's why they're so wary of strangers. There's something dark, even Gothic about it."

Bob leaned forward, his big hands clasped on the table. "I can't begin to imagine what it was like after that war: ruined homes, scorched land, people struggling to pick up the pieces of their shattered lives and all the while being hounded by carpetbaggers from the North."

"When you think of it, who can blame folks around here for their reserve?" Grace said. "I do admire their sense of pride of place."

Emily changed the subject. From under strikingly long lashes her eyes were soft and caring as she looked at Grace. "When do you start back tutoring?"

"Soon, I imagine. They'll call me after school's settled in for a week or two."

"Don't go to my old school. Come to my new one, Granny Grace," Tyler begged again. Grace tousled his hair.

"I'm committed to Caster Elementary, sweetheart. Know what committed means?"

"Sure I do, you made a promise."

"I did, and it's important to honor a promise."

He nodded. "I guess so." He looked so forlorn that they all laughed. As he sat in the seat beside her, Grace leaned toward him and hugged him.

"The dinner's marvelous, darling," Bob said.

"Love this duck," Russell said, helping himself to another breast and passing the plate.

"Grace's dinners are always terrrific," Emily said.

Grace blushed. "Why, thank you all."

They ate in silence, savoring the food, and then Emily asked. "How's Hannah's daughter? And when can I pay her a visit?"

"How is Laura?" Grace set down her knife and fork. Her brow furrowed. "I'm not sure. She's getting about, somewhat clumsily on crutches. She's withdrawn, depressed really."

"Who wouldn't be after what she's been through?" Bob said.

Well," Emily said, "I want to visit her, so let me know, Grace, when she's ready for company."

Several hours later, with their guests gone, leftovers stashed in the refrigerator, dinner dishes packed into the dishwasher, and the counters wiped down, Grace and Bob changed into pajamas and climbed into his king-size bed. Propping pillows behind them, they settled down to review the evening. "They certainly loved that duck you made. There's only a quarter of it left," Bob said.

"You can have it for lunch tomorrow, unless you're golfing."

"I'm staying right here and preparing for a class I'm teaching on Friday."

Grace fidgeted with the edge of the blanket.

Bob pulled her close. "What's bothering you, darling? I know when you're not settled in your mind."

"I've been avoiding telling anyone, even admitting it to myself."

"What," he asked, turning toward her.

She waved her hand at him. "I knew I shouldn't have said anything. You'll get all worried, and it's probably nothing."

"So tell me what nothing is."

Grace remained quiet for a time, then blurted out, "The doctor says that I have type two diabetes. I don't believe him. It doesn't run in my family, and I don't have all the symptoms."

"But you have some of the symptoms?"

"I'm fine, really. It's nothing, just running to the bathroom every few hours, probably because I drink so much water."

Bob took Grace's hands in his. He leaned forward and kissed her forehead. "This isn't something to make light of, my love. What does the doctor want you to do, take medication?"

"He says if I lose twenty, twenty-five pounds, I can control it. If not, then medication."

"How long have you known this?"

"Over six months."

His brows drew together, and his dark eyes became serious. "What do you want to do about it?"

"I'd rather not take pills. I've been telling myself for months now that it's not true, and I've been gorging on cookies and heaven knows what else, almost in defiance. If the sugar count's up when I go back next week, I guess I'll have to decide, won't I?" She sighed. "Bob, what am I going to do? It's so hard changing the way I eat. I love to cook. I'm scared I'll resent cooking if I can't taste things as I go along. The other day Amelia walked into the kitchen just when I'd started whipping up a cookie batter, and there I was scooping along the edge of the bowl with my finger, eating the sweet butter, sugar, and vanilla extract mix. I actually felt guilty." She flung herself against his chest and clung to him. "I'm scared, Bob. What shall I do?"

"For starters, we're going to go together to your doctor, and then we'll make a plan, and I'll help you, my love. Don't cry now. It's going to be all right."

But Grace wasn't so sure of that. She'd been trying without success to "get a grip," as Hannah would say, on the whole issue for months now.

5

Laura's Travail

As the days passed, there was much in the farmhouse that irritated Laura: the creak of the porch floor under the ladies' rocking chairs, the minuscule bathroom that forced her to leave the door ajar with her toes out in the hall. The sounds and smells of Grace's cooking brought heart-wrenching memories of the galley of the *Maribow*, and Marvin, who so loved to cook and to eat. She hated living in their dining room. She didn't go anywhere, so why not be upstairs, away from them all? Yet when her mother offered to help her upstairs, to wrap a plastic bag around Laura's cast so that she could take a shower, Laura declined. The steps did seem formidable. Instead, Laura hobbled on crutches to the kitchen counter once or twice a week to give herself what Grace called a "spitz bath." Some nights she sensed her mother hovering on the stairs, nervously waiting for her to be done. Damn, it annoyed her.

Grace seemed always cheerful. She did almost all of the cooking and baking, and seemed to enjoy it. Though her speaking voice was soft and soothing, the kind of voice that could lull a person to sleep after a bad dream, her singing left much to be desired, and Grace liked to sing. The phone rang off the hook: Bob for Grace, Tyler for Grace, eighty-one-year-old Lurina Masterson Reynolds for Grace, Brenda for Grace, Emily for Grace.

Social butterfly was the best she could come up with for Amelia. Laura hardly saw her. She was so different from the other two women. How had her mother and Grace ever made friends, set up housekeeping, with a woman like Amelia?

And her mother puzzled Laura. After checking to see if Laura needed anything, Hannah sometimes sat at the kitchen table studying what looked like architect's drawings. Plans, she had explained, for gardens, a children's garden, a water garden, an English garden. Laura lost track of the many types of gardens Hannah grew dreamy-eyed describing and over which she would be the director. The director? At seventy-two, or was it seventy-three? What was going on? "And who," she asked, "is this Max who keeps popping in?"

"His name is George Maxwell, Max to his friends," Hannah had explained. "He owns the dairy farm across the road and recently bought the land at the end of Cove Road. His wife, Bella, and I were friends before she passed away." Hannah wanted to kick herself. At a time like this, how could she speak to Laura of someone dying? She continued. "He's going to develop part of the land as a historic park with re-creations of olden times. It'll be called the Bella Maxwell Park and Preserve, after his wife."

Observing her mother and Max together, Laura sensed that there was more to it than that. In all her years growing up, her mother had exhibited only contempt for men. How incongruous, then, the plethora of ease and goodwill that flowed between her mother and this Max, and never a raised voice, compared to Laura's recollection of the shrill, angry woman interacting with her raging, screaming, sometimes violent father.

In this household, voices were raised in excitement, never in anger. How had these very different women achieved this level of cooperation and harmony? It pained her even to think about it when she had no one, no home, and everything she owned, clothes, books, dishes, pictures, every tiny memento of her life, lay at the bottom of the ocean. What did they know, or care, that guilt choked her soul? It was she, after all, who had proposed and nagged for them to move the *Maribow* to the Caribbean.

And making matters worse, her leg throbbed unbearably, especially at night. Tomorrow they would go to the doctor. Something was terribly wrong, and Laura knew it.

On uncertain crutches, Laura maneuvered down the steps of the front porch. With difficulty, she eased herself and her cast into the back of her mother's old station wagon. Exhausted by the effort, she could not summon up the energy to feel annoyed when she saw that Grace was accompanying them.

Dr. Gedlow's waiting room discomfited them with its tans and blacks, and its cold slick glass and metal furnishings. A nurse wheeled Laura away in a chair for X rays, and Hannah and Grace were left to wait. They thumbed through *Travel and Leisure, Golfing, Fishing Life,* and *Outdoors.*

Grace thought of her own doctor's pleasant waiting room, soft pink beige, with floral prints on the walls, where she and Bob would be going late in October. She still hadn't told anyone else, not even Hannah. And this was not the time to do so.

Ignoring the magazines, they sat in silence, fifteen, twenty, thirty minutes before Laura was wheeled back to them, and fifteen minutes more. She was agitated. "They weren't very gentle with my leg. It hurts worse now," she said. Moments later, a nurse beckoned them to one of Dr. Gedlow's examining rooms.

Stocky, of medium build, and with the high cheekbones of his Cherokee ancestors, Dr. Harvey Gedlow was reserved and disquietingly brusque. After a brisk nod at the trio, he headed for the light board on which the X rays were positioned. Holding each film up to the light, he scrutinized it, turned it this way and that. The only sounds in the room came from the whir of the air-conditioning unit somewhere outside and the snap of film against metal when he set each X ray back onto the light board hanging on the wall.

"The bone's not fit together right."

"What does that mean?" Hannah asked.

Dr. Gedlow pointed to a section of the X ray that none of them recognized. "The break was clean. The bones should line up. They don't." He shook his head. "I'm going to have to go in and reset the tibia, maybe pin it." He shook his head, and for the first time he looked at Laura, and his voice took on a kinder, less businesslike tone. "I'm sorry. You thought you'd be getting this cast off in a few weeks."

Gripping the arms of the wheelchair, Laura leaned forward. Her huge eyes glared at him. "Yes, I did. Aren't I?" She pointed to the cast.

"Not for another six weeks."

"God, no. I can't." Unstoppable tears came.

Moments later the doctor left the room. "I'll see you in my office," he said to them.

When she could talk, Laura whispered hoarsely, "I'll go crazy."

"You won't." Grace knelt beside her. "We'll take care of you. Time will pass."

"Six weeks is not the end of the world," Hannah said.

"It's already the end of the world," Laura moaned.

*

"Is it the fault of the doctor in Puerto Rico?" Hannah asked, when she had a moment alone with Dr. Gedlow.

"Possibly, but probably not. Might have been the trip. She should have been in the hospital longer. Damned insurance companies . . ." His voice drifted off as he jotted notations in Laura's file on his desk.

Surgery took place two days later. Dr. Gedlow emerged from the operating room to assure them that the bones were correctly positioned and secured with metal pins, which, down the road, could be removed if they bothered Laura. Laura, he said, would be going home in two days. "I want her up and about on those crutches every day."

6

Lucy Banks

In the first week of September, the hallways of Caster Elementary School echoed with the sound of children's footsteps, the cafeteria buzzed with their laughter, and Grace happily returned to tutoring second graders in reading. All that was missing was Tyler. Grace missed his hug and the way his dark cocoa-bean eyes danced when she handed him cookies baked specially for him to add to his lunch box and share with his friends. Sharing was important, she had emphasized, and was pleased when she had seen Tyler offering cookies to his friends.

The section of the school library where she worked with each child was hidden from the librarian's desk and tucked behind bookcases, so that Grace's voice and that of her pupils were muted. At the start of each week, as long as flowers bloomed in the garden, Grace gifted Jane, the librarian, with a slim vase bearing one bright flower.

In the library, Grace headed for the water fountain to fill the vase, which she then deposited on the librarian's desk. Within moments, eight-year-old Lucy Banks arrived. She's skinny, too skinny, Grace thought, but some kids were just that way, and Grace always brought her a bag of cookies. There were so many children in that family, seven, and Lucy the youngest. An advantage, perhaps, considering that older brothers and sisters could make good surrogate parents and/or confidants. Or, on the other hand, was there sufficient food in that home?

Lucy's problem was reading. She excelled at math, but letters frustrated and immobilized her. "They fly around," she said to Grace after their third time together, making Grace think the child should have her eyes examined. Probably, in Lucy's family, optometrists and eye examinations ranked at the bottom of the to-do list.

One evening last week, trying to devise a way to work with Lucy, Grace and Bob had cut out large letters and backed them with Velcro. These she now drew from her deep canvas bag and set two *t*s and two *g*s on the table as well as an *e*, an *a*, and an *o*. They would make the words *tag, got, get, gag, egg, ago, age,* and *tot.*

Lucy stared at the letters. She did not move.

"What are the letters doing?" Grace asked.

"Jumpin' round."

"Dancing?

Lucy nodded, then lowered her eyes.

"Do you hear music then?"

"Yes, ma'am." She tapped her foot and wiggled her shoulders.

"Can you stop the music?"

"Dunno."

"Would you try doing so for me, please."

Lucy closed her eyes and rocked a bit, then stopped and opened her eyes. "There, I done stopped it."

"Thank you. Do you know the names of these letters, Lucy?"

"Yes, ma'am."

"What are they?"

"*T, a, g, o,* and *e.*"

"Let's make words from them, shall we?"

Lucy nodded and grinned at Grace. Slowly she arranged the letters and sounded out "tag." Her brows drawn tight in concentration, she rearranged the letters to form *got,* then *get,* and after close scrutiny and speculation and with Grace's prodding, *egg.* "I wanna stop now. The letters are dancin' again." Her eyes closed for a mo-

34

ment, and then her shoulders bobbed up and down and her feet tapped the carpet.

"Lucy, I can see you know the letters and how to make words. Now let's read from this book." Grace opened a basic second-grade storybook. Bright pictures jumped off each page, along with several short lines of words. Lucy bent over the pages, turning them slowly from start to finish, then back to the beginning. "I like the pictures," she said, "but the words are floppin' all over the pages."

Grace read the story twice, then gave Lucy a bag of sugar cookies, bade her good-bye, and sneaked a hug. Don't touch the children was school policy, of course, but no one bothered Grace, not since Tyler, who had been so withdrawn and depressed after his mother's death, started drawing and talking about his mother and had jumped from his chair, rushed to Grace, and hugged her hard. Everyone at Caster Elementary said that Grace had a special way with children.

The librarian, a slender blonde, stuck her head around a bookcase. "Mrs. Tate would like to see you in her office when you're done here."

Grace rose. As she passed the librarian's desk, she slipped a bag of cookies into Jane's hand. "Enjoy," she said.

Brenda Tate sat behind her wide mahogany desk, glasses pushed high on her forehead, a pencil dangling between her fingers. A file lay open before her. "Lucy Banks," she said tapping the file with the eraser end of her pencil.

Grace nodded and took a chair across from the desk. Her eyes lighted on the Chagall print of the floating bride and groom that hung on the far wall over a worn, brown faux-leather couch. Kids who come in here to see the principal must get a kick out of that print, she thought.

"I'm concerned about Lucy," Brenda said. "Not only won't she read, but she's distracting the entire class with her movements, shaking her shoulders, tapping her feet, strumming her fingers, wagging her head."

"She's hearing music."

"What? Who told you that?"

"Lucy did. The letters move, she says, words dance. They won't stay still on the page. I think she ought to see someone, an optometrist perhaps."

"Or a counselor."

"She's a dear little girl, always smiling."

"Yes. I think that's what keeps Miss Kelson, her teacher, from branding her incorrigible and kicking her out of her classroom. But she can't teach, not unless they're doing math. Then Lucy shines. Almost like a savant, very skilled in math and dumb in other things."

"She isn't dumb. It's something else. I don't know what."

"Will you go on working with her?"

"As long as you want me to. I like her, feel sorry for her. One of seven kids, gets lots of hand-me-downs, I'm sure. Maybe she hears music to escape from all the noise at home, or whatever is going on there." Grace leaned forward, grasped the edge of the desk with her fingertips. "What is going on there?"

"I'm asking child services to find that out."

"You'll let me know what they come up with?"

"Certainly."

Grace started to rise. Brenda was a busy woman. "Grace," Brenda said, "please sit a bit."

Grace returned to her chair. "How is Harold?" she asked

Tears filled the eyes of the woman behind the desk, and she leaned forward, her hands clasped. "Not good at all."

Unselfconsciously, Grace handed Brenda her clean bandanna, and Brenda, with the same sense of ease, accepted it and wiped her cheeks and eyes. "He's going downhill. I see it. He's gone to bones. Bald now. His eyes are dark caves in his face."

"What does the doctor say?"

Dabbing at her eyes, Brenda sat back in her chair and squared her shoulders. "That it's different for each person. Some never lose their hair. They're giving him new drugs, more potent, more likely to bring about a remission, he tells me, but they're surely killing Harold."

"Surely not killing him."

A deep sigh issued from Brenda's chest. "Darn close. We don't know whether to stop the chemotherapy now, or finish the treatment, another six sessions over twelve weeks. I don't see how Harold can survive another six sessions. He can hardly raise his head, doesn't eat for days after each treatment." Her eyes appealed to Grace. "You lost your husband to cancer, didn't you, Grace?"

"Yes, but when they discovered it, it was what they called a type four and had already spread to his lymph system and throughout his body."

"Still, he went through chemo?"

"Ted insisted on it, wanted to hang on as long as possible." Remembering brought tears to Grace's eyes, and she forced them away. "He lost his hair, he lost every ounce of fat he had on him, and he cried a great deal."

"Harold cries too."

"It may be the medication."

Brenda nodded toward the Chagall print. "I wish I could fly away."

"I know. Watching someone you love suffer is horrible." After a moment, Grace asked, "What are you doing to take care of yourself?"

"People like y'all come over. Bring food. But most folks stay too long. It's exhausting." She smiled weakly. "How would they know that? We'd never ask them to leave. We're grateful you and others bring us a casserole or a pie. Ma would cook more except that the kitchen gets too hot for her. Thank God she's stayed on. I could never leave Harold home alone and come to work." Brenda wrung her hands. "And now, for the first time in my life, I'm not functioning efficiently. My mind's off with Harold most of the time. How did you survive it, Grace?"

"Pretty much like you are. Day by day. I was lucky to have friends, like you do. That's one of the advantages of living a long time in one place. People came out of the woodwork. Some people I thought I could count on weren't there for me, but miraculously others were. They hovered, sat with me to see that I ate. They spelled me with Ted, so I could get out to the beauty parlor every now and then, and to the market. Sometimes they dragged me to

37

a movie." She squirmed in her chair. "But when the lights go off, and you're all alone listening to your husband's raspy breathing, or his cough, or moan, or waiting for him to wake and call for you, that's when you're really alone, and it's scary, and your head won't stop working so you can sleep. You can't stop conjuring up worse case scenarios for him, for yourself." Grace raised her hands to her head. "I'm sorry, Brenda, going on like this."

"Everything you say is true. Your sharing it makes me feel less alone. I tell myself that you've survived, and that I can too, whatever the outcome. I remind myself that you picked up and moved on with your life. I take hope from that, if it should be that Harold . . ."

Leaning forward, Grace placed her hands over Brenda's. "Harold will recover. This part's the worse."

"Talking to you makes me feel less alone," Brenda said.

"Look, many nights I have insomnia," Grace lied. "Call me if you need to talk, no matter the time. Here's my private number. Bob sometimes calls late, and Roger my son too, so I had a separate phone installed in my room." She scribbled the number and handed it to Brenda.

"Thanks. That's incredibly kind of you. I won't abuse the privilege." Brenda dried her eyes again and smoothed back her hair. Grace sat quietly, allowing her time to collect herself. Then Brenda asked, "Your son, Grace, was he there with you, for you?"

"My goodness, no. Roger lived and worked in Saudi Arabia. He came home once to see his dad, again for the funeral, and one more time when he pressured me to rent my home and move to Branston in Pennsylvania. I'm not proud of it, but it took me a long time to forgive him."

"Molly, thank God, is right here, but have you looked at her? She's lost so much weight, huge dark circles under her eyes. She isn't sleeping worrying about her dad. I don't think her mind's on her teaching. She teaches math, you know, and she really needs to be on top of those kids."

"A hard time for Molly and for you. Do you ever take a day off just for yourself?" Grace asked.

"I went in to the beauty parlor one Saturday, and to a movie.

Halfway through the silly movie, I was certain that something was terribly wrong at home, so I dashed back, nearly hit a car getting off the highway. Harold was sleeping when I got there."

Grace nodded. "I had times like that, certain something was wrong and nothing was. Does it help to pray, Brenda?"

"Religion doesn't help me now. I'm angry with God. I don't want to see Pastor Johnson. He means well, old dear, but he annoys me with his platitudes. I doubt he's had any counselor training. Bowing to the will of God isn't what I want to do right now. I want to fight like hell for Harold, 'cause he sure can't fight for himself."

"Another opinion, perhaps? Emory University in Atlanta, or Duke over in Durham?"

"It's not that I distrust the medical team here. I think they're good, and they've got him on the latest mix of drugs. It's just that I don't think this particular mix is good for Harold."

"Have you talked to them like you're talking to me?"

Brenda shook her head. "I was raised up to think that 'doctor knows best.'" She hit the desk with her palm. "To hell with doctors knowing what's best. They're only people. I'll call right now, make an appointment with the surgeon and the oncologist together." A wisp of a smile touched the corners of her mouth. "Thanks, Grace, for listening, for sharing about your husband, for being my friend." She waved the bandanna as Grace opened the office door. "I'll return this after it's been washed."

"You needn't return it. Just let me know what the doctors say, will you?"

"I surely will. Thanks again."

"Nothing to thank me for." As Grace walked slowly down the hallway, she wondered, for a moment, that Brenda had been so open with her about Harold's illness and her despair. She was, after all, the outsider, the Yankee, and Grace was flattered.

7

A Friendship Grows

Laura was miserable. She hated not remembering things, hated that she lost words in the midst of a sentence. Sometimes, at night, Laura struggled in her mind to re-create the soft lap of gentle waves teasing the hull of the *Maribow*. Rocking her upper body gently back and forth, she attempted to simulate the roll of the ketch as it strained at its anchor and swung like a pendulum one way and then the other. But there were nights when she awakened alarmed and covered her ears to shut out the sound of tortured winds howling through and rattling the riggings of the *Maribow*.

One night Laura dreamed that she slid through the rollers with the anchor's chain into dark blue water where, buried to her waist in the sandy bottom, she clutched the anchor, like a child, to her breast. Then the anchor changed into Marvin's face, and she woke as enormous, nearly unbearable anguish punched her full force in the stomach.

As the days passed, Laura grew increasingly proficient on crutches. Still, she did not join her mother and the ladies for tea on the porch, though she envied them the stability, the sense of order and place it obviously provided them. Then one quiet night pregnant with moonlight, she awakened and, incapable of sleeping, moved cautiously to the porch. Settling into her mother's rocking chair, Laura extended her legs and for a moment reflected on the power of moonlight to divide the darkness into shades and tones of gray and black and shimmering silver whether the objects be oceans and islands or mountains and trees. All about her, everything suddenly appeared to reflect her sadness: the drooping branches of a Japanese cherry tree, planted by Hannah at the far corner of the house, and the hills falling away from Snowman's Cap Mountain seemed to hide their faces, one curved line behind another.

Amelia, coming downstairs for a snack, heard Laura crying softly. It would have surprised the other two women if they knew that of them all, Amelia identified most with Laura. She discerned Laura's sense of desolation, understood the loneliness of an unfamiliar place, with no friends to visit or to comfort. Would she consider it an intrusion if Amelia joined her on the porch? Timidly, Amelia rapped on the screen door. "Laura," she asked softly, "may I join you?"

Laura nodded, and moments later Amelia sat beside her and set her rocking chair in motion. For a time neither spoke. The power of light streaming from the heavens stirred Amelia's soul, and her photographer's eye traversed the strong graphic lines, grays and blacks, of shadows cast by the hills and trees, and Maxwell's farmhouse and windmill in the moonlight. "It's beautiful tonight," Amelia said.

From the corner of her eye, Amelia caught the lowered head and sagging shoulders of the younger woman. *Spiritless* was the word that came to mind, and Amelia's instinct was to assure Laura that things would get better, that she would smile again, laugh again, that one morning she would wake up glad to be alive and excited about what the day would bring. But Amelia knew all too well that such words would bring no comfort now; the loss was too recent, too raw, the anguish too immense. There were no right words at this stage of grief. She had merely to be there, to listen if Laura chose to speak, and that first night of their being alone together, Laura did not speak.

After a time, Laura stirred, eased to her feet, said a soft "good night" to Amelia, and placing her crutches carefully before her, departed for her room.

Amelia sat on the porch a while longer. She liked Laura, wondered, in the face of Laura's tragedy, why Hannah and her child could not bridge the gulf that separated them. Hannah loved Laura, worried about her, Amelia knew that, but words of affection or comfort did not flow like milk and honey from Hannah's lips. Too bad. Amelia rose. Forgetting the snack she had come down for, she went upstairs to her room.

Back in her bed, Laura stared up at the tray ceiling in the dining room/bedroom. She was tired yet afraid to sleep. Mornings were terrible. Each new day birthed again the anguished knowledge that Marvin was lost to her forever. Laura reached for the small calendar on the bedside table that Hannah had brought at her request. It was many weeks since Hurricane Arlene on July 18. Laura had learned, while still in Puerto Rico in the hospital, that a half dozen boats had been wrenched from their moorings in Hurricane Hole, a supposedly safe haven, a protected bay in St. John, Virgin Islands, and suffered an identical, final, cruel, and incomprehensible fate. Besides Marvin, five other people had been lost.

Laura picked up a magazine. The cover screamed COUNTDOWN TO THE MILLENNIUM. The *Maribow* had been chartered by a family of five from December 24 to January 3. They would know by then if computers failed, banks closed, stock markets crashed. She and Marvin devoted hours to drawing up a list of supplies, canned and dried food, additional first aid kits, Coleman lights and stoves, cases of bottled water, black plastic bags for garbage, games for the children, and more, in case the worst scenario played out.

"This whole Y2K thing, computers crashing, electricity going off, stocking food, people buying guns—it's all scare tactics, one huge hoax designed to make some people rich," Marvin had said to her one afternoon in mid-October.

"How can you be so sure?"

"You think the money brokers of the world, Wall Street, and governments in Washington, London, Paris, Japan can sit back and let the economy crumble? I bet they're hustling their asses and pouring millions into fixing the problem."

"Still, just to be safe, I'll fill this list of hurricane supplies they gave us at the boat dock: flashlights, extra batteries, plenty of canned food." And then they had gotten the charter, and Laura redoubled her efforts to stock up.

Was Marvin right? Now where would she be on December 31 at midnight? Her mother and the others never spoke of it. Weren't they preparing? Were they intending to?

Laura twisted her head toward the wall. What am I doing thinking about this now? I'm miserable enough. A picture of Amelia formed in her mind. A delicate-looking woman, still quite pretty, amazing eyes, blue and bright as fine sapphires. What was it she had heard her mother and Grace talking about? A man named Lance, and Amelia had fallen for him? At her age? A bounder her mother called him. What had happened between Amelia and Lance? Laura covered her eyes with her arm. Did she really care?

During the long, slow-moving days of her recovery, Laura attempted repeatedly to catch up on reading she had put off for years. At her request, Hannah replaced a paperback she'd had on the ketch for months, Frank Conroy's *Body and Soul*. She had read *Belonging* by Nancy Thayer and wanted to read several of her other books, *Three Women at the Water's Edge* and *Between Husbands and Friends*. Grace frequented Malaprop's Bookstore and Café and Accent on Books in North Asheville and picked them up for her, and they sat, mostly untouched, a small tower of books on a wide end table alongside the ugly but comfortable maroon recliner.

As time passed, and her leg itched, Laura was certain that she was healing. Adroit on crutches, she mastered the steps and even allowed her mother to help her tie a plastic bag around her leg so she could have a quick shower and wash her hair, which felt marvelous.

Laura was beginning to get a sense of her mother's housemates and their friends. Grace had chosen not to marry Bob. They had opened a tearoom, and sold it. Bob taught World War Two history at the Center for Creative Retirement at the university in Asheville, and Grace volunteered several times a week with children at Caster Elementary School where Brenda Tate was the principal. Bob maintained a strong and reliable presence in the house. She could see that he cherished Grace. Like kids, they laughed a lot.

Amelia was actually entertaining and whimsical. Mike was kind and gentle, always available for Amelia and willing to lend a hand to anyone else when asked. Amelia, off on a shoot most days, went out with Mike several nights a week to the theater or a movie or some café on Pack Square in the center of Asheville where, Amelia said, they drank coffee and watched the people.

"Colorful," was how Amelia described the scene. "We get a lot of young people, drifters with unkempt hair, body rings, tattoos, backpacks. They hang around the fountain in Pack Square. I wonder who their parents are, and if they know where their children are." Laura was welcome to come with them any time, whenever she felt like it, Amelia said.

Wayne Reynolds came and went. He was younger than Laura, late thirties perhaps. She would be forty-one on December 2. Wayne owned and operated her mother's former greenhouse and plant business, which still sat in the side yard of the farmhouse.

"Hannah's folly," Grace referred to it, laughing.

That her mother liked him was evident by her eyes and voice, which softened when Wayne walked in. She envied Wayne, might even call it jealousy. Why had her mother's eyes never lit up for her? Everyone treated Wayne as if he were a son of the household, and he had an enormous appetite. Grace baked endless trays of cookies and her special Vienna cake with its multicolored layers. Quite a menagerie of people.

One day at lunch, Grace asked if Emily might visit Laura, and Grace wanted to introduce Laura to Brenda's daughter, Molly Lund, and to Lurina Masterson. "Lurina's a wonderful character. I think you'd like her. At eighty-one she's quite an original thinker. Told me recently that since Adam and Eve lived in the Garden of Eden, which was obviously in the tropics as they were naked, and since apples don't grow in the tropics, the forbidden fruit was actually a mango."

Laura's disinterested hint of a smile came and went swiftly. "Please, Grace, I appreciate the thought, but could we wait a bit before I have to interact with new people."

"Of course."

How could she share her despair with strangers, make small talk or answer their questions? Even these women, who tried to be so kind to her, were strangers. Even her mother. Laura found it nerve-racking being around her mother. Hannah would ask some simple thing like, "I'm going to Mars Hill, can I get you anything?" or if she had been alone all afternoon, her mother would ask, "Would you like some company?" Hannah's queries grated on Laura like chalk drawn along a blackboard. Too many unresolved issues shifted and rubbed between them. She didn't want to get into rehashing the past with her mother, and they had no present to talk about.

So Laura smiled at Hannah and said she was fine, even though she hurt long after the stitches were removed from her arm, cheek, and face. She chose not to share the fact that she felt burdened by loneliness and nearly immobilized, or that she often wept alone and pined for her life with Marvin.

It puzzled her that her sister, Miranda, phoned their mother every week. When had they gotten so chummy? She chatted briefly with Miranda several times. "How are you?" her sister asked.

"Coming along. How's your business?"

"Going well. It's been nice working with Roger and Charles. You know the business bought a condominium near Bob's. We hope to come down before Christmas to see you."

"That would be nice." Would it? Laura dreaded it, even as deep inside it pained her to be so disconnected from her only sister.

It was complex, these intertwined, extended family relationships. Miranda and Paul in business with Grace's son Roger and his companion, Charles, who was HIV positive. Everyone nodded and smiled when they talked about his T cell count being high. God, didn't they realize that AIDS was a three-part disease: asymptomatic, which Charles was now; the development of symptoms; and finally full-blown AIDS?

The friendship between Amelia and Laura began over a bowl of coffee ice cream, Laura's favorite. Amelia brought them each a bowl out on the porch. They ate in silence, until Laura said, "Thank you, Amelia. Sorry I'm not better company."

"I'm fine with silence. Gives me time to make mental notes of things I'll photograph tomorrow or the next day."

"You photograph every day?"

"Not every day, several times a week. I'm working on a book, black-and-white photographs of Madison County. It's a big county and sparsely populated. I drive a lot, and I walk a lot, so I take every other day off to recoup. Not quite the gazelle I used to be."

"Pretty close, though, from what I see," Laura said, and that evening no more was said.

A few days later, on an afternoon when no one else was in the house, Amelia set up her light board on the kitchen table and asked Laura to critique her slides.

After studying the slides for a few minutes, Laura lifted her head from the light board. "You do beautiful work, Amelia."

"You learn, in time, what the best angles are, you learn about light." And Amelia told Laura how stupid she had felt at first and certain she would never grasp the basic concepts of photography.

"Mike was so patient, and your mother helped me a great deal."

"My mother? How?" Laura sat back and looked intently at Amelia. Her eyes issued a challenge. Prove it to me.

"I couldn't seem to grasp how light worked. I was trying to take a picture in the shade and again at noon in full light. Your mother told me she'd taken up photography once, learned the technical part

47

I was having trouble with, but she said she had no creativity. I was creative, she said, and you know Hannah doesn't give many compliments. She made suggestions for the picture I was struggling with, and she was right."

"I'm surprised she took the time to explain anything. I remember her never having time to explain things, and I always felt inadequate never doing anything right."

Amelia did not respond, and Laura rose to get a glass of water from the tap at the sink. She looked out of the window. "By the way," she asked, "what are all those cars doing parked down past the church lately?"

"People visiting Harold. Brenda says she hasn't cooked a meal since he had his surgery, in fact there's too much food some days, other days there's only dessert in their refrigerator. I take salads when Mike and I visit. Your mother and Grace have been down, of course. Harold's in terrible shape, physically and emotionally. It's clear he doesn't want to see people, but we feel we can't just stop going, for Brenda's sake, and her mother, Millie. Millie is there all day long with Harold."

"I understand his not wanting to see people. They probably exhaust him," Laura said.

Amelia wiped a smudge of some kind from her chin. "But how do neighbors and friends just stop going, taking food, trying to help?"

It struck Laura hard, right smack in the gut, then, how rootless and alone she was in the world. If the tragedy had happened in Maine, would people have reached out to her? Visited her? Included her? Their friends had been mainly Marvin's old boat buddies and their wives or girlfriends, and she hadn't needed a close woman friend. Marvin was all she needed or wanted. Besides, they all lived on boats that sailed in and sailed out, many wintering in Chesapeake Bay or as far south as Ft. Lauderdale or the Caribbean. Who besides Marvin had cared about her? Clamping her teeth together to still her quivering chin, Laura walked back to the table and returned to studying Amelia's slides.

8

Something More Meaningful

Twice a week Amelia joined Mike for lunch at a restaurant, often on Pack Square in the heart of Asheville. Then they browsed camera stores, purchased film, and picked up prints. This day, as they lingered over their coffee, Mike pouted. "Why do you need something else to do?" he asked. "Your photography keeps you busy, and you have another book in the works."

Amelia sipped her coffee. They had been sitting at their table for more than two hours, deep in conversation about Amelia's new black-and-white photography book. The room was very still. Amelia set down her cup, suddenly acutely aware that except for them, the restaurant was empty. Outside the thick glass walls that fronted Biltmore Avenue, cars and pedestrians hurried by.

Amelia toyed with an unopened packet of Sweet 'n Low. "What I do now is totally self-serving, can't you see that? I feel as if I'm being pushed to get involved in something larger, something dedicated to others."

"Like what, Amelia?" Mike asked.

"Well, like hospice, I . . ."

Mike gasped. "Oh, Lord. That's so hard working with dying people."

"You don't have to work directly with a dying person. There's plenty to be done to help the caregivers. They're overburdened, worn out, and need all the support they can get. Brenda's mother Millie's a case in point. The woman's worn out caring for Harold."

Mike shivered visibly. "It's so sad, Harold Tate. But why hospice?"

"Some people find working with hospice gratifying."

"True, but I can't imagine *you* going to some dying person's home."

"It's a toss-up," Amelia said, "between hospice and volunteering at the hospital, rocking babies."

"Oh, Amelia, hospitals reek with dreadful germs. Whatever is the matter with you?"

The waiter eyed them from the other side of the room, and Amelia realized that all the other tables had been set with crystal goblets and fancy rose-colored napkins for the dinner crowd. They had paid their bill and tipped their waiter well. He'd just have to tolerate their sitting a while longer. Sweetly, Amelia smiled at him. "We'll be gone soon." She finished the water in her glass and dabbed her lips with her napkin. "I told you, Mike. Ever since that day on the hill when I had that out-of-body experience, I've been driven to give of myself in a way I never have."

"Goodness sake. All those years working with your husband in the Red Cross. You must have helped hundreds of people all over the world."

"That was Thomas's life, not mine. I complied with whatever he required of me. My heart was never in it." The palms of both hands crossed over her heart. "In here, I know that I must help someone, an infant, or a dying person, or his family. I lie awake at night and think about this, think about my life and how vapid it's been. And I look at Hannah's daughter, and it reminds me of how unpredictable and chaotic life can be, how soon it's over. Seeing her reinforces my need to do something truly meaningful."

"Vapid? Your life is empty, pointless? How can you say a thing like that, Amelia? Making beautiful photographs is meaningful." Mike pouted.

"I'm sixty-nine years old, and I've been doing photography for only two years. All those other years I was merely a shadow of Thomas."

Mike looked utterly dejected.

"Oh, Mike. I won't give up my photography, not ever again." Amelia bit her lip, feeling guilty, remembering how, under Lance Lundquist's influence and his demands on her time, she had just about abandoned her camera, her friends, and Mike. But that was over and she had learned a hard lesson.

"My God, you're serious about this." Mike's hands gripped the edge of the table.

Amelia rested her hand over one of his and felt him loosen his grasp on the wood. "Please don't worry. It's just that I can't ignore this prompting to do more." Then Amelia looked at her watch. "Well, for starters, I have an interview with the volunteer coordinator at the hospital."

"Now, today, the hospital?" His eyes grew anxious.

"Dear Mike, please don't worry. I'm dedicated to my new book on Madison County and to our work together." She swallowed hard. It was difficult to speak of her relationship with the infamous liar, Lance, but now she did. "I'll never get over feeling guilty at the way I treated Hannah, and Grace, and you. How could I have been so taken in by such a duplicitous man? I'm so sorry."

"Don't worry your head about that, Amelia. It's over."

"It was all about him," she mused aloud. "But I've changed. This is about me giving something back to the universe. Don't you ever feel the urge to help someone who isn't as fortunate?"

"I help raise money for AIDS research." He hesitated. "I have a friend with AIDS. I help take care of him."

"I didn't know. That's so good of you." She covered his hand with hers. "You help care for your sick friend, so why get so upset about me doing it?"

"It's very hard, Amelia, very painful to watch someone die."

"But, you see, you do it and still have plenty of time for our work and your own work. So Mike, dear, it's as my father used to say, 'Busy people are the ones who always have time.'"

✦

Later that afternoon, as the three women sat on their porch, Amelia worked on the application the volunteer coordinator at the hospital had given to her. On a book she used for a tabletop, Amelia smoothed the ends of the application. "They ask for experience." She looked from Grace to Hannah. "They'll never take me. What work have I ever done?"

"Let me see that." Hannah extended her hand for the application. "Goodness, Amelia, just list all those things you did for the Red Cross, helping with inoculation of children in Thailand, all those years of relief work."

"I wasn't paid for any of that. They were volunteer jobs, not real jobs."

"Volunteer work is real work," Grace exclaimed. "All that's different about it is that you don't expect to be paid, but the hours can be the same, the amount of effort, the energy involved."

"And more satisfying sometimes than paid work you do because you must. Next time you go to that hospital," Hannah said, "step into the emergency room, go by the pharmacy, stop at the front desk, take a good look at the number of people wearing maroon jackets. They're all volunteers. Volunteers are essential to hospitals, to take just one example. That place couldn't run without dozens and dozens of them."

"And what about firefighters? Bob and Wayne both volunteer with our local fire department," Grace said.

Amelia tugged nervously at her scarf. "But I had to be there. They were trained."

Hannah eyed her curiously. They had shared a home, fought and made up, confessed their deepest secrets and feelings to one another, so when, she wondered, did anyone ever really know another person? She returned to studying Amelia's application. "Trust us, Amelia. Just list a few of the things you say you 'had to be there' to do, and while you're at it, don't forget to list your photography accomplishments."

A week later, Amelia dashed into the kitchen where Grace stood at the counter eyeing the bowl of sugar, butter, and vanilla extract she had just blended. Swipe or not to swipe her finger along the edge? Then, giving her head a vigorous shake, she swiped, licked the goodness off her finger, and reached for more. As she did, she turned to see Amelia in the doorway waving a letter.

"They're impressed with my application. It says so here, see?" Amelia shoved the letter into Grace's hand. "I have to take some training, and then I start. I'm incredibly happy." Amelia whirled about, waving her arms and humming a waltz. She grabbed Grace about the waist. The letter drifted slowly to the ground. "Come on, Grace, dance with me."

They swirled about the kitchen table until Grace grabbed a chair and flopped into it breathing hard. "Really out of shape," she said.

Amelia, hardly fazed by the exertion, picked up her letter and brushed her hair off her face. "Maybe you and Bob should sign up for dancing lessons, or come hiking all over Madison County with me when I go out on a shoot. Now that'll get you in shape." She walked to the counter and peered into the bowl. "What are you making?"

"The usual, sugar cookies."

"I never get tired of them. I guess you don't either." After pouring herself a glass of water from the tap, Amelia leaned against the counter and sipped it. "You must never drink water fast after exerting yourself, you know that. Want some water?"

"That would be nice, thanks."

Amelia ran the tap to make sure it was cold, then filled another glass and joined Grace at the table. "Don't you get tired of cooking, Grace?"

Grace scratched her head with two fingers. "Well, I see results pretty fast. It's relaxing."

"Always bothered me," Amelia said, turning up her nose. "You work for hours preparing food, and people devour it in five minutes, and then there's the cleaning up."

"I never think of it that way. I think that my cooking brings people together, gives them pleasure. You could call it satisfying volunteer work that I do at home." She set both elbows on the table like a tepee and leaned her chin on the back of her clasped hands. "Now, tell me what you'll be doing at the hospital."

"I'm going to be rocking very tiny babies."

"Sounds great. You have no problem going into a hospital now?" Because of Thomas's death and her burns, Grace knew that Amelia hated, even feared hospitals.

"It's time I got over that, don't you think? I admit I had a moment or two of real trepidation the other day when I walked into the hospital lobby, but it passed, thank heavens, and I'm excited. I can't wait to start."

Grace lifted her head and nodded. "Sounds like you're following the dictates of your heart."

Amelia's hand rested over her heart for a moment. "My heart, following my heart. What a lovely thing to say. I listened to my heart when we moved here, didn't I? And when I started doing photography. When I listen, life gets easier. Things just fall into place."

"How often will you go?"

"Once a week for two hours."

Grace set down the large spoon she had been blending the ingredients with. "You know how I love my work at Caster Elementary. Helping children learn to read is so satisfying. I'm glad you're doing this, Amelia. One day a week at the hospital's perfect. I'm proud of you, my friend."

9

Scars, Visible and Invisible

During the time that Amelia waited for the volunteer training session to begin at the hospital, friendship continued to develop between her and Laura. One afternoon, while they were having tea in the kitchen, Amelia invited Laura to play Scrabble.

"I don't play board games," Laura said.

Amelia set out the Scrabble board. "This is the only board game I play. Emily's mother, Ginger, got me interested. She's a difficult woman, very demanding. I tried to keep her out of everyone's hair those weeks before Emily and Russell's wedding. Ginger loves Scrabble, and I got hooked. She's traveling this summer, competing at Scrabble tournaments all over the country, and I've no one to play with."

"Oh, all right, one game."

Ten minutes into the game, Amelia placed letters that read *miglin*. "Twenty points," she said.

"*Miglin?* That's a word?"

Amelia tossed her head. "It means, very small, tiny."

"Let's look it up."

Amelia shrugged and reached for the dictionary. A moment later she looked at Laura, surprise written on her face. "It's not here."

"It's not a word."

"My mistake, then. *Miglin.* But you like the word, don't you? I do. It has class, does it not?"

Laura smiled for the first time since she had arrived in Covington, then immediately her face clouded. The smile faded from her lips, and her eyes misted.

"It's all right, Laura, a little smile's good for you."

Laura hid her face in her hands. "It dishonors Marvin for me to enjoy anything so soon."

"I don't believe that. Your Marvin would want to see a smile on that pretty face of yours."

"I'm not pretty—look at this scar."

Amelia rose. Slowly, deliberately she unwound the turquoise silk scarf from about her neck. "Sometimes we are left with invisible scars, sometimes with visible scars."

"My God, how did that happen to you?"

Amelia's fingers fluttered above the scars. "The accident that killed Thomas. There was a fire. They barely got me out of the car."

"Oh, Amelia, I'm so sorry. I didn't know."

"It's horrible to have to adjust to such things, but you can. It took me a long time."

The scars were pale, crinkled patches on Amelia's neck and shoulder, not disgusting, not meriting scarves, not terrible flaws to her beauty as Amelia obviously considered them to be. "I'm sorry," Laura said softly. "Would you think me insensitive if I said the scars are not bad? With a high-neck blouse or dress you wouldn't see most of them."

With a flourish Amelia replaced the scarf. "I see them in my mind the way they were at first, red and raw and horrid. I use scarves that enhance the color of my eyes." She made it sound manageable and resisted telling Laura about her fears that Lance, when she was dating him, would be repulsed by the scars.

Laura's hand touched her cheek, and she thought about warriors of old who wore their scars of war proudly across their faces. She felt only embarrassment about her scar, which could not be hidden by clothing, except perhaps by a chador worn by Muslim women. For an instant she imagined herself walking about in Asheville with her head and face covered. No. She had no intention of staying here. There was nothing here for her. Laura leaned across the Scrabble board, scattering letters. "Amelia, do you believe there's anything after death?"

"Yes, I do."

"What? Marvin believed there was nothing. 'When you're dead, you're dead, finished, that's it,' is what he used to say."

"I like to believe that the soul and the body part at death, the body is finished, gone, and the soul, well, I think it lives on. It soars."

"Soars?"

"Yes. Soars free, unlimited, above it all." Like Amelia had experienced only months ago after the painful debacle with Lance. Humiliated, despairing, and feeling empty and alone, she had climbed the hillside behind their home and rested on a fallen tree trunk. After a time of quiet, she unwittingly floated out of her body onto the bosom of the air and over Cove Road: light and free, relieved of guilt and shame and regret. She had only to close her eyes to relive the immense joy that had wrapped about her. The incident marked the turning point in her recovery from self-hate and humiliation and grief over Lance Lundquist, who had ardently courted and then betrayed her.

"I hope you're right, Amelia." Laura's voice put an end to Amelia's thoughts. "Marvin would like soaring." She leaned her elbows on the table. "He loved life. He'd been an mechanical engineer way back when, been married and divorced. Marriage, he believed, ruined a good relationship. I agreed. Neither of us wanted kids, so . . ." She shrugged. "Marvin and I . . . we were very close. One of us would start a sentence, and the other would finish it. And now he's gone." The corners of Laura's mouth drooped. Tears spilled from her eyes. She wiped them away with the balls of her hands. "If I could only believe he's somewhere, a spirit, energy, and not . . . well . . . just gone, I'd feel better." She looked away for a moment. "Marvin was special, always learning new things. If it wasn't a correspondence course in bookkeeping, it was studying astronomy or reading about sea turtles and coral reefs. His interests were boundless. When they told me he was, was . . . gone, I couldn't believe it. All I could do was scream."

If anyone understood, Amelia did. Some day, she thought, when I know Laura better, I'll tell her about my daughter, Caroline, dying in my arms when she was only nine years old, and about my breakdown after Thomas died, and even about Lance. I must reassure her how resilient we are, and that, remarkably, we can and do survive life's tragedies.

10

The House in the Pine Forest

Laura rarely looked in the mirror. The red scar marring her lower left cheek made her want to cry every time she saw it.

"It's going to fade until you hardly see it at all," Hannah had tried to reassure her. "Dr. Romano said you had the best plastic surgeon."

"So why didn't he tell me that?"

"Perhaps he did, and at the time you couldn't hear him."

Laura's vanity was her smooth and unblemished olive-colored skin that set off her blue eyes. When she was young, she wondered why her skin was shades darker than her mother's, or Miranda's, or even her father's. Finally as a teenager she had asked.

"Remember the Spanish Armada?" Hannah replied. "Some of the Spanish sailors made it to England."

"So besides French and English blood we have Spanish blood?"

"Indeed we do, somewhere back there."

Now, after all these weeks, the scar did indeed appear less angry. Of course, she could cover it with makeup, but Laura hated makeup except the occasional touch of lipstick. So she coped with the scar by avoiding looking at it when she washed her face or brushed her teeth, and since she hardly cared what her hair looked like, after several quick brush strokes, she yanked her shoulder-length dark hair back into a ponytail. "Please, Marvin, let Dr. Romano be right."

For the first, and not the last, time, Laura spoke out loud to Marvin and took comfort in so doing.

Several nights before Laura's cast came off, Amelia appeared in the doorway of her room with bowls of ice cream. As they ate, Laura asked, "How is that man down the road who had surgery?"

"Harold Tate? The chemotherapy's made him horrifically sick. Brenda's half out of her mind with worry. He won't see anyone. I went down there again yesterday afternoon. Their daughter, Molly Lund, was sitting in the porch swing, crying. She looked like an old woman, and she's only thirty-seven."

The news lifted Laura out of the morass of her own unhappiness for a moment. "I'm sorry. I hope she'll be all right. I hope Mr. Tate recovers from all this."

"I hope so too." A few minutes later, Amelia said, "*Chérie*, tomorrow I'm photographing in a special place way out in the hills. Would you like to go?"

Laura wiped a bit of ice cream from the corner of her lip and nodded. "Yes, I'd like that." She sat forward in bed, one leg up. "I've been reading about Madison County, trying to get a feel for it. Am I right it's very mountainous, mountains in the center, mountains to the north and west?"

"Yes. And the French Broad River runs right though the county, and there are many tributaries, which is why there are so many valleys and coves like Covington. Beautiful country, but the settlements were, and are, far apart."

"I've hardly seen any of it," Laura said. "I'll be very quiet, not disturb you while you work."

When her daughter died, a large part of Amelia's heart died with her. Love as deep and powerful as that was too painful to endure again, and yet, unwittingly, she found herself opening to this young woman, and Amelia resisted the desire to hug Laura and to hold her. Perhaps it would put Laura off. If she hugged Hannah, it would surely put Hannah off. Amelia gathered up the empty bowls. "Good. We'll do it tomorrow, then. Good night, Laura." At the doorway she turned. "Good night. Sleep tight." She blew a light little kiss.

"Don't let the bedbugs bite," Laura responded automatically. The door closed. Stunned by the memory it had evoked, Laura lay there. "Good night. Sleep tight." Her mother's words, loving words said to her at night, long, long ago. Had she been four or five? It was surely before that time when Hannah had roused her daughters and hustled them from their beds to flee from their father into a freezing February night. Laura closed her eyes and fought away tears. So many things had been lost, so much to weep about, then and now. Out of the past, Laura heard her own small voice as she blew a little girl's kiss back to her mother and whispered, "Don't let the bedbugs bite."

The unpaved road on which Amelia drove for the first half hour degenerated into a deeply rutted lane. Laura clasped her shoulders and shrank from the window as thick thorny bushes and low over-hanging branches reached as if to impede their passing. She felt like Dorothy on the yellow brick road in the land of Oz. When Amelia swerved to avoid a stand of protruding wild rosebushes, the car jolted through deep ruts. She's going to throw the frame of her car out of kilter, Laura thought.

Amelia chatted steadily, seemingly unfazed by the hazards of the trip. Now she spoke of Russell and Emily's wedding reception last June. "It was held in our yard. Roger and Charles came down and coordinated it. They had a dance floor built over the stream. Flowers everywhere, and twinkling lights. Magical. Beautiful."

Before Laura could respond, Amelia continued. "Tyler behaved terribly toward Emily when his dad started dating her. His mother, you know, was killed in an auto accident a few years ago, just before we moved down here. That's how Grace met Bob, while she was tutoring Tyler. Well, anyway, your mother asked them for dinner and got everyone talking. That broke the ice. After that, Tyler started to accept Emily."

"My mother as mediator?" Laura's laugh was tinged with sarcasm.

"Why, yes," Amelia said. "Without mediation, without compromise, how do you think three women as different as we are live together as harmoniously as we do?"

"I've wondered."

"You know how running water smoothes stones?"

Laura nodded.

"Friendships are like that. If they survive, it's because the jagged edges of the crises that inevitably occur from time to time get smoothed over. Like when Hannah set fire to the orchard . . ."

"My mother set trees on fire?"

"She meant to burn the leaves she'd raked. Thing was, I'm mortally afraid of fire. My neck, you know." Amelia fingered her scarf.

Laura nodded. "Mother must have been mortified."

"She was. I was terrified, wanted to pack and flee the house. But then the fire trucks came and stopped it before it reached the woods."

"What happened then?"

Amelia waved her hand in a dismissive manner. "I calmed down, and after a time we talked about it. That's how we handle things that come up. We listen to one another, we don't interrupt or argue. We aren't ashamed or afraid to say we're sorry, and we make every effort to accept each other's viewpoint, foibles and all. Our friendships have been tested and have survived." She looked quite pleased.

"Seeing you all together, I'd never guess there had ever been any problems."

Amelia laughed. "Three people sharing a house? To live without problems and some conflicts would be utopia, and impossible. But I am certain of one thing, *chérie*, when folks have goodwill toward one another, they can work things out."

They bounced along for a time. Laura supported her cast with her hands and hoped the tires would withstand being punctured.

Laura would have preferred silence, but Amelia skipped to yet another matter. "Mike's going to stop off at Roger and Charles's place in Pennsylvania on his way home from Indiana."

"He's from Indiana?"

"No, his folks retired there, near his sister." A worried expression crossed Amelia's face and settled in her eyes. "Several times, at Russell and Emily's wedding, I noticed Charles pouting, and Mike and Roger off in a corner deep in conversation. I told Grace, but she said I was being unduly suspicious, that Roger was utterly devoted to Charles. They've been together nearly twenty years. But I wondered. It's been six years since Charles's diagnosis of HIV, and Charles is older, maybe fifteen years older than Roger."

"You think because of HIV and Charles being older, Roger might be looking for a replacement?" Laura didn't really care, but Amelia had taken such an interest in her, she felt she ought to appear interested.

"I don't know. It's plain that Charles tires easily. They traveled a great deal while they lived overseas. They worked in Saudi Arabia for years, you know."

"Saudi Arabia? No, I didn't know that."

They were out of the overhanging trees now and the valley, backed by low hills, opened before them, wide and green and beautiful. "It's lovely, isn't it?' Amelia stopped the car, and they sat for a time breathing in the meadow air, laced now with the smell of fresh-mown hay. As if on their way to some grand fiesta, cumulous clouds raced overhead. "I lost a little girl when she was nine," Amelia said.

It was so unexpected that Laura jerked about to face her. "I didn't know. I'm so sorry."

Amelia's jaw tightened. "You'd think I'd have gotten over it by now."

"Does one ever get over the loss of a child?"

"I was just beginning not to cry every morning, when Thomas was killed and I was burned." Then, perhaps because she needed to change the subject she had just raised, she asked, "What will you do when you're fully recovered?"

"I guess, I'll head back to Maine, see who needs crew for their charter boat." She said it without thinking and was chilled by her words. Winters in Maine. Wasn't that why they had moved the *Maribow* to the Caribbean, for her, because of the cold? Her heart congealed with guilt and sorrow.

63

"I'll miss you. Don't you like it here, even a little?"

Laura shrugged. "It's not the ocean, but it is beautiful country. I need to work. What would I do here?"

"I don't know." It seemed, somehow, a day for confidences. "After my stay in the hospital," Amelia said in a bland voice, "I acted rashly, sold our home in New Jersey and traveled in Europe for months, until one day I found that I'd squandered a great deal of money. I came home to the States and had a breakdown. The hotel staff found me curled in a corner in my room. That's when I went to psychiatric hospital. After a time, my doctor there recommended Olive Pruitt's place. 'It's quiet and clean, and there are only one or two other women. You won't be alone, and you can afford it,' he said. What painful, dour days those were for me, Laura. But you see, like the phoenix, one can rise from the ashes."

"You really think that?" Bitterness oozed from Laura's voice.

"I know that." Amelia started the engine, and they rode on a good dirt road running along the perimeter of the meadow. "Look at me now. I have friends, a home, and Covington's a good place to live." Amelia stopped. "I'm sorry, Laura. It's quite too soon to be talking about a phoenix rising."

"I guess I need to hear it, even if it's hard to believe at this moment."

Amelia sighed. "You're a fine young woman. I like you very much, Laura Parrish."

Laura Parrish. How odd the name seemed. For seven years, everyone had assumed that she was Mrs. Marvin Binninger. Still, never having married, Parrish was her name, the name of a drunk who had, by his violence, forced her mother, herself, and her sister into that frigid February night. No wonder she hated the cold and especially disliked the month of February.

Pictures burst like fireworks before her eyes: her mother speeding so fast that Laura had covered her eyes, expecting them to crash, her father, his eyes bulging with rage, finding them at a gas station. The sound of his gunshot had sent streams of water arching from the radiator of her mother's car to freeze in midair. She shuddered, remembering the huge sixteen-wheeler truck and the cigar-smoking driver who took them with him to Pennsylvania. If the driver had been heading for Memphis, or Houston, or Santa Fe, that's where they would have ended up. And her mother, who had never worked outside the home, had cleaned other peoples' houses while attending night school to be a secretary. She'd worked long hours, been so exhausted. And she, Laura, had only made it harder. Tears clouded Laura's eyes. A whimper escaped her throat.

"I've upset you. I'm so sorry, dear," Amelia said.

"I was remembering how hard my mother worked to take care of us those early years after we left my father."

"Hannah's a hardworking, strong, reliable woman. I'm a better person because she's my friend."

Suddenly, Amelia veered from the perimeter road onto a rutted one-lane that plunged into deep pine tree woods. Sunshine vanished, and the air grew cooler. Amelia rolled down her window, inviting in the fresh clean smell of pine, while beyond the trees a weather-worn clapboard farmhouse, bounded behind by a precipitous hill, came into view.

There was about the place a sense of isolation. Slanting rays of sunlight spilled through trees to lend an air of enchantment. From the open doorway, a woman in a formless pale blue dress waved. Her smile welcomed them.

"Irene Ramsey." Amelia introduced them as they approached the steps to the front porch. "This is Laura Parrish, the daughter of one of my housemates."

"Broke your leg, did you?" Mrs. Ramsey asked, studying Laura. Her eyes grazed Laura's face, and Laura winced.

"An accident," she said. Would it always be this way? Would the scar remain to draw attention, to provoke explanations?

Before Laura could say anything more, Amelia said, "Mrs. Ramsey makes beautiful quilts, and she specializes in making the most lifelike cornhusk dolls."

"Twice a year, they comes up here from over in Asheville and gets my dolls to sell in that there craft shop they got." Irene Ramsey looked satisfied, and she laughed heartily and slapped her thighs. "Imagine folks wantin' to buy my dolls." She shrugged. "Well, guess we all's got somethin' we gotta have, like Miss Amelia here, she's gotta have her pictures." Irene Ramsey laughed again and addressed herself to Laura. "Miss Amelia's been tryin' to take a picture of this old face. Gray hair and all these lines. Tell you what I'm gonna do today. I'm gonna let her take my picture from the side, while I'm quiltin'. I seen them kinds of pictures in a book."

"Oh, thank you, Mrs. Ramsey," Amelia said. Delighted, she could have jigged the length of the front porch and back.

"Out here on the porch," the older woman said.

"That'll be fine."

Amelia helped Mrs. Ramsey carry out the straight-back chair she used for quilting, and the frame, heavy with a section of a Wedding Ring pattern quilt. Once Irene was settled, Amelia changed lenses on her camera, spread the legs of her tripod, and screwed the camera in place. For a long time she examined and considered the scene. What did she want to express in this photo? Loneliness, isolation, industry, purpose? Purpose, a meaningful life illustrated by the strong line of this widow woman's chin, her upright back, her steady fingers drawing the needle through layers of material and batting.

The film in Amelia's camera was black and white. The white boards of the house, Amelia knew, would represent the lightest value, white and near white. The dark blue shawl flung about Irene Ramsey's shoulders would provide the darkest value, while the quilt, the woman's thick, white bun pinned loosely at the nap of her neck, and the soft sunlight splashing across her lap and hands would infuse the photo with grays that would balance the photograph. Amelia adjusted her camera and began to work.

Deep wrinkles on Irene Ramsey's hands, her wide, thick knuckles, her silver thimble, and the ease with which one tiny stitch lengthened into a line of minute stitches transported Laura back to the *Maribow*, to Marvin, his brow furrowed, the tip of his tongue visible between his lips as he mended a section of sail. Pain sliced her heart, and for a moment she looked away, struggling to keep control of her emotions.

The shoot went on. Amelia moved the tripod more to one side, then the other, high, lower.

Laura studied Mrs. Ramsey's heavily lined and brooding face and understood that grief had the ability to toy with one's emotions. In reality, nothing about her resembled Marvin. "How long have you been working on this quilt?" Laura asked from her perch on the porch steps.

"Well into six months now."

"You do all this quilting alone?"

"My neighbor down the road a piece, Aggy Howard, comes when she can and helps, but mostly I been stitchin' on this one. Gotta keep at it steady 'til it's done." She nodded vigorously. Laura was sure that "slow and steady" characterized Irene Ramsey's life. Slow and steady. She'd heard that phrase used to describe Marvin.

*

On the return trip, Laura hardly noticed the crumbling roads, and when they cleared the woods they were greeted by a sky that could be described only as a wall of shifting color. Laura's spirits lifted as she watched entranced as reds turned to flame, flame to rust, rust to lavender, and finally lavender to gray. The wind picked up and swept past them with low moaning sounds. When they drove into their driveway, Laura was amazed at how welcoming the porch lights of the farmhouse were, and now pleased she was to see Grace and Mike waving at them from the kitchen window.

Moments later, the front door flew open, and Mike greeted them from the top of the porch steps. "Amelia, darling, I have the most fantastic news."

He took her camera bag, and she carried her tripod into the house. Laura followed, carefully managing her crutches on the gravel and up the steps.

"What is it, Mike? You're all flushed and excited." Amelia leaned the tripod against the wall of the foyer.

Mike paced the foyer, rubbing his hands together and smiling broadly. "Your work's been noticed. You've been invited to exhibit ten photographs at a gallery in New York City. *New Faces in Photography* the exhibit's called. They've selected six photographers from around the country. It's a great honor."

Amelia said nothing. She sat on a hassock and began to unlace her walking shoes. "Invited where, Mike?"

"New York City." He clapped his hands. "Soon all of New York will see your marvelous, sensitive, beautiful photographs." He frowned then. "It's a black-and-white show. Have we enough truly spectacular black and whites? We'll have to scrutinize everything we already have, and then there'll be weeks of shooting, selecting . . ."

"My photographs were chosen?"

"Indeed they were, my friend. Isn't it marvelous?"

"How did this happen?" Amelia asked.

Grace, a small bowl and a whisk in her hands, appeared in the doorway. "How do you think? Your greatest admirer and advocate, Mike, sent several of your photos off."

"You did that Mike? Without telling me?"

Flustered and worried, he was at her side in a moment. "Dear Amelia. Your work's too wonderful not to be seen by"—his arm made a wide sweep—"huge audiences. I didn't want you to fret and worry. If nothing had come of it, I'd have said nothing. Forgive me, please?"

"It's wonderful," Grace said. "Wonderful. New York." Her face spoke of adventure and excitement. "Our Amelia exhibiting in New York City. I can't think of anything more wonderful. Why are you staring into space like that, Amelia? Aren't you excited?"

"I'm overwhelmed, that's all. My mind's switched to neutral."

"It's a black-and-white show," Mike repeated.

Amelia nodded.

"Well, we'll have to get to work. First, we'll evaluate every black and white you've ever taken." Rubbing his hand together and smiling broadly, Mike walked back and forth in the small foyer. "We can do it. We'll get right to it tomorrow. I'll pick you up at seven."

One shoe in her hand, Amelia stared at him. "But Mike, I'm supposed to start at the hospital tomorrow."

"So put it off until this show's over."

"No, Mike, I won't put off my work at the hospital. It's too important to me. I start tomorrow. It's one day a week. The rest of the time you can work me until I drop."

Mike opened his mouth and snapped it shut. A thick silence filled the air. Grace whisked vigorously at whatever was in the bowl in her hand, then turned to go back into the kitchen. Laura followed her.

"When is this show, Mike?" Amelia asked.

"January tenth."

Amelia lifted her hand to his, and he helped her to her feet. "I don't talk about it much, but I worry what's going to happen December thirty-first. You'll come here that evening, be with us, won't you?"

"You're a love," he said. "But a couple of us are going to stay with Jamie, my sick friend." His eyes filled with tears. "He's near the end now, Amelia."

She rested her hand on her arm. "You care a great deal about Jamie?"

"I loved him once, years ago. We stayed friends. He was an excellent emergency room doctor over in Rutherford County." Mike turned so that she could not see the pain in his face.

"You're a good person, Mike. I'm sorry about Jamie." Amelia shook herself. "As you say, we have much to do. And thanks, Mike. I am grateful to you for sending the photos, and I'm very proud they chose my work." Taking his arm she guided him out onto the porch where, for a while, as he collected himself, they rocked and listened to jazz, the low, mournful sound of a saxophone that issued from a CD player in Laura's room. After a time Amelia asked, "You'll come to New York with me?"

He nodded.

It was not long before Hannah arrived home and joined them on the porch, and within moments, the tinkle of Grace's silver bell drew them all to the kitchen for dinner.

11

The Director Is Needed, Now

He came up behind her, his feet as silent as cats' paws, and when he spoke her name, "Hannah," she jumped and nearly toppled off her knees, and the spade fell from her hand into the soft cool earth. Hannah sank onto her haunches, then eased herself to the ground. "Max," she said, "I didn't hear you."

He came from his dairy farm across the road, and the smell of manure was faint but present. "Bella used to say I sneaked up on her. She never got used to it, even after all our years together." His smile faded. "It's not a year yet, Hannah, and it feels as if she's been gone forever. I miss her terribly." He lowered himself to the ground beside Hannah, reached for and handed her the spade. "I'm sorry I startled you. Can I help?"

She handed him a three-pronged digger. "Loosen the earth for me, and I'll pull the weeds."

Shoulders nearly touching, they worked for a time in silence. She liked George Maxwell. They had become friends after his wife's untimely death from some rare affliction that simulated multiple sclerosis. For months, since Bella's death, he had encouraged and supported Hannah's efforts to interest a land trust or conservation organization into purchasing Jake Anson's large tract of land that wrapped the end of Cove Road.

It had shocked Hannah, and stirred the fighting Irish in her, when Anson announced at a community meeting last year his intention to sell his land. With no zoning laws in place, irresponsible development—homes built directly on the floodplain of Little River, hillsides striped of vegetation to accommodate condominiums—had already taken place in Loring Valley just down Elk Road in Covington. A fierce determination to stop further local development motivated Hannah to purchase and become proficient on a computer. Surfing the Net, she identified, contacted, and appealed to conservancies, land trusts, as well as private and corporate foundations. But on discovering that upon the demise of his now eighty-two-year-old daughter, Lurina Masterson Reynolds, Grover Masterson had bequeathed his entire four hundred acres on Elk Road to the state for a park, their interest evaporated.

And then winter intervened, ushering in a storm so fierce that it wreaked havoc on nearly all of the homes and condos in Loring Valley. The swollen river spilled cascades of water and mud onto lawns and into homes constructed on the floodplain. Hillsides crumbled, washing away sections of new road and spewing muddy ooze under the doors of condominiums. Anson's deal evaporated, and Hannah rejoiced. But not for long. Within weeks, Anson's land came on the market again. It was then that Max had come forward and, using his wife's trust, purchased the seven hundred acres.

And now work was underway at the Bella Maxwell Park and Preserve. Plans included hiking trails and a limited number of campsites. There would be museums: a living Indian village; a museum to house the collection of Indian artifacts, dating back 7,000 years, that had recently come to light on the property; a homestead depicting the life and times of the first Scotch-Irish men and women who had settled the area. There would be gardens: a cottage garden, an herb garden, a canal garden, a children's garden for starters.

"Will you be director of the gardens, Hannah?" Max had asked her shortly after he told her about his plan to purchase the land.

"Director?"

"You wouldn't have to do any physical work. We'd hire a landscape architect and workmen."

Director! Immediately she visualized charming garden paths, trellises burdened with heavily scented roses, beds brimming with annuals and perennials, low stone walls, high brick walls, enchanted realms where water splashed and spilled into ponds. She heard the sound of children laughing as they worked with her to create their own whimsical garden space. "I'd absolutely love to do that," she replied.

"Good." Max had squeezed her hand. "I need you. I'm just an old dairy farmer. It's a whole new endeavor for me." He smiled.

That had been in the spring, and now it was nearly fall, and much had been accomplished. Anson's old house had been renovated and was now the park's offices. The brick walls of the cottage garden had been erected. The canal garden was well under way. Stands stood ready for soil from which would grow a bountiful herb garden. An adjacent space had been tilled and readied for the input of fifth and sixth graders whom Hannah taught gardening to at Caster Elementary School. Grace waited, eager to help. If only, Hannah thought, I could involve Laura. Gardening would surely help to heal her mind and soul.

Hannah's heart sank when she thought of Laura. Her daughter's lassitude was frightening. Her eyes lacked luster and animation. Laura had no appetite, often failed to remember words, and left sentences hanging as she gazed off into space. Hannah was certain that her daughter was severely depressed. In fact, there were days when Hannah was afraid to leave Laura alone in the house. Hannah's smile faded as she turned to face Max. "I'm very worried about Laura."

"Why? She handles those crutches like a pro."

"Her body's healing. It's her mind, her spirit I'm concerned about. She's quite depressed, at times, I think, suicidal. Whole life turned topsy-turvy and no support system."

"She's got you, and Grace, and Amelia."

Hannah's eyes clouded. "We're all so much older. Laura and I were never close. I hadn't seen her and rarely heard from her in more than seven years." The intensity of Max's questioning dark brown eyes unnerved her. "Whatever." She shrugged. "How can I be gone all the time? What if she needs me?" Her shoulders slumped in resignation.

"I was never good with sick people," he said. "Some folks are good at that, some aren't."

Hannah heaved a deep sigh. "Grace is the genius at caring for others. I'm not good at it either. Frustration sets in and anger, mostly at me, and I transfer it, I guess, to the sick person."

"You were incredible support to Bella."

"Why was that so easy, I wonder? I didn't sit there and think, 'Now how can I be supportive?' I simply did what seemed natural."

"But with your daughter?"

"Nothing seems natural. I'm always on edge trying to figure out what she's thinking, or what she wants or needs. Whatever I say to her makes her go tight. Guilt, Max. I left their father. Times were hard. So busy putting food on the table, I was an unavailable mother. I'm loaded with guilt, and now, again, I feel that I'm failing Laura." Hannah brought her knuckles of one hand to her mouth. "Always failed Laura. Here she is. She's lost everything. Never talks about any of it, not the storm, not Marvin, nothing. Bad to bottle things up like that." Hannah grasped his upper arm, then released it quickly, stunned by a sudden and powerful awareness of his strong male presence. Not this too, she thought. "Max, what am I going to do? How can I be gone all day every day of the week, and I'm sure Saturdays, in the beginning?"

Looking surprised, he drew back. "Laura's a grown woman."

"And I'm a mother who's failed her child. I have to at least try not to do that again."

"Let me think about all this," he said.

Several days later, just as Hannah drove her station wagon into the yard, Max appeared, walked to the wagon, and opened her door. Firmly, he took her arm and guided her under the great oak. "Sit," he said pointing to where Adirondack chairs were set in a semicircle. He wasted neither time nor words "Laura's depressed, right?

Inside all the time, no friends? I say we involve her, offer her charge of a project."

"Like what?"

"You decide. You know her better than I do."

"I wonder about that. Laura was never one for gardening."

"Was she always interested in boats and the sea?"

Hannah scratched her head. "Well, no."

"She learned, and it became her life, didn't it?"

"I'm sure Captain Marvin had a lot to do with that."

He leaned forward, turned his head, and fixed her with his eyes. "You're resisting, Hannah. Why? Are you afraid this work at the preserve may be too much for you, like your greenhouse?"

Anger flooded her. "I do have a legitimate conflict."

"Sorry." Max sat back. "Shall I start looking for someone to replace you, then?"

She whirled about, her eyes flaring with anger. "Are you serious?"

"We're ready to go. You're as important a part of this as I am, or Bella's money, even. This is your dream, my friend. It's your call now."

Hannah looked away. With men it was either yes or no, black or white. Well, it was more complex than that, or was it? Could Max be right? Was she hedging, using Laura as an excuse to mask an embryonic fear of failure? Success she knew built on success; but failure built on failure, and in Hannah's mind, having to give up the greenhouse and ornamental plant business was a failure, of judgment, if nothing else.

Hannah drew a deep breath and was suddenly aware of sunlight trickling through leaves, making patterns on her lap, on Max's shirt, on the earth. Her eyes traveled up along the ragged bark of the old oak and down again to the large bed of decorative hostas she had planted. Hostas were perfect shade plants. From the many species available, Hannah had selected three and planted them in great masses: *sieboldiana elegans* for its magnificent blue-gray, waxy, heart-shaped leaves; a smaller, white-edged variety, Thomas Hogg, and the pointed, narrow-leaved *lancifolia*. Tall spikes bearing bell-like lavender flowers swayed in the breeze. Nature could be so perfect, so benign, or—she thought of the hurricane that had shattered her daughter's life—so overwhelmingly devastating.

Hannah forced her mind back to the issue at hand. Would her back give out on her, or her knees? Why should they? This was a director's, not a laborer's, job. But would she have the patience to wait for others to do the things that needed doing now, this minute? Well, she darn well better learn how to let go of things. And she was hurt. Max's words had been harsh. Hire someone to replace her? Preposterous. Max had come up with an interesting idea. She'd create a job so appealing that Laura couldn't refuse. But what job? Laura hated gardening, and the prospect of talking to Laura about this chilled her. Her daughter's stare could render her speechless.

"Give me a day or two to work this out, think about this, Max, will you?"

Max patted her hand. "You're meant to be director, Hannah. You'll work it out." And he left her sitting under the tree, her stomach in a knot, listening to the crunch of leaves beneath his feet as he strode away.

12

A Walk in the Woods

"Take a walk with me up into the woods. I need to talk to you. I need your advice," Hannah said to Grace several days after her conversation with Max.

They left the house by the kitchen door, ambled past the greenhouse, where Wayne whistled as he worked, crossed the fresh-mown pasture, left behind the new apple orchard planted last year by Wayne and Hannah to replace the old trees destroyed by fire, and trekked up the hillside toward the woods. The wind picked up and blew their hair back from their faces. As they walked, Hannah talked steadily, telling Grace about her conversation with Max.

"Max wants you to do what?" Sweat bathed Grace's face.

"Create a job for Laura at the preserve and convince her to take it."

"Why?"

"Assuage my guilt, I imagine. Free me to start my own work, and for Laura, if she'll let herself, to come out of her shell. She needs a meaning in her life."

"You don't think it's a bit soon for meaning?"

"No. Wallow for months in self-pity, or get on with your life. Might not feel like singing, but at least there's a reason to get up in the morning."

The grade of the land changed, flattened a bit, and Grace stopped to catch her breath. "Let's sit," she said, resting a hand over her chest.

"I've told you, you have to take long, slow, deep breaths as you walk," Hannah said, but she joined Grace on a fallen tree trunk in the shade.

"I do so love the woods," Grace said. "I love the smell of pine trees and wild honeysuckle. Bob and I like to walk up here and sit and listen to the birds. There're so many birds. We keep talking about getting a book on birds and binoculars. But then we don't do anything about it." She brought her hands down on her thighs and leaned forward. "So, you want to create a project for Laura and talk her into doing it?"

"That's it exactly. So what can I offer her that she can't refuse?"

For a moment, Grace said nothing.

Hannah's eyes searched the sky as if she expected something to fall on them. Then she said, "Sometimes I see Laura sitting with a book open in her lap staring into space looking desolate, or I hear her crying in her room at night. It tears my heart out. Then I lie in bed and can't shut out my memories of Dan Britton and all the anguish following his death. I want to tell her about Dan . . ."

"He was the great love of your life. Why don't you tell her?"

"Haven't the foggiest idea how to start such a conversation. It's all I can do to approach her about a job at the preserve. Do you think she'd take it, Grace, or is she just waiting to get out of here?"

"Where would she go?"

"Maine. Must have friends there."

"If she did, why haven't they called or sent cards? Why hasn't she tried to reach any of them? You want her to go, Hannah?"

Hannah considered that for a long while. What did she want? Laura's presence evoked feelings of failure, frustration, and inadequacy as a mother. Yet she loved her daughter, empathized with her loneliness, understood her despondency, and despaired at the huge gulf, filled with gunnysacks of anger, hurt, and disappointment that lay between them. How had it gotten so out of hand, so divisive? "So far, any reaching out I've done to Laura's been politely rejected. I don't need that," Hannah said. "I'm sure she doesn't like me. Laura might say no just because I'm the one asking."

"I don't believe that. Laura loves you. I've seen the wistful look on her face when you're on the phone with Miranda, and she's jealous of Wayne."

"Of Wayne?"

"Don't you realize how pleased you are to see him?"

"I'm very fond of him. He's been like a—"

"A son to you."

Hannah's shoulders slumped. "I see what you mean."

"Back to your stubborn daughter. Wonder where she got that quality from?" It was said in jest, but Hannah did not smile.

"She is like me, too stubborn at times for her own good."

"True, but I think Laura knows that you care," Grace said.

"So much stuff we've never talked about."

"Maybe rehashing the past isn't necessary. Maybe what's needed now is to move forward. Laura could have a responsible position at the preserve, not working directly with you or for you, and that might help bridge the gap between you, instead of your having to analyze and understand everything in the past."

"Interesting viewpoint, my friend, and a good one. How did you ever get so wise?"

Grace smiled and tilted her chin. "Are you implying that living almost all of my life in Dentry, Ohio, population about five thousand disallowed for wisdom?" She laughed and felt warm inside. "People are people," Grace said. "Pain, loss, grief, joy—they're the same for everyone. I listen. That's all, my friend. I just listen."

"You listen well, and I appreciate that."

How marvelous, Grace thought, to have a friend like Hannah. She could confide in Hannah or confront her without Hannah taking umbrage. She trusted Hannah, could turn to her for counsel, and Grace knew that Hannah reciprocated her feelings. A twinge of guilt pinched at Grace. She had told Hannah nothing about her doctor's diagnosis. No need to speak of it before she and Bob went to the doctor. Besides, she felt fine.

Hannah kicked bits of bark and leaves with her shoe, and Grace rose from the tree trunk and brushed off her skirt. "Let's go a little farther, shall we? The other day I saw what I think was a sparrow hawk hovering."

"How did you recognize a sparrow hawk?"

"By its call, a sharp *killy, killy, killy.* Maybe they're nesting somewhere up here."

They strode toward the deeper woods to where the sun failed to pierce the thick, leafy canopy above them. Chunks of fallen bark, small limbs, and other forest debris crunched beneath their feet. The air felt cool on their arms and faces. They saw no hawks, but heard, in the distance, the caw of crows and the song of a cuckoo. Hannah held several long branches high so that Grace might pass. A thorn stuck her palm, and she gasped then sucked at it.

"Let me see that." Grace took Hannah's hand and turned it so that she could see the place, red now and swollen. "This looks like an allergic reaction. What was it? Blackberry bush, wild rose?"

"Didn't really look. It'll go away, always does."

"Let's go home and put something on it."

They started back down the hillside, exited the woods, and stood again in the clearing from where they looked down on the orchard, the pasture, and the red tin roof of their farmhouse. Grace said, "I've been thinking. Laura's interested in Madison County history. She asked me to get her some books."

Hannah nodded. "An A student, until she determined to fight any and all authority: stayed out all night, cut classes, colored her hair purple, blasted music, sassed me real good."

Grace nodded. How did any single parent ever manage to raise a child through those terrible teen years? "When does the cast come off?" she asked.

Suddenly, Grace slipped on matted leaves, and Hannah grasped her arm to steady her. "We're a pair, you and I," Grace said, laughing lightly as they slowed pace and braced against the steeper slope. "Your palm's swollen, and I'm about to twist an ankle." But she didn't, and they made it to the foot of the hill without further mishap.

Then Hannah said, "Laura's cast comes off in less than ten days."

"I'll bet you a twenty that Laura won't leave us if she's got something to throw herself into here," Grace said.

"You really think that?"

"I do. She's lonely. Can't you see that your daughter needs a friend? Haven't you noticed how much time she spends with Amelia?"

"Very odd to me."

"Amelia's asked her to go photographing with her. Your daughter's up for grabs, my dear friend. Who'll get Laura, you or Amelia?"

Hannah shuddered. "What a way to put it."

As they passed the apple trees, Grace rubbed her hands together. "Okay now, here's what I think Laura should do at the Bella Maxwell Park and Preserve. That name's just too long and ponderous. I think I'll call it Bella's Park. As I was saying, Laura should be involved with the early settlers' village. Who's coordinating that?"

"Maxwell, so far, and he'd rather be back at the farm with his cows." Hannah's voice rose with excitement. "Grace, that's it, of course. She's a capable woman. She can do it, I'm sure. Grace, I could hug you."

That was odd coming from Hannah, but Grace was not one to miss a hug. Turning to Hannah, they embraced briefly. Then Hannah smoothed her blouse and they walked swiftly up the kitchen steps.

13

Words from the Heart

Within days of Grace and Hannah's talk, Hannah and her daughter sat down on the front porch to talk. Hannah carried out tall glasses of lemonade and set them on the wicker coffee table. In a periwinkle-blue sky, pillars of white clouds towered above Snowman's Cap. From somewhere nearby, an unseen woodpecker tapped its Morse code into the bark of a tree. The last butterflies of summer, dark swallowtails and bright orange butterflies, perhaps a monarch butterfly on its way south, harvested nectar from the throats of bright red begonias. Falling leaves and nighttime temperatures in the low fifties heralded winter.

"Will it be a cold winter this year, do you think?" Laura asked.

"Almanac says so, and everyone around here says that all the signs indicate it will be."

Laura shivered. "I hate the cold. It goes right through me."

"That why you took the *Maribow* to the Caribbean?"

It was as if Hannah had slapped her. Her mother always had an uncanny sense of her deepest feelings.

Hannah's eyes searched her daughter's face and bore into her soul. "Now Laura, I hope you aren't blaming yourself for what happened. You aren't God, you know. You can't make or stop a hurricane."

Damn her mother. Tact had never been her strong suit. It still wasn't. Laura's anger flared. "Yes. If you must know, I feel guilty and responsible, and I don't believe there is a God." She looked away sharply. Suppressing the desire to cry made her throat tighten and ache. "Still, if we'd stayed in Maine . . ."

"I'm sorry, Laura." Hannah raised her hands in the air, then dropped them into her lap in a gesture of defeat. "I always say the wrong things, don't I? Always have. If anyone feels guilty, I do. I failed you when you were young, and I'm still failing you. Can't even comfort you now, let you know I understand, that I've been there too . . ." She hesitated.

"You mean running from Dad? How can that compare to what's happened to me?"

"I don't mean that." Hannah drew back her shoulders and lifted her head. She cleared her throat. Her stomach quivered. Keep your mouth shut, one part of her urged, while at a deeper level she knew that sharing her life, her love, her pain was the only way she might reach her daughter. Clasping her hands in her lap, Hannah began. "Long ago, when I was fifty-two, I fell passionately in love." She sighed deeply. "My one and only love."

The incredulous look on Laura's face nearly stopped Hannah. But she looked away, up at the huge hovering clouds, and continued. "His name was Dan Britton. He was married." It seemed that Laura was about to speak, and Hannah raised a hand to silence her. "Let me finish. He was Catholic. Four kids. I knew it going into it, but I loved him so much. We were together for three years, every other weekend, once or twice a week. If his wife knew, she never made an issue. He was all my life. I lived for our times together. It was, in fact"—she looked down at her fingers, ran her fingertips over her ring finger—"the happiest time of my life." Hannah raised her head and looked squarely into her daughter's eyes. "He was killed in a boating accident on a lake; a teenager racing his boat smashed into Dan's boat. For a year after he died, I cried myself to sleep every night and barely got through my workday, but I carried on."

"I didn't know." Laura blubbered. Tears ran down her face, tears for her own and for her mother's loss.

"No one knew. No one." Hannah gripped the arms of her rocker. She spoke almost fiercely. "Know what that was like? Couldn't attend his funeral. Couldn't show my grief in public, or talk about my time with Dan. Could only lie in bed at night and weep. Went to his church once, a church that forbade divorce. The smell of incense. All those statues staring down at me. I found no comfort there." She paused, then she said, "It nearly killed me. Then I started going to the lake in the evenings. I'd sit on the sand, let the water wet my feet, and cry." Hannah noted the empathy in Laura's face. She continued.

"Somewhere, I have a picture taken that year after Dan died. You wouldn't recognize me, Laura. Lost so much weight, everyone thought I had cancer. My eyes were sunk into deep hollows. Hair started falling out." She stopped and looked out at the road and beyond to the hills to the clouds, which were slowly changing shape.

"Where were Miranda and I?"

"Gone, off on your own, both of you."

Laura did the math in her head. When her mother was fifty-two, she would have been almost twenty-one and Miranda twenty-four. Miranda was newly married and she, Laura, to her mother's huge dismay, was hitchhiking across the country. She had never come home again until now.

"I'm so sorry." Leaning across the chairs, Laura touched her mother's arm lightly. "How did you ever survive it?"

"Thought for a good while that I wouldn't survive. Considered suicide but hadn't the courage for that."

Laura understood. She hadn't the courage for it either.

"Also takes courage to live and to grieve, to face the reality of a loss like mine, like yours, and to go on. I think the shock literally changes your body chemistry. And then there are all those 'if onlys,' especially when the death is sudden and violent. I berated myself: If only I hadn't gone to work that Saturday and been with him instead, he wouldn't have gone out on the lake, and so on."

Laura nodded and pressed her hands to her heart. "If only I'd found a way to handle the winters in Maine . . ."

"I understand."

After a time Laura asked "What did you do, Mother?"

"Worked my butt off. Forced myself out of that bed every day, got on that bus, and went to work. Office manager for a chiropractor then. Kept telling myself my work was meaningful, important. Worked hard at putting on a good face. So many years ago, yet when I think or talk about it, I still feel it." She placed a hand against her chest. "Two things helped me. When summer came, I went to the lake every day after work and swam. Something therapeutic about water. I'd open my eyes underwater. World down there was green, like Dan's eyes. That comforted me. Made me feel connected to him. Started talking to him. Started raising one pink geranium in a pot. I tended it and talked to it, told it all about Dan and me. Thrived and bloomed its little heart out. I was sure it understood."

"Is that when you changed jobs?"

"Had to see the results of my labor, to watch something grow. I went to work in a plant nursery." Hannah smiled at her daughter. "Started a whole new life, one that's sustained me through thick and thin."

"Through thick and thin," Laura repeated. Unconcerned, suddenly, with who might drive by on Cove Road, she began to sob deep wrenching sobs. When she could, Laura spoke for the first time about the hurricane.

"The night of the storm, the sky was clear, filled with stars, magnificent. The sea was like glass. We wondered if the weather reports were wrong. Marvin and I lay on the deck, very close, and we fell asleep. We woke being jostled about and the ketch rolling heavily. The stars had vanished. Moments later the rain came, pelting our skin like tiny nails.

"Somehow, we made it down to the cabin to see if everything was secured. No sooner had we gotten there than I was pitched against a wall, and Marvin, he was big and strong, couldn't maintain his balance. He fell. Many of the boat people had gone to stay with friends on the island or to the hotel. Several of us decided to 'ride it out' on our boats." She buried her head in her hands. "Why did we do that? The *Maribow* is, was, a big solid ketch, and we had two anchors down, and we were in a supposedly protected harbor. We didn't even realize we'd been torn from our moorings until the ketch lifted and heaved like a toy boat in a child's bath." Laura bent over and ran her fingers through her hair again and again before she could look at her mother. "We strained, both of us, to lift the hatch and get back up into the cockpit. There was water everywhere. I tried to bail out the cockpit with a three-gallon bucket. Stupid!

"It was raining so hard we couldn't see the islands. Gone, vanished, Mother, and then the boom swung, and Marvin almost went overboard. The force of the explosion when the mizzen cracked knocked us to the floor. We knew there were reefs, saw them one minute and not the next. It was surreal. I remember clinging to the wheel, yelling for Marvin to come to me, but he was involved with the main mast's riggings.

"I was terrified. The sky, the sea, were all so huge and empty, and the wind howling like a banshee, a banshee, Mother, a towering wave crested with white, white hair streaming." Laura's voice rose, a controlled hysteria. Her shoulders heaved. "The banshee took Marvin!" Laura broke down completely then and sobbed. After a time, she raised her head from her hands and looked at her mother with huge, sorrowful eyes. She seemed suddenly calmer. "That's all I remember, until I woke up in the hospital."

Laura brought her rocker to a standstill. The creak of Hannah's rocker on the floorboards sounded like hammer strokes. Hannah stilled her chair and handed Laura a handkerchief. Neither one of them moved or spoke for a long time.

"I feel better now. Thanks for letting me talk about this, Mother."

"Must have been hell itself."

"It still is."

They drank lemonade. Hannah pointed to the clouds, still changing shape. "Looks like a camel," she said and fell silent again. Time passed and then Hannah said, "I'm to be the director of the gardens at Bella's Park, as Grace calls it. There're to be living museums: an Indian settlement and the early settlers' village. When your cast comes off and you feel able to, Max would like to show you the land." She swallowed hard. "He'd like you to work with us."

"Work with you? Doing what?" Laura blew her nose.

"Developing the early settlers' village."

Laura was silent for so long that Hannah thought she had not heard her. Then she asked, "A proposal?"

"You'd be in charge of setting up the village. There'd be research on early settlements in Madison County so that every building, every screw and pot, every article of clothing worn is authentic. You'd have a staff, of course, one or two assistants of your choice. You'd write the script for the actors who'll portray the settlers as they lived, brogue and all."

Laura's brows drew together, and Hannah stopped. Fool that she was. How insensitive to suggest such a thing after what Laura had just told her. Much too soon. Grace was right. "You're thinking you can't do it. It's too much, at this time."

"Part of me's scared to death to do anything but hide. But something inside's urging me on, saying, 'Go at it, girl.' That's what Marvin would say when he assigned me some task I wasn't completely secure with on the *Maribow*."

"And I bet you never failed at the task."

"I never did. He was such a good teacher, Mother, and such a kind man. I'm sorry you never knew him. I loved him like you loved your Dan." She looked at Hannah, a worried expression on her face. "Do I have the energy to handle a job? I feel so listless, and can't keep my attention on anything."

"All our projects are just getting started. You could do much of the work at home, the initial reading and planning."

"But can I concentrate?" She held her head in her hands. "I can't read more than a page before my mind shuts down. Will I ever be normal, quick-thinking again?"

"I've been there. Thought I'd never be my old, competent self again. But in time it all came back, and it will for you too. Take it from old pros: Amelia, Grace, me. We've all been lost in that dark forest of the soul, and look at us now."

"I admit it has appeal, Mother, but I'm afraid I can't function efficiently, that I'll make a fool of myself."

"There'll be no one to account to but Maxwell, and he's suffered a loss recently, his wife. He's not over it, believe me. The dairy more or less runs itself. He's got a good man, José, who knows the business, and José's wife, Anna, puts dinner on his table and sees to it that his clothes are washed and put away. There are times when Max and I are talking and he goes blank, can't find a word, remember what he was talking about." She patted Laura's hand. "All his faculties, and yours too, will come back in time."

"Promise, Mother?"

"Promise. Don't decide now, Laura. Maybe, it is too soon. Take some time to think about this. Need more information, Max will sit down with you. When you're ready, we'd like to take you to see the property, what's been done, what's planned."

"Right this minute, it seems overwhelming."

"Do you have other plans, returning to Maine?" Hannah held her breath. More than she had realized, she wanted her daughter to stay, wanted to begin again with Laura, to become friends. Over Snowman's Cap the towering clouds had shifted from camel to amorphous mass and were drifting slowly to the east. Clouds shifted, changed form. Everything in nature, and in life, changes, Hannah mused, and has from the beginning of time. We move from foot to horse to buggy to vehicle, from wood fire to candles to electricity, yet when it comes to loss and change, no one explains the natural and healthy progression that accompanies grief. No one speaks of beginnings, middles, and endings, or about the realities of marriage or childbirth. In that moment Hannah hated her parents' stiff upper lip attitude, their puritanical ways, and the denial of feelings, positive and negative, that had prevailed in their household. It was painful to admit that she had been no better than her parents, had not nurtured her children as children deserved to be nurtured, or prepared her daughters for the vicissitudes of life.

"I'll think about this," Laura said, breaking into her mother's train of thought. "I really don't have any plans for my life. Until this minute I didn't think I had a life."

At that moment, Molly Lund drove by, honked, and waved. Hannah waved. Unwittingly, Laura raised her hand in greeting.

89

"Molly's father's having such a bad time," Hannah said. "Her mother too, the whole family. Hard to watch someone you love suffer."

Reaching over, Laura touched her mother's arm lightly. "I know. It's been hard on you seeing me this way, Mother."

Hannah nodded.

"At least Mr. and Mrs. Tate have familiar things and people around them."

"Yes," Hannah replied, "life's tougher when we're faced with illness or the loss of a loved one and have no support system close at hand."

"Like me here now," Laura said softly.

"Yes. Like you here now."

They set their chairs to rocking again and rocked in silence.

14

Beginnings

Bella Maxwell Park and Preserve curved in horseshoe fashion around the southern and farthermost end of Cove Road. Acres of pastureland drifted into rolling hillsides and stretched upward to meld almost imperceptibly with higher and higher forested mountains. As Hannah, Max, and Laura walked across the tightly mowed, lush green lawn, invisible plumes of warm, humid air swirled about them. Laura walked more slowly than the others, using a cane for balance. Hannah wiped her brow, brushing away minuscule gnats that circled her face. Only her sunglasses, wrapped snug about her temples, protected her eyes.

Forest green vinyl siding had replaced the battered wood, and fresh white louvers framed every window of Anson's old farmhouse. The porch, during its renovation, had been widened to accommodate a row of cane-back rocking chairs and small tables. Entering through double doors, painted purple—Bella's favorite color—that had replaced the narrow front door, they stepped into a room transformed from dim and dingy cubicles to a well-lit and open reception area, in the center of which sat a high, circular desk.

"Didn't this floor turn out well, Hannah." Max pointed down at the large squares of white and green tile. "I like the look."

Hannah agreed, and for a short time they gave their attention to the floor and its diagonal pattern. Then Max led them upstairs and along a narrow hallway, past rooms on whose doors black letters identified offices: Sam Ainsley, Coordinator—Native American Settlement; Ed Thomas, Construction Manager; Hank Brinkley, Landscape and Park Architect. Here Max stopped and knocked. When no reply came, he opened the door and stuck his head inside and, finding no one, shut the door. "Wanted you to meet Hank. Nice young chap, very talented," he said to Laura.

Max had searched in Atlanta for a landscape architect with a park development background, someone a bit offbeat, creative, open to possibilities. It did not take him long to hone in on Hank Brinkley, a quiet yet intense young man. "It's virgin territory," he'd told the landscape architect. "It's a chance to make a name for yourself, put your own indelible stamp on the land like Frederick Law Olmstead and Central Park. Now, that's immortality." Hank was everything Maxwell expected. Young, with no wife and no family nearby to impinge on his time, he designed and supervised, working day and night, which accounted for the rapidity with which things had proceeded.

They moved on past the offices of the park and trail development supervisor and the museum curator, neither one of whom had been hired yet, and past several unmarked rooms to a pleasant corner office with wide windows. "This office is earmarked for the coordinator of the early settlers' village."

Hannah leaned against a wall, her hands shoved deep in the pockets of her slacks. "Must come up with a better name."

"That'll be the coordinator's job." With long strides Max moved swiftly from corner to corner as if measuring the distance. "I learned from Bella it's best to let a woman design her own workin' or livin' space." He grinned at Laura.

He had switched on the air-conditioning when they entered the building; cool air from a vent three quarters of the way up the wall lifted wisps of Hannah's hair. It felt good, the coolness on her face. She studied her daughter. Shoulders concave, arms crossed tightly about her chest, Laura looked as if she felt trapped. Max was assuming that they had a deal. Hadn't she made herself clear to him that Laura was fragile and could not be pushed? "Or a man," Hannah said, "if a man takes this job."

"Is there a job description?" Laura asked.

"Figured we'd let the coordinator write her, or his, own," Max said. "I haven't the slightest idea what this job actually entails, research, yes, but will the coordinator have to travel to visit other living museums? The Museum of Appalachia in Norris, Tennessee, more than thirty buildings, is a labor of love of John Rice Irwin. His ancestors settled in the area back in 1784." Max's brow scrunched to form a bushy salt-and-pepper bridge above his eyes. "There'll be plenty of organizing, supervising, coordinating, and God knows what else. Let the coordinator write her or his own job description."

"I, I'm not sure . . ." Laura avoided Max's eyes and sought those of her mother. "Where's your office, Mother?"

"Ground floor, off to the side of reception. Groundskeeper and I have our offices down there. Easy access to the outside world, I imagine."

"Can I see the rest of what's been done?"

Back in the reception area, Max stopped to inspect a join in a section of wallpaper, then pulled a tape measure from his back pocket and began to measure the height of the desk from the floor. Hannah led her daughter out the back door and onto a wide, circular flagstone patio. "It's a huge task we have ahead of us, but exciting," Hannah said.

Several wood and wrought-iron benches hugged the shade of the building. A workman's ice chest stood alongside one of them, and a fast-food cup lay on the ground near a trash container. Hannah walked over, picked up the cup, and disposed of it. Ahead of them stretched an arbor constructed of heavy wooden beams. Hannah waved her daughter under the arbor. "Bare as bones now, but imagine this arbor draped with purple wisteria." They moved along a path heavily mulched with bark that crunched beneath their feet.

"Where's the Indian site and the early settlers' place going to be?"

Hannah pointed to the left. "Indian site's over behind that hill, along Bent Bucket River. I don't think Max has located the early settlers' village yet."

"Bent Bucket River. That's an odd name for a river."

"Story is that a wagon carrying buckets overturned by the river. When the buckets were retrieved, they were bent and battered."

The arbor opened into a walled rectangle of fresh-turned earth and walkways. From a well in the center, cobblestone paths radiated in four directions, disecting the lawn into what would become four symmetrical, lush flower beds. Hannah bent and scooped up a handful of rich, loamy soil. "Nothing like a well-prepared flower bed," she said, rubbing the grains in her fingers. "Want to feel?" She extended the handful of soil to her daughter.

Leaning on her cane, Laura stared disinterestedly at her mother's hand. She shook her head. "What will you plant in here?" she asked, pointing to one of the beds.

"There will be trellises along the brick wall and pink climbing roses, evergreen shrubs for backdrop and perennials, lots of perennials."

"What are perennials?"

"Flowers that come back year after year for many years, and of course mixed with them will be summer-blooming annuals like petunias and delphiniums. And of course there'll be benches and some small trees, like dogwoods, near them for shade."

"You see all this in your head, don't you?" Laura asked.

"I do, and I see it as a calm and relaxing space, as the Germans say, gemütlich. My version of an English cottage garden."

"You mean like a comfy room that wraps itself around you?" Laura said softly.

"Like a comfy room, yes. Well put."

"Nice," Laura said.

She's being polite, Hannah thought. Doubt if she's even interested in this garden, in any garden. Well, in the beginning, tending my single geranium in a pot, neither was I. Discovering. That's the joy of it, the adventure of it. Francis Bacon, back in the sixteenth century, had called gardening "the purist of human pleasures . . . , the greatest refreshment of the spirits of man." Hannah agreed. She knew firsthand the benefits of gardening. People, seeking to escape the chaos of their lives, would find calm and beauty in this garden, of this she was certain. Then, their spirits refreshed and restored, they might credit their experience in the garden as having healed their hearts. It gave her deep satisfaction just to think about it. In fact, Hannah had not been this excited in years, or felt more alive or more creative. "I want these gardens designed as rooms, where people can come and feel comfortable, get a sense that things, life is under control . . ." She stared at Laura. Huge tears rolled down her daughter's cheeks.

"Laura . . ."

"I never felt so empty, so unhappy. I can't do this job. It's too immense, this whole concept is too big for me."

Hannah raised her hands. "You don't have to take this job. I'm sorry for pushing you."

"You haven't. It's Max. He seems to assume that we have a deal. We don't, we don't." Her blue eyes were like far-flung islands adrift in measureless seas. "How can you plan like this? What about the millennium? All the computers and electronics that keep things going in the world could fail. Don't you have concerns about it? Why don't any of you talk about it? We may not even be here three months from now."

In that instant, all Hannah could think of was a quote from Martin Luther, of all people: "Even if I knew certainly that the world would end tomorrow, I would plant a tree today." When she had first read it in a gardening magazine in some dentist's office, Hannah recognized her own philosophy: live now, today. She had spent too many of her younger years focused on misery, worrying about tomorrow. She would never do that again.

For a brief moment, a wave of impatience swept over Hannah. A part of her wanted to take her daughter by the shoulders and shake her. Didn't Laura understand what a boon this job could be? She could take it at her own pace among caring people, and no one looking over her shoulder. Hannah tried to keep the irritation out of her voice.

"Yes, we've done what we could. Go look in the basement. You'll find paraffin lamps from the Amish, cases of food and water. There are two full tanks of propane gas behind the house, wood in the shed behind the greenhouse. Grace bought air mattresses for all of us in case the electric goes off and we have to camp out in the living room and kitchen where we'd have heat. Can't make it happen, or not happen, so we do what we can, don't dwell on it and go on with our lives. Does that answer your question?"

"You sound so angry." Laura brushed her hand across her cheeks. "I was just asking."

"No, you weren't just asking. You're grappling for an excuse not to accept this offer, so you can go on hiding in your room, avoiding people, wallowing in self-pity . . ." Hannah stopped, appalled at what she was saying, and for a moment she covered her mouth with her hands. "My God, I'm sorry, Laura. It's your life, your loss. Live it the way you want. Stupid of us to suggest that you work here. What's Covington got to offer you?"

Laura's mouth trembled. She exploded, sobbing and yelling at the same time. "My mother, that's what. I want a mother who'll comfort me, like you want this place, this place"—she waved her arms wildly—"to comfort total strangers." Tears cracked her words apart, and Laura buried her face in her hands. Her shoulders, her entire body shook.

Laura had thrown down the gauntlet. Stunned by the outburst, the total honesty, the uncensored plea, Hannah knew that she must respond. If she failed her child now, she failed them both forever. Yet hugging, kissing, saying "I love you," had always felt and still did feel decidedly artificial. Why couldn't she be spontaneously demonstrative, tender, affectionate like Grace, or effusive and cheery like Amelia? Feeling clumsy, self-conscious, and awkward, Hannah slid her arm about her daughter's shoulders for a moment, then withdrew it, and stood silent for a time, feeling frustrated, arms dangling at her sides. "Laura . . ."

"What?" Laura eyes were bright and defiant.

Hannah had grown into adulthood denying hurt and anger. Fearful of risking her emotions, she had become expert at acting brave and pretending not to care. Opening her heart, she had risked loving Dan; the resulting anguish had nearly crushed her. And again, years later, she had invested great affection in Grace and had spent sleepless nights worrying that Grace, by marrying Bob, would no longer be her housemate or her friend. "When I was a little girl, no one in my family showed any affection to anyone. No one ever said they loved me, or held and hugged me, or comforted me. I never learned how to do that naturally, I guess. I'm sorry. I do . . . love you. Tears my heart out to see you so miserable. Forgive my impatience. Stems from my need to see you smiling again. Selfish."

Somewhere Hannah had read, "Not risking is a sure way of losing." Clenching both fists now, she brought them together again and again in such a forceful manner that, if a fist striking a fist was capable of creating music, drumbeats would have filled the air. Hannah realized that she must dig deep inside to uncover a different way of acting and reacting, no matter how uncomfortable that might be. Grasping Laura's shoulders, Hannah spoke rapidly, knowing that too much thought would smother the words in her throat. "I love you, Laura, more than I've ever told you. Whatever you decide to do is fine. Move upstairs and stay with us as long as you want to or need to." Leaning forward, Hannah pecked her daughter's wet cheek. It was easier than she had imaged. Tentatively, she lifted her hand and smoothed Laura's hair back from her face. Laura did not move or speak. "You're so pretty," Hannah said. "Always were."

"I am?" Laura's face paled. Her voice was suddenly that of an uncertain, frightened child needing reassurance.

"You are. Losing Marvin was dreadful. Unfair. There's no answer to why. Stay with us, won't you?" She hesitated for a moment, then said, "I'd like you to stay."

"You would?" A glimmer of light appeared in Laura's eyes. She smiled. "Whether I take this job or not?"

"That's right."

Laura threw her arms about her mother's taut, angular shoulders and hugged hard. "Then I'll stay."

For a span of time, which seemed like ages to Hannah, they clung to one another. Feeling awkward, Hannah wondered how long to hold the grasp, how long before her daughter would let go. From the arbor came the clomp of Max's boots on the path and his voice calling, "Hannah, Laura, where are you?" and she eased her hands from her daughter's back and stepped away from her.

Entering the fledgling garden, Max stood watching them, his feet planted wide apart, hands on his hips. "Come on, you two. We've got lots more to show Laura. Let's go."

Silently, each deep in thought, the women followed Max back through the arbor and across the wide expanse of pasture. Cleared of roots and rocks, the grass felt soft and springy beneath their feet, and Hannah slowed her pace to match her daughter's. Laura, she thought, was regaining her strength quickly.

They moved along, first up an incline, then crested a low hill from where they could see, perhaps two hundred yards away, a river and trees along its banks. The hill at this point sloped sharply down. Hannah offered Laura her hand. Fiercely independent, Laura declined. At one point, when she stumbled, Hannah grasped her daughter's hand and was immediately puzzled by the rough and callused palm. Then she considered that working and living on the *Maribow* must have entailed hard, physical labor.

A fast walker, Max reached the bottom many minutes before they did. With his head cocked, he seemed to Hannah to be listening intently to something.

The rush and tumble of water grew louder as they approached Max. Bent Bucket River was no longer languorous and shallow as Hannah remembered. Now it raced at a hectic pace, lapping its banks, swirling and whirling, forming helixes and tearing them apart, skimming the tops of boulders, kicking up foam. Smooth rocks tumbled along its sandy bottom. Several trees, their roots exposed, clung to a pittance of washed-out bank. Still, and dense as pudding, the air offered no relief from the heat and humidity.

Laura scratched her arm and swatted her face. "I'm being eaten alive," she said.

"Where's that bridge, anyway, Max?" Hannah asked.

"I wish I knew." He swatted a mosquito clinging tenaciously to his cheek, then wiped the crushed creature off his palm. "I've always come at it directly from the road. I think it's that way." He pointed to their left, and stepping away from the dankness of the river, they moved swiftly down the pasture until a narrow wooden footbridge appeared. "This won't do," he muttered. "This bridge has got to be wider and much higher."

Across the river, upturned earth indicated that site preparation had begun. Max hit his forehead with the ball of his hand. "How'd I miss that when I looked over the plans? We can't put a settlement this close to the river. Anyone can see it's in the floodplain. I've got too much on my mind these days. What I need is an assistant. How about being my assistant, Laura?"

Hannah saw Laura flinch and step back, as if she had been stung by a wasp.

Max laughed. "Just kidding. Now, if your mother wasn't so hell-bent on having all those gardens, well, she'd be all I'd need to help me get this entire project up and running properly."

"Maybe you should talk to Molly Lund, Brenda and Harold's daughter," Hannah suggested. "She teaches high school math, but I get the sense, with her dad so sick, she'd be glad to work closer to home."

"Look, I'm distracted. I don't need a distracted assistant." He gave Hannah a curious look.

"From what I hear, Molly's superorganized, and gets things done in a quarter of the time it takes other people. I bet she could handle it. She's smart, she knows all the suppliers in Weaverville and in Asheville. She grew up on a farm right here in Covington, remember, and rode out shopping with her daddy every Saturday when she was a girl. Molly knows everyone."

He bent, plucked a long blade of grass, and yanked at both ends as if testing its tensile strength. "How do you know all this?"

"Brenda told me. Oh, never mind, Max. Do what you want. I've enough to do with my gardens and the holidays coming. Miranda and her family will be here for Thanksgiving, and then Grace's son and Charles will be here for Christmas."

"I know," he said. "Just kidding. You're as busy as a person can be."

The tweet and twitter of unseen critters filled the air about them. Birds chirped, and the indifferent sun beat down on them. Hannah's legs felt tired and heavy. Sweat dripped unceremoniously down between her breasts, and she could see the stains along the back and underarms of Max's shirt. Smidgens of damp hair dappled Laura's forehead. Hannah read the tiredness in her daughter's face and saw, by her slower pace, the effort this was taking. Meanwhile, Max strode back in the direction they had come from.

"Where are we going, Max?" Hannah asked as she began to follow him. Then stopping, she wiped her brow with one of Grace's bandannas, which she pulled from a back pocket.

"There." Max pointed to a flat area on a rise. "That's perfect. It won't be affected if the river floods, yet it's close enough to Bent Bucket River. I'll get the crew on it tomorrow." That settled, he turned and retraced his steps to where they waited. At the too-narrow bridge, Max offered Hannah a hand to help her across, and smiling, she took it for a moment, then released his hand. They moved apart and walked along then with Laura trailing. A smidgen of a breeze stirred the thick, hot air. Hannah felt as if she were breathing through cheesecloth. What must my daughter think of Max and me? she wondered briefly.

But then Max started talking about the Cherokee, and it was immediately clear that he both admired and respected them. "Folks think all Indian tribes lived in tents and moved around a lot. Some did, of course, but the Cherokee were settled folk, livin' in solid houses made of vertical log poles, woven vines, and plastered with mud to make them airtight, and they built them inside stockades. They had dome-shaped roofs constructed with interwoven saplings covered with long grass and reeds that rain couldn't penetrate. Their women farmed, wove cloth, made pottery, and educated the youngsters. The men trained the older boys to hunt and fish and fight when the tribe had to. They'd developed quite a strong social organization when white settlers arrived on the scene." Occasionally, he looked behind to include Laura.

"They had this New Fire ceremony markin' their new year. All the fires were extinguished and the hearths in their houses cleaned out. Then they had this big dance around a freshly lit fire from whose embers they started new fires in all the hearths." He turned back toward the hill, shaded his eyes with his hand, and nodded. Apparently satisfied with whatever he was looking at, and seemingly unaffected by the heat, he continued his running commentary. "Cherokee had their own creation myth, of course," Max said. "And many, many ceremonies, like when they planted corn, and another when they picked it."

His voice grew sober then, and he shook his head. "It took less than a hundred years before the Cherokee lost all their land to white settlers, driven out one rainy October mornin'. Soldiers yanked them from their houses, rounded 'em up, loaded 'em like cattle into wagons, six hundred and forty-five wagons, and started west." He stopped, and Hannah and Laura automatically stopped. The lines of Max's craggy face tightened, and his eyes seemed to travel back, to see it all as if he'd been there and witnessed the horror, the inhumanity of it. "One hell of a trail of graves they left from the Smoky Mountains to the Western Territory. Case of genocide if I ever saw one."

He picked up his pace then and made one last remark about the Cherokee. "We owe them respect, and the best presentation of their lives and times, and I'm damned well determined to give it to them."

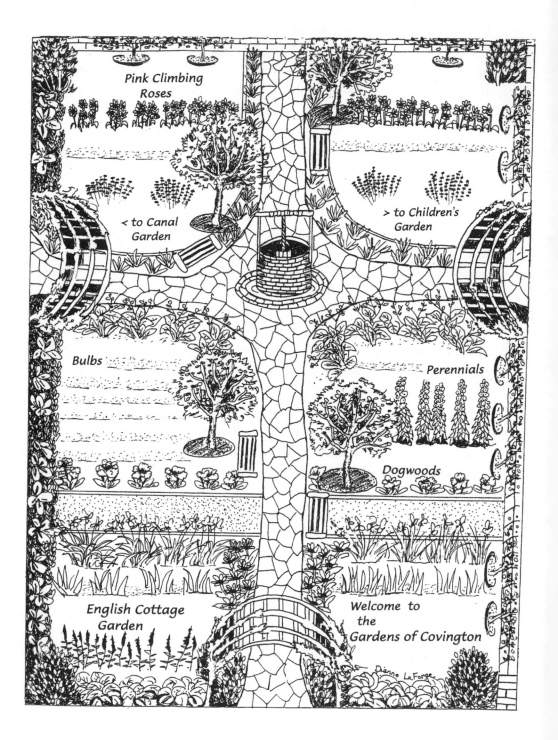

15

Good News and Grave Concerns

"Hannah, Amelia," Grace called. She couldn't wait to tell them the news and to hear from Hannah how Laura had reacted to Bella's Park. When neither answered, Grace stepped into the pantry off the kitchen and onto the back porch from where she again called, "Hannah."

Hair hanging in straggles about her face, Hannah poked her head from the greenhouse. There was a smudge of damp dirt on her chin. "I'm here." She waved an arm. "Be right out. Got to wash my hands." She vanished.

The greenhouse was forty feet long. Rather than move it to Wayne's home up in the mountains near Tennessee, they had decided it would remain where it was outside the farmhouse kitchen. "No different, really, than your going to an office to work," Hannah had said to Wayne, and he agreed.

She worked with him as the mood took her, without a set schedule, which was a change for Hannah and had taken some getting used to. "Even though I don't have to, it feels odd knowing there are jobs in the greenhouse to be done, and me propped up in bed watching one of the morning shows. On the other hand, I kind of like the freedom," she told Amelia and Grace one afternoon while sitting out on the porch drinking tea and chatting about their day.

Now, as she waited for Hannah, Grace lowered herself onto the top step of the small kitchen porch. Her eyes strayed to the vegetable garden close by. Beans hung heavy on wooden tepees. Tomato plants, supported by heavy wire rings, ripened daily. Hannah could never plant only one or two tomato plants from a flat of four or six. It was impossible for their small surrogate family to eat the harvest, so Wayne helped by toting baskets of tomatoes, yellow squash, beans, cucumbers, and other vegetables to the tailgate market in Weaverville every other Saturday. It sounded romantic, selling produce at the tailgate market. Once she and Bob had taken the vegetables, but standing in the scorching hot parking lot steamed the romance out of it for them.

Smiling and wiping her hands on the blue denim apron about her waist, Hannah stepped from the greenhouse. She untied the apron as she mounted the steps, slung it over the railing, and lowered herself beside Grace.

"Where's Amelia?" Grace asked.

"Gone with Mike and my daughter out somewhere." She frowned a moment, then said, "With that cast off of her leg, Laura's doing fine, isn't she?"

"Seems to be."

"I told Laura about Dan."

"Oh, Hannah. I'm so glad. What did she say?"

"She was empathetic. I think we actually connected."

"That's wonderful." She leaned over and hugged Hannah, who looked embarrassed. "And remember, if Laura takes this job you owe me twenty dollars."

Hands on her thighs and leaning forward, Hannah turned to her friend. "Now tell me, what's up?"

"Two things, one terrific, one worrisome."

"Terrific thing first."

Grace's face beamed. "The good news is that Emily's three months' pregnant. We'll have a spring baby."

"A baby we can all spoil. And look at you," Hannah playfully poked Grace's shoulder. "For someone who thought she'd never have grandchildren, you've got Tyler and now a baby. I'm happy for you."

"For us all." Grace flushed with pleasure. She hugged herself. "I'm a lucky women."

"The Richardson family's lucky to have you."

Grace's face grew sober. "Do you think that'll be a problem down the road with those children?"

"Problem? How?"

"Bob and I not being married. You realize I'm what you might call an illegitimate grandmother."

"Grace, the things you find to worry about. Everyone in that family loves you. Tyler adores you. Kids are fine when people love them and are honest with them, and you give Tyler so much time and attention and love. So," she changed the subject, "they know if it's a boy or a girl?"

"Emily didn't say."

"Now let's get the worrisome news over with."

"Our neighbors the Herrills are stocking up as if the world's coming to an end. I met Velma at the market yesterday. Two of her daughters were with her, and each had a brimful cart of food, water, bags of dried beans and rice. Are we being foolish to assume nothing's going to happen when the year turns?"

"Guess it wouldn't hurt to add more staples to our larder," Hannah said, "but I refuse to get all worked up about this. Still think New Year's going to come and go, and our lives and the computers and electricity won't fail us."

Grace frowned. "But what if the electricity does go off, even for a few days? It's winter. We won't have heat or water."

Hannah patted Grace's leg. "So let's each of us pick up an extra gallon of water every time we go to the market or the drugstore."

"What about food?" Grace asked.

"Food!" Hannah said thoughtfully. "Canned, dried. Guess it won't hurt to stock up a bit more, if it'll relieve your mind. Nothing happens, we use it up in a few months. The propane gas tanks will be topped off by early December."

Grace nodded. "We do have five air mattresses and a foot pump, for us, Bob, and Mike. I'll get an extra mattress for Laura. You never know. We might have to sleep in the kitchen or the living room for warmth." Talking about this with Hannah, deciding to put in additional supplies bolstered her sense of control. Deep inside, Grace didn't think anything would happen, and neither did Bob, but just in case she'd have things ready. "Another thing," Grace said. "Velma went on and on about how Charlie and their sons were off at a gun show buying extra guns and ammunition. Charlie feels if they're well stocked, others might come with guns to try to take it from them. Isn't that a horrible thought? If someone came to their door hungry, why wouldn't they share their food?"

"I guess they feel if they did that, it wouldn't last long."

"The whole thing's too much for me," Grace said.

Their conversation ended abruptly as Wayne, his shirt wet from watering plants, strode from the greenhouse. His face and arms were brown as toast from tending his own garden and that of his grandfather, Old Man, and his new step-grandmother, Lurina. After their wedding last spring, Old Man had moved from his mountain fastness with his horse and his beloved pigs to Lurina's home on Elk Road. He muttered a great deal about it being "too darn hot in this here valley." Yet many an afternoon, Old Man moseyed down to P. J. Prancer's Hardware Store to sit on a wooden bench by the front door and wile away the hours with old cronies he'd hardly seen living way back up in the mountains as he had for so many years.

"Miss Lurina's asked me to clean up around her family grave-yard," Wayne told them. He stood a few inches taller than Hannah and was slender with dark brown, almost black, hair and eyes. His teeth, having never been a priority, were uneven, and there was a missing tooth halfway on one side, visible only when he grinned, as he did now. "You never seen nothin' like it," he said. "Old Man feedin' his pigs and Miss Lurina feedin' her chickens and the both of them sittin' out on the porch holdin' hands." He chuckled. "Sure hope cleanin' up the Masterson Cemetery ain't gonna raise an issue again about where they're gonna be buried."

"I though that was all settled, the Reynolds Cemetery would be their final resting place," Grace said. Last winter she, Hannah, Amelia, and Mike, as Lurina's representatives had tromped, with members of the Reynolds clan, into the woods behind Lurina's farmhouse to inspect her family cemetery, and then up to the mountain to the Reynolds Cemetery. It had fallen to Grace to convince Lurina that the Reynolds Cemetery was by far the better maintained and assuredly the more aesthetically pleasing. But words had failed to sway the old woman. Finally, Amelia's pictures, spread out on the kitchen table before Lurina, finally convinced her of the sad disrepair of the Masterson Cemetery. With that settled, a major impediment to the wedding had been overcome.

Wayne said good-bye, strode across the front lawn to his big black truck whose massive tires held it suspended above the road, and drove away.

"I swear, a California earthquake couldn't shake the ground more than that truck does," Hannah muttered.

16

Making Plans

Leaves on tender plants curled and wilted. Stunning rose-colored caladiums spilling from pots on the front porch steps had withered, their juicy stems frozen by a thirty-degree nighttime temperature aided and abetted by the windchill factor. Still in her bathrobe, Amelia stood on the porch just outside the front door. She shivered head to toe. "It's only October twentieth, too early for a freeze. I'm not ready. All my winter things are still stored."

"Better unstore them," Hannah said. She had flung a jacket over her pajamas before coming out to inspect the damage to her plants.

The door behind them opened and closed, and Grace, dressed appropriately for the day in dark blue sweats and a blue knit cap pulled over her ears, joined them. "Every year when we have the first freeze, I have to remind myself that spring's only five months away." She hugged her shoulders. "I've always dreaded fall, even though it's beautiful. It ushers in winter."

"I agree," Amelia said. "If only it were summer all year."

"Could move to Florida," Hannah said.

They looked at her. "Have you ever been to Florida in the summer? Now that's hot, really hot, and it's so flat," Amelia said.

Hannah walked to the porch railing. Thick stems of wisteria snaked their way up the post alongside the steps. She slid a hand along its twisted bark. "They'll sleep, and then it'll be spring, and they'll come awake. It's worth it to me, the winter, just to experience spring and new life everywhere. It's only October. Chances are it'll warm right back up and not freeze again for weeks." Hannah reached up to remove a cluster of lavender flowers from a branch. "These got zapped too." The look on her face said, Well, that's that.

"What is it, thirty-five degrees?" Grace moved to the side of the door and read the thermometer. "Forty-two. It feels colder."

"It better warm up. I still have a dozen rolls of film to shoot before Mike and I select the photos we're sending to New York. They want them by November fifteenth."

Grace looked at Hannah. "How far do you think you'll get with the gardens before winter?"

"We'll be laying out several gardens this week."

"Which ones?" Grace asked as she headed for the front door.

The others followed her into the house, where the aroma of fresh-brewed coffee drew them to the kitchen.

"The canal garden and the herb garden for sure. I want to wait for the children's garden. Brenda's assigned us an area at the school. This winter we'll be working on design and plant materials. Clay's the predominant soil around these parts. I'll have the children bring a sample from their own yards, and we'll examine each to determine how heavy it is and how to amend it."

The coffee mug was warm, and Hannah relaxed. "Know how you tell about clay?" she didn't wait for their reply. "You form a ball and squeeze a handful of it, and then let the ball dry out. The worst clay soil will dry rock hard. You wet it again and it's slick and slippery, won't absorb water well. They'll learn what's needed to amend it, lighten it with compost, peat moss, sand, manure, there's a blend you can buy called nature's helper. By the time spring comes, they'll understand soil and they'll have chosen the kinds of plants they want for their garden."

Amelia toyed with the lid of the sugar bowl. She looked at Hannah and smiled. "Well, I'd better get dressed. Mike's coming for me at ten o'clock."

Amelia flitted from the room and whistled as she mounted the stairs. Hannah smiled. "She tries." Then Hannah unrolled a sheet of engineering graph paper that had been stashed against a wall in the kitchen. "Hank gave me this," she said. "Nice young man. Maybe he and Laura . . ." She waved away the thought. "Nonsense. Too soon. Foolish."

Grace helped her secure the graph paper flat on the table with the sugar bowl, the creamer, and two glasses. "Have to lay out the entire garden." She gazed at the wall behind Grace's head. "Imagine a shade garden, a wildflower garden, woodland garden, oriental garden, rose garden . . ."

"There's no end to it, is there?" Grace said.

"I guess there really isn't."

"We'll have to have a greenhouse and a potting shed, of course, for mixing soil, starting seeds."

"It'd be nice if you had the greenhouse for the winter," Grace asked.

Hannah smiled. "If I hadn't sold my greenhouse to Wayne, we could just move it over there."

"Ever wonder if Wayne has second thoughts about running a plant business? He's less of a free spirit these days."

Hannah stared at Grace. "I never considered that."

"You might ask him."

"I might just do that. Oh, I forgot. You might be interested in this. How about putting in a medicinal plant garden?" Hannah's eyes and faced were flushed with excitement and pleasure.

Happiness, Grace thought, is Hannah in a garden.

Hannah moved a ruler over the graph paper, then threw it to one side and scowled.

Grace studied Hannah. "What's the matter?"

Hannah's face softened. "Sorry. I suggested to Laura that she stay with us, move upstairs even if she doesn't take this job. I made the offer on the spur of the moment without checking with you and Amelia. She'd like to stay."

Grace's hand moved slowly across the table to cover Hannah's hand. "That's fine. Laura belongs here with you. I bet she says yes to Max too." Grace rapped the table with her knuckles. "And when she does, just remember you owe me twenty dollars."

"How could I forget, you remind me often enough." Hannah sobered. "Sometimes I jolt awake early in the morning. I think I hear a car door slam, and I'm sure Laura's called a cab and left."

"She wouldn't do that, Hannah. Not after what you told me about your talk at Bella's Park. She needs to be here, and you need her here. Amelia was saying the other day how nice it is having a young woman in the house. Reminds her of when she was young and several generations lived in one big house." Noting that Hannah still looked troubled, Grace said, "Don't worry, Hannah. It's going to come out just fine."

A wry little smile touched the corners of Hannah's mouth. "She'd be more inclined to stay, don't you think, if she had a friend her own age, like Molly or Emily?"

"Maybe." There was a long pause, then Grace said, "It's time for us to have a little dinner party, the Richardson clan, Mike, Max. Max can bring Hank. If Zachary's back we can ask him too."

"Zachary's been gone since his mother died. Max misses him."

"I guess he must."

Just talking about entertaining electrified Grace, candles glowing on the table, Amelia's lovely china, laughter, talk, good company. "Let's get Laura settled upstairs, have storage bring back our dining room furniture, and then we'll have a party."

"That would be nice," Hannah said.

"You get to help. You can chop onions."

Hannah raised her hands to her head. "What have I wrought?" They laughed just as a horn blew.

"I'm off," Amelia called. Her light footsteps descended carpeted stairs, tapped across the porch and down the steps. The crunch of gravel, and a car door slammed.

"Exciting preparing for a show at a New York gallery," Grace said.

"It isn't a major gallery, you know that? It's somewhere down in the Village."

"Does it matter? It's wider recognition than Asheville, a real boost to Amelia's ego."

"Of course," Hannah replied. "Hope the city doesn't seduce her with all its glamour, excitement, theater, art galleries, fancy stores."

"Are you suggesting that Amelia might be enticed to move to New York?" Grace's eyes were wide. She crossed her arms over her chest.

"No," Hannah said. "Maybe she'd go there every year for a visit, something like that."

Grace tapped a finger against Hannah's arm. "That's not what you meant, Hannah, and you know it."

It grew still in the kitchen. The ticking of the clock and the hum of the refrigerator seemed to compete for their attention. Finally Hannah replied. "Can't fool you, Grace, can I?"

"No, you cannot."

"Well, the way I see it is this. People move at the drop of a pin. They're more committed to change and money than to relationships. Children leave home and move great distances. Couples retire to Arizona and Florida, far away from their kids. Friends are discarded in favor of change. My underlying concern is that eventually one of you, us, might, for whatever reason, decide to move," Hannah said.

"Like me moving in with Bob? Is that what you're thinking, Hannah?" Hannah was silent. "Tell me," Grace insisted.

Hannah sighed. "Well, yes, I worry sometimes that that might happen."

"Oh, ye of little faith." Grace leaned forward. "And I just gave Tyler a talk on commitment! Listen to me, Hannah. Because I never left Dentry in all those years doesn't mean that people I cared for stayed in Dentry. Roger, my only child, left. Three good friends, women I loved, confided in, depended on, moved away. For a while it seemed that someone was always leaving, and I was having to adjust to the hole their going left in my life and in my heart. I like things here just the way they are, don't you understand that?" Lifting her hands in exasperation, Grace continued. "Men and women. So many things, large and small are involved in a male/female relationship. The minute you move in or get married, things change. One or the other may develop a sense of ownership, and the result is a decided lack of personal freedom. It seems as if someone's always giving up a part of themselves, the man as well as the woman. At this stage of our lives, who needs it?"

Hannah nodded.

"Long ago, Hannah," Grace continued, "I took a correspondence course in anthropology. I wanted to know if there were any essential truths about marriage that were universal and existed within all the tribes and races of mankind. Know what I found out?"

It was unusual for Grace to get on a soap box, and Hannah stared at her. "What?" she asked.

"Some form of marriage, whether it be monogamy or polygamy, is universal among all the peoples of the earth, and some form of family group is universal, although their compositions may differ. There are matriarchal societies in which an uncle, not the father, raises a boy child to manhood, and property is passed through the mother. And every single culture in the world has a cosmology explaining the origin of the universe, man's place in the scheme of things, and a belief in something greater than themselves. There are even cultures that encourage a man in his forties, after his children are raised, to leave his wife, sometimes for a few years only, in order to develop his spiritual side, to connect with his god."

Hannah nodded.

"Now, a real surprise to me was that war's not universal," Grace continued. "The Eskimos have no word for it in their language. I guess when you're struggling to survive against the elements there's no time or energy for fighting."

Hannah shifted in her chair. Picking up a pencil she gazed anxiously, for a moment, at the graph paper. Then she raised her hands. "Okay, Grace, what's the point? Are you saying that you're never going to move in with Bob?"

Grace's mouth snapped shut. She blinked. Her hands rested on her hips and she laughed. "That's right. So you can just relax. Now show me what you have to do with that ruler and all those lines."

17

The Daunting Task of Being a Caregiver

The following morning, Grace lay in bed considering turning over and going back to sleep, when the phone on her bedside table rang. It was Brenda. "Grace, how are you?"

Immediately, Grace was wide awake. "I'm fine. How are you? How's Harold?"

Brenda sounded rushed and harried. "I'm calling to ask you for a huge favor. You know my mother's been here with us taking care of Harold, and today she's got some errands she wants to run in Asheville. It's short notice, I know, but could you possibly spell her for a bit this morning?"

"Of course. What time?"

Grace could hear the relief in Brenda's voice. "Is ten all right?"

"Ten's fine. What will I need to do for Harold?"

Brenda's voice tightened. "Ma will tell you. Probably he'll be sleeping. You sure, now, I'm not interfering with things you have to do?"

"Brenda, I'm glad for the chance to help. I'll be there at ten. Want me to call your mother and tell her I'm coming?"

"I'll let her know."

In the background, Grace heard the school bell ringing. "Gotta go." Brenda said. "Got a meetin' with the counselor and social worker. Bless you, Grace."

For a brief moment, Grace wondered if the meeting had anything to do with Lucy Banks, then she set the phone on its cradle and lay there thinking about Harold for a time. Harold worried her. She'd been to see him at least once a week, sometimes twice, since his surgery. She'd taken food, sent flowers. She'd assumed that everyone else on Cove Road did the same. In the beginning, before he started chemotherapy, Harold had been optimistic. "I'll beat this thing," he'd told her.

And why not? Many people did. Repeatedly, during the following weeks, Grace had offered to help, but Brenda had said, "Thanks, we're doing fine. Ma's here, and she's terrific with Harold." But Grace had this sense that things were not good with Harold, and her apprehension grew when, in the last several weeks, Harold would not see her when she visited. So she sat awhile on the porch with Brenda, or Molly, or Millie, Brenda's mother, and each time, after a brief "He's coming along," they never spoke of Harold. Why?

There had been that one time in the school office when Brenda shared her worries with Grace, but she had never used the phone number Grace gave her, until this morning. A decidedly uneasy feeling nagged at Grace. She flung back the covers to begin her day.

🖋

The door to the Tates' farmhouse swung wide. The stout little woman, looking utterly frazzled, stared at Grace through tired, pale blue eyes. She ran her fingers through cropped white hair.

"Millie." Grace reached for the woman's hand. "Brenda asked me to come."

Millie clasped Grace's hand in both of hers. "I hope it's not too much trouble."

"Not at all. I'm glad to be able to help."

Brenda's mother beckoned Grace in, a finger to her lips. "Harold's sleepin'. I just gave him his medication. He should sleep all the while I'm gone."

Grace hung her jacket on the coat rack in the entrance hall. "Is there anything I can do for him, or anything at all, while you're gone?" Grace asked. "Fix dinner, maybe?"

"We've got more food than we could eat in a month what with people dropping off casseroles every day. You just sit and watch some television." Millie reached for her jacket and hat, a wide-brimmed affair with flowers on one side, and fidgeted with her handbag. A horn sounded. "That's my ride." Grace held her jacket, and she slipped her arms into it. "Be back in two hours, Grace. I can't thank you enough for spelling me this morning."

"Don't worry about anything."

Holding onto the porch railing, Millie made her way cautiously down the front steps, leaving Grace with many unanswered questions. Chemotherapy made you sick, she knew that, but usually after a week, there was a rebounding, one felt better, more able to function. But Harold had not. Why not? Was depression smothering his ability to fight back? Had his cancer metastasized? Who helped Millie care for Harold during the week when her daughter and granddaughter were working? How much care was required? Grace had had to bathe, and change and turn and feed Ted, and she couldn't have managed as he grew more debilitated without a home health care LPN who came three times a week. Well, Grace would have to wait for answers, but answers she would have.

Grace looked about her. The house was quiet. No papers or magazines cluttered the large leather chairs or couch. The clicker for the big TV set in the corner rested alongside a heavy glass ashtray on an end table. Grace wondered that they had not disposed of all the ashtrays in the house. A few minutes later, Grace wandered into the 1950s kitchen. There were no dishes in the sink. A glass cover protected a chocolate cake on the table. Grace lifted the lid. The aroma whetted her taste buds. She knew that she would be welcome to have a piece, but did she really need a piece of cake this early in the morning? Just a few days now before that appointment with her doctor, the one Bob was coming to with her. She better not have such rich cake. Satisfied with this decision, she replaced the cake cover. As Millie had said, the fridge was jammed, as was the freezer. Why wasn't some effort being made to coordinate who brought food and when?

Several hours later, when the key turned in the lock and the front door opened and closed, Grace was settled in a chair watching Martha Stewart talking about Thanksgiving table settings. Clicking off the television, she rose to greet a dispirited Millie. "He's been asleep all the time you've been gone," she sought to reassure Brenda's mother.

Without removing her jacket and hat, Millie sagged against, then slumped into a chair in the living room. "Don't know what's wrong with me. I haven't much energy anymore and I'm irritable all the time these days. Snapped at Alma going and coming. At the store, I couldn't make up my mind about anything. Alma was right good puttin' up with me. She's a decent woman, not much aware how things are with other folks, but a decent woman."

A year ago, Alma had been to the ladies' farmhouse for lunch along with the Tates and the Lunds. Grace remembered her as parochial and self-righteous and decidedly uncomfortable through-out her visit. Grace said nothing. There was an edgy silence. Grace waited, sensing that Millie had more that she wanted to say.

After a while, Millie removed her hat and let it drop into her lap. Seemingly unaware, she plucked at the flowers. When one came loose, she cradled it in her hand for a moment, then dropped it, along with the hat, onto the floor beside her chair. With slow, heavy movements she unbuttoned her jacket and eased her arms out of it. The jacket bulked behind her in the chair. When she finally spoke, it was slowly and wearily. "What's Brenda gonna do when I go home?" Tears filled the corners of her eyes, and she dabbed at them with a handkerchief. "Lord, I'm plum worn out. I'm not young no more. I can cook meals, do some dustin', but this watchin' after a man who's so sick has just about undone me." She dabbed at her eyes again.

"I came up here full of energy, thinkin' I could really help Brenda. I feel guilty leavin' her." She shook her head. "I never thought Harold'd be one to cave in like he has. He acts like a child, keeps askin' for things, especially when Brenda's home. He wants her with him all the time. She's up half the night as it is, and what with workin' all day." Millie heaved a deep sigh.

She closed her eyes for many moments, and when she opened them, she looked crestfallen, and her voice was grim. "Just heard earlier this week that Harold's got cancer in the lymph nodes." She sucked in her breath. "The chemo nearly killed him. They had to stop it. Now this."

Shock hammered Grace's body. Her heart plummeted. Impossible. It couldn't be true. Harold was a strong man, a young man, a friend. "Isn't there something that can be done, with all the research going on?"

Millie shook her head. "Molly's lived on that Internet, checkin' and makin' phone calls. Far as I can understand, the cancer's too far gone. What can be done is being done." She fell silent again, and Grace waited, her mind racing and her anger raging at the thought of Harold's fate and the stunning loss to his family. Memories of Ted, of cancer gobbling his life away, of turning everything upset down, and of fears about suffering and dying spun wildly in her mind. She wanted to yell, "No, no." Millie's voice served to calm her. "I'm a private person," Millie said. "Not used to tellin' my troubles to strangers."

Grace pulled herself together. "Sometimes it's easier to talk to a stranger."

Millie nodded and fell silent. "When I leave, Brenda's gonna have to stop workin'. She can't work and take care of Harold, and that's what she's intendin' to do. Who's gonna help my daughter?" Tears came, and sobs, and Grace ached for her, sat silent, and respectfully allowed Millie her grief.

"Don't you have people who come in give you a hand, or stay with Harold while you go to the market?"

Millie shook her head. "People come and go on as they will. Brenda doesn't like to ask for help. She shops on her way home."

"Doesn't the church help?"

"They got people who pay a visit one time to the sick, make a hospital visit, but the congregation's small."

A long pause again. Cars drove by on Cove Road. A kettle Grace had put on for tea began to whistle. Grace rose. "I was making myself a cup of tea. Would you like one?"

"Well that's right nice of you. Yes, I think I might do with a cup." Millie started up. "Let me help you."

"No, no. You sit and rest. I'll get us each a cup. Sugar? Lemon?"

"No. Just black, thanks, Grace." Millie's head sank back against the headrest of the chair, and she closed her eyes again.

When Grace returned, they sipped their tea in a more comfortable silence. Amazing how quiet a house can be, Grace thought. Millie set her cup on a table near at hand and sighed again. "Friends drop in, of course, but I think it's more out of pity or duty than anything else. I guess they don't offer to help 'cause they don't know what to do."

"You're probably right."

"Mostly I'm here alone with Harold all day long, no one to talk to, sometimes feelin' trapped, and guilty for feelin' that way. Times are I want to run away and hide."

"I know," Grace said softly. "I nursed a husband with cancer for many months. Even with the kindness of friends, and help from hospice. I felt isolated as if I were the only person in the whole world doing this job, and no one could really understand the loneliness of it and how scared I was."

Millie nodded, then stirred herself. "God bless you, Grace, for comin' and for listen' to me. I feel better just talkin' a bit about it." She leaned forward and tilted her head up. "I think I hear Harold." Millie patted her hair and stood, a trifle unsteadily. Then, with a worried frown, she pulled herself together and started up the stairs.

Grace washed the teacups, put them away, and tiptoed from the house. The lightness of air, the blue of sky, the glorious soft green hills like protective arms behind the farmhouses on Cove Road brought a sense of relief and pleasure, followed instantly by sadness for Brenda and her family. Bowing her head, Grace whispered a prayer on behalf of them all.

18

The Best in People

The pace of Hannah's life accelerated. Often she found herself checking her watch as she dashed between Bella's Park, Wayne and the greenhouse, and Caster Elementary School. Her garden at home lay neglected and cried out for trimming, cutting back, and mulching. No longer was there time to sit and muse about the shape of clouds, or pay attention to birds courting, or, worst of all, to have tea with Grace and Amelia. Why was it that the first thing to go from their busy schedules was teatime? And yet, Hannah thought, the more harried I get, the more I need quiet time with my friends.

On a glorious afternoon in late October, she and Grace sat on the porch, drinking tea and having a catch-up chat. After the killing freeze earlier in the month, the stalks of annual zinnias, salvias, and impatiens had wilted and turned black, and much too early, brown-spotted and golden leaves drizzled from the branches of the great oak and rustled across the porch. One or the other of them was forever sweeping leaves away.

Grace brushed a leaf from her skirt. "Colors coming early this year."

"It's as if someone turned on a switch."

"One day there are whispers of fall, and a week later whole tree's turning saffron, or cinnamon, or paprika color."

"Goodness, Grace," Hannah laughed, "you take the kitchen out into the countryside, don't you?"

"They are those colors. Look and you'll see."

"I guess they are," Hannah conceded.

After a time, Grace said, "Do you realize how busy you've gotten, how much you're gone lately, Hannah? How do you keep up with it all?"

Hannah raked her fingers through her thick hair. "You were busier than I am when you had the tearoom. But you're right, I haven't time for a haircut. Might try the place opened up in the new shopping center on Elk Road." Her eyes sought Grace's, and she asked, "So what do you suggest I give up?"

"I don't know. You're exhausted at night. You're bedroom light's out by nine-thirty most nights. You used to read until at least eleven."

"You used to come into my room, and we'd chat." Hannah rubbed her chin with her thumb and forefinger.

"I don't want to disturb you."

"And then there's Laura. I worry about her. She's moved upstairs, but she's not what I would call all right." Unwittingly, Hannah's fist curled into ball and she brought it down lightly on her knee. "I just wish she'd say yes to working with us at Bella's Park and get on with it."

Grace's voice was firm. "You tell your daughter she can stay regardless of whether she works or not, but you don't really mean that. You want her to pick up and make a life, fast."

"True. But I've managed to keep my mouth shut, haven't I?"

"I know how you really feel. Maybe Laura knows also."

Lord, Hannah thought. I don't want to talk about these matters. All I want right now is to sit quietly, rock, sip my tea, and enjoy the colors. "Dogwoods go first," she said, pointing across the street. "And sassafras trees turn curry colored as you'd say."

"And sourwoods turn the color of paprika." Grace smiled.

Hannah studied trees as far as she could see. Clusters of trees on hillsides had bowed to color. Some had donned full fall regalia. "I love working with the kids at school, adore my work at Bella's

Park. I must spend at least a portion of the next six months helping Wayne. He's getting the hang of the business, making friends of the shopkeepers in his own inimitable way. There'll be enough money by next spring to pay a part-time bookkeeper. Then I'll wash my hands of it."

"You'll never wash your hands of that greenhouse as long as it's sitting right outside our kitchen. Have you talked to him about selling it to Maxwell for the park?"

"No, but I will, maybe." Hannah brought her rocking chair to a halt. "Grace, what would you have me do? I know I'm harried at times, and tired at night, but I'm happy."

"I'm sorry, Hannah. When am I going to learn to butt out?"

"Need you to butt in, you're my friend. But just now's not the time for me to rein in. When the park's up and running, things will quiet down."

Grace doubted that. She set her cup down. "I have sad news," she told Hannah. "Harold may not make it."

Hannah's rocking stopped abruptly. "Not make it?"

The muscles of Grace's throat tightened, and she struggled not to cry. "Millie told me that Harold's cancer has metastasized. The chemo made him so sick they stopped it."

"What are you saying? There's no hope for Harold? With new drugs, new treatments going on in medicine every day?"

Grace shook her head. "His cancer's spread everywhere. They're not telling everyone, not yet, anyhow." She clutched at Hannah's arm. "They haven't enough help. No one had come in to relieve Millie until I did the other day. She's been Harold's sole caregiver all day long these past months, and she's worn to a frazzle. She's going home to South Carolina. Molly, she says, is taking leave from teaching; Brenda will cut back her hours at the school. They need help. I want to help them, Hannah."

"How? Certainly not with Harold's physical care. You'd be in bed yourself after a day of trying to turn or lift him."

"I know that. But I could try to organize our neighbors so that someone's available several hours each day to help, even if just to spell them. Harold's caretaker, whether it's Millie, or Molly, or

Brenda, would be able to rest or get out of the house for a time."

"What's the church doing?"

"Not much. Pastor Johnson's old. I doubt he's much of an organizer."

"And what makes you think our neighbors are going to respond to you, the outsider?"

"I'm going to ask Amelia to go with me to Velma Herrill. Remember, last fall, Amelia took beautiful pictures of Velma and her roses? Velma likes Amelia. I'll explain to Velma, ask her help in getting something started."

"Good luck, my friend. I'll be glad to do some shopping, pick up a prescription, something like that." She raised her arms, palms toward Grace. "Just don't ask me to sit with someone sick."

Long moments passed in silence. What was there to say? Grace knew exactly what lay ahead for the Tate family. A west wind stirred the branches of the great oak, seeming to electrify it. Suddenly it seemed that dying was everywhere. Golden leaves, despairing of holding on, released their grasp and floated for a moment before seesawing to earth. Drifts landed on the porch and scudded along, curling over their shoes. Grace bent, lifted several leaves, smoothed them on her knees, and studied them. Brown spots dotted the gold. "Like the spots on my hands," she said, "all dried up and shrunken like poor Harold." She heaved a deep sigh. "The cycle of life."

Later that afternoon, when Amelia returned from the day's photo shoot, Grace commandeered her into the living room. "I need to talk to you," she said.

"What's up?"

Grace spared her nothing of Harold's illness and the strain and stress on his family. "They're about to come apart," she told Amelia, "and we have to help."

"How?" Amelia fidgeted with the buttons on her blouse. "Her hair was wind blown, her cheeks rosy from wind and sun, her fingernails unpolished and cut short, and her delicate hands chapped and red. Amazing, Grace thought. She's so absorbed in preparing for her New York show that she hardly notices how she looks anymore.

They sat side by side on the couch in the living room. Earlier, when the temperature dropped, Hannah had turned on the gas jets in the fireplace. Curling her feet under her, Grace snuggled into a corner of the couch. Amelia, at the other end, did the same. "So what can we do?" Amelia asked.

"Velma Herrill likes you. I thought if you'd come with me, we could tell her what I've told you, except the metastasis part, of course. That's for Brenda to tell people. We could ask her help to organize the neighbors on Cove Road."

"What would we ask them to do?"

"Sign up for a time when they'd be available to the family for an hour or two so Harold's caregiver can have a break. Maybe shop for the family, see that everyone doesn't bring food on the same day, it's spoiling over there now. At least until hospice comes in."

"Hospice?" Amelia shifted, leaned toward Grace, her hand tight on the back of the couch. "Don't they come in when, when . . . ?"

"When Harold . . ." Grace found it hard to say, so she nodded. Tears filled her eyes. "Millie said it could be six months, or as soon as two months."

"*Mon Dieu.*" Amelia's hand covered her mouth. Wide, frightened eyes fixed on Grace's face. "I can't bear for Harold to die. He's been so good to us."

"It tears my heart," Grace murmured. "I can't bear that he's suffering so, or for Brenda to be left alone so young."

Amelia sat up straight. "I'll call Velma right away." Reaching for the phone on the table close by, Amelia set up an appointment with Velma for herself and Grace to visit that evening after dinner.

"Charlie and the boys are off to another gun show. She'll be there by herself," Amelia told Grace when she hung up. She shook herself. "This gun stuff gives me the willies. I never heard so much talk about guns until we came here."

125

They would have walked the short distance down Cove Road to Velma's, but the temperature was dropping rapidly. Next week they would turn back the clock. Rain began to fall as they hastened from the car to the house.

Velma greeted them at her door and ushered them into the living room, where a roaring wood fire crackled. Grace and Amelia peeled off coats and sweaters.

"It's warm in here, isn't it?" Velma cracked a window. "Charlie got that fire going before he left. I'm not good at startin' wood fires, and with what he calls his touch of arthritis, he likes to come home to a warm house. I tell him he's either got arthritis or he doesn't. No such thing as a touch of arthritis."

Her words struck the pit of Grace's stomach. All the denial in the world wouldn't change anything. There was no such thing as a touch of arthritis, or diabetes, or cancer.

As expected, they chatted about the weather turning cold. Would it warm up? Was there time to get in the round bales of hay that stood like ancient monuments in the pasture? It was raining now. "They'll have to dry out before we can put them inside," Velma said.

Grace nodded. "The weatherman says we'll have sunshine to-morrow."

Velma frowned. "The weather's so darn unpredictable in these parts." Then she asked, "How's Hannah's daughter?"

"Her cast's off," Amelia said.

"She's walking better every day, and going to physical therapy three days a week. Laura was in excellent physical shape when she was hurt, so I think it's easier to get back her strength," Grace said. She itched to get to the real subject, but there was this game that had to be played, talk of weather, ask about family, relax a bit. There was a pause then, and Grace felt that she could speak of the real matter. "Harold's having a bad time of it."

"I figured so," Velma said. "I used to stop by every few days, but he let me know right soon that he preferred being alone. Y'all can imagine how hurt I was, at first, until I realized it was his illness talkin'."

Grace spoke with deliberate slowness, making it clear that although Harold was a difficult patient, the chemotherapy had made him sicker than it did most people, and that Millie was worn out and about to return to her home in South Carolina. "Harold needs someone there all the time, if only to get him a glass of water, or see that he takes his medicine." She didn't really know if he took medicine, or what kind, but it sounded right. Then Grace proposed a volunteer team that would be available for short stints, perhaps two hours at a time, whom Brenda could call upon for respite care if nothing else.

Velma, a small woman, looked lost in Charlie's big chair where she sat with her hands clasped in her lap listening attentively, her wide gray eyes sober with concern. "Of course I'll help. No one's had any idea what to do. I'll bring it up at Bible study Wednesday night. Would you like to come, Grace, and explain it yourself?"

Grace hesitated. "What do you think is best? I don't want to be the outsider coming in to tell people what to do."

Velma nodded. "You may be right. I'll tell 'em. What you think we ought to do?"

"How about presenting Brenda with a schedule of folks who are willing to help, and the hours they'd be available." Grace suggested. A trickle of perspiration slid down her back, making her want to scratch. The heat in the room was getting to her.

"Brenda or Molly could then call someone when needed," Amelia suggested. "I'll help any Saturday from noon to three." Then she scowled. "Except now, when I'm rushing to get my photos ready to go to New York in January."

Harold, Grace thought, might not make it to January. She held her tongue. Amelia, however, went on telling Velma how Mike had sent her work to a New York gallery, and how ten of her photographs had been requested for a show. Then, suddenly, as if remembering why they had come, Amelia turned to Grace. "Will Brenda call folks for help do you think?"

"She'd be a fool if she didn't," Velma said. "Folks will be right proud to help. One time or another we've all nursed a sick relative, or cared for an aging parent. Folks would be downright insulted if Brenda never called them."

So it was decided. Velma would tell the Bible study class about Millie leaving, and Brenda and Molly needing help, and she was certain folks would more than willingly sign up to help. Grace would talk to Brenda. She did not tell Velma about Harold's diagnosis. Lung surgery for cancer and chemotherapy were bad enough. A final diagnosis was Brenda's to tell, not hers.

"That turned out well," Grace said as they drove back home. The car's wipers scraped and hummed as they worked steadily to maintain visibility through the now heavy rain. Thank God, Grace thought, we haven't far to go, and she thought how a crisis brings out the best in people. At nine P.M. on Wednesday night when the phone rang, she knew instinctively that it was Velma.

"Everyone wants to help. Thirteen signed up, including Alma's sons and our boys. There'll be plenty of help, and no one will feel burdened."

"Bless you, Velma," Grace said. Now she would talk to Brenda.

19

A Time to Reap

The very next morning Grace knocked lightly on the door of Brenda's office.

"Come in," Brenda called. Her face brightened at the sight of Grace. "Good to see you, Grace. Come in. Sit you down. I was about to call and ask you to come see me. I've news about Lucy Banks." She opened a folder on her desk. Several sheets of official-looking papers were clipped to it. She slipped on her glasses. "This is the report from Francie Dimillio, the social worker." She shook her head. "Sad. Lucy's father's considerably older than might have been expected, in his sixties. And he suffers from emphysema. Her mother works the night shift sewing labels on uniforms. They live in a three-room trailer back of Marshall in the hills. Only heat's a wood stove. Dangerous. The older kids chop the wood. The little ones gather kindling. You were right, there's not much food, clothes are hand-me-downs. The twins trade shoes from the Salvation Army and take turns coming to school." Brenda removed her glasses and closed the file. "No wonder Lucy can't learn. She lives in a dream-world, hears music. Fairies talk to her in the woods, her older sister says. I've asked for a psychiatric evaluation for Lucy."

"Is there anything I can do?"

"Just what you're doing. It's a matter of getting them government services. Ms. Dimillio thinks the father will qualify for Medicaid. They certainly can get food stamps, and probably a housing subsidy, maybe even medical insurance for the children. Ms. Dimillio will see to all of that."

"I'll get Lucy some clothes for Christmas."

"Remember there are seven children in that family, so don't get carried away." Brenda shook her head.

In the small silence that followed, as Brenda closed the file, Grace grabbed the opportunity to speak of Harold. "Your mother told me about Harold."

The light in the room seemed to dim. Brenda's face crumbled. The corners of her mouth quivered. "You know, then? Oh, Grace, what am I going to do?"

"Exactly what did the doctors say?"

"You know how sick Harold was from the chemotherapy. It was killing him. Even the doctors saw that. They did more tests, and then they called us in. I've been crying myself to sleep ever since that day." She paused to gain composure. "They said we might as well stop the chemo." She brought the knuckles of one hand to her mouth. The pain in her eyes went right to Grace's heart. "Oh, Grace, Harold's cancer's in his lymph system, in his colon and . . ." She clasped both hands over her mouth. "In his brain. His brain, Grace. My God, his brain."

"Oh, dear God," was all Grace could say. A darkness as heavy as a tarpaulin settled over the room, shutting out light and air to breathe.

"What am I going to do?" Brenda whispered, her eyes brimming with tears.

"You could tell people what's really going on and stop trying to do it all by yourselves, you, your mother, Molly." Then Grace told Brenda about Velma talking to the Bible study class and their response. "People want to help, even your cousin Alma's sons. They just don't know how."

"Harold refuses to let anyone come near him but my mother, Molly, and me."

"Harold's a proud man, but maybe he's not thinking clearly these days. Maybe he shouldn't be making these kinds of decisions now. Your mother's about collapsed, soon it'll be Molly, and then you. What happens then?"

Brenda looked away, and for what seemed an interminable time she stared out of the window. "The ladybugs are back," she said. "Ladybug, ladybug, fly away home."

"You've never used the phone number I gave you except that one time," Grace said.

"I couldn't dump my troubles on you."

"If I felt like that, I never would have given you the number. You may be too proud for your own good, Brenda."

"That's what my mother always said about me. Missy proud foot, she called me when I was growing up."

"This isn't the time for pride, for secrets. You and Harold have helped many people; it's their turn now. You've sowed. Now it's time for reaping."

Brenda nodded.

"We can't help with Harold's physical care, but there must be times when he's sleeping and someone could stay in the house, like I did for Millie, so you can get away for a few hours. You could make a list of things that need doing, things Harold would usually take care of like cleaning the gutters." In her mind she saw the rolled bales of hay in the Herrills' field, "Folks could help get in the hay, shop for any food or anything you need."

Brenda started, as if shocked by an electric charge. "Lord, how am I ever going to get through all this?"

"If you'd allow it, you can have plenty of help."

Brenda looked crestfallen. "Ma wouldn't have burned out like she has if she'd had some help, someone to visit with her, even, while Harold slept. It's my fault." Brenda broke down then, lowered her arms and head onto the desk, and sobbed. "I haven't wanted to face the truth."

Footsteps stopped at the door of the office, then hastened away down the hall. Somewhere in the belly of the building, a jarring bell rang. Children's voices echoed, and a rush of feet tromped down hallways. Doors slammed.

"Blaming yourself isn't going to help Harold or Molly or yourself."

Brenda lifted her head and began to dry her eyes. "Yes. You're right. Good, wise Grace."

"I'm not so wise. Lord, I make mistakes all the time."

"Reaching out like this, setting things up for me. Bless you. I hadn't the energy. I hardly sleep nights."

A low, rumbling sound of school buses preparing for the afternoon run poured in through the open window. Acrid exhaust fumes drifted into the room. Brenda covered her nose with her hand and rose to shut the window. "Every bus around here needs a new exhaust system. You'd think the service department would do something about it."

"You'll let your neighbors and friends help you, won't you?" Grace asked.

Brenda turned from the window. "I will. And thank you, Grace. You'll come see Harold regardless if he's a bear?"

"Of course, just say when." Grace rose. Brenda's body was shaking when Grace hugged her. Then Grace walked slowly along the freshly painted hallway, down well-lit steps to the lower floor, past student lockers and locked classroom doors, past the gym, where the thump of a bouncing ball indicated that basketball practice was under way, and out into the parking lot. In the nearly empty lot a gust of wind pounced upon her, and Grace staggered back. Lowering her head onto her chest, she pulled her jacket snug. How unfair and utterly irrationally life seemed at times. Of all the men she knew, Harold Tate was among the best and the kindest. She would miss him very much.

20

Toad-in-the-Hole

When Grace walked into the house, the phone was ringing. Moments later, before she had a chance to take off her gloves and jacket, Charles was asking her to write down a recipe. Her ear to the phone, Grace struggled to remove her jacket. "Wait a minute, Charles, let me take my gloves off and get to a proper place to write."

In no time, she grabbed a pad and pencil and pulled out a chair at the kitchen table, glad that she'd had the foresight to buy a long cord for this phone. "Go ahead, now," Grace said into the mouthpiece.

"It's called Toad-in-the-Hole, my favorite recipe from home. For years, since Granny turned up her toes, I've been trying to make it the way she did. Today, I found her recipe in a scrapbook I've had for eons and hadn't opened. When I sat down with it this morning, straightaway I saw the recipe. You ready?"

"I'm ready. I take it you want me to make it for you when you come down?"

"Wouldn't that be wonderful." His voice dropped. "Roger's not keen on it, but I'd adore it. Well, here goes, Mother Singleton." That's what Charles had called her from the first day, and still did. Back then, it had seemed too formal, but no longer. It was just a name, and the caring behind it was obvious in his tone of voice and in the courtesy and affection with which he had always treated her.

"I can smell them already," Charles said. A pause, then, "This only makes four servings. You'll need to double it, Mother Single-ton."

She lay down the pencil. "Just give me your dates and I'll have it ready when you get here, how's that?"

"You are a saint."

"I have some news," Grace said.

"Oh, dear, not bad news, I hope. Okay, go ahead, what is it?"

She told him about Harold.

"That is bad news. Dear God in heaven, that's tragic. Such a nice man. I am terribly sorry."

"I've good news also," Grace said. "Emily's pregnant and we'll have a spring baby. Everyone's excited."

"Now that's brilliant news. Is Tyler excited?"

"Tyler especially. He's old enough not to be threatened by a sib-ling the way a young child might be."

She could picture Charles twisting the phone cord in his fingers, shifting from leg to leg, eager to be off the phone to relay it all to Roger.

"There's more. Several of Amelia's photographs will be exhibited at a gallery in New York. She and Mike will go up for the opening January tenth."

"How absolutely marvelous," Charles said, "I'm rushing off to tell Roger. Stay well. See you soon. Love you." And he was gone.

Grace realized she hadn't asked how he was. He had been in good health for several years now, although he claimed to have slowed down some. She had come to take it for granted that Charles would continue infection free. Now, suddenly, she was swept with a sense of anxiety. Oh, God, she prayed silently, keep Charles well.

The front door opened and closed, and a draft of chill air drew her back to the room and to Laura, who stood in the doorway, her brown hair windblown, her arms loaded with books, her gait steady

Toad-in-the-Hole

(sausages baked in batter)

1 cup all-purpose flour
2 eggs
1 cup milk
½ teaspoon salt
Freshly ground pepper
1 pound small pork sausages

Preheat the oven to 400°. In a blender, combine flour, eggs, milk, salt, and pepper, and blend at high speed for 2 or 3 seconds. Turn off the machine and scrape down the sides of the jar. Blend again for 45 seconds. Refrigerate the batter for an hour.

Place the sausages in a heavy skillet and prick them several times with a fork. Sprinkle them with 3 teaspoons of water, cover the pan tightly, and cook over low heat for 4 minutes. Uncover, increase the heat to medium, and cook, turning frequently, until the water is evaporated and the sausages begin to brown in their own fat.

Arrange the cooked sausages at least an inch apart in a baking tin or dish about 6 by 10 inches. Moisten them with 2 teaspoons of their own drippings.

Pour the batter over sausages. Bake in the center of the oven for 30 minutes, or until the pudding rises over the top of the pan and is crisp and brown. Serve at once.

and no cane today. "I try to get a sense of the places where I live, what makes the natives tick." Laura spilled the books onto the kitchen table. *A History of the Civil War* topped the pile, coming to rest above a biography of Robert E. Lee. A paperback of Cash's *The Mind of the South* almost slid off the table, but Grace caught it and placed it to one side, and as she did she remembered what

Emily had said about the South being the only part of America that had ever lost a war.

That was well over a hundred years ago, yet the mystique of the South lay in this event, which was deeply imprinted in the psyche of its people. It was as if the pain and humiliation of the past were expressed from mother's milk and imbibed by generation after generation, setting Southerners apart. Yet even in the South, the mythic memory seemed to differ from state to state and section to section of the state. Mountain people disdained the people from Florida or south Georgia or along the North Carolina coast, flatlanders they called them. City folks were contemptuous of Appalachia. "Did you find people in Maine standoffish?" she asked Laura.

Laura finished stacking the books. "They tolerated us, I think. Mainly they stuck to themselves. Looking back, I wonder if we weren't just as standoffish. Boat people are a subculture, you know. We think of ourselves as unique. Maybe we created the separation, maybe we didn't recognize a hand held out in friendship." Her brow knitted. "I don't want that to happen here."

Grace studied Laura's serious face. She had Hannah's blue eyes, and height, and like her mother her smile warmed her face. "You've decided to stay awhile with us, then?"

"I think so."

"I'm glad. I know your mother likes having you here, and so do Amelia and I. We enjoy a young woman about. It keeps us young."

"I haven't told my mother yet, but I've about decided to work for Mr. Maxwell." She lifted a hand. "Not full time, but I can begin to do the research. I've always loved history, any kind of history."

"I'm attracted to ancient history," Grace said. "I never tire of reading about ancient civilizations."

"Was history your major in college?"

Grace laughed. "I didn't go to college."

"In a million years, I'd never have guessed that."

"Why, thank you."

Laura leaned across the table. "You know, Grace, when I first came here I resented everything and everyone. But I found a solid stability, kindness, and acceptance here from all of you. It was exactly what I needed, although if I'd had someplace else to go, I probably would never have come." Idly, it seemed, she ran her fingertips along the scar on her cheek. "Why do I have this scar? Tell me, was it fated?"

"Do you think so?" Grace asked.

"I don't know," Laura replied thoughtfully. "Again and again, I question whether it was fated that Marvin die and I survive, or was it an arbitrary event without meaning? A book I picked up at the library today suggested that everyone, even an infant a few hours old, dies at the appointed time. Does that mean everything's fated?" She bit her lip. "Do you ever wonder, Grace, what life's all about?"

"I wonder all the time," Grace replied. "When I was young I was quite religious. God, the benevolent old man, sat somewhere in heaven waiting to help me. My parents believed that the Bible was literally the word of God. They lived by rigid rules. But later, when I was older, I'd look at the heavens at night, a sky salted with stars, and try to imagine ancient man sitting in the mouth of his cave trying to fathom that incredible display of moving lights. Surely he worshiped the stars. How could he not? That's when I began reading about other religions. My parents didn't appreciate my questioning their beliefs. They'd quote the Bible. They agonized, quite genuinely, that I'd go to hell."

Grace shifted in her chair, crossed and uncrossed her legs. "I married about that time and got on with my life. Ted's was a more tolerant background, but I didn't discuss it much with him or with anyone really." Grace fell silent for a time, then said, "Talking to you has brought it back, all the questions I have about meaning, about purpose."

"Some folks seem to have all the answers," Laura said.

"Not anyone in this household," Grace said.

"That's a blessing, anyhow," Laura replied. "I appreciate your listening and sharing your feelings about this." Gathering her books, Laura smiled at Grace and left the kitchen.

21

Dinner with Friends

"The success of a dinner party," Grace said to Hannah, "hinges on fine food, pleasant company, and everyone's willingness to be cheerful, talkative, and interested in others."

And so, on a blustery evening in early November, the ladies enthusiastically welcomed the Richardsons—Bob, Russell, Emily, and Tyler—and the Reynoldses—Old Man, Lurina, and Wayne—as well as Max, Hank, and Mike to their home for dinner. They arrived, one close upon the other, smiles on their faces, cheeks pink from the cold, and wrapped about in snug coats, scarves, woolen hats, and mittens. Seams of snow laced the ground, and they all stomped their feet on the thick, wiry mat placed on the porch for just this purpose.

Grace waved them into the living room where finger food waited. Max sank to the floor on the rug near the fireplace and crossed his legs. Hank, looking shy and uncertain, took a straight-backed chair nearby and the others settled into chairs and sofa. Bob bustled about helping Grace and Hannah serve drinks, mostly spiced cider and a beer or two. Suddenly, Tyler sprang from the couch and raced to the window.

"It's snowing, look everyone. Can we make a snowman, Dad, please, please?"

"Tomorrow," Russell replied, "if there's enough snow."

Max pushed up from the floor and joined Tyler at the window. "There'll be enough snow. It's coming down hard."

"Maybe we'll get snowed in and have to sleep over," Tyler said, running back and bounding onto the couch between Emily and his father. Then he remembered that Laura now had his room upstairs.

"If it gets really bad, I've plenty of room for you-all across the road in my big old empty house," Maxwell volunteered.

"How's the park coming?" Russell asked.

"Just fine," Max replied. "Hank's doing the plans and supervising. It's going like clockwork."

Russell smiled and nodded. As a collector of antique clocks he understood clockwork.

"Laura's coming on with us soon," Max said. "When she does, most of the staff'll be in place."

"Miss Hannah showed me the gardens yesterday," Wayne broke in. "Never done seen nothin' like that canal water garden with fake fish flyin' in the air. Real different."

"How do you like Covington, Hank?" Mike asked. "Big change from the city, eh?"

"Atlanta is too big and too busy. I was ready to leave," Hank replied. Sandy hair fell across his forehead and stopped just short of clear hazel eyes. Shyly, he looked away.

Squiggling in her chair, Amelia talked about her pending New York trip. "I'm so excited. It's been years. New York's such a thrilling place."

At that moment, Grace appeared in the doorway. At the sound of her silver dinner bell, everyone rose and started toward the dining room.

"You outdone yourself, Grace. It's sure pretty," Lurina said. And it was, for all down the center of the table white candles of varying heights rose like flowers from among leathery green leaves. A graceful cream-colored lace cloth hung low on all sides. Crystal goblets glimmered in the candlelight, and Amelia's lovely floral china was stacked on one end of the buffet table.

Max waved Lurina first. Lurina held her plate carefully with both hands as Grace offered crisp chicken thighs, plenty of stuffing and gravy. "Get you some of this here asparagus soufflé Grace made," Lurina said, turning to look at Old Man, who was shuffling along directly behind her with Wayne close on his heels. "You ain't never tasted nothin' like it before, I reckon."

When their plates were filled, Grace led them to the far end of the table, close to where she would sit. She had neglected Lurina these last few weeks. Not that Lurina needed her the way she had prior to her marriage to Old Man, but Grace genuinely liked her and enjoyed visiting. She even enjoyed Lurina's amazing stories about who died, when, where, and about their funerals. Lurina seemed never to run out of tales, and once all were seated and the meal under way, she began a story that captured everyone's interest. Even Tyler sat transfixed, his food growing cold on his plate.

"Wayne was a cleanin' up the old Masterson Cemetery," she began. "He found him a grave I done forgot about all these years. Cousin Sally Masterson." Lurina shook her head and looked sad. "Young, too young to pass, only seventeen. Happened on Halloween night a long while ago.

"Bunch of young uns out partyin'. Comin' home, they had to cross a wood bridge over by Sandy Mush. They was piled in a buggy, and an old horse pullin', doin' his best. But something . . ." She paused. Her eyes widened and her eyebrows shot up as she scanned everyone at the table and settled on Tyler. "Somethin' big." Lurina leaned way forward. "Maybe 'twas a lost soul, or a bear—there was bears in them hills that time—crossed that old horse's path. He took to boltin' and started off at a run. When they reached the bridge, he like to went crazy raisin' up on his hind legs, and that old wood bridge gave way. Horse, buggy, and all those young uns smack-dab landed in that crick. Wasn't deep, plenty of rocks, though, so most of them got bumps and bruises, except for Sally Masterson. Poor Sally got her head knocked on a rock and she passed, poor thing, right there in that crick."

Lurina nodded, sat back, and adjusted her slight frame in the chair. "Old Man gave a low whistle. "Well, I'll be derned," he said.

Grace knew it wasn't over, there was still the burial to tell. After taking several forkfuls of dinner, and a long drink of water, Lurina continued. "Plenty of folks gathered for Sally's funeral, so many the preacher had to move it outside the church and preach about Sally from a stump in the yard. A real mournful service it was, everyone sobbin', and callin' the Lord to keep her soul. I was fourteen years then. I seen three women faint and carried out right past where I was sittin'. Some said it was from the heat. Way others told it, was the spirit took them. Old Lady Springer, she went about tellin' people she done seen Sally a sittin' in a tree behind the preacher. I could see that tree real good from where I was, and I never did see no Sally sittin' there."

Finished now, Lurina folded her hands, satisfied that the tale had been well received by all, and Sally Masterson would live on in their memories. "The departed live as spirits in heaven long as they're remembered," she'd once told Grace.

Ghost tales seemed in order then, and Max had one, and Bob, and everyone feigned fright, even Tyler, and laughed, and ate, and Grace smiled to see that even Laura seemed to be relaxing. She even chatted with Emily, who was seated alongside her, about Emily's pregnancy, and when Emily suggested that they have lunch one day in Mars Hill, and Hannah offered to lend Laura her car, Laura accepted. But Laura ignored Hank, who sat alongside Hannah and across from Laura. Except for responding to questions put to him occasionally by Hannah, he was silent throughout the meal.

Later, after the dishwasher was stacked and whirring away, Laura said good night. Wayne drove off with Lurina and Old Man. Much to Tyler's disappointment, it stopped snowing by the time he and his parents departed. Amelia had trotted off to bed, saying that she had a long day tomorrow shopping for clothes for New York, and Mike bade them all good night, leaving Max, Hannah, Bob, and Grace sitting in the living room. Bob drew a hassock close to the couch, lifted Grace's feet, removed her shoes, and massaged her feet and toes.

"Feels good." Grace leaned back into the cushions. "Thanks."

Max turned to Hannah. "Laura's going to do a fine job coordinating the early settlers' village." Then he said, "I admire what you ladies have accomplished here. You came to Covington knowing no one, and you've created a family."

"Seemed to unfold," Hannah said.

"Nonsense. Things happen because we choose to take action and make them happen," Max replied.

"Or was it fate?" Grace asked, opening her eyes.

"Was what fate?" Bob asked.

"Olive's boarding house was hardly the location of choice for any of us, yet circumstances placed us there. Was that fate, luck, what? Amelia's cousin surfaced out of the mists of the Blue Ridge Mountains and left her this property. If I'd not been assigned to tutor Tyler, I might never have met you, Bob." She ran her fingers along his cheek. Grace craned her head and looked from one to the other of them. "I want to know how much of all this is destiny, or is it all accidental?"

Hannah moaned and held her head. "Too late at night, too tired for this conversation."

"I think it's interesting," Max said. "But it is late." He yawned. "Excuse me. I'm pooped, and tomorrow I have to be on site at sunrise. Those site preparation people must get up at four in the morning, they start so early. I don't want the early settlers' village site in the wrong place, like they did the Indian site." He heaved up from the rug where he had been sitting near Hannah's chair. "Thanks y'all for a delicious meal, and the pleasantest evening I've had in ages."

Hannah walked him to the door.

Briefly, he took her hand. "Thanks for including me."

She nodded, forcing back the lump forming in her throat. After the door closed, she waited, listened to his heavy tread on the porch, the crunch of crusted snow on the steps. He was whistling, but she could not make out the tune. From the small glass pane in the door, she watched him stride past rosebushes laced with garlands of snow. A trail of dark footprints marred the virgin snow. When he had crossed Cove Road, Max turned and looked back once, then hastened up his drive to his front porch. A slant of light appeared, then vanished, as he opened and closed his door.

From the frame of the old farmhouse door, cold air indigenous to the old house seeped in, chilling Hannah's arm and shoulder. Hannah reached for a sweater hanging on the coat rack nearby. Max was a friend, a colleague now, absolutely nothing more.

22

No Such Thing as a Touch of Diabetes

On a blustery day, with fog hugging the low spots on the roads and the mountains hazy and formless on the horizon, Grace and Bob drove into Asheville to see Dr. Grimes, Grace's internist. Had Bob not picked her up, Grace would have used weather as an excuse to cancel her appointment. Perhaps other people had done just that, for the office was amazingly empty, and within five minutes Grace was being escorted, with Bob in tow, into a pleasant examining room with a mural of a waterfall covering one wall.

The nurse weighed her and took her blood pressure, which was fine. In a few minutes, she said, Dr. Grimes would be in.

Chart in hand, glasses shoved high on his forehead, Dr. Grimes ambled into the room. A man of medium build and height with a warm smile, he never appeared hurried and seemed attentive and interested. Grace liked and trusted him.

Bob had questions. "Are you certain that Grace has type two diabetes?"

"She does, and so far, I can't get her to take it seriously." He looked mournful and shook his head.

"I'm aware of how serious diabetes can be over the long haul," Bob said.

Dr. Grimes tapped the chart. He gave Grace a wry smile. "What are we going to do with you?"

"I'd like you to lay it out for Grace again. She's got to start taking this seriously. Spare none of the gory details."

As Dr. Grimes talked, a frightening picture emerged. Grace could lose her sight or her toes or legs; she could suffer heart disease or kidney failure, go blind, and more. "I can prescribe medication," he said.

"I suggest you take the medication, darling," Bob said, taking Grace's hands.

"Medication's an aid, not a cure. You're still going to have to go easy on carbohydrates, white rice, potatoes, pasta, white bread, and sugar," Dr. Grimes said.

"So what's the point of taking medication?" Grace asked.

"As I've told you, any weight you lose, and an exercise program, just a fifteen-minute walk a day, can help keep this whole thing under control. When you lose weight, the body can use insulin better and thus lowers blood sugar. Lost weight could add years to your life and avoid complications down the road."

Grace felt cornered, and angry with Bob for being so amenable to everything Dr. Grimes said. And then, suddenly, the whole frightening prospect hit her. Her body had betrayed her. An insidious illness had crept up on her, and she would have to come to terms with it and make changes, major lifestyle changes. "Okay," Grace said. "So I have diabetes. I must change the way I eat. I'll even take your pills, but when I lose the twenty pounds, if I can, I want to go off the pills."

Dr. Grimes nodded and looked pleased.

So what if he attributed her change of attitude to Bob's presence and influence? Grace knew otherwise. For the past six months she had moved, albeit slowly, from denial to bargaining, through anger, to this day, to acceptance.

Tears filled Grace's eyes. "I'm a diabetic."

"It's manageable, Grace, if we work together." Dr. Grimes smiled and made notes on her chart.

"What are you thinking?" Bob asked as they left the building.

"That now I have to rid the kitchen shelves of white rice, flour, sugar, noodles." Her heart sank. She squeezed her eyes shut and immediately lost her balance and had to grasp Bob's arm to keep from falling.

"Grace, what's wrong?"

"I closed my eyes to see what blindness might be like."

Bob squeezed her arm. "You can lose weight, Grace. I'll help in any way I can. Why," he patted his stomach, "I could take off some pounds myself." Nonchalantly he asked, "Wouldn't it be easier if you moved in with me for a few months, easier to cook just for the two of us than for all the ladies?"

She slapped his hand gently. "You never give up, do you?"

"Nope. You know what they say, hope springs eternal. I wish we lived together, married or not."

"Keep wishing. I can handle this thing. Come on, let's stop at the market. I might as well start buying vegetables and salad greens."

The habits of a lifetime resist change. The mind protests, initiates cravings, demands satisfaction. The mind sends messages to the stomach, which then howls for potatoes, thick creamy soups, casseroles, cookies. Lying in bed at night, Grace struggled with food cravings by conjuring up unnamed illnesses and sores that would not heal and clogged blood vessels. But that was all so amorphous. It was impossible to imagine any of it happening to her.

And then one day she began to gather cookbooks: Pritkin, Weight Watchers, and a half dozen cookbooks that specifically boasted "real food" or "delicious recipes" for diabetics in their titles. Propped up in bed at night, she perused the pages and started a file of recipes with reduced fat and sugar, skim milk for whole, sweetener for sugar, reduced-fat cheeses, brown rice for white, sweet potatoes for white ones. The pictures accompanying some of the recipes actually were appealing.

It wasn't easy. Where before she didn't have to think twice in preparing a meal, now she had to plan carefully. Could she still make meatballs and prunes, she wondered? Why not? She could brown the meatballs and the onions in Pam rather than oil. But one shouldn't eliminate all oil from one's diet. A little olive oil wouldn't hurt. Jumping from bed, Grace trotted down to the kitchen to check the back of the box of pitted prunes. Five prunes contained eleven grams of sugar. She would use twelve, one tucked in the center of each meatball, and at least another dozen in the sauce. Roughly, that would be over fifty-two grams of sugar. No, more. There was sugar in the tomato paste. But she wasn't going to eat twelve meatballs, only two or three perhaps. As she returned the box of prunes to the shelf, she decided that it wouldn't hurt occasionally to enjoy meatballs with prunes and gravy. Back in her room, Grace extracted the stained recipe sheet from between two pages of an old cookbook and studied it. This calculating was going to drive her crazy.

The first meal Grace cooked on the new plan, broiled swordfish steaks, filled the house with fishy smells that lingered on the stairs, in the hallway, and their bedrooms, and brought pleas from Amelia and Laura that they never, ever have swordfish again unless they purchased an outdoor grill.

What Grace missed most and longed for was sugar in her tea. Even in November, there were days when the temperature reached seventy, and they took their tea on the porch. But tea without real sugar, even with artificial sweetener, tasted bitter, and she felt angry, at whom or what she wasn't sure. So Grace decided to enjoy a teaspoon or two of sugar in one cup of tea, only one, and no dunking cookies, and there was a decided limit on finger sandwiches.

It was Hannah who unwittingly helped her cope with her growing antipathy to tea. "I'll start taking lemon in my tea instead of sugar," Hannah announced one day. "I can see what's coming. Soon you won't want to have tea, or even sit with us. I'd detest that. I want it to stay as it's been."

It was the "as it's been" that got Grace's attention. Shame brought a flush to her cheeks. Her immaturity and crankiness were affecting the others. "No," she said. "This is my problem. I have to learn to cope with it." She held her head in her hands for a moment. "I am sorry for making such a fuss. I read labels, and it seems there's

Meatballs and Prunes
a recipe from Netta Orlouski

1 can tomato paste

4 cups water

2 medium onions, chopped

Olive oil

2 pounds ground round or sirloin

Salt and pepper to taste

2 eggs

Seasoned breadcrumbs, as needed

1 box pitted prunes

Combine the tomato paste and water and mix well, then place in large pot on stove.

Sauté the onions in olive oil until golden. Drain well. Stir into the tomato paste liquid.

Put the meat in a deep bowl. Season as desired. Add the eggs and work into meat with a fork or your hands. You may have to sprinkle some breadcrumbs into the mix to hold it together.

Form round meatballs of desired size. Insert a pitted prune into the center of each one. Be sure that the prune is surrounded by meat and not visible. Coat each meatball with a light dusting of breadcrumbs.

Heat olive oil in a skillet. Brown the meatballs on all sides. Remove and drain.

Add the meatballs to the tomato paste mixture and add water to cover. Add the remaining prunes and check the seasoning. Cover. I use tin foil under the cover for a better seal.

Bring the liquid to boil. Reduce to medium heat (bubbling slightly) and cook for 30 minutes. Lower heat and simmer for 1 hour. Check now and then, to be sure the liquid is not boiling off. Bring back to boil and cook, uncovered or until the gravy has become thick.

Serve with rice or other starch. Bob likes it with mashed potatoes.

Should make 8 to 10 meatballs.

nothing I can eat anymore. Sugar's in everything—fruit, cereal, bread, milk. Fiber, now that's good for you." She skinned up her nose. "I've never liked beans. But I guess a few in soup or casseroles aren't so bad." She grew pensive and cupped her chin with her hand. "I've denied this diabetes thing for months. I can't anymore. I'm working on it. Once I get my mind turned off of sugar especially, it won't faze me what anyone eats." Would this ever be true, she wondered?

"We could still sit together and not have tea," Amelia said.

Grace looked intently at them. She had shared with them all that her doctor had said. "No. I live in the world, and I can't let myself be affected by what others eat. This is my problem, and I have to remember the long-term complications of diabetes, which are really awful. I have to get a grip on this food thing. I've found some great-sounding recipes, creamy potato casserole, almond cake using sweetener. It's a new way of cooking. I'll master it in time. I have to."

23

Acts of Love

Grace dawdled in the market as she located items needed for new and healthier meals. Some items, like liquid nonegg egg mixture, she'd never heard of and sounded unappealing. She skinned up her nose at fat-free yogurt, sour cream, and cottage cheese but bought them anyway. Grace lingered at the ice cream freezer, debated, and succumbed to a small container of frozen raspberry yogurt that beckoned to her from behind glass doors. On arriving home, before unpacking the groceries, she sat at the kitchen table alone, and with her eye on the door she gobbled down half of the container of yogurt. It soothed and satisfied her. When she turned the container around, Grace was appalled to see that each serving contained 25 grams of sugar and 136 calories. "I blew it," Grace muttered and dumped the remaining yogurt into the trash.

It was quiet in the house: no jazz drifting downstairs from Laura's room, no Amelia roaming the house complaining, as she did every year, about ladybugs that once again colonized their ceilings, no Wayne in the greenhouse blasting country music on his radio. Grace slipped off her shoes, sat at the kitchen table, and stretched her legs. She wiggled her toes. Was that a slight numbing in her left big toe? Concerned, she rubbed the toe. It seemed fine. She was turning into a hypochondriac. Barefoot, Grace turned to consider each new item and the recipe involved. Then she rose, unpacked, and put away the groceries, until finally only four unlabeled plastic baggies, whose contents were of similar color and texture, remained on the counter. Which was the wheat germ, which the wheat bran, which was whole-wheat flour, and which oat bran? Scooping them from their bins at the market, she was certain that she would remember. Now, before making oat bran muffins, she'd have to return to the store to identify the contents of the bags.

The phone rang, jarring her.

"Grace?"

"Yes."

"Can you come over?"

"That you, Brenda? When? Now? Okay, be there in ten minutes."

Grace folded and smoothed the paper bags. She stored the four bags in the refrigerator. As she turned to leave the kitchen, her eyes fell on November's picture on the wall calendar, a rugged wooden porch half in shadow with green wicker chairs set back close to the log walls of the house. A lake, shrouded in fog, filled the foreground. November fifteenth already. Stupid to start a diet with Thanksgiving so imminent, and Miranda and her family coming.

Suddenly she could hear Dr. Grimes's voice. "Exercise is important. Walk as often as you can, rather than drive." Well, she could start doing that now.

Grace checked the thermometer outside on the sill of the kitchen window. Forty-two degrees at three in the afternoon. It would be colder on her walk back. Grace put on her old down jacket, the one that made her look like a barrel teetering on the edge of a hill about to tumble over, pulled a red knit cap over her head and ears, and headed at a brisk trot down Cove Road.

Blue jays, gorging intently at the bird feeder in the Tates' yard, reminded Grace that she'd forgotten to purchase birdseed. Every winter, Hannah maintained four bird feeders in their yard. They all enjoyed watching the birds. Anxious creatures, birds, ever alert for larger, more aggressive members of their species, like blue jays, to swoop down, pounce, and dislodge them from their perch on the feeder.

Brenda opened the door and welcomed Grace inside. In the living room, the couch was littered with comic books. A worn brown leather jacket dangled over the arm of a chair, and a pair of frayed sneakers peeked from under another. Soda pop cans and crumpled potato chip bags cluttered the coffee table. "Please ignore the mess," Brenda said. "Molly's boys are here. They're upstairs now watching TV with their grandpa. They're the only visitors he tolerates." She handed Grace a sheet of paper that proved to be a list of neighbors and family.

"They all signed up to do something. Help me with this, will you please? By the time I get home from school, my mind is hash."

As they talked, they moved to the kitchen, and sat at the 1950s vintage table with its red Formica top, which stood, as in many farmhouse kitchens, in the center of the room. Brenda brewed tea. Grace chose Sweet 'n Low from a crock Brenda placed on the table. Maybe if she used less of it, it would taste less bitter. Her cold hands welcomed the warmth of the cup.

"Who'll be here after your mother leaves on Sunday?" Grace asked.

"Molly's resigned her teaching, starting Monday."

"Has Molly ever taken care of anyone as sick as her dad?"

Brenda shook her head. "I need to contact my insurance agent about home health care, but every time I head for the phone, I stop to do something else like wash a dish, take out the garbage, or let the cat in. One day I even plopped into a chair to read an old magazine dated June twenty-third, 1998. I can't seem to get anything important done."

"How about making a list of things that are important, and let's see which of our neighbors could help with what. Could your cousin Alma call the insurance agent for you?"

Brenda drew back. "Heavens no. Asking her to do that would be like hanging our dirty linen on the front lawn."

"Can Molly do it?"

"Maybe."

"It would take Molly, what, fifteen minutes to get some information?"

Brenda drummed the list with her fingers. "Oh, Grace, how can I ask all these people to do things for me, for us?"

"There's a time for rugged independence and a time for cooperative effort. You must let people help you now." Grace deliberated on the list. "Alma, Velma, Hannah, Amelia, and me, and the men of course. I don't see Maxwell on this list. Guess he doesn't go to Bible study."

"I wouldn't expect him . . ."

"I would. He's a good man. Bob too. They'll both want to help." Grace set the list on the table and added both of their names and phone numbers. Then she looked intently at Brenda. "Would you like me to check on the insurance and get the information about home health care services?"

Brenda's shoulders relaxed; the relief on her face was evident. Grace wondered why Brenda hadn't just come out and asked her to make these calls, and she also wondered why it was easier for Brenda to seek and accept help from her rather than her relatives and old neighbors. "Give me the name of your insurance agent and the policy number. If they can't recommend someone, I'll look up the health care agencies in the phone book." She studied the list again. "Alma's sons want to help. Would Harold sit out on the porch in a lounge on days when it's warm? We'll undoubtedly have some warm days in November, maybe into December."

"He might. It would be good for him to get out of that old bed."

"Can he get about on his own?"

"He's weak, but he refuses to use a walker. Every time he starts downstairs, I die watching him, scared he'll fall."

"What do you think about asking your cousin Alma's sons to help him outside, sit with him for a while, and help him back in?"

Brenda nodded, then reached over and lay a hand on Grace's arm. She spoke not a word, but her tear-filled eyes expressed gratitude and relief.

Gently, Grace circled Brenda's hand in both of hers. "Right now, you need someone to help you make these arrangements, don't you?"

Brenda's chin quivered. "Why can't I handle this? I've always been the one to get things done."

"Too much stress is overwhelming. It's immobilizing. The less able we feel, the more certain we are we'll never be able to function the way we did. Believe me, I know. I also know that eventually the old brain starts to work again the way we want it to. So now let's figure out exactly how the neighbors can help. But I think it would be best if Molly phoned everyone. Sound all right to you?"

Brenda held her head in her hands. "The stairs wore my mother out. I feel so guilty."

"Your mother's a grown woman; she could have said something," Grace replied. She sounded like Hannah and felt strong in that awareness. "Don't use precious energy punishing yourself. Have you considered making Harold a bedroom downstairs?"

"Yes, but I haven't been able to organize things. The dinning room, I guess."

"Let's have a look at it."

They moved across the hall into the dining room, a moderate-size room but large enough to hold a bed for Harold, a small rocker, a dresser, and a TV. For a brief moment, Brenda brightened. "He could look out the window here, see people go by, lights at night." She flopped into a chair and for a moment covered her mouth with her hands. "Why didn't I do this weeks ago?"

"Because you're human. You do what you can, when you can."

Brenda turned worried eyes to Grace. "You really think I'll be my old self again?"

"I'm sure you will be. Now let's get back to the list."

Putting her arm about Brenda's shoulder, Grace led her back to the kitchen. "Let's see. How about asking Alma to bring her sons and husband over on Sunday after church and move Harold downstairs? Would that give you enough time to prepare him, ward off his objections?"

"He'll object all right. Wants me right there next to him all night long."

"Brenda, are you still sleeping in the room with him?"

"In the bed with him. I have to. He's so afraid. I am too, but I hold him and tell him he's going to be well again. But I think he knows." She stifled a sob. "It breaks my heart."

"Ted knew. He wanted me right there all the time also. I couldn't do it. Ted was restless all night. He tossed and moaned. I couldn't sleep. I could hardly function. Finally, I moved into our guest room. It was that or my sanity."

"I've wanted to sleep in another room for weeks, but Harold made such a fuss, and what would my mother think?"

"Millie? She probably wondered why you didn't."

"I can't think clearly."

"Not sleeping won't help. Once Harold's settled downstairs, don't you start sleeping on the couch down here. If you feel you have to be downstairs, then put a comfortable bed for yourself in the living room."

"Good thinking," Brenda replied.

Grace looked deep into her friend's eyes. "You've got to listen to me, please, Brenda. You're going to fall apart if you don't sleep and if you don't let others help you. If you come apart, who's going to benefit?"

"I'll ask the doctor for a stronger sedative for Harold, so he'll sleep nights, and I can also."

They talked then about Harold's medication, his sleep patterns, feeding and bathing, and other things about the house that cried out to be handled, as well as things that needed doing on the land.

"The hay's baled in the pasture waiting to be brought under cover," Brenda said. "Tobacco's drying in the barn. It needs taking to market."

"And leaves from your oaks needed raking and bagging," Grace said.

"Harold likes old John Wayne movies," Brenda said. "Can't make it through a whole one, he's not comfortable in one position for too long, but if someone could get videos and put them in that darn machine and sit with him awhile, that would help. I haven't the patience."

Grace made notes. Soon they had a list of things to be done and matched them with neighbors. It was not until the grandfather clock in the hallway bonged five times that they realized it was dark outside, and Grace hadn't even decided on dinner. She rose from the chair. "I have to go now. I'll call you tomorrow. Just give Molly this list and the phone. Let me know about Sunday. Any help you need moving down sheets, blankets, whatever from his room, let me know."

"How can I ever thank you, Grace?"

Grace smiled. "Don't thank me. I'm your friend doing what friends do."

On the brisk walk home, Grace raised her eyes to a clear, cloudless, moonless sky. There would be multitudes of stars tonight. Later, much later, when the others were asleep, when Cove Road lay wrapped in deep, soft darkness, she would throw a light blanket about her shoulders and step outside to hail Orion's progression across the southern sky. Flinging back her head, she would breathe deeply of the cold night air, ask for strength, and thank the universe for its many blessings. But now, as she strode along Cove Road, glad for the puffy down jacket, her queries about meaning seemed suddenly to be answered by a growing awareness that kindness and love and cooperation were among those things that gave life meaning and expunged the seeming randomness of the universe.

24

A Sense of Urgency

It was hard for Grace to maintain a balance between a life that flowed unhurriedly along, and the pressures and urgencies of assumed responsibilities. She made phone calls for Brenda, worried about Harold, worried about Brenda and Molly. Early on Sunday morning, she and Hannah and Amelia helped Brenda carry down sheets, pillows, clothing, medical supplies, and other paraphernalia of Harold's life. When Frank Craine and his sons arrived to move his bed and dresser, Frank hung Harold's hunting rifle, empty of shells, on one of the dining room walls alongside a framed picture of a man tramping through the woods accompanied by hounds.

"We sure had some good old huntin' times before we got us married," he said.

Then Harold, supported by two of Frank's strapping young sons, came slowly down the steps. For Grace it was déjà vu seeing him this way, emaciated, haunted, sunken eyes, nearly bald, and hardly able to walk across a room unaided. But his mind was still sharp, though not for much longer, Grace knew, and once installed in bed, he joked about second childhood and one's dotage.

Propped against his pillows, Harold's expression changed, and it was apparent to Grace how exhausted he was and close to tears. And yet, some of his kinfolk seemed oblivious and remained to chat among themselves and help themselves to food from the generous plates of fried chicken and potato salad Molly had set on the kitchen table.

After that, Grace dropped in briefly almost every day to check on Harold. As Thanksgiving approached, Harold's shrunken body had deteriorated and his mental faculties declined. Ted's illness had progressed slowly, allowing more time to say good-bye, and more time to grieve. Harold slid downhill rapidly, too rapidly, it was clear, for Brenda, whose distracted eyes had sunk deeper into her pale, pained face each time Grace saw her. With Thanksgiving looming, and Miranda and her family arriving in a few days, Grace had less time to devote to Brenda. She determined, however, to prepare a complete Thanksgiving meal for the Tates. Because of the size of her oven she would have to cook and deliver the meal several days before the holiday.

"Look at you," Bob said as she pulled the Tates' turkey from the oven. "You look exhausted. You're all flushed. I've never seen you so agitated."

"I know. I took on too much, but I had to, Bob. I can't be with them as much as I'd like. This is the least I can do."

They were in the kitchen of the farmhouse. Bob sat and drew her onto his knee. "You're too kind and generous for your own good, my love."

"I have to help Brenda."

"You've helped her a great deal already. You can't make Harold well, or take away the pain that family's feeling."

She nodded soberly, smiled at him, and then her eyes clouded. "Can you believe I forgot cranberry sauce? Come to the market with me." She untied her apron.

"There are days yet to Thanksgiving."

"I know. But I need not to have it hanging over my head."

"Fine." He rose and reached for her land. "Let's go."

As they drove toward Weaverville on darkening country roads, a sliver of a new moon crested the hills. "Do you ever make a wish on the new moon?" Grace asked.

"Can't say that I do."

"Well, I did."

"What did you wish for?"

"Charles's health. I'm worried about him. On the phone last night, he said he wasn't feeling up to snuff."

"I'm tuckered out by two in the afternoon," Charles had said. "I should be beavering away in the shop this time of year. Instead, I go home and sleep for hours."

"I have this sense of urgency that increases with each day as the holidays get closer," Grace said. "I feel agitated."

"All the pressure, Harold and Brenda, Miranda and family coming, two turkey dinners. Couple of days, Thanksgiving will be over. Things will settle down. What say we take a little drive to Florida sometime this winter?"

"Maybe," she said distractedly. "Watch that car, it's turning."

He slowed, then reached over, lifted her hand, and kissed it, and she was soothed by his touch.

Grace was not alone in her agitation; everyone in the ladies' household seemed to be edgy: Amelia and Mike spent hours pouring over contact sheets, sorting and selecting from among dozens of black-and-white prints.

"I don't like the way the printer did this," Mike said, holding up a photograph of a pathway through the forest. "He's burned this area rather than allowing the light to stream through." He slammed the print onto the table. "The only way to control the final print is for me to do it, with you standing right there. How can some stranger in a darkroom understand your intention? If we do it ourselves, we can do the cropping, the darkening or lightening where needed, and not end up with someone else's version of your photograph."

He was right, Amelia knew. That's how it was with black-and-white prints, very subjective, highly personal, but the smells of the darkroom fluids bothered her eyes and caused her to sneeze and feel miserable. And now, with the gallery in New York waiting for the prints, Amelia found it hard to choose among the twenty she and Mike had finally narrowed it down to and must narrow, again, to a mere ten.

They worked for hours until finally ten prints stood hip to hip on the mantel. One of the photographs was of Irene Ramsey, a portrait whose expressive power lay in its subject's qualities of patience, endurance, and calm. The color values were perfect, from the near white boards of the house to the almost black frame of the quilting stand, and with her clothing and the patterns in the quilt running the gamut of light to dark grays. Then there was the woman herself, hands on the quilt, determined jaw, head tipped, squared shoulders softened by the lines of her hair, and the full, loose bun at the nape of her neck. It was a photograph that viewers would not pass lightly.

"I think we've made good selections. Now it's time to send them off," Mike said.

Amelia's face was a study in anxiety. She wrung her hands and walked closer to the mantel. "Are you sure these are the best?"

"I am. You've taken gorgeous photos these last few weeks, and we've chosen smartly, I'm sure." He put his arm about her shoulder. "Of course you're nervous. I am too. But I trust the quality of these photographs, and time's run out. We must mail these tomorrow."

She nodded, knowing he was right, yet in her stomach, butterflies continued to flutter.

Laura's voice startled Amelia. "They're wonderful, those pictures. Mrs. Ramsey's beautiful, powerful." Laura waved her hand. "They move me, all of them."

"They really do?"

"Yes. They really do."

Hannah entered the room. She wore gloves and carried clippers in her hands. "Rosebushes cut back and mulched, put to bed for winter. What's going on in here? Haven't sent your photos off to New York yet?" She joined Laura in front of the fireplace. "Great work," she said. "Good luck, Amelia." Then, turning, Hannah muttered something about sunflowers and left the room.

Minutes later, Mike slipped the photos into a special box with separators designed for shipping photographs. A quick peck on Amelia's cheek, and he was off.

Laura followed her mother to the pantry off the kitchen and leaned against the doorframe while Hannah stripped off her gloves, stashed clippers and gloves in cubbyholes in a cabinet, scrubbed her hands at the sink, and doused them with alcohol.

"Why do you do that, Mother?" Laura said.

Hannah dried her hands. "Read somewhere it kills whatever germs you may have picked up from the soil."

Laura nodded. "I'm nervous these days," she said. "It's been more than fifteen years since I've seen Miranda. Sammy was walking and Philip crawling. How old are the boys now?"

"Almost twenty and just eighteen."

"I don't know Paul at all."

"Who knows Paul? Your sister's husband's a quiet man. He seems content to be around everyone and not talk much, so don't worry about it."

"Doesn't that make you uncomfortable?" Laura asked.

"You get used to Paul. He's a decent man, and he and Miranda get on well."

"Both of your daughters found good men. Didn't you know what dad was like when you married him?"

Hannah sighed. Her shoulders slumped as she pulled out a chair at the table and sank into it. "It's been years since I've thought about your father." Her eyes sought and held her daughter's. "When I met Bill Parrish, he was handsome and gregarious. He sold cars, was quite successful, and seemed to have the world by the tail. I knew Bill liked a beer or two, and twice while we were courting he got drunk and screamed at me. Of course, he was abjectly contrite afterward, and I was only too eager to forgive him. I didn't think one could be an alcoholic drinking beer." Her voice grew bitter.

"Your grandfather drank gin by the bottle." She shuddered remembering. "Once my mother hid his bottle. He tore the place up hunting for it."

"You married my father, and you had two children." Laura's voice was almost reproachful, and Hannah leaned back from the table, from her daughter.

"I needed to get away from the situation at home. Youth may be short on wisdom, but it sure abounds with hope and enthusiasm." Hannah squared her shoulders. "It wasn't bad at first. Your father'd get drunk maybe twice a year, rave, rant, and fall asleep on the couch. Five, six years before he lifted his hand to me."

"Is that a euphemism for hit you?"

Hannah nodded.

"How terrible that must have been."

"It was. I should have known from day one, but who ever told me that right from the start, people's behavior tells you exactly who they are? In my family no one ever spoke of anything personal, anything that really mattered." Her fingers tapped the table. "What I do blame myself for is staying with your father after he hit me the first time." Her eyes clouded. "You were an infant. I'd no place to go, no education, no trade, and he'd moved us to that godforsaken house on the lake in Canada. Didn't have a car." She shook her head. "Can't imagine how I tolerated it as long as I did."

"I don't remember much. Miranda saw him hurt you. I only remember a lot of screaming and yelling."

"Glad you didn't see him hit me."

"He never touched us," Laura said. It was as much a question as a statement.

Hannah's eyes clouded. She stared into space. "Last time he hit me, he swore he'd kill us all. That's when I took the car and you kids, and ran. I didn't care where to, or how we'd get by. Always bless that truck driver at the gas station in Michigan who offered us a ride away from him."

Laura rested her hand lightly on her mother's clenched fist. "I'm sorry I asked. I've upset you."

"Time to talk about these things. Too many secrets."

"Thanks for telling me, Mother. Marvin used to urge me to talk to you, get to know you."

Hannah smiled. "Feel better now?"

"Yes, I do. And I understand why you were gone from us so much, working, going to school, trying to better yourself, make it better for us." She hesitated, uncertain, afraid of rejection. "Thank you for taking us away from him. You were incredibly brave." Again she hesitated.

"I had no choice."

The Laura said, "I was a monster, wasn't I?"

"I thought so at the time. Looking back, I realize it stemmed from unhappiness. I can't recall ever sitting down and explaining things to you girls. I wish I had."

"Would we have listened at that time, I wonder?"

"Water over the dam."

"What do you think will happen when Miranda comes?" Laura asked. She nibbled at her lower lip.

"You'll talk, get reacquainted."

"That easy?"

"Miranda's looking forward to seeing you."

"Why am I so scared to see her again?"

Leaning across the table, Hannah's fingers briefly touched her daughter's cheek. "Don't be. You'll like her."

Laura grasped her mother's fingers and held them fast, before Hannah, visibly embarrassed, rose and strode from the room.

For a long while, Laura sat at the table remembering: a dreary, cramped apartment, crying herself to sleep, plotting to run away to Canada, to her room in their house with its view of the lake. Sometimes Miranda had held her and tried to sooth her. Miranda cried too, but she had seen their father strike their mother. She tried to tell Laura. Laura covered her ears. Not until they learned that their father had died of a stroke did Miranda grow sullen and silent, and Laura's pain and anger turn overt and subversive. She fought her mother on every issue, arguing, failing in school when she knew the work, dressing like a tramp when she was older, and staying out until all hours of the night.

As an adolescent, Laura wove fantasies. She would run away, east or west it didn't matter so long as she reached the ocean. But remembering her mother's worn face and swollen legs after cleaning other people's houses all day, Laura realized that she needed an education. Community college led to an associate degree in computer science, a new name, as she saw it, for a career as a secretary. Still, it served her well, carried her west across the country to San Diego, where she worked for years before heading back to the Atlantic Ocean. In Maine, working as a waitress—the money was better—she had met Marvin.

Pushing back her chair, Laura rose and ambled to the window. For a few moments she watched Amelia and her mother chatting on the porch, before Amelia turned and walked back into the house. Amelia had been so kind, making Laura's decision to stay in Covington easier. Well, the Atlantic Ocean wasn't going anywhere. She could always return to its shores, but would she want to without Marvin? Pain resurfaced just thinking his name, and she pressed her hands hard against her chest. She couldn't bear talking to anyone now, not even Amelia. Hastening from the kitchen, Laura scrambled upstairs to her room, where she flopped on to her bed and cried for a time before she lay there staring at nothing, thinking about her mother's life and about Miranda coming.

They arrived, the rack on the top of their big sedan loaded with suitcases, and pulling a small trailer. Miranda sprang from the car, embraced her mother, Grace, and Amelia. Then she turned, smiled at Laura, and opened wide her arms. Laura moved into the circle of her sister's arms and held on as if for dear life.

"I'm so happy to see you," Miranda said. Her eyes brimmed with tears.

Laura responded with the urgency of the little girl who had so loved and depended on her older sister. "I'm so glad you're here."

"And these are my sons. Philip, Sammy, your Aunt Laura."

They emerged from the car, muscled and still tan from summer, followed by their father. How different they are, Laura thought.

Sammy's tall and sandy-haired, like his dad, and Philip's shorter but gorgeous with those blue eyes and dark hair. Why, he's inherited the Spanish-English mix and looks like me. It was, for Laura, love at first sight.

They came inside, everyone talking at once, carrying armfuls of brightly wrapped Christmas packages, which they stacked on either side of the fireplace in the living room. "Not to open until Christmas," Miranda said turning to Laura. "I dub thee keeper of the gifts. No one's to get to them until Christmas Eve. Promise?"

"Promise." Immediately, Laura felt happily drawn into conspiracy with her sister.

After a time, Miranda said to Paul, "Let's go on over to the apartment and unpack. I could use a hot shower and fresh clothes. You coming, boys, or staying here?"

Disappointment flooded Laura when Philip volunteered to go with his parents.

🌱

Sammy surprised his grandmother when he announced that he would stay. Two summers ago when the boys spent several weeks in Covington, it had not been a happy encounter. A drunken Sammy crashed his car, and Hannah's reaction had been immediate and irrational. Miranda, she demanded, must come to Asheville the very next day and take her sons home, no matter that they were battered and stitched and bandaged. Sammy had entered a treatment center and, as he assured Hannah on the phone, his strongest drink now was Coca-Cola. This was their first meeting since those disappointing days.

"Can I see your greenhouse, Grandma?" he asked.

"I've sold it to Wayne, remember him?"

"The guy who tripped you up in the hardware store?"

"He didn't trip me. I wasn't looking. But yes, that's the one. We're quite good friends now." They left the others and headed for the back porch and out to the greenhouse. In contrast to the chill November day, the interior of the greenhouse was warm and humid. Lush plants lined the shelves. Every few seconds a light mist, sus-

167

pended from jets set in a bar along the ceiling, sprayed water.

"A misting system," Sammy said. "I remember you talking about that. Looks like it works real good."

She studied him. He had grown and was taller now than she was. The stubble on his chin and cheeks indicated a beard in process. Long, sandy hair curled about his ears. She wanted to ask if he planned to shave, wanted to remind him that his hair needed cutting, but she refrained, remembering how she had chided and nagged him about one thing or the other when he was here before. She bent to pick a leaf off the ground and tucked it into her pocket. "You've grown into such a handsome young man, Sammy. How do you like college?"

"I like it fine. It's more work than I imagined." He walked along the row of shelves, touched the glossy leaf of a plant, then stepped back to avoid the spray. "I'm going into computer networks. Computers are where it's at."

"Probably right." She was about to tell him about having bought a computer and then donating it to the elementary school, but not wanting to sound ignorant, she refrained.

They stood a few moments longer. Sammy fingered the glossy, wet leaf of a gardenia. "Mom says you force these with fertilizer, and they bloom out of their usual time."

"That's right. People want flowering plants in their homes in winter."

"Are you glad or sorry you sold it?" he asked.

"Glad, and glad it's here, and I can work with Wayne when I feel like it." Hannah swallowed hard. She still felt chagrined admitting that she hadn't been able to handle the sheer magnitude of the work, constant transplanting, lifting, bending. "Selling it was the best thing to do."

Hannah started outside, but Sammy called to her. "Grandma, wait up a sec."

Half inside, half outside, she turned to face him.

"I want to apologize for what happened when I was here. I was awful, and I'm really sorry. I'd like to make it up to you. Can I help you in any way?"

Tears filled the corners of Hannah's eyes. All these feelings, all this emotion was getting to her. She cleared her throat. "There is something. Make friends with your Aunt Laura. She's more a stranger than an aunt, but she's . . ."

"Lost everything, I know."

"The man she loved as well."

With two long strides, he was beside Hannah. "Sure, I'll do that. What does she like to do?"

For a moment Hannah was silent. What were her daughter's hobbies, interests? "She likes boats and water."

"That's easy, then. We'll go down to South Carolina, rent a pontoon boat, and take her out on Lake Jocassee. We can all go, make a picnic of it."

"If the weather's nice."

"We heard the weather report. It's to be in the low sixties tomorrow and the next day, before it turns cold. It's always a good seven or eight degrees warmer down in South Carolina. If we went tomorrow, we'd have a fine day."

"You want to get into a car and drive after just coming from Pennsylvania?"

"Sure. Why not?" He shrugged, smiled, hooked his arm through Hannah's, and marched her up the back steps and into the house where he announced, "Grandma and I have a surprise for everyone. You want to tell 'em, Grandma?"

"You do."

"Tomorrow, if I can rent a boat, we're going on a picnic and boat ride on Lake Jocassee in South Carolina." His face was all smiles and twinkling eyes, his enthusiasm infectious.

Grace frowned and shook her head. "I can't go. I've got too much to do."

"Nonsense," Hannah declared. "You, of all people, deserve a holiday. Then we'll all help with whatever needs doing here."

25

Lake Jocassee

Folding chairs and food hampers topped the two vehicles. Hannah, Miranda, and her sons rode in Hannah's station wagon with Sammy driving, and Laura, Emily, Bob, and Grace followed in Paul's large sedan, with Bob at the wheel. Paul stayed behind. Bob had introduced him to Emily's father, Martin, and had scheduled eighteen holes of golf.

The drive down the mountain—to what Sammy called the Lake Country of South Carolina and South Carolinians referred to as the Golden Corner of their state—took an hour and a half, most of it along Scenic Highway 11, which hugged the valley floor. The lush, soft, rolling land boasted mild winters, rich soil, bountiful crops, and copious rivers, streams, and lakes.

Lake Keowee, long and sinuous, snaked past the towns of Salem, Seneca, Clemson, and beyond, sharing its coves, bays, and stretches of shoreline with homes and condominiums. Farther south, Lake Hartwell boasted marinas and houseboats and shared a shoreline with Georgia. To the north and east, with its waters lapping pristine mountainsides, and with its waterfalls, Lake Jocassee remained the jewel in the crown.

The day was as warm, bright, and languid as a summer's day, and when they crossed a bridge over a section of Lake Keowee,

Emily drew a deep breath. The development that had taken place on this lake seemed well planned and executed. The few homes that dotted the shoreline were placed well back from the lake, surrounded by trees. Distant mountains framed the scene. "Oh, I wish we could stop. It's so beautiful," Emily said. Turning her head, she strained to see the lake long after the car had crossed the bridge and the view was swallowed by heavy woods.

"You think this is beautiful, wait until you see Jocassee," Philip said.

In the other car, Laura sat quiet, saddened by the sight of water and memories of Marvin. She regretted coming.

Moments after they reached the inauspicious plank boat ramp, they carried the food and drinks hampers and folding chairs onto the flat-bottomed boat that floated on huge rubber pontoons and was powered by a large outboard motor. A tarp stretched from end to end over the boat, providing shade. Sammy took the wheel. From this location, a view of the lake was limited by jutting hillsides. But when they shoved off and rounded the bend, Lake Jocassee, shimmering in sunshine, opened its width and breadth to them.

"A magnificent lake," Bob said, moving close to Grace.

"Good choice, Sammy," Hannah said, slapping her grandson's shoulder gently. "Good choice."

"Jocassee's four hundred feet deep, and they have trout fishing and bass tournaments here," Sammy said.

Under shade, in the front of the pontoon boat, Bob set up the folding chairs, then ambled about making sure the hampers were out of the sun, that Grace was comfortable, that everyone had something to drink. Then he wandered to the rear to chat with Sammy and Philip, and to the railing, where Miranda, Laura, and Emily lolled. Bob pointed and waved, and the younger women nodded and laughed at whatever it was that he was showing or telling them.

"Maybe Laura and Emily will get to know and like one another," Grace said to Hannah. "They seem relaxed and interested in whatever it is Bob's saying."

"Hope water doesn't trigger Laura's depression," Hannah said.

"It's part of the process, isn't it?" Grace asked. "Grieving happens over time, first it's all-pervasive, then less so, then it washes over you on certain occasions. It's only four months, but even years later when you think you're done with it, you see something, read something, smell something, and bingo, you feel the pain as if it were yesterday."

Hannah nodded. "I know. But I can't bear seeing Laura suffer."

"You old softee." Grace poked Hannah's shoulder then smoothed it gently. "We've all had our share of suffering. Laura'll be fine. It's glorious today. Put worries aside and enjoy."

"You're right," Hannah said. "I'm glad we did this."

Sammy steered the boat along the shoreline to minimize the effect of the wake of a speeding boat. Bounded as the lake was by hills and mountains, the roiling wake heaved and tumbled like a miniature tsunami until it splattered against eroding banks, where trunks of stunted trees clung mournfully to exposed networks of gnarled and twisted roots. Below, when calm returned, the shallow water glowed green, the bottom tan, sandy, and gently shifting.

It wasn't long before the pontoon boat, lapped by waves and rolling slightly, lumbered across the width of the lake toward the mountains. "Wait until you see the waterfalls," Sammy said. And when he cut the engine and sank the anchor, they stood at the railing awed by great gushes of water spilling from some dark dragon's mouth high up the rugged mountainside. Twisting and turning, the long cords of water tumbled down the rock cliff past jagged outcroppings to finally slip into quivering pools before spilling smoothly into the lake. It reminded Grace of a great symphony, the crash of cymbals, the swell of violins, the mellow sounds of a flute. Fine spray dampened their faces and arms. For an indeterminate time, they stood transfixed, and then Philip's voice broke the spell.

"There are two other waterfalls. We'll try to see them all. What do you think of Lake Jocassee, Grandma?"

"I think it's a gem," Hannah said.

Everyone clapped. Amid murmurs of "lovely," "wonderful," "beautiful," Grace, Miranda, and Hannah returned to the front of the boat, to their chairs in the shade. Laura rushed to help Bob haul up the anchor, and moments later Sammy revved the engine, and they were off.

"Are you all right?" Bob asked Laura.

"Good as can be expected," she replied, turning away.

After a time, Philip joined the older ladies in the shade and squatted beside the food hamper.

"How did you boys know about this lake?" Hannah asked.

"That summer we were here, we came down one afternoon with a bunch of guys from Mars Hill," Philip confessed, grinning. He rubbed his stomach. "I'm hungry. What's in the hamper, Grandma?" Bending, he undid the clasp. "It's bound to be good, if Grace made it."

"I didn't have much time . . ." Grace began, but she was cut off by Bob who plopped onto the bench seat nearby.

"Right you are, Philip. Anything Grace makes is delicious."

By then Philip had the top of the hamper up and was lifting out wrapped sandwiches. "What kind?" he asked holding a sandwich toward Grace.

She took it from him and eased up an edge of the foil wrap. "Roast beef. I broiled a flank steak and sliced it thin. There's extra mustard and mayonnaise in the basket."

"Growing boys have hollow legs," Miranda said. "They go off to college and the food bill drops."

"Anyone else hungry?" Philip called.

Emily and Laura shook their heads, but Sammy called, "Bring me one, Phil. Any kind, and a soft drink."

"It's wonderful here, isn't it?" Grace said to no one in particular.

"A lovely way to start the holiday," Miranda said. "It's great to be with you." She looked over at her sister and Emily who were standing at the railing close to Sammy. "Laura looks well. She's had tough luck. I'm not sure I could handle it as well."

"It's been hard," Hannah said. "She's far from over it."

"I didn't mean to make light of her situation." Miranda gave her mother a quizzical glance.

"We know you didn't, dear," Grace said. "It's been hard on your mother too, harder than she'd ever admit."

Hannah looked at her watch. "Almost noon. Anyone else hungry? I'm starving." She began to unpack the hampers, stacking cans of soda, bottles of water, sandwiches, condiments, and bags of chips on a table built into the boat. Sammy maneuvered into a wide cove, from where a waterfall was partly visible and highly audible.

At the railing, Emily drew back sharply. "We're awfully close to the rocks."

Recognizing the concern of those unfamiliar with boats and the sea, Laura touched Emily's arm. "It's okay. Pontoon boats have a shallow draft."

"What does that mean?"

"It's got a flat bottom. It can glide over shallow areas safely."

Emily's hand rested on her heart. "I'm glad to hear that." She leaned heavily against the railing.

"When's the baby due?" Laura asked, turning her head toward Emily.

"Late March, early April."

"How are you feeling?"

"I've had some morning sickness, but it's gone, thank goodness. I was a bit nervous about coming today, but"—she straightened up and patted her tummy—"so far, so good. I feel fine." Lifting her head, she took a deep breath. "Air's so fresh and clean, and it's so beautiful. I'm glad I came."

"So am I," Laura said, thinking that she also had had doubts about coming though for far different reasons. "Did you always want children?" she asked.

Emily positioned her elbows on the railing. "Yes, always. Two or three at least. At thirty, when I hadn't met anyone I wanted to marry, I started to feel time was running out. If I'd never married I'd have had artificial insemination."

"Really?"

"Yes. I have a friend in her forties who did that. Then I met Russell. Who'd have thought I'd find my soul mate in Covington of all places?" She laughed.

"Russell's a good man, like his father." Laura startled herself saying that. She liked Bob, and even Russell, and Tyler too, more than she ever imagined she could.

Emily nodded. "And I love Tyler."

"Grace considers him her grandson. She'll feel the same about your baby, I'm sure."

"Could any child have a more loving, caring grandmother?" Emily asked. "Wish I'd had a grandma like Grace when I was little."

"I don't remember my grandmother. My grandfather was an alcoholic, and we kept our distance."

"I'm sorry. That must have been hard on your mother, on you girls."

"My father drank too." Why was she telling all this to practically a stranger?

"These days in my law practice I see that sort of thing and how the kids suffer. There's one judge who insists that alcoholics enter treatment centers, but you know, they come out, and some of them go right back to drinking."

"You must see a lot of sad things in your practice."

"In Florida I didn't practice family law or divorces. Here, because I'm new at the firm, I get handed cases involving child and spousal abuse. I prefer corporate, wills, trusts, even real estate. It's different here. For example, our firm's been asked to send someone along with a social worker to check out a family living, as they say, back behind Walnut. Seven kids, father doesn't work. Mother works the night shift."

"Why? They think he's abusing the children?"

"They haven't quite said that. Maybe the family can't take care of all those kids, maybe they should be in foster homes, some of them." She shrugged. "I guess I'm the one they're sending."

"I pray he's not abusing the children." Laura changed the subject. "I hope you don't mind my asking, but how do you like living here? Must be a big change."

Emily nodded. "It is, but there are so many compensations, and it's a beautiful place. How about you?"

"I miss the sea. Covington's not my first choice, in fact there are days when I wonder why I've agreed to stay."

"You're staying, then?"

"I'm going to work at Bella's Park as Grace calls it."

"I'm glad. I've wanted to visit you. I'm sorry about the storm, about everything."

Laura wiped her forehead with the back of her hand. "Thanks. I'm getting hot. What say we join the ladies in the shade?"

"Fine."

In one unrehearsed, fluid moment, the two women straightened their backs and shoulders, turned, and walked slowly, balancing against the movement of the boat, toward Grace and Hannah. Emily's loose cotton shift caught in the breeze and billowed about her. In her khaki knee-length shorts, Laura's legs, one thinner, the other stronger, looked white and hairless. She limped slightly, but the doctor had assured Hannah that eventually her daughter would regain full strength and mobility.

Everyone crowded into the shade for lunch. In the cove, the lap of water contrasted sharply with the ruckus of the last of the summertime crickets. The whine, then sting, of a hungry mosquito caused Grace to slap her leg. She missed the critter. Occasionally a fish arched above the water, then vanished, creating circles of ripples. They waved to folks in sailboats and in motor boats.

With Philip urging him on, Sammy told silly jokes that everyone laughed at. He seemed so gregarious and so in his element out here on the water that Hannah wondered about computers as his career choice. Life in a cubicle, she thought. Once she had stopped trying to find funding for Anson's land, she found the Internet annoying to navigate and hard on her eyes. Before long she donated her computer to Caster Elementary School.

After they had eaten, Sammy started up the engine, and for a time they circumvented the lake, stopping periodically at waterfalls that cascaded down curving steps carved into the hillside by the action of water. There were times when the tumult of rushing water prevented conversation. By four in the afternoon, sunburned and weary, they were ready for home.

✽

That night, insomnia visited Grace. After tossing and turning, she rose, pulled a robe about her, and eased down the steps to the kitchen. The house was still and satisfyingly peaceful. Grace opened the refrigerator. Onions, green peppers, and celery cried out to be chopped. Why not? She wasn't sleepy. She was surprised when Amelia joined her.

"I walked so much today, my legs ache. I can't sleep. Tylenol hasn't kicked in yet. Can I help?" Amelia asked.

"If you don't mind chopping." Grace nodded toward the onions and green peppers.

Amelia positioned a chopping board close to the edge of the counter. "Tell me everything about your trip today. How'd Hannah and the boys get along?"

"Fine. The boys have really grown up. Sammy apologized to Hannah."

"On the boat? In front of everyone?"

"No. Here, before, when they first arrived."

"Well, I'm glad of that." Amelia chopped vigorously. "Laura, how was she, being on water again?"

Grace removed the turkey from the refrigerator, set it on the table, and removed the neck and giblets and set them aside. "She seemed okay."

"She and Miranda get along? Laura worried so about her coming."

"Seemed fine."

"Laura and Emily talk?"

"Yes," Grace said, rubbing the turkey's skin thoroughly with seasonings.

"Did they get along well?"

"Seemed to be."

Amelia dropped the knife among the vegetables. "You know, Grace, you are absolutely no fun to gossip with."

Grace laughed. "I'm sorry." Covering the turkey, she returned it to the refrigerator, then pulled out a chair at the table and sank into it. "The day was perfect. The lake was beautiful. A little long. I could have done with half a day. The sun gets to me after a while, even sitting in the shade."

"Sitting in the shade, and the sun gets to you." Amelia laughed. She pushed the pile of chopped onions away from her.

"Glare, I guess. See, my nose is red. It'll probably peel." Grace moved to stand beside Amelia, took another chopping board, and began to chop green peppers.

"Now you're chopping, after I've done most of the onions." Amelia said, one hand on her hip.

"Certainly."

"You took Brenda her turkey?"

"Bob and I did, the day Miranda came."

"They keeping it until Thanksgiving?" Amelia asked.

"Brenda said it smelled too good. They decided to have an early holiday feast yesterday. Harold can't eat, but at least the rest of the family could sit down together. They invited the Craines. Alma will help Molly with cleanup." Grace's eyes clouded. "It's probably Harold's last Thanksgiving."

Amelia's knife clunked onto the wooden board. "Harold's that bad? He's going to die." She stared wistfully into space. "I like him so much. Why is this happening to him? Why not an old creep like Jake Anson or that dreadful Lance Lundquist?" Then her voice cracked, "Why my Thomas and my Caroline?"

"You're not suggesting I can answer that, are you?"

"Not really." She smiled then. "*Chérie*, I like to bombard you with my deeper, more philosophical questions. Your brow knits; you look so serious. I think, maybe Grace will have some great insight."

Grace cut a strip of pepper and beat it against Amelia's hand. They were chopping and laughing when Hannah entered. "Such a ruckus, what's going on?"

"Grace is attacking me with green pepper."

"You probably deserve it," Hannah replied. "Need any help here?"

"Just reach in that drawer by the fridge and get out a couple of plastic bags for these vegetables. When you're done, you can help chop celery."

"Mistake coming down here, I can see that," Hannah declared as she proceeded to do as asked. For a time the only sound was that of their knives hitting the chopping boards. Then Hannah said, "It was a lovely day. You should have come with us, Amelia."

Amelia shoved a pile of chopped onions toward Hannah, who reached over, scooped them toward her, and swept them into a plastic bag.

"I can taste onions for hours after chopping them," Amelia said, shutting her eyes tight for a moment. "They've got my eyes watering." She looked at Hannah. Hannah's hair stuck up and out on the sides and a chunk rose from the top of her head. She'd obviously not bothered to brush it. It amazed Amelia, the ease with which Hannah usually handled her hair. No matter how it sprawled or bunched in the morning, a few sweeps of a brush, and every strand obediently returned to its designated place, high, back from her face, and neat. Even cut short, Amelia's hair was so fine and soft that it took regular perms to keep it curled and manageable. The beautician said that coloring it would give it more body, but she liked the white, silvery as it was.

"Cove Road won't be the same without Harold. He was so good to us. How long do you think he's got?" Amelia asked.

A heavy sigh issued from Grace's chest. She set down the knife and rubbed her eyes with the heels of her hands. "They don't know. Could be weeks, or months. Brenda's arranged for a male LPN from a health-care agency to come every day from seven in the morning until three in the afternoon. Physically, she can't bathe Harold or turn him, or change his bed. It's all she can do to give him his medication. Her insurance policy, however, covers only three months of home care."

"Then what?"

"Then she has to pay for it, or do it herself."

"I'd like to suggest right now," Amelia said, "that we call an insurance agent and look into getting long-term health care policies for all of us."

"I'll call someone," Hannah said. "Think Bob would be interested?"

Grace nodded. Her hands lay still on the counter. She stared out into the dark night. "Where has this year gone? Why does it seem to go so fast? Now that we're older we could use a bit of time standing still."

"Agreed. And now we have this millennium thing to worry about."

"Thanksgiving," Amelia said. "Focus on Thanksgiving, and we'll worry about Christmas and the millennium after that. Talking about it makes me a nervous wreck."

They resumed their chopping.

26

Thanksgiving Day

Blustery wind whipped coat flaps, nipped noses, and stung ears of the arriving guests. Hannah's grandsons' eyes watered. The boys had not expected the weather to be as nasty and cold as in Pennsylvania. The bitter cold wrested past the layers of their clothing, and with reddened cheeks they hurried after their parents into the farmhouse. Everyone sighed with relief as they removed knitted caps, gloves, sweaters, and coats.

"How cold is it out there, anyway?" Philip asked as he rubbed his hands together.

"With the windchill, it must be ten degrees," his father, Paul, said, smoothing back his son's hair, which stuck straight up with static electricity.

Thanksgiving odors filled the house: cinnamon, vanilla, pumpkin pie, turkey roasting in the oven. Philip and his dad headed for the kitchen, but Grace shooed them away. "Out, out all of you. I'm ready to take the turkey out of the oven." Turning to Bob, who had come earlier, she nodded toward a bowl of eggnog. "Take this in and serve it, will you?" she asked.

Bob extracted a small flask from his jacket and poured some of its contents into the bowl. "A touch of rum's what folks need to warm up," he said.

Grace gave him a look from the corner of her eye, sighed, and produced another bowl of eggnog. This she handed to Philip with the admonition that no liquor be added under any circumstances. "We've got a huge meal, so don't fill up on eggnog," she said.

Philip nodded.

It wasn't long before Max and Hank arrived. When she joined them all in the living room, it seemed to Grace that Hank was less shy and anxious than he had been the last time he'd shared a meal with them. Miranda had cornered him and was asking him about his background, his family, his work at Bella's Park.

"I was born in Canada, in Guelph. My dad was a professor of horticulture at the university there. Mom's from Atlanta. She detested the cold, so by the time I was four, we'd moved to Atlanta. That's where I grew up." He was an only child.

"I always wondered what it would be like to be an only child," Miranda said. She sipped slowly from her cup of spiked eggnog. "What was it like?"

"Sometimes lonely, sometimes great."

"When lonely?" she asked, feeling warm from the rum.

He seemed not to mind her probing. "When I was sad, troubled, angry at my folks, hating homework."

"And when was it great?" Laura joined them. "Hi, Hank. How's it going?"

He blushed beet red, regained his composure, and answered her first question. "It was great when we traveled, when I had my parents' undivided attention, having my own room, having most of the packages under the Christmas tree be mine."

Laura looked at her sister. "Remember how we used to fight about everything?"

"Like that pillow fight, and Dad came in and threw both our pillows out the window into the snow."

Instantly, Laura's eyes clouded. "I can't smell scotch without remembering that night, the liquor on his breath." She walked away.

"Uh-oh. Obviously that's a sensitive subject," Miranda said, and by way of explanation, "We haven't seen each other in so long, I don't know what upsets my sister. Excuse me, Hank, I have to make it right."

*

Hank watched the sisters. Miranda, slender, tall, long dark hair pulled back, her eyes warm and caring, very much the older sister. In the light of the fireplace, Laura's hair glowed auburn. The pain in her eyes when she spoke of her father had touched him, and that surprised him, for he had pegged her as cold and unapproachable. Laura faced her sister with tear-filled eyes. A short time later they hugged, and she brightened. Seeing her smile, the tiny crinkles flittering away from her eyes, Hank wondered at the loosening in his chest.

*

Tyler couldn't sit still tonight. He skipped from Bob, to Russell, to Grace in the kitchen, and out again. He climbed on Emily's lap and tugged at Hannah's jacket, and he even pestered Amelia with questions, though he knew that her patience with children was limited. He ought to sit or stand quietly, have a cup of plain eggnog, hang around Philip, maybe, but something inside of Tyler itched and tickled and prodded him to action.

Maybe it was all those packages piled about the fireplace waiting for a home under the Douglas fir that he, his father, and grandfather would cut from a field and deliver to the ladies' farmhouse. He was dying to investigate those big boxes, see which were for him, but knew better then to rummage among them. Looking at the packages, Tyler considered what Hank had said about being an only child, like he was. He loved it. Soon he wouldn't be anymore. A baby would cry and fuss, and everyone would pamper and cuddle it, even Granny Grace. He'd be left out. He'd be lonely. Why were they having a baby when they had him? It was going to be a disaster.

*

Although each week that passed lessened the pain of losing Bella, guilt assailed Max whenever he realized he had not thought of her

185

during an entire day. Then he'd stop and remind himself that she wanted him to be happy. In those last days, Bella had made him promise to get on with his life. "Don't spend the rest of your life alone," she'd said. She had even suggested that, in a proper time, he court Hannah, or even Amelia.

Amelia. That was a joke. She was too, what would he call it, theatrical? Artistic? Bella had been an artist, but she'd been solid, her feet on the ground. Amelia struck him as capricious, reckless, or was she merely gullible? He remembered that foggy day, last year, when Lance Lundquist crashed into the rear of her car, and he had come along in his pickup and given Amelia a ride home. She'd thanked the fellow, Lance. Imagine that! He'd hit her car, and she'd thanked him. And then she'd dated him. Definitely, Amelia was not his type. But Hannah? Bella had been small, and soft, and gentle, and flexible. Hannah was tall, and angular, and strong willed. He admired her mind; they had common interests. He respected her, took pleasure in her company, enjoyed working with her, valued her efficiency and no-nonsense approach, but romance?

The rum in the eggnog warmed his body and filled his mind and heart with goodwill toward all. He looked to where Hannah stood chatting with her son-in-law, Paul. She wore a grayish blue, ankle-length suede skirt with matching jacket over a pale yellow blouse. Not pretty, but a handsome woman sometimes, and sometimes not. Odd the way her mood changed her looks. But no, he had no romantic interest in Hannah. They were friends and neighbors, and now collaborators in the creation of Bella's Park and Gardens, and that was enough.

*

Mike swung his car into the driveway, parked behind three cars, and stepped out into the bitter afternoon. He was late. In the driving wind, his face felt cold as marble. His coat whipped about him as he hurried along the path and up the steps, to be welcomed, moments later, by friends and the warmth of the fireplace. He was satisfyingly and totally at home in this house. Here he felt loved and accepted, and it would remain so as long as he held silent the secret that tortured his mind and his heart. Mike had fallen in love with Roger Singleton.

It had happened the night of Russell and Emily's wedding. Working with Charles on the flowers and music had been fun, but it was Roger's handsome face, the curve of his jaw, the flashing blue eyes that drew his attention, captivated him, and left him desolate. They were essentially decent men, all three of them, and none of them promiscuous. A few weeks ago, he had visited their home in Branston on his way back from visiting his family up north. In a private moment, Roger had expressed interest in Mike yet made clear his commitment to Charles.

"Sorry," he'd said looking mournful, "just one of those things."

Back at home, Mike couldn't stop thinking about Roger, nor could he risk the loss of the acceptance and love he garnered from these women, or his warm welcome in this house. Life had been so simple. Now he felt restless and distracted, and Amelia, he was sure, suspected.

"What's wrong?" she'd asked.

"Nothing's wrong. I'm a trifle nervous about New York." He wasn't at all nervous. He knew the city. New York thrilled him, but this explanation satisfied Amelia. Perhaps it reflected her concerns and insecurities.

With all the laughter and good cheer in the room tonight, Mike felt alone. Once he had been neurotically stuck in a relationship in which there had been little communication. He'd felt alone in bed with his partner, alone when they dined out, alone moments after his partner walked into the apartment at the end of a day, alone as he did now. It saddened him, made him morose. Charles and Roger would be here for Christmas. He would avoid them. But how? There would be dinners, casual evenings with friends chatting, playing cards or Scrabble. What excuse could he offer for not coming? He'd leave town. Yes, that's what he'd do. Take a hotel in Atlanta, perhaps, or Charlotte. Or even spend the holiday with his friend who was dying of AIDS in Forest City.

Someone poked his arm. Amelia. "Come on, Mike. Turkey time." She slipped her hand in his and led him in for dinner.

The dining room table had been extended to its fullest and glittered with candles of differing heights that rose like yellow tulips from among clusters of tiny orange pumpkins strewn along the length. The sideboard buffet staggered under platters of Thanksgiving fare: mounds of dark meat, mounds of white meat, white mashed potatoes, candied sweet potatoes, creamed corn, tiny green peas and onions, green beans drizzled with butter and toasted almonds, gravy, stuffing, cranberries, hot rolls and butter.

They ate with barefaced gusto as if attending a Roman banquet. They related stories, told silly jokes, and laughed a lot. Even Laura was caught up in the camaraderie of the evening.

"I have a joke," Sammy said.

"Which one, son?" Paul asked.

"The taxi driver/preacher one."

"That's fine. Go ahead."

"There's this preacher and a taxicab driver. They die and find themselves with Saint Peter, who's busy fitting them with wings. The preacher notices that his wings are old and battered, and the taxi driver's are exquisite, shining golden wings. 'Why in heaven's name is this old taxi driver getting such beautiful wings while I, who so diligently spread the good news, am handed this worn-out pair of wings?'

" 'Well, it's like this,' Saint Peter said. 'When you were on earth supposedly spreading the good news, people fell promptly asleep. However, when this taxi driver was on earth, people in his cab prayed as if their lives depended on those prayers. That sir, is the difference.' "

There were laughs all around. Then Mike asked, "Where are Lurina and Old Man and Wayne?"

"Off to Tennessee to visit the nieces," Bob replied.

Dessert followed, and the evening stretched on until Emily looked at her watch and announced, "It's ten o'clock. Way past Tyler's bedtime."

Tyler gave Grace an aggrieved look.

"Time to go, son." Russell swung his arm about Tyler's shoulders.

Outside a deep, cold darkness had settled in. Beyond the house, the wind howled. In the dining room, the shuffle of chairs brought conversation to an end.

"It's been a wonderful evening. Dinner was delicious, Grace. Thank you," Miranda said as she rose. She looked from one to the other. "In fact, this has been a wonderful vacation." Paul and her sons scooted back their chairs and started around the table, shaking the men's hands and kissing their grandmother and the other ladies. Philip patted his belly.

"Boy, I ate enough for three people. Sorry to say, Mom, but this was the best Thanksgiving meal I've ever had."

Paul's arms straddled Sammy's shoulders. "It's been wonderful sharing this meal with all of you." And to his son, "Get our coats, will you, Sammy?"

Their going signaled the departure of others. "Thanks for including me," Hank said to the women. "The food was great, and the company also."

"We're glad you came. You'll have Christmas with us?"

"I'd love that. Thanks, Grace."

As she shook his hand warmly, Grace noted the long look Hank gave Laura before departing.

Mike pulled on his coat and yanked his knit cap low over his ears. At the door, he hugged Amelia. "Sorry I wasn't my usual self."

"You were fine. *Bonne nuit, mon ami.*" She kissed his cheek, and then he opened the door and exclaimed, "Goodness, they're sitting in their car waiting for me to move mine. I'm sorry. Coming. Coming." Mike sprinted down the steps, hands on his head, holding his cap from being blown away by gusts that whipped about him.

Closing the front door, Amelia stood a moment burdened by the unease she sensed in Mike. Not for a second did she believe that he was nervous about New York. And then an image of Mike and Roger huddled in a corner last summer and sneaking guilty glances at her, and at Charles, came to mind. Amelia shook her head and hastened back to the kitchen. "Can I help?" she asked.

"Bob's loading the dishwasher. Won't take long. I did most of the pots before we ate. Just these bags to fill with leftovers and slip into the fridge. We'll have lots for lunch tomorrow and dinner too."

"I'll go on up, then," Amelia said. "You outdid yourself, Grace, the food, the table setting, everything."

"I had help from my friends, remember." Grace leaned against the refrigerator and sighed. "I ate too much, but what the heck, it was my last calorie-intensive meal for a while."

Amelia started upstairs followed by a yawning Laura. "I could use a push up these steps," Amelia said half joking. Placing both hands on Amelia's back, Laura pushed gently and, chatting lightheartedly, they ascended the stairs.

With the dinning room table cleared and things under control in the kitchen, Max asked Hannah to join him in the living room. He wanted to talk to her. Last to arrive, last to leave, Max flopped in a chair, his long legs sprawled toward the fireplace. Hannah sat across from him. When Bob came to the door, they were engrossed in conversation.

"Grace and I are turning in. You kids don't stay up all night, now."

Hannah looked up at him. "You two don't gossip until the rooster crows."

"Turkey's the elixir of sleep, remember? We'll postmortem this party in the morning," Bob replied.

"That's right." Grace came up behind him. "We'll do our who said what, who did what, and why in the morning propped up in bed with a good cup of coffee." Grace reached for Bob's hand. "Night, Hannah, Max." Moments later they were climbing the stairs.

✻

The house fell quiet save for the low swish of the dishwasher from the kitchen. Gusts of wind sluiced along the porch, moaning. Max's voice droned on. Perhaps he can't bear going home to an empty house, Hannah thought stifling a yawn. Max was talking about the Indian site, and she was too tired for that just now.

"Will it freeze tonight, I wonder?" she said.

Max lurched forward. "I should go, you look tired."

"Not tired," Hannah replied, suddenly wanting him to stay. "I have something I want to talk to you about."

Max reached for his coffee, balanced the mug on his knee, settled back into his chair, and waited. "So, talk."

"My head won't stop making gardens. I finish planning one, and I'm onto the next. Left to my own devices, I'd have ten gardens, not five."

"Who's stopping you?"

"Do I have space limitations? Are there funds for additional crew for maintenance? What parameters are there? What kind of budget's assigned to gardens?"

"I hadn't thought about that, so I guess there's no limit." Stretching out his arms, Max cracked his knuckles. "Make ten gardens."

"Really, just like that?"

He set the mug on a table and loosened his tie. "It's gotten warm in here. Mind if I turn down the fire?"

"It is hot." She moved quickly to turn the dancing flame in the gas fireplace down to a mere glow. "You'd think with all the bodies gone from the room we'd be chilling, not heating up." Hannah spoke casually, without thinking, and was suddenly embarrassed at the implication. She flushed. "I didn't mean . . ."

Max sank back in his chair, crossed his legs, and waved his hand. "I know. It's fine. Tell me more about gardens. What do you want to add?"

Hannah spoke in longer, more languid sentences than she usually did. "All entry would be through the lobby, of course, then out onto the patio and through the arbor. I'd like to see a sign, WELCOME TO THE GARDENS OF COVINGTON, over the first arbor. Within the gardens, all pathways should be a minimum of four rather than three feet wide." She gazed off, seeing the future. "Between some of the gardens there'd be covered walkways and, off to the side of each, gazebos with seats for relaxing or resting. Others, like the herb and kitchen gardens, or the rock garden and woodland garden, could flow into one another."

Hannah spoke with animation. *She's almost handsome*, Max

191

thought, and he delighted at their being so enlivened and energized in their seventies. Listening to Hannah, planning with Hank, walking the land alone, he felt aroused and enthusiastic as he had years ago when starting the dairy farm. Forty years old, that's how he felt, and he wondered if Hannah felt the same. "You look about forty when you speak of your gardens," he said. "Do you feel fortyish?"

A sentence died before it birthed, and Hannah stared at him. Then she leaned forward, grasped her knees, and rocked slightly.

"I mean," he said, flustered, "creating this park has revitalized my life, made me feel young and eager to tackle new things."

"It's had somewhat that effect on me," Hannah replied cautiously. "But I want to tell you about the other gardens."

That smoothed it out somehow, and he sipped his coffee and settled back to listen.

"What do you think about a garden composed almost entirely of decorative grasses of various heights and colors?" She paused and looked at him.

"I don't know those grasses, but if you choose them I'm sure they'll be wonderful and instructive to visitors," Max said.

"And how about a wildflower garden and a shade garden? People are always wondering what to plant in shady areas of their yards."

Max stirred. "Hannah, my dear, it all sounds great. You make as many gardens as you want. Bella never stopped gardening until she had to. Seems to be you gardeners are never finished. Left alone, you'd garden every inch of earth in sight."

"The funds?"

"Have your Gardens of Covington. There are funds for whatever you want to do and all the staff you need to plant and maintain it."

Before she could express her appreciation, he rose and took a step toward her. With his hand on the back of her chair, he bent slightly, then hesitated. Hannah's heart caught in her throat. What was he doing? Would he kiss her forehead as he would a child, or her cheek?

Max appeared to deliberate. He looked down at her, then patted her shoulder and smiled. "Good night, my friend."

A wave of disappointment swept over Hannah, followed by relief.

Before she could get up, he stood in the foyer pulling on his fleece-lined jacket. The front door swung wide, admitting a gust of cold, damp air that swirled and swished into the living room where Hannah still sat. With a quick backward glance and a wave of his hand, Max was gone.

Hannah started up. She locked the front door. Through the square of glass she watched Max tromp down their driveway, his hands shoved deep into his pockets, and hurry across Cove Road. Hannah shivered. She needed to talk to Grace, but Grace had Bob, and even if their light was on, she would never discuss her strange agitation over Max with Bob. A great tiredness settled into her bones. Using the banister to aid her ascent, Hannah moved slowly, almost laboriously up the stairs to her bedroom. For many hours she lay awake thinking, or trying not to think, unable to shake the feeling of embarrassment and alarm at her unwitting response to George Maxwell.

It was over, this kind of silly quickening of the breath, skipping of the heart. It was inane and schoolgirlish, and made utter fools of women, especially women her age. But did it have to do that? With Bob, Grace beamed and walked on air for a time, but she never went completely bone headed and ridiculous as Amelia had with Lance. With Dan, there had been those exuberant highs when he walked in the door and the spiraling lows while she waited to see him, or when calling him—her heart catching in her throat when the phone was picked up, hoping it was he and not his secretary—and waiting for him to call. Never again. No roller coaster for her. Mellow, even keeled, uncomplicated, that's how she liked it. It pleased her, relieved her mind to remind herself that she was mature, recognized a possible entanglement, and could avoid it. Finally, at five in the morning, Hannah fell into a deep and dreamless sleep.

27

Days of Questions, Days of Change

🍂 The days after Thanksgiving simmered with activity. Tearfully, with tight hugs and promises to return, Miranda invited Laura to visit them in Branston, and the boys insisted that Hannah come too. As their car turned out of the driveway, and the waving stopped, Hannah descended the porch steps and stood, hands on hips, in front of a scarecrow perched on a bale of straw with faux blackbirds pecking at his flattened hat and snow-crested shirt. "Let's do Christmas lights."

Amelia's hands covered her head. "Not Christmas decorations so soon. I hate shopping, worrying what to buy, and all the rush and frenzy."

"If you'd shop all year for presents like I do it wouldn't be so stressful."

Amelia grimaced. "We should have asked Philip and Sammy to help us put up decorations before they left."

🍂

The following morning, when Grace arrived at Caster Elementary, she found a note in her box requesting that after tutoring Lucy Banks she come to Brenda's office. Lucy was bright-eyed and smiling as usual. They worked on the words *meet, met, meat, meal,* and *make*. Grace kept Lucy focused for perhaps five minutes longer than usual before the child's attention drifted, and she began to write columns of numbers, add each, and go on to the next. "What are you doing, Lucy?" Grace asked.

"Someone brought us a turkey for Thanksgivin', in a basket, and I learned me the numbers on the slip at the bottom of the basket."

The sales slip. Whoever brought the basket had not removed the tab from the market. Grace looked at Lucy's list. There must be twenty items. "All these things?" Grace asked.

"Oh, yes." Lucy beamed. "Nuts and candies, too, and cans of pumpkin for puddin'. I like puddin'. Do you, Mrs. Grace?"

"Yes, I do."

"We had it for dessert instead of pie. Ma ain't much good at bakin'." For a moment she appeared crestfallen. "Pa can't read, and he cooked the turkey too much, Ma said." Lucy brightened again. "Still, we had candies and apples. I sure do like apples."

Her father can't read. He can't find work. This child, Grace thought, has an indomitable spirit even if the words dance on the page. Grace hugged her. "Next week we work on *L* words." She handed Lucy a paperback dictionary. "This is for you, from me. Now you can pick the words we work on. Look under *L* and find five words you like the sound of, and we'll study them."

Lucy's smile stretched from ear to ear. "My own book?"

"Your own book."

"Wait till I show Pa. My own book." She opened it. "It's even got little pictures on some of the pages." She hugged the dictionary to her chest.

✳

Lost in thought, Grace walked slowly down the hall and up the stairs to Brenda's office. Classes had started. The halls were empty except for a latecomer, a boy of about ten, who dashed past her. His book bag struck her hand. "Sorry," he called, turning the corner. Grace stood still for a moment, relieved that he had not run into her.

Pictures drawn by second graders lined the stairway. One caught

Grace's attention. *Lucy Banks* was scrawled in uneven letters in a ragged line across the bottom. Grace stopped. Green lollipop trees framed the picture. Rose and plum and orange flowers adorned the pasture. Seven black-and-white Jersey cows with sticks for legs lolled among tall flowers. It reminded Grace of the story of Ferdinand the Bull who loved flowers and would not fight.

When she knocked on Brenda's office door, Brenda called, "Come in." She waved Grace to a well-used brown leather chair across from her desk. "First, Grace, I want to thank you for the turkey dinner. I hadn't expected all the trimmings too. We all enjoyed it so much. We ate leftovers and loved every morsel. Thank you so much."

"I'm glad you liked it. How's Harold?"

"How is Harold?" Brenda's shoulders sagged. "Not good, but it's better since we moved him downstairs. We can get him outside now. I've replaced our couch in the living room with a futon. Molly said it would be more comfortable to sleep on, and she's right. I couldn't rest easy being upstairs with Harold down. Down's easier, with the kitchen right there." She was silent for a time. "I'm cutting back to part time after the holidays. Velma's organized folks bringing supper on different nights. That's been real helpful."

"The Herrill boys get in the hay?"

"They sure did, and the Craines carried our tobacco to market. Tobacco prices down again this year, but every little bit helps." She sighed. "Harold can handle about an hour of any one visitor. We've got us a sign-up list on the fridge like you suggested, and folks stop by and put their names. If Harold's too sick, or he just doesn't want to see anyone, we call and ask them not to come; otherwise, he's got company some part of every day. Makes him feel cared about and sure takes the pressure off Molly and me. Bless you."

"People always wanted to help. I'm glad you've let them."

Clearing her throat, Brenda sat straight in her chair, and Grace uncrossed her legs and sat taller. "What I want to talk to you about is Lucy Banks."

Grace nodded. A curlicue of anxiety wiggled in her stomach.

"Once the paperwork's done, the family will get food stamps and

197

other services." She leaned across the desk, hands clasped, her eyes earnest. "Grace, I don't want to pussyfoot around this, so tell me, have you any reason to suspect that the father might be molesting Lucy?"

"What?" Grace grasped the arms of the chair. She racked her brain for some clue. "Why, no. Does the social worker suspect that?"

"The human services department asked a law firm in Mars Hill to assign someone to go with a social worker to check on the family, the father home all day and not working, and all."

"And?"

They're sending Emily Richardson, Russell's wife." Brenda sat back. "Frankly, I don't think she's had any experience with this kind of thing, or with mountain folks. She's raised the issue of abuse, so I'm asking, what do you think? Anything about Lucy that indicates such a thing?"

Grace thought of the crayon drawing on the stairs. She thought of art therapy and how children drew things that provided clues to their inner lives. Lucy's drawing was light and bright, with cows in pasture smelling flowers. Nothing sinister in that picture. But who was she to answer on such a matter? Maybe Emily knew things she did not. Grace heard herself saying, "No. I've never sensed anything, and there's nothing about Lucy that's morose or guarded. She speaks about her father freely and with affection, even with pity since he can't read. He overcooked the turkey someone brought them."

"He cooked a turkey?"

"Tried to." Concern filled her eyes. "Tell me, Brenda, how would a child who's being abused, sexually or otherwise, act in school?"

"It might manifest in the kind of unruly behavior Lucy sometimes exhibits in the classroom, or she might be morose, lose interest in her studies, her friends, withdraw, her grades drop."

"Other than her jumping around and distracting the class, has she withdrawn or have her grades dropped?" Grace asked. Blood pounded in her head. By the time she left the office, she would have a headache. Just the idea that Lucy might be . . . It couldn't be. But these things did happen, and the father was home day and night, alone with the children, and his wife sleeping days, working nights. Suddenly it seemed feasible to Grace. She turned apprehensive eyes to Brenda. "What about the other children?"

"I've talked to all their teachers. Some of the kids are bright and doing well. The fifteen-year-old boy's at that rebellious stage, but he's keeping his grades to a C at least, and he does show up for class every day. I sometimes think that for kids like this, a father without work, probably insufficient heat in the house, that school's a refuge. About Lucy, I'm not sure there's anything to this. The social worker's new, and she wanted someone else with authority along in case the children were being neglected and needed to be placed in foster homes. This is Emily's first case of this kind, and the idea of abuse came from her."

"Sounds like the blind leading the blind," Grace said.

"True, but they can intervene, break up the family, and years later, when they're wiser and more experienced, they'll look back with regret and call their actions precipitous. Our counselor and I will talk to the social worker. We wondered if you'd have a chat with Emily, find out why she thinks this? Maybe it's a generalization from some book she's read."

"Isn't this kind of thing confidential?"

"I wouldn't think so at this time. She hasn't been out there yet, and no charges have been filed. The family's having a hard enough time without officers of the law swooping in on them, yanking the kids out of their home and into foster care on a suspicion of a novice attorney." Leaning forward, Brenda lifted a glass paperweight from one stack of papers and brought it down heavily on another stack of papers. "On the other hand, if there's a real reason for suspicion, is it fair to leave the children in the situation?"

"You think Emily would talk to me about such a matter?"

"I have a feeling she'd be happy to. You know the child involved, and from what we gather, Emily's a bit insecure about this. Insecure people often act to prove they're not insecure, you know what I mean?"

"Yes. I'll have a chat with Emily, see what I can find out. Can I introduce her to Lucy casually, or is that interfering with the law, or what do they call it, tampering with justice?"

"It's not that kind of thing, yet. I hope it never gets to that."

The chance to speak alone with Emily came just a day after Grace's conversation with Brenda. Emily stopped by on her way to the Tates' to drop off a custard pie. She no longer wore skirts and jackets but had switched to maternity clothes, mostly shapeless blue or black denim shifts over long-sleeved turtleneck shirts. "Someone said this is Harold's favorite kind of pie," she said "Store bought. I haven't time to bake."

It had rained all morning, then turned dry, blustery, and cold. Grace drew Emily into the living room to the warmth of the fireplace.

"Thanksgiving was wonderful," Emily said. "I was glad for the opportunity over the holiday to get to know Laura a little. I'm happy she's staying on in Covington."

"It would be nice if you two young women became friends," Grace said. "Laura's lonely. Amelia, bless her heart, has been wonderful to her, but Amelia could be her mother."

"I think Hank likes Laura."

"Heavens," Grace said, "don't mention such a thing to her. It's much too soon."

Emily scratched her head. "Yes, of course, you're right." She was silent for a few moments, and Grace wondered if she should bring up Lucy. Then Emily said, "Grace, help me with something. You tutor a little girl, Lucy Banks."

Grace nodded. "She's a happy child, and very good with numbers."

"And disruptive in class, they tell me."

"What about Lucy?" Grace asked. The back of her neck tightened. Light from the window hurt her eyes, as did the glow of the fireplace. Changing chairs, Grace put her back to the fireplace. Abuse, or anything like it, was way beyond her education, way beyond her ken. What could she say or do to prove or disprove an accusation so terrible, and if it was made by a lawyer? She cringed for Lucy. What if it were true? How could she help the child? "Let me get us some tea," Grace said starting to rise.

Emily lifted her hands. "No, please, no tea. Don't go, or I'll lose the courage to speak about this."

Grace folded her hands in her lap. "Well, then, tell me what's on your mind."

Emily rose and paced, hands clasped behind her. "You know, I've never practiced family law. Now they've given me this case." She stopped, ran her fingers through her hair. "I'm to observe, they said, get a feel of what's going on in that child's home, evaluate the father and the children." She stopped moving and scowled. "There's a general assumption in my firm that any man who's home all day, and his wife sleeps, and she's gone at night, would automatically entertain himself by sexually abusing his kids." The pacing began again. "What do I know about such things? What am I supposed to think? Time must hang heavy on the father's hands. What does he do all day? What does he do after the kids come home?" She raised her brows as if to say, "You know what I mean."

Grace knew, and every fiber of her being rejected the idea. She would have sensed something from Lucy. The child was open and eager to talk about her family. She seemed not to harbor secrets. "I don't think anything like that's happening," Grace said.

Emily ceased pacing and looked intently at Grace. "Why don't you?"

"Because Lucy's open and cheerful. She talks about her father often and kindly. I get no sense of any secrets there, and you can't have abuse without secrets."

"How do you know that? Are you trained to recognize such things?"

"Are you trained in these matters?" Grace demanded, then held her breath. This was Tyler's stepmother, someone whose goodwill was important to her and to Bob. She waited, watching Emily's face for signs of anger, but there were none, only resignation and concern.

The younger woman sank into a chair. "What can we do to find out?"

Grace's hands were shaking. Again, she considered art therapy and how it had helped when Tyler was lost in grief. He had finally, after many months, drawn an angel and identified it as his mother, and the process of healing had begun. "We could take Emily's teacher into our confidence, ask her to have the children in her class draw pictures about their family, what in their family makes them happy, what makes them sad."

"What will that do?"

"It's a method used by art therapists. The colors and the topics a child draws often indicate a lot about the child's psyche."

"It's a start. I don't want to send the child to a psychotherapist until we know more," Emily said.

Grace's head pounded. "A psychotherapist?"

"They have dolls, you know, and games they play with the children to help them show what's going on."

Grace's hands shot up. "Please, Emily, wait on that. Let's talk to her teacher about drawings."

"Fine. We'll try it your way first. Thanks, Grace. There's no one else I could admit my ignorance to in this matter."

They were walking to the front door now, and when Emily put on her coat, without realizing what she was doing, Grace tucked Emily's scarf about her neck and buttoned the top button as she would have done had Emily been her ten-year-old daughter. Suddenly aware, Grace drew back, worried that she had overstepped her bounds, but Emily reached to embrace her. "Thanks for being you," she whispered.

"I'm so glad you married Russell," Grace replied. She wanted to say, "I'm glad you're in our family," but didn't. After all, it was she, Grace, who was not really in the family, and that raised doubts in her mind, again, about the legitimacy of her role in the Richardson family. Once Emily had gone, Grace took two Tylenol and went upstairs, undressed, and got under her covers. She needed to sleep off this headache. And it was there, at five in the afternoon, that Brenda reached her.

The ringing phone tore Grace from a deep sleep and set her head throbbing again.

"God, Grace," Brenda sobbed into the phone. "Harold's in the hospital. He's had a seizure. Molly called nine-one-one." Sobs now.

Grace froze. "I'm sorry. Where are you?"

There was the sound of people coming and going, of a door closing, and then Molly came on the phone. She sounded stunned but controlled. "We're at Mission Hospital intensive care unit. Can you come?"

Grace's mind raced in circles. Why had they not called their cousin Alma or Pastor Johnson? Lord, she didn't want to go to the intensive care ward. Sweat formed on Grace's lip and along her hairline. Her hands trembled. Could she even drive her car to Asheville? The old fear of driving on a highway flooded back. If she managed to get to Highway19-23, she could crawl at forty miles an hour, the way she'd done that time when they'd first come to Covington. But there were a tangle of curved streets in Asheville, and lights, and finding a parking place once she got to the hospital. One phone call, a mention of intensive care, a dying man had flipped her. She hated her weakness, her cowardliness. She wanted Bob. Where was Bob? What had he told her about today? Was he playing golf, teaching at the university? Her mind went blank.

"Are you there, Grace?" Molly asked. Grace heard Brenda sobbing uncontrollably in the background, and a man's deep voice, probably the doctor.

"What's happening?" she asked Molly.

"They don't think Daddy's going to make it. A stroke, and then another." Molly's voice remained unemotional and detached. Grace understood. She understood Brenda breaking down.

"I'm not dressed." Grace's voice faltered. "I'll dress and try to find Bob. I'd rather he drove me. One way or the other, I'm coming. Tell your mother I'm coming. I'm so sorry, Molly."

"I'll tell Mom."

Bob was not at his apartment, or at the golf club, nor was he teaching. She would have to get there by herself. If only the call had come when Emily was here. Emily could have driven, or

Wayne. Pulling on a robe, Grace hastened to Hannah's room from where she could see the greenhouse. Wayne's truck was nowhere in sight. In the bathroom, Grace slapped icy cold water on her face. A woman with frightened eyes stared at her from the mirror. "Get a grip, Grace," she muttered.

Back in her room, Grace dressed deliberately, carefully shoving one leg and then the other into warm slacks, selecting a white blouse, a dark brown vest, a tan sweater. How did one dress at a time like this? "What does it matter?" she asked herself and ran a comb through her hair. "Sit down and breathe," she said out loud. "I can do this. What I'm feeling is merely old anxieties associated with Ted's illness and death, that's all. It'll pass once I get going. Brenda needs me. I can do this." Two more Tylenol and she'd be fine.

Cautiously edging her Subaru onto Cove Road, Grace turned left onto Elk Road and drove slowly past Loring Valley, past Lurina's land and farmhouse, past Elk Road Shopping Center, and onto the two-lane to Mars Hill. There was no traffic on the road, and in Mars Hill she rounded the college, noted the post office on her right, and soon swung into the entrance to the highway. Immediately, Grace wanted to pull off the road, onto the grass, but a car was close behind her, and she kept going, around a curve and onto highway 19-23, and suddenly she found herself moving with traffic at fifty-five miles an hour. Gradually, a sense of calm settled over her, and she kept her eyes fastened on the road and her hands glued to the steering wheel.

❧

Harold's funeral would be talked of for years, perhaps for generations. It snowed that day in December. Max's backhoe cleared Cove Road and the churchyard. Icy cold hindered no one from coming. Bundled in topcoats and scarves and hats, Harold's friends from as far away as Tryon, Waynesville, and Bryson City braved snow-covered roads to pay their last respects. And when the little church failed to accommodate the mourners, Max came to the rescue by sending men to set up loudspeakers outside the church and an old school bus he'd bought, for reasons known only to himself, where people could sit rather than stand out in the cold.

Folks would relate that Harold, laid out on beige satin in his copper coffin, looked as if he were sleeping, and that folks, not just the family, sobbed uncontrollably. So many people rose to offer tribute to the man that Pastor Johnson limited each to five minutes to allow time for all to eulogize. Hannah spoke on behalf of the ladies. People would recount how she broke down and cried twice while describing Harold's kindness, and how he had taken them under his wing, and the goodness of the man's heart.

Folks would speak reverentially of the snow-blanketed cemetery behind the church where Harold was laid to rest, of how hard the earth was, and how the grave was dug by Maxwell's big yellow backhoe, and the way the sun spilled from heaven as the coffin vanished into the ground. A good omen, they all agreed.

Folks' eyes would shine, and they would salivate recounting the tables of food prepared by Grace and Velma and Alma that awaited them in Brenda's parlor after the service and burial. They would smirk relating that old lady Lurina wore a long purple dress that smelled of mothballs, and laugh good-naturedly when divulging that Old Man, bless his heart, had flirted with all the young ladies.

That night after Harold's funeral, after rubbing and soaking her aching feet in Epsom salts, after bidding her housemates good night, Grace slumped into her rocker near the window in her room. Questions of life and death haunted her. Am I afraid of dying, she wondered, or am I afraid of how I'll die? Guaranteed an easy and painless death, would she be afraid? There were nights, of late, when she lay in bed, squeezed her eyes tight, held her breath, and tried to imagine nonbeing. An impossible feat.

What did it mean to lead a useful life? Had she regrets? Would she be happier, more satisfied if she'd lived her first sixty-seven years as openly and freely as she'd lived the last few years? "I feel I've led a perfectly useless life," she'd said to Bob one day recently.

He'd looked at her in amazement. "A useless life, you, of all people? For years you baked and cooked and served a meal to the homeless on Sunday afternoons in your church's basement. Didn't you tell me you registered donors for the Red Cross blood drive twice a year? You spoke proudly of being on the committee that sold used books to raise funds for the library, and the money raised bought computers, furniture for the children's room, and air-conditioning for the entire building. You're a loving woman, a devoted friend. I'd hardly call that living a useless life."

"I could have done so much more: gone to college, taught history, inspired young people. I could have traveled to Egypt, Pompeii, Crete, Machu Picchu."

"You could have, yes." Bob's eyes were serious. "I don't think anyone comes to our time of life, Grace, without reevaluating one's life. Everyone has something he wishes he'd done or not done. I read that Golda Meir, even though she was foreign minister and then prime minister of Israel, felt she'd failed her children, regretted not having been a better mother."

"Are you saying that even people who do amazing things, win an Olympic gold medal, the Nobel prize, write a best-seller, lead a country, have some area of their lives in which they feel they've failed, or at least could have done more with or about?"

"You've got it."

"Are you rationalizing to make me feel better?" she asked.

"I read a lot of autobiographies and biographies. If the author's honest, he tells it all, good and bad, dreams unfulfilled, mistakes made, achievements. Everyone regrets something."

"What do you regret?"

This silenced him for a time. "Not being around for my son when he was a kid and teenager. At that time my career was more important than anything else. Now I believe there are other career choices I could have made and done as well in, and certainly there's more than one person any of us could have been fairly content being married to. I bet there are many people who think they should have been better parents. And so it goes. It's a lot more positive to look back and think, I did the best I could with what I had to work with at the time."

"I thought I wanted to travel. Why haven't I?"

"You tell me, honey. I've suggested we go to Italy or France."

Grace looked off into the distance. "Because it's not important, and the details stop me cold. Planes are forever late. They're uncomfortable. You sit for hours with swollen ankles and then have jet lag. And all those hotel rooms, hard beds, soft beds, rooms too hot or too cold. All the walking, food your system's not accustomed to. I guess when it comes down to it, I'm a creature of habit and prefer my creature comforts."

"And that's just fine."

"Besides," Grace said, taking his hands in hers, "everything I want is right here."

But now, Harold's short, intense illness and death had unnerved her, and she could not rest easy, so Grace sat and rocked and stared into the darkness beyond her window and thought about Ted. She had fallen in love with him in high school, married him right after graduation, and wrapped her life around him. Why? Because in her family college for a girl possessed no value? Had she hankered to attend college? Had she envied friends going off to college? No. If anything, she'd felt smug. They'd be sitting in a classroom for years waiting to start life, while she'd be Mrs. Theodore Singleton and ready to start a family. As for travel, her church and the Lions Club, where Ted was a member, sponsored travel overseas. She'd toyed with the idea of going to Israel, put down a deposit, and withdrawn it months prior to the trip. So why all this stewing about meaning, unfulfilled dreams, time's wingèd chariot, and all that? Grace pressed her toes to the floor, stopping the rocker. Bob was right. She had tried to be kind and cooperative, tried in her own small way to make a contribution to her community. She had done the best she could within the framework of her life and her conditioning. Yet it seemed fitting to evaluate her life in light of the death of a valued friend.

28

A New Career

On her first day of work, Laura wore black jeans, a black shirt, a black jacket. It seemed appropriate for a widow of fewer than five months, and that's how she thought of herself. Feeling anxious and downhearted, Laura walked down Cove Road, arms hanging listlessly, face joyless, chin trembling. The early morning frost sat heavily on the grass and on the stubble of tobacco stems in untilled fields. Dew dripped like diamonds from barbed-wire fences. To avoid an oncoming car, Laura stepped from the road onto the grass, slipped on slimy matted leaves near the edge, and nearly fell. She steadied herself, glad for her sailor's sense of balance and her solid walking shoes.

So much had happened in five months: deep and abiding grief, but there was also a fledgling reconciliation with her mother and reuniting with Miranda. So many new people were now in her life: Amelia, kind and caring; Emily, who might become a friend; Maxwell, who had offered her this job. She'd be working with Molly Tate Lund. She remembered her mother suggesting Molly as Max's assistant. Since her father's death, Molly had no interest in returning to the classroom and jumped at the opportunity for new and creative work. So why wasn't she, Laura, more enthusiastic today? She had been given a generous budget to furnish her office and urged by Max to purchase a top-of-the-line chair. It would be interesting watching her mother create gardens. Quite a woman, her mother, tough, resilient, guarded, yet with a well-girdled soft underbelly.

Laura quickened her pace against the chill of morning. Did any children really know their parents? She thought not. Trapped as they were in childhood fantasies, childhood memories, and clichés, an adult child could come to understand a parent only slowly, over time. But this required living near a parent, interacting more than once a year. Miranda had had that opportunity with Hannah living so close for years, and it was clear that her mother and Miranda understood and respected one another. How had that unfolded? At what intersection in time, and with what memories, had they come together? There hadn't been enough time to discuss any of this with her sister. Perhaps she would go to Branston in the spring. Then they could go off alone and talk.

Looking up, Laura was surprised to see that she had arrived at the shockingly purple front door of the office. Inside, she greeted Mary Ann Lipton, the receptionist, with a smile. Perched behind her high circular desk, bright-eyed and smiling, Mary Ann welcomed everyone warmly.

"Your office furniture arrived," Mary Ann said. "I had it sent up. Need someone to move it about, just buzz me. I'll send up a workman."

Unwittingly, Laura's spirits lifted. "Thanks, Mary Ann," she said, feeling suddenly at home. For a moment she considered going into her mother's ground-floor office, then, eager to see how her furniture looked, she headed for the stairs.

Voices issued from Hank's office, Max's and Hank's and some other man's. Laura hesitated a moment but refrained from stopping, and soon she stood with her back pressed against the closed door of her own office. Someone had positioned the walnut desk at an angle to afford the best view of the mountains out the large window. At right angles to it sat the computer table. In the center of her desk, a single vivid orange rose in a slim bud vase caught her attention. Tears welled in her eyes. No doubt the rose was a welcome from her mother. Walking to the desk, Laura leaned across it and bent to smell the fragile petals. Beneath her palms, the smooth, satiny feel of the walnut surface pleased her, gave her a sense of satisfaction.

Her seven-hundred-dollar chair boasted wide arms that lifted and descended, a well-padded seat that adjusted back and forth and up and down. Her budget allowed for a small love seat covered in a large blue and yellow plaid, two simple armchairs, a small walnut coffee table. Two chunky walnut lamps had been placed in the center of matching end tables.

Laura reached for the phone. Now this was where she was going to have trouble, all those lines, one, two, three, four, and a hold button, a call-waiting button, a line at the top to display caller ID. Oh, for a simple one-phone line. Pressing a button, she picked up the receiver. Someone was talking. Embarrassed, Laura set the phone back on its cradle. She would ask Mary Ann to give her lessons on how to use this piece of equipment.

Someone knocked on the door. "Come in," Laura, said expecting Hannah. Hank stepped into the room. No tie, a shirt pulled half out of his pants, mussy hair, the man looked as if he'd slept in his clothes.

"I took the liberty of setting up your furniture. If you'd like anything moved, just say so." He blushed and looked away. Marvin had been so self-assured; this man seemed either inappropriately insecure or unbelievably shy.

"I like everything just the way you placed it. Thank you." She looked down at the desk. "Did my mother bring me this rose?"

"No," he said, looking directly into her eyes, "I did."

Now it was her turn to blush. "It's lovely. Thank you."

Hank turned formal, professional. "Call Mary Ann for a desk set: blotter, calendar, pens, stapler, pencils, that kind of stuff. Your computer will be delivered tomorrow. They'll train you on it and be available for any questions you have."

"That's a comfort. I'll need a lot of training."

He walked to the window. "Nice view."

"It's lovely, isn't it?"

Turning, he moved toward the door. "Well, see you around. Anything I can help you with, just holler." His aftershave, pleasant and lemony, lingered.

*

A few minutes later, Laura went downstairs to find her mother.

"Miss Hannah," Mary Ann said, "is in the gardens. Have you seen the canal garden? It's pretty amazing. I never heard of such a thing."

"Neither had I until my mother got all excited about it. Seems she saw one at a botanical garden somewhere. A long canal down the center of the garden, I think."

"You'll absolutely love it." Mary Ann's voice bubbled, that was the only word Laura could think of to describe it. With blond hair that puffed like a halo about her face, and her huge blue eyes, Mary Ann looked positively angelic.

"I'll go right out and have a look at it," Laura said.

Workmen bustled about the patio, which appeared to be a staging ground for bags of soil amendments, as she would be told the peat, manure, ground seashells, and humus were called.

"Going through, miss." A burly man in a camouflage-colored jacket wheeled a barrow overflowing with bags of mushroom compost.

Laura stepped aside, then followed him through the arbor and into what she recognized as Hannah's English cottage garden. The wide perennial beds, abundant with dark, rich soil, perfumed the air with their fresh, clean odor much like dry earth smells after a much-needed rain. In summer these beds would bear a profusion of flowers. Tags indicated that a variety of bulbs had been planted: snowdrops, golden winter aconites, hellebores, purple iris reticulata, yellow daffodils, and tulips. Later would come daylilies, peonies, poppies, roses, and other perennials and annuals to fill the gaps along with purple-leaved heuchera, silvery cardoons. Laura imagined the clematis and climbing roses clambering up and over bare trellises that now stood waiting at attention. Two arched doorways, one on either side of the cottage garden, spilled into other garden rooms.

212

Canal Garden

to English Garden >

Dianne LaFonge

"Which way is the canal garden?" Laura asked.

"Follow me," the man said, heading to the left.

Stepping through the arched opening, Laura followed the man and his wheelbarrow along a flagstone path bordered by beds bearing tall tags naming a variety of irises and daylilies. Laura imagined spikes of purple and yellow irises followed by brilliant orange and yellow daylilies in May and June.

The walls of the canal garden had been constructed of fieldstones gathered on the land. The stones were round and grayish tan. Set in concrete, they rose in perfectly matched layers about six feet high on all sides, broken only by an arched opening that led to yet another garden. Down the center of this space, a concrete trough, six or seven feet wide and perhaps three feet deep, had been constructed. Fieldstone walkways on either side of the canal had been finished with a battleship gray grout. Wooden benches with wrought-iron arms and feet offered places to relax, and behind them, in two long rows, deep-planting beds stretched to the walls. No plants had been installed. In a nearby corner Laura noticed a protrusion of tumbled rocks descending to a small round pool that measured perhaps four feet in diameter. Suddenly, a great gush of water exploded from the rockery, spraying her arms, face, and hair. Laura stepped back, just as Hannah entered the garden.

"Goodness, I'm sorry. Didn't know you were here. We're testing the waterfall." She came to stand beside Laura and handed her a terrycloth towel that hung across one shoulder. Accepting it, Laura wiped her arms and face. "Well," Hannah said leaning back, "what do you think?"

Having settled into its appointed course, the water flowed rather than gushed down rocks, to a large flat surface close to the bottom from where it formed Lilliputian waterfalls that spilled with hypnotic pings and plinks into the pool. "It's beautiful," Laura said.

"Maybe it's too much in here with the canal," Hannah said. "Still, there's something wonderful about the sound of falling water."

"What will be in the canal?" Laura asked. "Besides water, that is." She felt foolish.

"Metal sculptures of fish jumping through reeds, and orange and white koi. We'll sink containers with water lilies, so we can change them and always have something in bloom."

"And in the beds?"

"Tall, wide, leafy plants, some tropical like antheriums and bananas. We'll bring them from a nursery."

"Interesting." Laura studied her mother. Hannah's hands were red and rough, her fingernails caked with dirt. Her damp hair stuck out every which way about her face, and her cheeks were flushed. But her eyes were those of a totally happy human being, and Laura envied her mother her passion for gardens.

Upon returning to her office, Laura found Max sitting at her desk with papers strewn about him. Seeing her, he swooped up the papers except for a small pile and waved her to her chair. "Sit, Laura. I've brought you some information." One by one he shoved brochures at her. "Plimouth Plantation in Massachusetts. The Shaker Museum in Kentucky. The Museum of American Frontier Culture in Staunton, Virginia. Here, this Appalachian museum in Norris, Tennessee's probably going to be the most helpful to you." He tapped a sheet of yellow pad paper with a short list of names and phone numbers neatly printed. "Take a good look at the Shaker Village in Kentucky too." He leaned over and peered at a glossy, colorful brochure. "These folks have developed quite an industry around their museum. When visitors leave there, they know something about the Shakers."

"I'll look over the material and call them all," she said "I have a lot to learn."

"If you feel you want to visit any of these, just let Molly know. She'll make travel arrangements for you. Keep me posted." Efficient and to the point, Maxwell did not waste time or words. She could see why her mother liked him. Now he strode to the door, turned, and looked about the room. "Nice choices. Good chair. Glad to have you aboard, Laura." He smiled and she felt officially welcomed.

Laura picked up the Shaker Village flyer. It was packed with information and pictured costumed interpreters singing in the meeting hall, making cheese, shoeing horses, milking cows. Too fancy for the Appalachia that was Madison County in the 1880s. When she reached for the phone, Laura remembered that this was the mystery instrument and she'd have to talk to someone about unlocking its mystery. Walking briskly down the hall, she passed Hank's office, then stopped, retraced her steps and knocked.

"Come on in," he called.

Amazingly, Hank's office was shipshape. Rolls of plans sat in a retired umbrella stand by his drawing board. Papers on his desk were organized in orderly stacks and his pencils and pens efficiently placed in metal cups on desk and drawing board. A pencil stuck behind Hank's ear looked as much at home there as a rose on its stem. A dichotomy, she thought, the way he looks versus the space he works in. Hank grinned and waved her to a brown leather wing chair. "You look like a cat who's just eaten all the cheese and missed being caught in the trap."

"Look at this." She handed him the Museum of Appalachia material. "They have more than thirty buildings, starting in the 1730s."

He turned a page of the brochure, studied the section, turned another page and did the same, nodding each time. She appreciated that he took his time and that he took her seriously. After folding it carefully, he returned the brochure to her with a big grin and a nod. "It looks like they have examples of just about everything from hog pens to outhouses to two-story log homes with candelabras." Perched on the end of his desk, his leg swinging slightly, he looked like an overgrown seventeen-year-old. "So what's next?"

Laura hadn't thought about the next step. They were all so pragmatic around here. Thinking fast, she said, "Well, I guess I'll go see Molly about my going to Norris, Tennessee."

"You know, there's an Appalachian center at the college in Mars Hill, and there's the Vance Birthplace in Weaverville, and lots of books. I'd talk to a couple of librarians. You might want to look at *Our Southern Highlanders* by Horace Kephart. He writes about real mountain folk. And there's an oral history I like called *Our Appalachia* by Shackelford and Weinberg, I think. Read that and discover that onion hulls made yellow dye and walnut hulls made brown dye, and about the rhymes the old folks said when they drank their whiskey. The book's full of homey anecdotes. I think you'd enjoy it."

He was trying to guide her, to gently point the way. It annoyed her, yet she was grateful. She could teach him, or anyone, how to sail or how to handle a yacht, but this was all new to her. "Thanks for the help," Laura said. "I appreciate your interest and your suggestions."

"That's what we're all here for, to help each other make this a fine, accurate, living history park."

She said good-bye then and went to ask Hannah if she would take a short break from her work and drive with her to Norris, Tennessee, less than a three-hour trip by car, Molly informed her.

"Let's see," Hannah tapped her pencil on her desk then pulled her calendar closer and studied December, flipped to January, then February, March, and back to February. Laura's heart sank. She wanted to go now, tomorrow, next week. "I could do this with you in February. Never know what the weather'll be like that time of year, of course." Looking up at her daughter, Hannah read the disappointment in her eyes. "You want to go right now, don't you?"

Laura nodded. Deep within, the old resistance ignited, and for several moments Laura struggled to squelch its spread. She could argue with Hannah, say she'd go alone, walk out in a huff. Or she could hold to their new "adult" relationship and appreciate that her mother's schedule was as busy as one she might soon have. Laura sank into a straight-backed chair alongside Hannah's desk.

"Have you talked to Max?" Hannah asked. "He's considering revamping the early settler idea and going for a Covington family settlement. Try to replicate the original cabins and homestead old Patrick Arless Covington and his brother built when they came here in the 1880s." She studied the material her daughter handed her. "I can see where what these folks have over in Norris would help a lot. You're on the right track." Hannah eased her chair closer to the desk. "Sorry, Laura. It's hard to change bad habits. I shouldn't tell you what to do." She studied the calendar again. "February works for me. I can go with you then if you still want me to, and we have decent weather." She leaned forward, her eyes fastened on Laura's. "Or you go alone tomorrow, or next week."

"I tend toward impulsive, as you know," Laura said drawing a breath. "I'll wait. If I research first, I'll be better equipped to identify what I really need in order to implement our settlement, whether it's generic or focused on the Covington family." She wished Max had said something to her, instead of letting her find this out via her mother.

✣

Without being asked, Mary Ann had delivered a box of supplies to Laura's office. Laura placed the blotter in front of her, set a canister of pens and pencils to her right. She stacked in- and out-trays and shoved them to her left. As she worked she found herself humming and stopping periodically to enjoy the view from her window. On a mound in the distance, earth-moving machines reconfigured the land, flatting areas, mounding others. Was that the site for the first settlers' village? She'd need the site plans and a quick lesson on how to read them. Laura picked up the phone and punched zero. Mary Ann's cheery voice came on. "How can I help you?"

"Think I could get a hard hat?"

"Of course. I'll send one up right away. Want an orange vest too?"

"Why not? Thanks, Mary Ann."

"Always a pleasure," the cheerful voice replied.

Laura was used to providing what former bosses, and then what Marvin, needed. Picking up the phone and requesting whatever she needed would take some getting used to. For a moment, Laura found Mary Ann's sweetness cloying. Why was Mary Ann so darn cheerful? Well, she was young. Probably life hadn't kicked her in the stomach, zapped the optimism out of her yet.

When the knock came, Laura assumed it was a messenger with a hard hat, but Amelia breezed in, a straw basket on her arm. "*C'est magnifique,* your office." Setting the basket on the coffee table, Amelia sat and trailed her hand along the arm of the loveseat. "Very

218

nice," she said. After testing both chairs, she ambled to the window. "What a great view. *Chérie,* I brought lunch. Come over here." She moved to the couch. "We can have lunch on your coffee table, *oui?*"

Amelia seemed nervous and agitated today, Laura thought. "That would be fine," she said, joining Amelia, who removed a tablecloth from the basket and spread it over the low table. A plastic bowl filled with chunks of fresh fruit followed, along with a knife and a stack of toothpicks, a bowl of egg salad, a package of crackers, and a jar of pitted black olives.

"I adore finger food, don't you?" Amelia asked. "Who can bother with all that paraphernalia?" A wave of Amelia's hand indicated that they would spread egg salad on crackers and spear fruit and olives. There were no cups. She opened a bottle of ice tea with lemon. "Well," Amelia said between swallows, "I'm impressed with what Max has done here. It was a shack when that awful man, Jake Anson, lived here."

"It's a nice place to work," Laura said.

"You like it, *chérie?*" Amelia's voice was hopeful.

"Yes, I think I'll like working here."

Amelia sighed, and squeezed Laura's hand. *"Très bien.* I'm happy then."

Laura finished the cracker she had just spread with egg salad. "Are you ready for New York, Amelia?"

"Am I ready? I'm nervous. It's been years since I've been to a huge city like New York."

"But you used to breeze in and out of cities, right?"

"Yes. In and out. Sometimes we lived six months or a year or two, like in London. A classy city, London. Marvelous theater. Everyone, it seems, gardens." She rolled her eyes. "In New York everyone moves fast. I'll be afraid to cross a street, even with the lights, with all those taxis and bicycle messengers dashing by."

"You'll have Mike. Hang on to his arm."

"I certainly shall." After a moment of silence she frowned and leaned toward Laura. "What if my photographs . . ." Her palm closed over the arm of the couch. "I'm worried whether I'm good enough for a show in New York City."

"Of course you are, Amelia, or they wouldn't have asked you. Your photographs astound me, astound us all."

"You're kind to say so." Amelia cracked her knuckles. "Oh, *mon Dieu*, I nearly forgot why I came." She bent over her deep canvas bag and lifted out a framed photograph, which she handed to Laura. "A little gift for your office."

"Amelia, it's Irene Ramsey. I love the way the light strikes the side of her neck and chin, her hands. Thank you so much."

"And here's another one. You must have a matched pair."

The second photograph was of an old and rugged mountain man fly-fishing. He stood thigh deep in a stream, his rod poised above his head. Ripples fanned out from the spot where his hook struck the water, and light streamed through willows that drooped nearly to the water on the opposite bank.

Laura held the framed photos before her. "They're a wonderful pair. Do they know one another?"

"Matter of fact they do. It was Irene Ramsey who suggested that I go and see her old friend Fred Page. He's quite a character. Ninety years old, lives alone. He attributes his longevity to the fact that he eats mostly fish, which he catches."

A short while later, Amelia rose and brushed cracker crumbs from her slacks. "I must run, now. Mike and I are having an early dinner with friends of his in Hendersonville. It'll take us an hour to get there. Cocktails at five, and I still need to have my hair done, and my nails, and get dressed." She covered the bowl of what was left of the egg salad.

"Leave that. I'll wrap it all up and bring it home."

"Thanks, *chérie. Adieu.*" Bending, she kissed Laura's cheek, and moments later the door closed behind her. Another knock on the door brought Laura's hard hat and orange safety vest.

29

Christmas Season

A week before Caster Elementary School closed for the Christmas holidays, Brenda asked Grace to come to her office. A one-burner hot plate sat on a table against a wall. Steam spewed from the curved spout of a potbellied yellow enamel kettle. Two mugs, several tea bags, sugar, and a sliced lemon filled a small tray next to it. "Have a cup of tea with me," Brenda said, rising to fill the mugs.

Grace accepted one level teaspoon of sugar and squeezed a lemon into her tea.

"I miss Harold so much. When will the pain stop?" Brenda asked.

The question set Grace remembering: a time in Branston when a lawn mower started up, and a sandy-haired man who resembled Ted and who was mowing his lawn had reduced her to tears. And once in a restaurant about a year after Ted's death, the tilt of a man's shoulders sent her leaning hard on her chin to keep from crying.

"When, Grace, when will it stop? You've been through this. Tell me." She took a chair alongside Grace's. "I can't do Christmas. It's three weeks away. I don't want to shop. I don't want a tree. There's nothing to celebrate."

"I understand. Christmas was hard for me for years after Ted died. I don't think I enjoyed the holidays until we moved down here to Covington."

"That long?"

"It takes time. The pain will ease. I know it doesn't feel that way, but it will."

Brenda's chin quivered; she struggled for control. "In the meanwhile, while I'm waiting for time to kick in, how do I cope? How do I go on working? I hate everyone coming to me for decisions. I'm considering resigning, or at least a long leave of absence."

"Think that over carefully. If you didn't have to get up and get dressed each day, if you isolated yourself from people, you could become very depressed."

"I'm already depressed. People. I don't want to see them. I don't want to hear that some child may be the victim of abuse, or that a big kid's bullying a small kid, or that a case of basketballs has been lost in shipping, or that the new desks for the fifth grade are too small for the children and have to be sent back."

"Isolation could make it worse," Grace said.

"Why did this happen to Harold? To me?" Brenda's voice turned bitter. "Sometimes I hate him for smoking. You know how often I begged him to quit? Damn him. Oh, God, I hate myself for feeling this way." She struck her fist on her desk and the next moment dropped her head onto her hands and wept.

Grace said nothing. She did not rush to put her arms about Brenda. She did not try to sooth or placate her with words, but sat quietly, her eyes fastened on the frayed edge of the raffia rug upon which their chairs sat. Grace waited for Brenda's anger and pain to vent themselves.

"I'm sorry." Brenda lifted her head and dabbed at her eyes and cheeks. "I can't seem to control myself these days."

"If there's any advice I can offer you, Brenda, it's don't isolate yourself."

"What am I supposed to do, dress up and go to some holiday party?"

"No. I didn't mean that, but I imagine you have to have Christmas for your grandsons."

Brenda's chin quivered. She nodded. "I'm not going to make it, Grace."

"You are. I did. You will too."

As the days closed in on Christmas, Grace thought of Brenda often. A few days before Christmas, Grace stood at the sink chopping vegetables for the stuffing of yet another turkey. Near her on the counter fat green peppers sidled up to long stalks of celery, and onions spilled from papery skins. She made a mental note to call Brenda before the family left for Brenda's mother's home in South Carolina. As she prepared the stuffing for the turkey, Grace's mind drifted to Harold's wake and all the food that she and their neighbors had prepared, and of all other life events: weddings, births, anniversaries, all kinds of celebrations that centered around food.

Over the years, Grace had gone out of her way to honor the food traditions of her friends: corn beef and cabbage for the O'Malleys, latkes (potato pancakes) for the Franks. When Andre and Maria Marinopolous entertained relatives from Greece, Grace prepared stuffed grape leaves, and she had welcomed the Russian couple from Yakutsk in Siberia, whom the town had sponsored, with borscht. When she saw the borscht, Anna Kierof had hugged Grace hard.

Now as she chopped onions, Grace's mind drifted. She wondered if language had evolved in a cave over food as primitive people hunched around a fire and planned the next day's hunt. She thought about an African tribe she'd read about somewhere that believed that sharing food established a kinship among people. She recalled reading that to the ancient Egyptians, the onion symbolized the multilayered universe, and they swore oaths on onions, as we do on the Bible. She had passed that bit of extraneous information on to someone at church in Dentry one day. The woman had responded with a shake of her head as if to say, Poor Grace, where does she get such nonsense from?

The onion stung her eyes, causing them to burn and tear. Grace held the onion for a moment under cold running water. Chopping vegetables reminded her of long ago when she'd help her mother prepare for Thanksgiving, and how her father had insisted that they all sit down to dinner together every night—no grabbing food on the run—which at the time she had considered a bore. Looking back, however, she knew that it was there that she learned table etiquette, and how to listen and not interrupt others, and how morose and silent a man could be when he hated his job. She had also learned that men ruled the home and required women to be compliant and cooperative.

Grace raised her eyes to the window just as a sedan with darkened windows turned off Cove Road and crunched its way up the long driveway to the house. The car was unfamiliar, and it was not until Roger and Charles disembarked that she realized that it was Tuesday, the day they were expected. She had anticipated their going directly to the apartment they had bought, with Miranda and Paul, in Loring Valley, or had they already been there? Why was she standing here like this with the doorbell ringing? Dropping the half-cut onion in the sink, Grace wiped her hands and started for the door calling, "I'm coming."

Tiredness ringed their eyes. "We drove all night," Roger said. His fair hair was windblown, his blue eyes bloodshot.

"Good heavens, why?" Grace asked as she hugged them and helped them off with their coats.

"Just eager to see you, Mother Singleton," Charles said, hugging her again. "Why, you look absolutely wonderful. Covington must have a fountain of youth." The pouches under his eyes had deepened and widened. For an instant a shadow crossed his face. "I could sure use a drink of that water."

"Just wanted to stop by and say hello before we go unpack," Roger said. "I'm starved. I smell onions. Making chopped chicken liver?"

"Already made, in the fridge," Grace replied, warmed by his hunger for her chopped liver. The Russian woman, Anna Kierof, had taught her how to make it.

They headed for the kitchen, where the aroma of onion perfidiously charged every molecule of air. "Wow, that's powerful," Roger said.

They seemed oddly disconnected from one another, each following his own train of thought and interrupting one another with impunity.

"So good to be here." Charles sank into a chair at the table. His blue flannel shirt hung loose and puckered about his waist.

He looks exhausted, and he's lost too much weight, Grace thought, but who am I to talk? I look a wreck. My shirt's got paint stains, my slacks have a hole in one knee, and Roger's so conscious of clothes. Positioning herself behind Charles's chair, Grace placed her hands on his shoulders and watched Roger bend into the refrigerator, shove aside this jar and that bottle, and find the plastic bowl of chopped liver. Without giving her a second glance, he brought a plate and knife as well as a box of crackers from a cabinet to the table and dug in.

"What would you boys like to drink?"

"Water for me, please, Mother Singleton," Charles said.

"Hot tea would be nice." Roger heaped chopped liver on a cracker and ate, closing his eyes so as to savor the taste. He mounded chopped liver atop a half dozen crackers, placed them in a neat circle, and shoved the plate toward Charles. "Have some."

"Thanks." Charles helped himself. "Delicious, Mother Singleton."

"I wish you would just call my mother Grace." Roger's tone was unaccustomedly peevish.

Charles turned his head and looked up at Grace. "It's a comfortable habit. Do you mind?"

"It's a mouthful to say, but I certainly don't mind. You eat. I'll get your drinks and finish chopping this onion." Grace moved to the sink. Oh, well, perhaps the trip. They were tired. "When you're done, maybe you ought to go to the apartment and rest a bit. Bob's taking us all out for dinner tonight."

"Mike and Amelia joining us?" Roger asked.

"Only Amelia."

Charles's voice turned sarcastic. "Poor, Roger, will that make you sad?"

Grace spun about. "What's going on?"

225

Anger and pain tinged Charles's voice, yet he replied, "Nothing at all, just being silly."

But Grace knew from their strained faces and barely restrained hostility that this was untrue. She remembered, then, that last June at Emily and Russell's wedding Amelia had noticed the amount of time Roger and Mike spent together. What had happened recently when Mike visited them in Branston?

"Mike and Amelia are busy these days getting ready for her show on January tenth in New York," Grace said.

"Mike going with her?" Roger asked.

Charles stiffened. In his eyes, an expression of surprise quickly turned to hurt, and he looked away. Abruptly, he pushed back his chair and stood. "We'll, if you're finished stuffing yourself, Roger, we'd best be going."

Roger waved a hand at Charles. "Oh, come off it. Sit down. I'm just trying to catch up on people around here." He turned to his mother. "How's Mrs. Tate doing?"

"Not well. She's got her daughter close by." Their disaffection was affecting her. Suddenly, Grace wanted to strike out at her son, to berate him for vanishing the day so long ago after his father's funeral, leaving her further bereft. "It's just a few weeks since Harold died," she said.

"And Laura," Charles asked. "How is she doing?"

"Laura and Hannah seem happily occupied at the new park down the road. We're all fine. Are you?" It was bold of her, intrusive, yet she was glad she'd asked it.

In that instant they could have heard a pin drop. Grace found herself listening to her own breathing. Then came a flurry of activity as the back door swung wide, ushering in Hannah and Laura, their hands filled with bundles, and bringing with them the smell of woodsmoke and a blast of freezing air. "Lord, it's cold out there," Laura said. She looked at the men. "Why, hello."

"Laura, meet my sons, Roger and Charles." The "sons" was deliberate, meant to let Charles and Roger, too, know where she stood.

The men rose, hugged Hannah, and shook hands with Laura.

"I'm delighted to finally meet you." Laura joined the men at the table. She helped herself to a cracker piled high with chopped liver. "So good. Where have you been hiding this, Grace? I didn't know you could make chopped liver."

"For me," Roger said. "Mother knows I love it."

"Enjoy," Grace said. "Take some with you to the apartment. I made plenty." She took a covered casserole dish from the refrigerator and handed it to Charles. "This is for you, toad-in-the-hole, just like the recipe you gave me. I hope it's what you expected, like your granny's."

Charles's eyes lit up. "May I taste it now?"

"Certainly." She handed him a plate and utensils, and as he scooped a spoonful she watched the crust split apart, revealing fat little sausages. Charles's eyes closed as he savored the taste. "Just like Granny's," he said. "Thank you so very much, Mother Singleton."

"If it weren't all baked together, I'd call it pigs in blankets, little hot dogs rolled in pastry dough," Hannah said. "Remember them, Laura?"

Laura rolled her eyes. "Do I ever? We had pigs in blankets twice a week sometimes."

"End of pay period. Money was low then," Hannah said. "Certainly not the good old days." Hannah turned to Roger. "Can you give me a hand with the bottled water and drinks from the car?"

"Bottled water?" Roger asked.

"Laura likes bottled water," Hannah explained.

Laura nodded. "They have well water here. Maybe there are minerals in it that I'm not used to."

"Well, let's get the water." Roger pushed back his chair and followed Hannah out of the kitchen door. Another blast of freezing air caused Grace to shiver. But she knew that it was more than the cold air that affected her. It was Roger and Charles and the sense of something sad and unpleasant lurking just below the surface waiting to pounce on these two men whom she loved.

Later, when they had gone and Laura was upstairs, Grace asked Hannah, "Did you sense the tension between the boys?"

Hannah jostled Grace's arm. "Boys? You still calling those grown men boys?"

"Be serious, Hannah. I sense trouble between them."

"What kind of trouble?"

"Remember how Amelia felt there was an attraction between Mike and Roger? I pooh-poohed it."

"I agreed with her; they were just a touch too cozy."

"Looks like you two were right. The mention of Mike's name and each of them bristled, and the snide remarks started."

Hannah sank into a chair and scratched her head. "When, I ask you, do things run smoothly and stay that way?"

"There's always something, isn't there? Life seems to be about meeting challenges, solving problems with time-outs, of course, to recoup. Wouldn't want to knock us out in the second round, even the fourth."

"Stop, Grace. It's almost Christmas. Supposed to be a jolly old time. Don't start with your questions about the meaning of life."

Grace laughed. "You're right. Let's all have a jolly old Christmas."

Hannah sighed. "Who's coming for Christmas Eve dinner?"

"Max, Hank, the Richardsons. Mike's going out of town. Lurina, Old Man, and Wayne can't come. Wayne's been staying with them, painting and fixing up the old farmhouse, and Old Man's nieces and their families from Tennessee are coming to them for the holiday. The nieces are doing the cooking."

"We don't see Lurina as much as we used to," Hannah said.

"I know, but I'm glad for her. When she married Old Man, she married a family."

"They are cute together. Ever seen them in the market? They push the cart together and discuss every can of fruit and box of cereal they buy." They fell silent for a time. Hannah toyed with the edge of the empty chopped liver bowl. Then she asked, "Brenda coming Christmas Eve?"

"No, she and Molly's family are going to South Carolina to Millie's place."

"Shame Harold passed so close to the holidays."

"It sure is." Grace counted on her fingers. "With the Richardsons and all of us, there'll be thirteen. We'll extend the table and squeeze together like we did at Thanksgiving."

"I have this urge to buy all new decorations for our tree," Hannah said.

"That's odd coming from you. You hate to shop."

Hannah shrugged. "If I'm in Asheville, and I make it to Biltmore Village, I may go into a Christmas store, if not," she shrugged, "too bad."

🍂

Amelia found them in the living room, Hannah rummaging through a box of ornaments and Grace absorbed in a Christmas catalog. "What's new?" Amelia flopped into a chair close by the fireplace and loosened the ubiquitous scarf about her neck. "It's cold out there." She rubbed her hands briskly and pressed them to her red cheeks. She sniffed the air. "What do I smell?"

"Pine branches." Hannah pointed to a tall clay vase that reminded Grace of clay vessels that women in biblical times used to carry water from the well. It stood in the corner of the room and was filled with pine limbs Hannah had cut that day. "Good backdrop for poinsettias, don't you think?" Hannah asked.

"When's our tree coming?" Amelia asked. "Not until Christmas Eve again?"

"Tomorrow, three days earlier than usual. Emily prodded Bob and Russell into going to Little Switzerland to cut us a tree earlier this year."

"Why can't they just cut one closer?"

"Habit," Grace replied. "Russell's been getting his tree over there for years now."

"Next Christmas we'll have a baby to shop for." Amelia kicked off her shoes, extended her legs, and wiggled her toes. "This baby's going to have three grandmothers."

"Four." Grace placed her hands behind her head and leaned back. "You forgot about Ginger."

Hannah stopped rummaging and looked at Grace. "I forget about Ginger all the time."

"She's quite forgettable," Amelia said.

"Well," Grace said, "she's away a lot."

Amelia brought her feet to the floor and leaned forward, elbows on knees, chin on hands. "Do you think Ginger's really playing Scrabble all over the country, or has she got something else going?" Her eyebrows shot up.

"Do we care?" Hannah asked.

"Whatever. Life's easier for Emily, isn't it, when she's gone?" Amelia seemed eager for gossip. "Emily's closer to her father, isn't she?"

"Yes," Grace said. "Martin, unless he's eating at his club, has dinner with them when Ginger's away. Martin's fond of Tyler. Tyler was teaching him to fish last October. He, and Bob, and Martin got all dressed up in vests and fishermen caps and trotted off with their boxes of flys, and hooks, and bait. They were cute, and funny too. They rarely brought home their catch. Dumped it back. They hadn't the heart, they said."

Amelia sat back in her chair and extended her legs. "Less than three weeks, and I'm off to New York."

"Excited?" Hannah held up and scrutinized a clear, round ball frosted in faux silver. "Maybe a silver theme for the tree this year?"

"*Je suis très nerveux.* Excited and nervous. I used to adore traveling. Now I hate getting on a plane," Amelia said.

The catalog slipped from Grace's knees. She bent to retrieve it. "It's going to be all right, Amelia. I feel it in here." Her hand covered her heart.

Hannah returned the ball to its box and rummaged past tinsel and plastic stars and diminutive crystal angels. "Trust Grace's intuition."

Amelia's eyes grew dreamy. "It might be wonderful. We got pre-opening tickets for *Annie Get Your Gun,* and Mike's gotten tickets for some play with Alan Alda. I just worry about finding a cab after the theater. He says, if we have trouble, which I'm sure we will, we'll find a restaurant and have a late supper. By then, there will be cabs. I hope he's right." Her face changed, brightened. "How could I forget? When we went to the theater in London, Thomas hired a private limousine. It would be waiting and the driver waving a sign with our name. We could do that in New York, I'm sure."

"Feel better about it?" Hannah asked.

"Yes." Amelia straightened her shoulders and sat erect. "I do feel better." Then she looked at Grace. "My goodness, what are you wearing?"

Grace smoothed her paint-stained shirt and tugged at the red-and-white-checkered bandanna hanging loosely from her waist. "Comfortable clothes."

"Your moccasins, look at that left one, the stitching's come out. What if you got sick, and the ambulance came, and you're dressed like that?"

"Am I hearing, right? You think I should dress up all the time, even when I'm cooking, in case I get sick?" Grace laughed. "Amelia, you can't be serious."

Amelia's face fell. "You're right, of course. Who would want to dress up to cook?"

"Thought you'd gotten past that kind of crap, Amelia," Hannah said.

"Hard to believe, my mother's voice speaking and at my age," Amelia said. "Her mantra was, 'Always be properly groomed.' When-ever we left the house, even to run around the corner for a bottle of milk, we put on makeup and stockings. Maybe there'd be a fire, she'd say, or an accident, or we'd have a heart attack in the street. Did she really belief that stuff, I wonder? And here I am mouthing her words. I'm sorry, Grace."

Grace patted Amelia's arm. "As I grow older I hear myself saying things that came straight from my mother. I remember swearing I never would. Like I mumble and talk out loud to myself when I cook and I'm alone. Mother did that when she thought she was alone. I remember catching her at it and mimicking her behind her back." Grace lifted an eyebrow. "Now I do it. And I'm going to continue wearing grungies when I'm cooking, and mumbling to my-self."

"Your taste in grungy, however, is deteriorating." Hannah laughed. They all did, and Grace pushed up from her seat and pranced about the room, her hands on her hips, her head thrown back. "You mean to say I don't make a fashion statement?"

"Let's have a day a month when we dress in the funniest combinations of clothes we have," Amelia suggested. They laughed again, and Hannah remarked, "Are you thinner, Grace?"

Sobering, Grace returned to her chair. "I may have lost a few pounds. It tends to come off my waist first." Grace related how the doctor had finally scared her out of complacency, and that she planned, after the holidays, to eat differently. "But I'll make sugar cookies for you, Amelia, and Vienna cake for you, Hannah, same as ever."

Amelia swallowed hard. She adored Grace's cookies. Tea without them would not taste the same. "That's so good of you . . . ," she began. The exasperated look on Hannah's face stopped her, and she shook her head. "No, that'll be too hard on you." Amelia's chin tilted up. "I can do without them."

"We'll forgo sweets and eat whatever you make for yourself," Hannah said firmly, and Amelia agreed.

With "Jingle Bells" on their lips and the numbing cold at their backs, Bob, Russell, and Tyler delivered an eight-foot Douglas fir three days before Christmas, and the ladies cheered. That night the Richardsons, along with Roger and Charles, joined them for a light supper, after which they decorated the tree. Hannah had not made it to Biltmore Village, and everyone's ornaments, old and new, large and small, found a home among the branches. Bob supported Tyler on the ladder as he set an angel on top, and Emily was given the honor of plugging in the lights.

"Get the gifts from the car, will you, Russell, please?" Emily said.

Tyler raced ahead of his dad, and they returned with boxes beautifully wrapped in red and silver and green holiday paper with huge bows. Laura brought down the gifts Miranda had left in her care, and the ladies added their presents. Soon the tree seemed to wade in a sea of color. Grace produced a bowl of unspiked eggnog and her special multicolored Vienna cake, which she had cut into finger-size pieces.

"Dessert at last," Tyler said. Plate in his lap, he snuggled close beside Grace on the couch. "It's a happy tree, you know," he whispered.

"How can you tell?" she asked.

He swallowed a piece of cake. "It stood in the field and waved its arms at me. It called to me. My real mommy, who's an angel now, told the tree to call to me."

"What did it say?"

" 'Tyler,' it said, 'I've been waiting for you,' and I heard it."

"I'm sure your angel mommy is watching over you." She concentrated on the tree, studying its size and shape. The angel's hair touched the ceiling. "Yes, I can see that it's a happy tree, and it's made us all happy."

"I know," he said, snuggling closer. "I don't talk about Mommy to Emily, you know. I don't want to make her feel bad."

Grace nodded and hugged him. Such a dear boy. Taking the empty plate from him, she held and loved him, loved them all, and said a silent prayer of thanksgiving that she was surrounded by these dear people at this special time of year. Roger and Charles, she noted, seemed to have settled down; perhaps they had merely been tired. Mike was conspicuous by his absence. The skin on her arms prickled. Since they had been in Covington, he had celebrated the holidays with them. As if reading her mind, Tyler asked, "Where's Mike?"

"Mike's spending the holiday with a sick friend down the mountain in Forest City," Amelia explained.

"Oh," Tyler said.

Grace noticed that at the mention of Mike's name, Roger's jaw tightened, and Charles fidgeted. Grace said, "Why don't we sing? I've the song sheets from last year." She rose and, with Tyler in tow, went to the dining room.

"But Mike's not here to play on the portable keyboard Miss Lurina gave us last Christmas," Tyler said.

233

"We'll sing a cappella, without music. Everyone knows the melodies."

He nodded and, hands filled with sheet music, returned to the living room to distribute it.

Music worked its magic, and by the time they all stood in the doorway shivering against the penetrating cold, avoiding the frost that rimed the doorframe and bidding one another good night, Roger and Charles seemed, once again, relaxed. Roger slipped his arm about Charles' shoulder as they started down the steps. Then the women returned to the living room to plump pillows, straighten hassocks, and pick up the last of the glasses and plates.

"After tonight, Christmas Eve will seem anticlimactic," Hannah said.

"It's fine by me if it's quiet," Amelia said.

"It's nice that our holidays include more people every year since we're here," Grace remarked.

"I look forward to the holidays, and I'm always glad when they're over." Hannah snapped off the light.

"My bones will appreciate my bed tonight," Grace said. But Grace had no sooner settled into bed when a light rap sounded on the door. "Come in," she called softly.

Wrapped in a pink fleece robe, Amelia slipped into the room. "Grace, did you see it?"

"See what?"

"Roger and Charles's faces when Tyler asked about Mike." She pulled the robe snug about her slender frame. "I knew it. I knew it last summer. There's something between Roger and Mike." Amelia plopped on the edge of Grace's bed, and Grace scooted over to make room and to get her toes out of the way.

"Mike visited them when he went north to see his folks. He's never mentioned that visit, and that's not like Mike, not at all. He tells me everything, everything." Amelia gestured wildly. "He's going to be gone all holiday season."

"He's helping a sick friend, isn't he?"

"Well, yes." Amelia folded her arms over her chest. "A friend with AIDS."

"I'm sorry."

"I think he's really avoiding your son and Charles. I knew it. I knew something was brewing."

Grace was certain Amelia was right, but why stir things up further? Better to placate, calm, and reassure Amelia. "If there is anything, and we have no proof there is, Mike's taking a wise course of action, wouldn't you say?"

Amelia turned anxious eyes to Grace. "Do you think so?" She considered that for a moment. Grace had opened her window an inch at the top. Wind chimes suspended from the curtain rod tinkled softly. "But what if Roger and Mike have a thing going?"

"They're sensible, basically good people. They'd make every effort to do the right thing."

"How naive you are, really. I'm a good person, wouldn't you say?"

Grace nodded.

"Remember how I was with Lance? I changed, was insensitive to you and Hannah, cruel to Mike."

Grace swallowed hard and crossed her fingers under the covers. "Your imagination's working overtime, Amelia. Mike's friend is sick. It speaks well of him that he's chosen to spent the holidays with him. You're worrying unnecessarily."

"You think so?"

What else could she say? "I think so," Grace replied, shifting her legs. "Aren't you tired?"

Amelia smiled uncertainly, then brightened. "You're probably right, and yes, I'm tired. You are too. I'll let you go to sleep now."

But for a long time after Amelia left her room, Grace's mind hummed with concerns. Rising, she opened the window further and drew a deep breath of wintry air. Winter was early this year, too early. It would seem endless until spring. How she longed for hot summer sunshine. To the east, above the hilltops, the full moon sculpted the landscape. Harried by a restless wind, trees dipped and swayed. On the ridge of the hill behind their house, bare-branched trees appeared to have been sheared by a sharp scissors, leaving a brush cut on a rounded pate. Shivering, Grace closed the window and hastened back to bed to snuggle under her down comforter.

30

If You Love Me, Mother

On Christmas Day the world lay silent. Branches sagged beneath their burden of snow. Snow sprinkles wafted away on imperceptible breezes. Grace was finishing the inevitable cleanup that follows a large holiday meal and an evening of gift giving: putting away platters, returning Amelia's sterling silverware to its protective case, jamming overlooked bits of ribbon and Christmas wrapping into trash bags waiting to be sealed. When Roger rang their doorbell, Grace welcomed him into the cozy yellow kitchen. Snow grazed the shoulders of his coat and dappled his blond hair silver.

"Sit. Let me get you a cup of coffee."

"That would hit the spot," Roger said. Removing his coat, he shook it, then folded it carefully and lay it on the back of a chair. Drifts of snow settled on the kitchen floor where they dissolved into pellets of water. Taking a roll of paper towels, Roger bent to wipe the floor. "Last night was one of the nicest evenings I've had in years. Everyone was so relaxed. I like it that we have dinner and then open gifts on Christmas Eve."

"In this household, we adhere to the principle that no one should be on her feet working on Christmas Day. It's a day to kick back and relax."

"I'm going to adopt that principle." Damp hair toppled forward into his eyes. Roger brushed it back over his forehead. "I have to talk to you," he said.

Grace placed a steaming mug of coffee before him, poured water for tea for herself, and they sat facing one another across the kitchen table. Cookies baking in the oven dispatched mouth-watering aromas. For a moment a log popping inside the wood-burning stove distracted them. "That stove was a good idea," Roger said. His fingers drummed the table.

Grace covered them with her hand. "Relax, son. Tell me what's on your mind."

He raked his fingers through his hair. His face, Janus-like, shifted from tiredness to exasperation, from longing to anxiety. He lowered his eyes. "You're very perceptive. You must know."

"Know what?" She knew, but he would have to tell her in his own words.

"About Mike and me."

"Mike and you?"

"Mother, don't act dumb. I'm sure you know."

"I can see that you're upset. Charles is worried. But whatever's going on is not clear to me."

"Charles is much older than I am."

"Yes."

"Do you realize he's over sixty?"

"Why, no. I never did the math, I guess."

"He's closer to your age than mine," Roger said.

"So? Drink your coffee." Grace needed time to digest this fact.

Roger's hand slammed down on the table. "Don't treat me like a child, Mother. I'll drink coffee when I feel like it."

"Sorry," Grace murmured, looking away to hide the tears beginning to fill her eyes.

He reached for her hand. "I'm sorry. I'm a nervous wreck."

She waited. He sat back and crossed his arms over his chest. A thud against the windowpane sent Grace dashing to the window. "Oh, Roger, it's a bird. It flew into the window. It's fallen into the snow."

"Mother, forget the damned bird. I need you now."

She could not forget the wounded bird, nor could she ignore her highly agitated son, so Grace returned to the table to hear him out, wishing all the while that Hannah would appear and take care of the little creature lying in the snow.

"It's not that I don't love Charles," Roger said. "We've had great years together, but HIV has really slowed him down. He's lost his zest for life. He doesn't talk about it, but he lives in fear of AIDS. I've been humoring him, urging him to rest more, seeing that he eats right, exercising with him. Lord, Mother, you know I've always hated exercise."

She nodded. "You've been good to him and for him."

"It's your damned fault that I can't just leave him. Loyalty, honor, that kind of thing—I learned it at your knee."

Grace smiled. He was cool, reserved, and unapproachable most of the time. She never imagined having had any lasting influence on her son.

"Anyway, I'm not going to walk out." His eyes were fixed on some spot on the wall behind her. "Besides, we have the business together, and Charles insisted on putting our home, which was bought with the inheritance from his granny, in both our names." With an abrupt movement, Roger shifted, nearly knocking over the coffee mug. "What's wrong with my wanting to spend time with Mike occasionally?"

"What about Mike? Does occasionally work for him?"

Roger's chin tilted upward. "I'm committed. He knows that."

"Are you speaking after the fact, Roger? Have you and Mike . . . ?"

"Damn it! No. We've never talked about it, but Charles knows. He's gotten whiny and needy. Lord, I can't stand it when he acts like that."

"How would you expect him to act?"

"I knew it. I knew you'd take Charles's side."

"Roger, stop it. You're my son. I love you. I love Charles, too, and Mike, and I don't want to see anyone get hurt."

"In something like this, someone gets hurt," he stated, his voice hard.

239

"Not someone. Everyone," Grace said softly.

"Okay. Everyone, then." He leaned toward her. "I need your help. I need an excuse to spend time with Mike. I don't want to hurt Charles, so I need a reasonable excuse to get away. Any ideas?"

"No. None at all."

"Would you consider asking Charles here for a visit, then?"

"Without you? He'd know immediately."

"But at least he wouldn't be alone; he'd have you to talk to. He trusts you. You could reassure him, bring him around to accepting the situation. He and I can go on as we are, and I could see Mike a couple of times a year. It would take adjusting to, but if you talked to him, Charles would come around." He raised thick eyebrows and his voice filled with pain coupled with an edge of sarcasm. "Charles had a fling once."

Grace's shoulders sagged. "And the price was HIV," she reminded her son.

"Mike's been checked. He's clean. So am I."

It had gone that far! Grace's head ached. All she could think of now was the bird lying in the snow. That was simple. She could do something about it. She rose. "Sit here. I'm going to get the bird."

"You're what?" His voice was incredulous. "I've got this huge problem, and you're worried about a damned bird?"

She was out of the kitchen, yanking on a coat in the foyer. Her boots plunged into foot-deep snow, which spilled over their tops, making her feet cold. Drifts from the roof salted her hair and shoulders. All but the bird's tiny red crest lay blanketed in white. Moments later, Grace returned to the kitchen, indifferent to the snow she tracked on the floor. Cradled in her palms, a baby cardinal shivered. "I think his wing's broken," she said, setting the bird gently on a kitchen counter. Then she pulled a shoe box from a nearby shelf and lined it with a kitchen towel. The little creature chirped sadly. "Poor baby," Grace murmured. She looked at Roger. "There's a vet in the new strip mall on Elk Road. I wonder if she'd see him as an emergency."

"Mother, I want an answer from you."

Grace turned to face him, and her eyes were serious, almost

fierce. "Roger, I can't give you an answer on something as serious as this in two minutes. I have to think about it. I'm going to talk with the others too."

"I'd leave Amelia out of it," Roger said flatly.

"You think she doesn't know? She noticed something at Russell and Emily's wedding, and she's been worrying ever since."

"So why worry her more?"

Grace clutched the shoe box to her chest. The bird's needs involved no moral issues. It chirped, and chirped again. "It's okay, baby," she whispered. "We'll get you fixed up."

Precipitously, Roger shoved back his chair and stood. "Some help you are. You're my mother, remember?"

He towered over her. Again, as she had many times before, she marveled at the genes from some unknown ancestor whence had come his height in a family of short people.

"I'm out of here," Roger declared.

She stepped toward him. "Please, Roger, wait. I'm sorry."

But he had snatched up his coat and was halfway to the front door.

"I need time to think about this," she repeated.

"Forget I came here," he called back to her. "I don't need your help."

"I will help, I promise. I just need a little time." She was at the door now.

Whipped by gusts of wind, cold air sliced her like a knife. Grabbing the door before he slammed it, Grace closed it behind her son and peered through the glass inset. Roger reversed rapidly down their drive. His horn sounded loudly before he backed into Cove Road. Drive safely, my son, she thought. Then, moving slowly to the steps, she grasped the banister and called, "Hannah. Amelia. Please come down. I need to talk with you."

※

Fifteen minutes later the three women sat at the kitchen table. Hannah had called the veterinarian's service, and Dr. Marva Pinkerton would meet them at her office in an hour. The cookies had browned too much but were crisp and, Amelia assured them, delicious as she dunked one after the other in her tea. "These will be my last for a while," she said.

Grace told them what Roger had asked of her. "I don't think there's any talking him out of this. Do you think, Amelia, that it would help to talk to Mike?"

"He called late last night. He sounded as if he were walking on air, so he and Roger must have made some arrangement earlier."

"I have my doubts about interfering in this business," Hannah said. "People have their own lives to live. They mess up, but if they're lucky they learn from it."

"I'm more concerned about Charles than I am about Roger," Grace said.

"You want to invite him here, go ahead."

"We have a full house. He'd have to stay at Bob's. I'll talk this over with Bob. Like you, Hannah, Bob will probably advocate a hands-off policy. I just wonder." Grace shook her head. "If Charles did come here, what would I say to him? That it's okay for his partner to go off with someone else, even temporarily?"

Amelia piped in. "Charles did it once. He just might be willing to go along, to close his eyes to the situation."

"I say leave it be." Hannah looked at her watch. "I've got to get dressed if I'm going to take this wee creature to the vet." She looked out of the window. "So much snow. Good thing you traded your car for a four-wheel drive, Amelia. May I take your Subaru? The county won't get to plowing Cove Road for days."

"Ask Maxwell to have his machine do it for all of us," Grace said.

"I forget he's got the equipment," Amelia said.

They could hear the fifth stair creak as Hannah ascended. "I'm surprised at her attitude," Amelia said. "After all, she was instrumental in getting Laura to stay with us. That's interference, isn't it? And she had plenty to say about Lance."

"I imagine it's just an initial reaction. If Charles comes for a visit without Roger, she'd welcome him. We all would."

"Indeed we would. Dear Charles. He's always been so good to you, Grace. For that alone I'd help in any way I could, but I hardly think, in this matter, I have any influence with Mike." She sat there, twisting her grandmother's narrow diamond and sapphire band, which she wore on the third finger of her left hand. "Why do grown children come running home with their problems?"

Grace laughed lightly. "Who else would have them? In all his adult life, Roger has never turned to me for anything." She hastened to correct herself. "Except money that time to go into business. In one way I feel needed, and in another way put off, almost angry that he waits for something like this."

"What will you do?" Amelia dunked yet another cookie in yet another cup of tea.

"Try to help. It would be worse for Charles, don't you think, alone in Branston?"

"I imagine so."

Rising from her chair, Grace slipped several additional pieces of hickory wood into the iron stove. Hickory might be hard to get started, but it burned wonderfully, slowly and steadily. "I'm chilly all of a sudden."

"Grace," Amelia said, "I hope this business with Charles and Roger won't upset you unduly. It's been forever since I've seen you take any nitroglycerine."

Grace knocked on the table. "Knock on wood," she said. "I haven't had to take it in so long, I forget to carry the pills with me."

"If it were me, I'd be wary and carry them with me all the time."

"You think this news of Roger's might upset me so much that I'll have chest pains?"

Amelia nodded and nibbled at the edge of her lower lip. "Maybe."

"Don't worry. I'm fine. I'm a happy woman. Happiness is a great healer, and remember it was years ago, and they had to do an angioplasty in only one artery."

"I just want you to stay well. You're a good, kind person, always here for all of us. Doesn't it ever get to be too much?"

Grace thought a moment. Her brows knitted. Then she replied, "If I can listen to someone, help someone, I figure it's one of the reasons I'm on this earth, or I'd like to think that."

"I feel so selfish compared to you," Amelia said, twisting her ring

"We all have different skills. You give in other ways. You create beauty that many people enjoy."

Amelia's finely shaped brows drew together. "Remember how I felt that Thomas had a rich and meaningful life, while mine was insignificant?"

"I certainly do. I'm happy you no longer feel that way."

"Sometimes I do, especially when I think about how much you do for others."

Grace rose and stepped behind Amelia's chair. Reaching across her shoulders she hugged her. "Dear Amelia, there's a wonderful, childlike quality about you that I love. Please, don't ever change. Thomas did what he had to do, and now you're doing what you have to do. Your life is full and creative, so don't worry about little things, or wallow in the past, or fuss about what was or wasn't. At this stage of our lives, there's no time for regrets."

Amelia turned to look at Grace. "I've come a long way, haven't I?"

"You have indeed." Gently, Grace squeezed Amelia's shoulders.

"Thanks, Grace. I needed reminding."

"Don't we all, at times?" But it troubled Grace that her words to her friend belied the nights when she lay in bed worrying about this or that, about Hannah and Laura, about Emily's new job and its pressures and the coming baby, about Brenda's enormous grief, about little Lucy Banks. She worried if Hannah would have the energy to oversee all those gardens, and was Amelia going to be all right now that there was no man in her life? It seemed to Grace that she worried enough for all three of them. But she had spoken truthfully about regrets. Bob had helped her see that whatever decisions she had made, whatever she had done in her life, had been done with good intentions and to the best of her ability at the time. What more could a person do? And now she was being asked to aid and abet a situation that went against the grain of who she was and what she valued. This troubled her deeply. How could she resolve this problem, how could she decide what course of action to take?

31

Simple Gifts

While Grace pondered, Roger acted. Within days after they returned home, Charles called. The desperation in his voice reminded Grace of her own sense of helplessness and despair when Roger had insisted that she leave her home in Dentry and move to Olive Pruitt's boarding home for retired ladies.

"Roger minced no words, Mother Singleton. He said flat out that he needs a change, wants more fun than we've had for a while, and he's planning on meeting Mike in New York after Amelia's show, after she goes back to Covington."

Grace knew the hardheaded resolve her son could muster. Her heart ached for Charles, and she found herself inviting, then urging Charles to return to Covington, not to stay alone in their house in Branston.

"How can I do that? We can't both walk out on Miranda and the business. I'll have to stay here. I'll keep busy."

"I'm so sorry. What can I do for you, Charles?"

"Say it's okay for me to phone you every day, cry my troubles."

"Of course. I'm here for you."

They talked a while longer, Charles struggling in vain to control his tears, Grace listening and being careful not to say anything that might make matters worse. When they hung up, Grace felt glued to her chair by her window and stared out at the gray, chill morning. Rain had held sway for four long days, and everyone in the household, it seemed, felt as bleak as the weather. It reminded Grace of rainy Saturdays when she was a child. "I don't care if it's only a drizzle, it's still rain," her mother would say, and she would insist that Grace and her brother remain indoors all day long, when they would rather be out running in the rain, or at least visiting a friend.

"It's warmer today, in the fifties," Grace said aloud. "I'm going for a walk in the rain." Rousing herself, she pulled on a long-sleeved turtleneck and a pair of jeans and trotted downstairs, where she donned a yellow raincoat, a matching yellow rain hat, and black galoshes.

From the kitchen window, Hannah watched Grace march down the front steps, hesitate momentarily, then square her shoulders and button her raincoat snugly about her neck. Grace strode down the driveway with firm steps, her heels coming down hard. At the end of their drive, she turned right on Cove Road. Grace is worried about something, Hannah thought, stifling the impulse to join her friend as she tromped along in the rain. Leave it be, she told herself. Had she wanted company, Grace would have asked.

At Elk Road, Grace turned left. Feeling exhilarated, she strode past Masterson land on her right, past the dilapidated gas station where Buddy Herrill, the manager, was unlocking the gas pumps. He stopped and waved at her. "Mighty strange weather we done been havin'," he said, to which she nodded, waved, and did not stop to chat.

Rain—the kind farmers pray for, the kind that sinks deep into the good earth—fell softly and steadily. Holding her yellow rain hat, Grace looked up at the leaden sky. Raindrops splashed onto her face and trickled along her cheeks. She licked her lips. The water felt cool and tasted sweet on her tongue. Soon she had passed the Cottage Tearoom. At P. J. Prancer's Hardware Store, several old-timers, smoking and chatting, sat in chairs pushed back on two legs on the covered porch. "Howdy," they called.

She waved. "Howdy," she called back.

Ignoring raindrops that pattered onto the wide brim of her hat,

Grace plodded on, unmindful of the distance until, suddenly, she found herself standing beneath a brightly lit sign on a tall billboard. ELK ROAD SHOPPING PLAZA it said in bright yellow lights. Plaza? No one's ever going to call this anything but a shopping center, Grace thought. In the newly paved parking lot, water puddled between jalopies, sedans, pickups, and trucks held high on monster wheels. Avoiding puddles, Grace wended her way through the lot and headed for the market.

Do we need anything? she asked herself. Eggs? Milk? Grace shook her head. As she approached the market, the automatic exit door slid back, and Velma Herrill stepped out. Plastic bags of groceries weighted her hands.

"Hi, Grace," Velma said. "How you doin'?" She set the bags in her right hand on the ground and rummaged in her purse, apparently for her car keys.

"Fine," Grace replied.

"I been wantin' to tell you, everyone's mighty appreciative the way you organized all that help for Brenda. We didn't realize what was goin' on. Brenda's sure a close mouthed person, ain't she?"

"Everyone stepped in to help, especially your family," Grace replied.

"Brenda's takin' Harold's passin' right hard, ain't she?" Velma asked.

Grace nodded. "When you've been happy with someone, it's even harder to lose him."

Velma shifted her weight from one leg to the other. She nodded and was quiet for a moment, as if she were considering Grace's words. Then she said, "Sometimes I think it's better not to care too much about a person." She shrugged. "Well, see you. Better get goin' before it comes down cats and dogs." Picking up the grocery bags, she trotted off, sending spikes of water skittering about her shoes as she hurried to her car.

Grace stood for a time, thinking about another bit of extraneous information she'd acquired recently about cats, dogs, and rain. Long, long ago, when houses were built with thatched roofs, the roof was the place where animals went to get warm, and when it

247

rained, as it was raining now, the thatch grew slippery. Animals sometimes slipped and tumbled off the roof. Thus the expression "raining cats and dogs." She must share that little tale with Velma next time she saw her.

Rubber boots squeaking, Grace meandered along the covered sidewalk that ran the length of the shopping center. Tiny white Christmas lights still framed the window of Lily's Beauty Salon. Inside, Alma sat stiff as a poker in a beautician's chair. Grace waved. Alma raised her hand to her eyes to cut the glare. Recognizing Grace, she waved back.

P. J. Prancer dashed from Frank Craine and Son's auto parts store and nodded as he hastened past her. The video store was jammed. Rainy day entertainment, she thought. A sucker for books, Grace lingered outside the newspaper and paperback bookstore. Not today, she decided. Not with this rain. Instead, walking gingerly to avoid the puddles, she crossed the parking lot and was poised to step onto Elk Road, when a horn blasted, jarring her and setting her nerves rattling, as her mother would say. Never had she seen such traffic on Elk Road. Grace stepped quickly back onto the wet, slushy grass on the shoulder to avoid sprays of water spewing from tires.

Originally, one entered Masterson land from a point closer to Cove Road, but the entrance had been relocated to the far side of the shopping center. Nevertheless, Grace decided to go to Lurina's and phone Hannah for a ride back home.

Wind gusted, whipping branches and tweaking her nose. A paper wrapper fresh from a fast-food store flew from a passing car and struck her leg. Although annoyed at the way people littered, Grace bent, picked up the paper, wadded it, and stuffed it into a pocket of her raincoat with the result that her hands were now wet and felt dirty. Digging her other hand into her empty pocket, she walked faster.

Faster, however, proved stressful, for several times Grace had to stop to rub the cramps that gripped her calves. She was decidedly out of shape, and longed for warmth, a comfortable chair, and a cup of hot tea.

For a short while, the rain moderated to a soft, light drizzle, and in time she reached the Masterson property and crossed the pasture. Ahead of her stood the old bridge, a bridge seldom used before the road was moved. The grass of the pasture, spongy with an excess of water, gave way beneath her feet, then sucked at her rubber boots, making walking burdensome.

When she reached the bridge, Grace heaved a sigh of relief, grasped the railing tightly, and started across. Underfoot, the shiny, slippery boards glistened. Bad River, usually languorous and shallow, now raced along as raucous and noisy as a passing train. Leaning against the rail, Grace peered down into the tumult of thick, curved branches of a tree that were jammed against a column supporting the bridge. The blockage reduced smaller branches and matted leaves to a spiraling mat of debris around which the river swirled, having carved a new bed by eroding the bank in a widening C. Water can be Machiavellian, she thought. Nothing deters its fierce determination to push on, to win at any cost.

Absorbed in the drama below, Grace failed to steady herself as she stepped back from the edge. Her right leg shot out in front; her left leg buckled beneath her. Her back and head hit the boards. Pain traveled up her leg and into her back. "Oh, my Lord," she cried. Injured, afraid to move, and feeling foolish and embarrassed, Grace indulged in self-pity. She wept. Dizziness followed, and regret at not having brought a snack with her in case, with all the exertion, her blood sugar level dropped. Stupid not to have paid more attention to her doctor's admonitions.

And then, from a distance, came the high-pitched sound of a fiddle, and a memory of a tale that Old Man had related about the old days and hunters gathering around a campfire and fiddling wild, shrill melodies to repel wolves. Who was fiddling and singing, and where? Old Man's nieces at the farmhouse?

The lilting Shaker tune "Simple Gifts" sounded full-bodied now, with many voices raised. " 'Tis a gift to come down where we ought to be." Grace considered the words literally. She'd "come down" all right, but what kind of gift was it to be twisted like a pretzel on an old wooden bridge in the rain? The opening lines of the song started again, " 'Tis a gift to be simple," and in that moment the fullness of the music enveloped her, lifting her above pain and fear and faintness, until the notes scattered and floated away, and Grace found herself pinioned to the bridge by pain so fierce that even turning her neck, limited as that was by stiffness, was agonizing.

Rain lashed the bridge and beat down on her face and body. Inside the raincoat her clothes were wet. Gritting her teeth, Grace eased her left leg from beneath her and slowly, tentatively, managed to bend the other. Bruised, painful but not broken, thank God. But her neck and shoulders, her back and legs, every muscle and bone in her body hurt from the wallop she had taken. You must get up, she told herself. You've got to get to the farmhouse. But her efforts to do so proved fruitless; Grace desperately needed a hand up.

And then, below, something snapped, shaking the structure, and the nightmare of being washed away with the detritus and wreckage pressing against the piling below compelled her to action. An arm's distance away, the railing beckoned. With superhuman effort, Grace edged closer to the rail, but her attempts to lift herself failed, and her outstretched arm thudded back onto the slick, quavering boards. Then came the ache in her chest, and the rapid beating of her heart. Once more she floated and heard the song again. "To turn, turn will be our delight." Pain shot along her left leg. Grace welcomed the darkness that enveloped her.

When she opened her eyes again, Grace knew she must try to get off the bridge. With a lurch, she managed to roll over into the center of the bridge. On hands and knees, she inched her way across the slippery, uneven decking of the bridge, nicking her fingers on jutting nails and snagging her raincoat on splintered wood. After what seemed an interminable time, her palms touched thick, soppy grass, and she eased forward until her knees and shoes sank into the waterlogged pasture.

32

Facing Serious Matters

Paralyzed by fear, Grace lay on the sopping grass until, as if in a dream, she heard familiar voices. They had found her. Gratefully, Grace slipped her arms about Bob's neck as his strong arms lifted her. She closed her eyes and once more floated, and again she heard parts of the song that haunted her: "To turn, turn will be our delight." They reached the farmhouse. Roused by the warmth, and the smells of mothballs and sautéed onions, Grace opened her eyes. Then she recognized the familiar spoke of broken spring in Lurina's ancient Victorian couch. At Bob's urging she accepted a tiny nitroglycerine pellet under her tongue, and wondered, had she had them in her pocket all along? The worried faces of Hannah, Amelia, and Bob leaned over her. Someone handed her a small glass of orange juice. Grace sipped it slowly.

"Are you all right?" Bob asked. "What in God's name happened?"

"I went for a walk in the rain. I guess I walked too much and too fast. Crossing the bridge, I fell and for a while I couldn't get up. I'm sorry for causing everyone so much trouble."

"Ain't no trouble helpin' you, Grace," Lurina said from behind the couch. She circled and sat beside Grace for a moment.

Grace made to get up, but Lurina's hands, small but strong, pushed her gently back. "You ain't goin' nowhere until the doc comes and says it's okay. Now I'll get you some broth that'll cure anything that ails you."

"Brace yourself, Grace," Old Man said. "It's mighty powerful broth, like she says, but it sure cures whatever ails you." He chuckled.

Grace looked around. "Where are your nieces? Who played the fiddle when you were singing 'Simple Gifts'?"

Old Man shook his head. "Nieces been gone a full day now. Me and Lurina were checkin' the pigs, and we noticed somethin' yellow, your raincoat, over yonder by the bridge." He lifted his eyes heavenward. "Lord, we near to died when we seen it was you, lady. Lurina waited with you while I phoned Hannah. Weren't no more than a blink of a pig's eye, she and Amelia were here."

Grace looked at Amelia. "What are you, psychic? Just this morning you asked about the nitroglycerine. I haven't needed it in so long."

"Promise me that in the future you'll carry some in a pocket or purse," Bob said. He sat beside her now, held her hand, felt her forehead, her cheeks. "No fever," he said.

"Why should I have a fever? I fell on the bridge, and I ache everywhere. And the oddest thing was, I heard that Shaker song 'Simple Gifts' being sung. You sure your cousins aren't here?"

"Cousins gone. No singin' round here this mornin', not with all the chores to be done," Old Man assured her. "Must've dreamed it."

When had they undressed her and wrapped her in this ancient plaid bathrobe reeking of mothballs? Lurina wore a size six, and Old Man was slight and short, so the bathrobe probably belonged to Lurina's father and had not seen the light of day in many years.

Bob tucked the blanket closer about her, and Grace dropped the subject of singing. The doorbell rang. Lurina's Doc Jones, from over near Walnut, stood dripping in the doorway. "Bless you fer comin', Doc." Old Man helped the doctor out of his rainwear and led the lean, slightly bent man with a balding head and drooping mustache into the living room just as Lurina returned from the kitchen with a steaming cup of broth.

252

"Took you long enough to get here. Just fixin' to tend Grace myself," she said.

"Your bridge may not last the day," Doc said. "Hope you've got a way for me to get back to Elk Road, or you've got one more for supper and the night."

"You'd be mighty welcome," Lurina replied.

Old Man said, "The other bridge is still there, only the road ain't no more since they plowed it under, but if you've got a four-wheeler you can cross that pasture back to Elk Road."

"What's wrong with the bridge?" Bob asked as he folded back the blanket so Doc could check Grace.

"Seems like one of the pilings holding it up is busted, and the river's mighty fierce and rising steady." Doc opened his bag and rummaged for his stethoscope. "What have we here?" he asked, looking into Grace's eyes.

Falteringly, she admitted being diabetic. "I probably did too much too fast, and my blood sugar level dropped. But I fell first. The bridge was slippery and I fell."

Doc nodded sagely. "You should always carry nuts, cheese, fruit, something to offset falling sugar." Carefully, he bent Grace's arms at the elbows, lifted each, and set each back beside her. Then he checked her legs, asked her to wiggle her toes, to bend her knees, her neck.

Grace mumbled through the thermometer between her lips. When Doc removed it, she said, "A thick branch wrapped itself about the piling, and all kinds of debris accumulated behind it. The river's created a new channel. I thought I heard the branch snap."

"Probably you heard the piling crack," Bob said. "Darling, that bridge might have given way with you on it."

"A miss is as good as a mile," Hannah said. "Grace is safe, and the bridge is still standing."

"Not for long," Amelia called from the window. "It's tottering. My God, it's splintering and falling into the river." She opened the window, and beyond and above the patter of rain on the roof, the crash of timber sounded in their ears. "It's gone. The bridge is gone," Amelia cried, shrinking from the window.

The fall on the bridge did more than batter and bruise Grace's body. For days, everything ached, and some parts of her ached for weeks, especially her lower back, but more than that, the experience triggered feelings of helplessness and a growing apprehension about her diabetes and its relationship to her heart.

"This is a serious matter, Grace," her doctor had said on more than one occasion. "People with type two diabetes run the risk of heart disease and stroke if they don't take care of it, and that starts with losing a good ten to twenty pounds. Take it off slowly, very slowly, a pound a week. Take it off fast, it'll come back fast. You can do it."

Words, mere words, until yesterday. There might have been a time, years ago in her fifties, during menopause, when depression came and life seemed meaningless, but today she treasured every aspect of living, and being healthy was an important part of that. She would, she must, do something about her weight, but Lord it was hard to get a grip, to shut that refrigerator door, to pass up a fresh, glistening doughnut calling to her from behind glass doors in its case in the market.

Aside from health worries, the fiddle and the song haunted her. Were they a figment of her imagination caused by confusion and stress? "Bob, will you buy me a cassette of 'Simple Gifts'?" she asked.

And when he brought it, she played the cassette repeatedly, seeking a clue, until she memorized the song. Gaining no insight at all from the words, Grace eventually shoved the cassette in the back of her pajama drawer and dismissed it from her mind.

In the days that followed, Grace complied with Doc Jones's prescription: plenty of bed rest, hot baths or showers, ibuprofen for aching muscles, and some little amount of walking each day. "We can't let those muscles atrophy now, Grace," he'd insisted. Enervated as she felt, she cooperated with Bob, who walked with her back and forth in the upstairs hall, but she refused to venture downstairs. The remainder of the days she spent propped in bed taking phone calls from Miranda, Charles, Brenda, Lurina, even Velma Herrill, who heard via her son Buddy about Grace's fall and the bridge washing away.

"Folks are sayin' you were clingin' to that bridge when it snapped," Velma reported. "And Bob jumped in with all his clothes and shoes right into that icy water to rescue you."

"No. I was well away from the bridge, in Lurina's house in fact, when it tore apart."

"Well, I'll be darned. Such stories you hear. I'll just be settin' that right with the gossips."

"Thanks, Velma," Grace said, understanding that Velma relished knowing more than others, having "gotten it directly from the horse's mouth" so to speak.

Brenda came the moment she heard and hugged Grace hard. "Thank God you're all right, and you didn't get smashed with that bridge."

"I was off the bridge and being well tended to when it went," Grace assured her.

Brenda sat on the edge of Grace's bed and shook her head. "You and Bob are quite the celebrities around Covington. You go down with the bridge. Bob rescues you. Heroic. The truth would disappoint everyone terribly."

"It would have been horrific going down with the bridge. The water was raging, filled with branches and heaven knows what else. Don't people realize how badly I'd have been injured, maybe killed?"

Brenda patted her hand. "Grace, dear, they don't think that far, just the heroics of it, no injuries."

"Thus are tall tales born," Grace said. "And to think I trusted oral history." Then she asked, "How was your holiday, Brenda? How's your mother?"

"Mother's fine, rested up now. She was so happy to have us, went out of her way with the tree and everything. The boys got lots of presents. We went to her church, Unitarian. Never been to one of those. The sermon was about how early Christians adopted pagan holy sites and festivals and made them into our holidays, and not a word about the baby Jesus. At the end they sang 'Simple Gifts.' You know the song?"

Chills started along Grace's spine. " 'Simple Gifts.' Yes, I know it." Several lines popped into Grace's mind.

> When true simplicity is gained,
> to bow and to bend, we will not be ashamed.

And then it struck her. She was ashamed of having diabetes. Every time she said the word, it stuck in her throat. Having diabetes implied a lack of self-control, a weakness of character. There was more to it, however. There was the incipient shame of being over-weight, something she thought she had long since gotten beyond. In that instant, a resolution took shape in Grace's mind, and a steel door lowered on appetite, on lust for food, on those cravings that sent her sneaking to the kitchen late at night. She could, she would lose weight. Weight loss would only benefit her, help control her diabetes. Her doctor had said that often enough. This disease could kill her, and life was too precious to aid and abet her own demise.

Grace would have told Brenda about hearing that song, and its meaning for her, but Brenda was dabbing at her eyes and speaking about Harold. "We went every year to a Christmas tree farm. We'd choose a tree that matched Molly's height each year. As she got taller, so did the tree." She blew her nose. "Mother's tree was huge. It took up too much of the living room. But what difference did it make, anyhow? With Harold gone, it was sad and lonely."

Grace listened, nodded, and commiserated. What else could she do? Brenda and Harold had been happy together, depended heavily on one another. It would take a year, maybe two or longer, and Brenda needed to tell and retell stories about their life. As long as she needed to do so, Grace would listen.

33

The Last Night of December

On the night of December 31, Mike, Maxwell, and Hank joined the Richardsons and the ladies for dinner at the farmhouse. During the meal, no one spoke of the millennium, or expressed a nonchalant attitude, or allowed his or her deepest concerns to surface. Only the many candles, thick ones and tall ones and some on the sideboard and on the table, suggested that the electricity could fail.

Grace served hot, rich vegetable soup, laced with tender bits of sirloin, and crusty homemade French bread. They spoke of mundane things, of the new dry cleaners in the shopping center, of a post office at the back of the newspaper and paperback bookstore, of Emily's plan for a garden at her new home. Occasionally Russell told some silly joke. After dinner, they retired to the living room, each one carrying an unlit candle or two, and set up bridge tables to play Scrabble and gin rummy. They talked little and sneaked frequent glances at the clock. Tyler fell asleep on the couch, his feet touching Grace's thigh.

At fifteen minutes to twelve, Max raised his wineglass. "To us. To the future, no matter what."

They toasted, set aside the cards and Scrabble boards, and fell silent. Emily nuzzled close to Russell. Tyler awakened and snuggled next to Grace. Max and Bob and Mike walked to the window. "Look, it's starting to snow," Mike said.

"It's gotten very windy," Bob said. "Your chairs that we pulled close to the house are rocking."

Hannah strode over to them and lowered the shades. "It's nearly time. Let's watch the ball come down in Times Square."

On the television, Dick Clark began his countdown, and the great globe of light began its descent. They hardly breathed. From the hallway, their clock, jarringly loud in the silent room, struck midnight and continued to do so past the moment when the globe reached its destination, and the crowd in Times Square roared its welcome. Had they watched television earlier, they would have seen Japan and Indonesia, Paris and London welcome the New Year with fireworks and jubilation. In the living room of the farmhouse on Cove Road, everyone sighed with relief and hugged one another as a reporter flashed back to midnight in Tokyo, Singapore, Calcutta, Frankfurt, and Belfast.

"I knew it," Hannah declared. "All that fuss and stocking up for nothing."

"*Mon Dieu*, but I'm so relieved."

"I must admit, I was more concerned that I let on." Bob squeezed Grace's hand.

New Year's greetings filled the air. When Max hugged Hannah, an innocent hug, she stiffened. He looked at her and pecked a kiss on her check. Remembering it was New Year's, she smiled and returned his good wishes. Amelia noticed that when Hank placed his arms about Laura to hug her, Laura drew back. Then, as if remembering the occasion, Laura stepped forward, hugged Hank briefly, and wished him a Happy New Year. Then she walked from the room. Amelia immediately followed her.

"Laura," Amelia called, "come on into the kitchen."

About to climb the stairs, Laura turned. In the kitchen, Amelia hugged her gently. "Happy New Year, dear," she said. "I know how hard it is this time of year."

Flinging her arms about Amelia's neck, Laura wept, and Amelia held her until the younger woman's grief was spent.

"I'm sorry," Laura said wiping her eyes and cheeks.

"Don't be," Amelia replied. "It wouldn't be normal at a time like this if you didn't feel sad and cry."

"Will I grieve for Marvin at these occasions the rest of my life?"

"For a time you will, and then less often, but every now and then something will trigger memories and pain, and you'll shed tears."

"Do you, still?" Laura asked.

"I do. Your mother does. We all do. It's life. Now, do you feel able to come back and share some champagne with us all?"

Laura shook her head. "I'd rather be alone. Marvin said it would be this way, the lights on and no cause for panic."

Back in the living room, Bob's glass was raised and he was making a toast. "May we all be blessed with good health and happiness in the year 2000, and may all our dreams come true."

"Here, here." Max lifted his glass and looked directly at Hannah, who flushed and looked away.

A half hour later, the men drifted off to their homes, except Mike, who lived on the south side of Asheville and hated driving in snow. Using the electric foot pump, Mike inflated one of the mattresses, and Amelia helped him put on the sheets and a blanket.

The lights were turned off and everyone in bed when Laura knocked on Hannah's door. "Mother, may I come in?"

Smugly satisfied at being right that nothing out of the ordinary would happen on December thirty-first, Hannah lay awake thinking about Max. Theirs was a professional relationship, and she wanted to keep it that way. At hearing her daughter's voice she flipped on the light by her bed. "Come on in."

Laura pulled a chair close. "I want to apologize for my behavior these many months and say how relieved I am about tonight. I'm glad to be here with you and the ladies."

"I'm happy you're here with us," Hannah replied. She wanted to yell it loudly and hug her daughter, but did not.

They sat in silence for a time, then Laura said, "It's still snowing. The world's so beautiful and calm when it snows. Makes me want to bundle up and go outside."

Hannah threw back her covers. "So let's do just that."

"Really? Oh, goody."

Swept along by a surge of youthfulness, Hannah felt forty again. Five minutes later, bundled in fur-lined boots, heavy coats, with thick woolen caps pulled over their ears, they stood in the foyer. As quietly as possible, so as not to disturb Mike in the living room, Hannah opened and closed the front door, and mother and daughter stepped onto the porch.

The wonder of it stifled words. Tufts of white decked the limbs of trees and shrubs. A comforter of white camouflaged the earth, merging driveways, lawns, and pastures with Cove Road. Red-roofed buildings floated like so many cherries on whipped cream. Bearded with snow, solitary and still, the vanes of Maxwell's windmill stood motionless. From a distance, a dog howled, startling them. Closer, a dog barked back. Moments later, from around the corner of Elk Road, a truck with bright lights glaring turned into Cove Road and lumbered past Number 70 and the women standing on the porch, past Cove Road Church, defacing and leaving behind scars as if from the lashes of whips in the snow. Finally, it turned left into the Herrills' driveway.

"Now what's that boy Brad doing out on a night like this?" Hannah said.

"I hate civilization," Laura said. "Out on the ocean, it's clean and pure."

Hannah thought about fish disappearing, whole industries dying, about the slime of pollution encased at the lowest depths beneath what appeared to be the pristine surface of oceans, coves, and bays. But she remained silent. Cold air stung her nose, and she covered it with her gloved hand. "Glad we had that time before the truck went by," she said. "Well worth getting out of a warm bed for."

Laura turned and hugged her, and Hannah found herself responding, hugging her daughter back and liking it. Laura's skin smelled of roses. Her breath was sweet, and the grief had, for a moment, vanished from her eyes. What a lovely girl she is, Hannah thought. My daughter chose to stay in Covington. Pride and pleasure swelled in her chest.

Eight days later, on January 9, an agitated Amelia and an animated Mike boarded a plane at Asheville airport. They would change flights in Charlotte, and arrive at La Guardia by midafternoon. Six days later, Hannah and Grace would return to meet a weary but starry-eyed Amelia at the Asheville airport.

"Well, tell us everything," Hannah prodded, as they walked to the baggage claim area.

Amelia stopped, clasped her hands across her chest, "New York City. *C'est manifique*, spine-tingling, humming with life. I'd forgotten how thrilling the city is. Everything was fabulous."

"After the theater, you hired a limo to pick you up?" Hannah asked.

She shook her head. "We walked. We found a delightful restaurant, and ate and talked, and after a while there were plenty of cabs, just like Mike said there would be." She grabbed their arms. Her eyes danced. "They loved my photographs. One reviewer wrote that when I photograph people their very essence jumps off the page, or something like that. Every one of them sold, imagine that, and for a good price too."

"Wonderful," Grace said. "I'm so proud of you."

Hannah was as pleased for Amelia and wished she could be more ebullient. Instead she quoted Grace, "Proud of you," and patted Amelia's shoulder.

They reached the baggage carousel, and after a few anxious minutes located Amelia's bags. Then, each one carrying a bag, they crossed the road to the short-term parking lot, loaded all into Hannah's old station wagon they called Nelly, and departed for Covington.

It was Amelia's moment. She chattered about her adventures in New York, her excitement at seeing her works hanging in a gallery, her elation at watching people stop and exclaim over her photographs. As they passed the Weaverville exit, she told of her initial disbelief, followed by a sense of quiet satisfaction and pride, when informed that all her photos had been sold, and the gallery owner asked for more.

"I thought I'd faint when he said they'd sold them all, every last one of them. And he gave me this check." She rummaged in her purse, couldn't find it, waved her hand, and said, "Later. I'll show you later. But just imagine, I have an outlet for my work in New York City."

They were turning off the highway now, taking the exit to Mars Hill. "The lights of Broadway. I got all dressed up, and guess what? Hardly anyone dresses. People even wore jeans to the theater. I couldn't believe it. But once the lights went off and the curtain rose, *mon Dieu,* it was magic." If Amelia had not been buckled into her seat, she might have floated out of the car window.

Except for the theater experience, Amelia did not speak of Mike, not until they were all in their nightclothes and settled in the living room for a last cup of tea and to wrap up the day. "*Je ne comprend pas.* Why Roger? When Mike said he was staying on, I was upset and frightened for him, for the three of them."

"People do things they're sorry for later," Hannah stated empirically.

"It's Charles I'm worried about," Grace said. "He's devastated. How will he ever come to terms with this?"

"You heard from him already?" Amelia asked.

"Immediately after Roger left for New York," Grace said.

"Unfortunately," Hannah said, "some people have to come to terms with much worse."

"This is a sad state of affairs. But at least Charles has his work, and he has you, Grace." Amelia took the last sugar cookie from the plate, held it up, and looked sadly at it. "What did Hamlet say when he held up that skull, 'Alas, poor Yorick'? I say, alas, poor cookie, last of your kind to please my palate." They laughed, glad not to be further embroiled in a discussion of the disturbing triangle.

"Not the last," Grace said, feeling confident about her ability to lose weight. "I've become indifferent to sweets. I'll bake again soon."

Amelia dunked the cookie and took tiny bites, savoring the taste. "I'll live," she said. "Don't do anything that makes this diet harder for you."

"I can't think of it as a diet. I've done that too many times, and I've felt so deprived I couldn't wait to cram forbidden food into my mouth. I'm going with Weight Watchers. Their new program lets you eat what you like, using points. So many points for each food, so many points a day."

"Laura and I will cook two days a week, if that'll help." Hannah said, then wondered if her daughter would even want to.

Grace almost said no and decided that anything Hannah and Laura did together was good. "That would help. Thanks."

"I've come to love the peach-colored walls in here. They glow in the light of the fireplace. Good choice, Hannah," Amelia said. "Remember how I worried it would be too much color and hard to live with?" She tossed her head and laughed lightly. "You know how conservative I am about color. White and off-white, and off-off-white's about as courageous as it gets for me."

As it had been nearly from the beginning, conversation among them flowed and often required no reply, or it veered in odd directions, or drifted into speculation. Hannah's mind fastened on the water garden and her concern that she had not made the canal wide enough. Just thinking about New York, the smells of grocery stores pungent with take-out foods, the delight of shopping at Bergdorf Goodman, the thrill when velvet curtains rose at theaters, was enough to fill Amelia with excitement. How would she ever settle down and readjust to Covington?

Amelia's eyes moved to Hannah in her worn, casual slacks and black-and-white checked shirt, legs stretched before her in her chair by the fire, and Grace in her sweats, sprawled contentedly on the couch. Their faces glowed pink in the firelight, and Amelia knew that it was not about location, but about people. People mattered. She smiled. "I love you both so much," she said. "New York's thrilling, great to visit, but my life's here and so is my work."

"Now that's nice to know. I love you too," Grace said, relieved that their household would not change. Once again, Hannah found herself in the uncomfortable position of wanting to say something she termed "mushy" and being unable to do so. "Ditto," she said.

34

At Bella's Park

Ragged loops of clouds caught in tall pines and oaks; fog curved about the waist of mountains. Hannah's impatience with winter had no limits. February had bounded in with snow and sleet, and too often the day's high dipped below freezing, confining her to the house or to her office at Bella's Park. Already she pined for the jade of April, ached for the smell of fresh-turned earth, longed for purple crocuses and Wordsworth's host of golden daffodils fluttering and dancing in the breeze. Not much longer, she consoled herself. It's nearly March.

Today, Max arrived in his truck to take her to the office. "Did you see the beautiful sketches Hank made of the gardens?" she asked as they drove down Cove Road. "The man's a genius. I described each garden to him, and he sketched as I talked, then he colored them. I've pinned them to a corkboard in my office. Days like this, I sit back and relish the possibilities." She turned to him. "Tell me spring's just around the corner, Max."

"Spring's just around the corner, my dear."

Hannah froze.

Max continued blithely, and Hannah assured herself that his use of "my dear" was merely a figure of speech. "I'll stop in and have a look at your sketches." He leaned forward squinting, then slowed as they approached a dark, shiny spot in the road. "Black ice," he said. "Never brake on black ice."

"I don't drive when it's like this," Hannah said, then stiffened as his thickly jacketed arm reached across to brace her as the truck slid to the right and came to a halt just short of the ditch. Max said not a word but shifted into low gear. Moments later they inched forward.

"Almost there," he said, ignoring the incident. "I'm glad you like Hank. He's the kind of young man I'd hoped Zachary would be."

"Where is your son?" Hannah asked. Zachary had left home shortly after his mother died and had not come home at Christmastime. At least he phoned his dad then, and again for New Year.

"That boy's got a wanderlust. Says he's working his way around the world on a freighter. For all I know, he may be in Singapore. Well, let him get it out of his system. These days it takes a long time for young people to find a direction, to settle down. I don't think he'll come home to be a dairy farmer, however."

"Would that upset you if he didn't?" Hannah asked, suddenly deeply aware of how lonely he must be in the big empty house across the road.

They pulled into the driveway of Jake Anson's old farmhouse–turned–office building. Max did not switch off the ignition, and the motor hummed. He stared ahead of him, and Hannah noticed the twitch at the side of his cheek. Max heaved a sigh and moved head and shoulders as if to shake off his concerns for his only child. "Long ago I relinquished such expectations. Zachary was very close to his mother." With a snap he turned off the key and unbuckled his seat belt. "Wait," he said, "I'm coming around to help you."

"Why? You think I'm made of crystal?"

"You're too tough for your own good, Hannah." In a moment he reached the passenger side of the truck and extended his hand. On the pavement she slipped. "See what I mean?" He laughed, and she did too, and did not refuse his proffered arm. Together they walked gingerly up the slippery walkway.

Laura used snowshoes to get to work that day. She had bought them recently at a sale in Asheville with the intention of visiting Wolf Laurel, the closest ski resort. Snowshoeing was the only sport she and Marvin had participated in during the long Maine winters. Being alone on a snowy trail would bring her closer to Marvin, she thought, yet the lethargy prevailed and she made no effort to carry the idea to its conclusion.

When she entered her office, the first thing she noticed was a sketch of a rough-hewn log cabin and its outbuildings centered on her desk with paperweights. Hank, she thought, appreciating his thoughtfulness as well as the high caliber of his drawings. He had obviously researched late-nineteenth-century log cabin construction. Laura studied the sketch.

There had indeed been a change in plans. Rather than develop an entire Appalachian settlement dating back to the 1700s, the drawings represented the first homestead of Harold Tate's ancestors, the Covingtons, and included the original homes, outhouses, corncribs, springhouses, chicken coops, and pork-curing houses. A site had been chosen for its proximity to the forest, whose rich harvest of trees had provided the Covingtons with chestnut and oak for logs and floorboards for cabins and other buildings, hickory for the best fire, locust for fence posts, walnut and maple for furniture.

Laura turned from her desk, pulled a cassette player from a deep canvas bag, and placed it on a table near the couch. Harold Tate had been revered as keeper of family lore, and Molly had questioned her father and recorded their conversations. She had loaned the tapes to Laura.

Pad and pencil in hand, Laura settled on the small couch at the other side of the room and pressed the Play button. Harold's voice, sometimes firm and clear, sometimes low and frail, issued from the machine.

"Our people came to these mountains back in 1881, more than a hundred years after the first settlers. We weren't the richest folks in these parts, nor the poorest. Earlier settlers with money had bought up the valleys where the rivers ran. We paid out hard cash for this land." He paused. "What especially you want to hear about, Molly girl?"

"Tell me about the log cabin your great-grandparents lived in."

Laura leaned forward, pencil ready, eager for details.

"That time, chestnut trees were plentiful in these mountains. They grew straight and tall, easy wood to work, and it lasted forever. They used it for logs for the cabins, plank for floors, strong fence rails, even for caskets. Back then, cabins didn't have many windows or doors. Walls were chinked inside and out. Stone chimney for heat and to cook over the open hearth. Grandma said they had a main room, kitchen, living and all, and two small rooms off of it, one for her parents, the other for the four children. The outhouse was turned nearly on its side but still there when I was a boy, and the old smokehouse too.

"Great-grandpa and his brother figured on growin' cotton, same as they done down in the flatland. Cotton don't like these hillsides. Then a big snow brought the cotton barn down, Granny said, and they built them a new barn, closed in for the sheep and horses, when she was a young woman with a baby on her hip." He was silent a moment.

Although Harold was gone, his shallow breathing mixed with the low whine of the tape saddened Laura. She hadn't known him, but from all the ladies said, he had been a good man, a kind man.

Molly's voice drew her back to the tape. "When they decided to settle here, where did they live while the men built cabins?" Molly asked.

A sharp intake of breath, and Harold replied, "In tents and the wagons. Way Grandma told it, she was a young un then, and it was spring. The air was sweet and fresh, and the meadows green with wildflowers poppin' up everywhere, same as they do today, and the mountains all about them. Why, the older folks thought they'd died and gone to heaven it was so much like home, like Northern Ireland." He stopped speaking for a moment. "They were Scots, you know, set- tled in Northern Ireland long ago. Scotch-Irish we're called.

"It was two families came, Patrick Arless and his brother, Samuel, and strapping sons among them. Once they set to cuttin' trees and rollin' them down the hill, they worked together to build cabins for both families." Again silence, before Harold coughed deep, gut-wrenching coughs.

"Let's stop for today, Daddy."

"Just you give me a minute, girlie. I'll be fine in a minute." And after a short time, he resumed his story. "Soon as the men felled the trees, the women planted Indian corn and potatoes among the stumps. Later, when they'd cleared fields, they sowed grains like oats and wheat and rye by hand. Later they harvested with a sickle and threshed with a flail, right in the center of that old cotton barn. When they had a harvest of corn, everyone husked the corn together. Those times, people worked together to get the job done. Of course, with the cornhusking, there was an incentive, a big jug of liquor hidden under that corn." He mumbled something Laura did not get and went on to talk about bedding.

"Granny showed me a straw mattresses she kept long after they switched to feather mattresses. Ticking stuffed with straw it was, and they'd lay it over rope nettin' attached to wood frames. Come summer, she said, they'd empty out the straw and sun it real good. 'Smelled sweet and clean,' she said, 'as the day it was made.'" He laughed.

"Did they eat venison from deer they killed in the forest?"

"No. They'd brought a cow or two for butter, but hogs were the meat of choice. Used every darn last part of a hog, feet, snout, all of it; cured and smoked a lot of it for winter." He chuckled. "There were rules. Even when I was a boy, we killed hogs at the right time of the moon, at the full of the moon."

"Why was that, Daddy?"

He chuckled. "If you didn't, when you cooked it you'd get shrunken meat and plenty of grease." He paused a moment. "Granny'd make scrapple. Haven't had scrapple in years."

Laura could hear him shift in his chair and his feet shuffle on the floor.

"What is it? I'll make it for you if you'll tell me how," Molly said,

Harold laughed and coughed again. "You wouldn't like doin' that, Molly girl." His speech slowed considerably now. "To start with, you'd have to get you a pig's head, remove the eyes, cut off the ears,

269

clean it good to get all the hair off it. Then you'd season and boil it 'til all the meat came off before you removed the bones from the pot. After that, you'd add cornmeal, cook it 'til it got thick, then pour it in a mold and wait for it to harden. Granny used to cut it in slices and fry it real brown. Sure was good."

Laura imagined Harold leaning back, closing his eyes, memory stirring the taste on his tongue, the smell in his nostrils. She thought about the actors/interpreters who would be employed to staff the buildings. How would some modern woman react to making sure all the hair was off and then boiling a pig's head until the meat came off the bone? What did it smell like while cooking? she wondered. Laura returned to listening to the tape.

"I'll make it, if you want me to," Molly said.

Now, that girl really loved her father, Laura thought.

"Thanks, Molly girl, but these days I couldn't hold it down in my stomach."

"You need to rest now," Molly said. "Next time you can tell me about things they did by the moon and planets, like planting."

"Ah, yes." Weariness permeated Harold's voice. "The signs. They're still important."

"Next time," Molly said, and the tape clicked off.

Downstairs in her office, Hannah sat back in her desk chair and viewed the sketches taped to the corkboard. Hank had widened the waterway in the canal garden, narrowed the walks, and widened the planting beds. His proportions brought symmetry to the whole. By removing the rocks and waterfall, the canal became, as it was meant to be, the focal point of the garden. She smiled. It was satisfying to direct others and not to labor herself. Max insisted on a crew of workers and a foreman who took orders directly from her. She wasn't used to giving orders and often had to stop herself from grabbing a rake, or reaching for the handles of a wheelbarrow, but she was learning, and it was getting easier. And, she had discovered, the men expected to be instructed.

"Think of yourself as the queen of Babylon. Your gardens will be renowned for generations to come," Max said.

That required a stretch of the imagination for Hannah, who was only too aware of the vagaries of wind and weather. "Climatic conditions in these parts don't allow for that kind of posterity," she replied. "Babylon had the advantage of an arid climate and shifting sands that preserved the things it buried."

"Well," he replied, "think of yourself as the queen of the Gardens of Covington."

"That reminds me," Hannah had said, "how about that sign at the entrance of the first arbor, where folks enter, WELCOME TO THE GARDENS OF COVINGTON?"

Max had bowed slightly. "Take care of it today. Your wish is my command."

She did like working with this man.

Someone knocked on her door. "Come on in," she called, anticipating Max or Laura, and was surprised to see Amelia lugging her tripod and camera bag. "I thought you'd like a record of your work. I'm here to shoot." Her arms framed the air. "I will make you a record of your gardens on film."

"Really? What a great idea, Amelia."

The idea had been Grace's. Earlier that day, as they sat in the kitchen over breakfast, Amelia had bemoaned the gray and cold of winter, and Grace had suggested that she use her time and talents to record the progression of the gardens. "It would be a marvelous gift for Hannah," Grace said, and Amelia responded with a big smile and a yes.

"I'll do it," she declared, and within an hour was off to Bella's Park to discuss it with Hannah.

Hannah listened, amazed at Amelia's proposal. "I'll create a visual record, start to finish. I'll take pictures every season and even shots of you and the men working." Amelia set down her equipment. "I'll begin with black-and-white film." She made sweeping circles with her arms. "Winter's grip on the land. Sleep time, death, and then regeneration." Her magnificent sapphire eyes sparkled. "In spring,

271

I'll use a diffuser on the lens to soften the shots: pale green shoots breaking above brown earth, sticky bronze leaves clinging to thorny rose stems, dogwood blossoms unfurling. Fuji film will bring out the vibrant colors of summer." She stopped and looked intently at Hannah. "What do you think?"

Hannah was taken aback by the whole proposal, by Amelia's enthusiasm and effervescence. Then her heart warmed. How good of Amelia to make this offer, and how splendid it would be to have a record of her work, especially afterward, when gardens sparkled with warmth and color and no one remembered the work involved. The men, she was sure, would appreciate the note taken of their contributions.

"What's wrong?" Amelia's face fell. "Don't you want me to take photographs?"

Hannah smiled "Yes, I do. Certainly do. I'm overwhelmed by the generosity of your offer. I realize how much time it'll take, and on a quarterly basis."

"It's my pleasure, my gift to you, Hannah." Amelia came to stand in front of Hannah's desk and leaned forward, placing her hands on the smooth shiny surface. "Don't you know what a role model you've been for me, showing me how to be independent and not be afraid to take a risk? There's no way I can ever thank you for your friendship, your tolerance, your sage advice that time with Lance, having him investigated." Seeing Hannah's face turn red with embarrassment, Amelia stopped and straightened up. "So, how many gardens are there?"

"Let me see. We're farthest along with the cottage garden, and the canal garden, and we've laid out the herb garden and next comes the children's garden."

"I'll start with the cottage and canal gardens, then."

"Now?"

"Now. Take me to them, give me a chair to sit on while I speculate. " She flipped her head and made a sweeping gesture with her arm. "And leave me to myself with my camera."

"Cold outside. Shouldn't you wait for a warmer day?"

"See?" Amelia dug beneath her shirt to show Hannah the several layers of clothing she wore. "I'm prepared."

"And I'm impressed."

Back in January after Roger and Mike's tryst in New York, and after an oddly sullen and taciturn Mike returned to Asheville, Charles had phoned Grace.

"Mother Singleton," he began in a high-pitched and almost delirious voice, "can you imagine, Roger's a new person since he came back from New York. Not that he says what happened, and I don't ask, of course. All I want, really, is not to be abandoned and to be treated kindly, and with respect, and he's doing that. If it keeps up like this, I can live with him and Mike, you know."

Caught off guard by this news, Grace hardly knew what to reply, so she said nothing and waited for Charles to continue. There was a long silence on the line. "You still there, Mother Singleton?"

"Yes, I'm here. You're all right, you say?"

"I'm fine. Roger hasn't said much, but you know what they say, actions speak louder than words. He's kinder and more caring toward me than he's been in months."

Grace's mind raced. Perhaps Roger and Mike had found their encounter disappointing. Had Mike confided in Amelia? But days later, when she questioned Amelia, Amelia professed to be puzzled.

"Mike's uncommunicative," she said. "Believe me, I've pried."

"Odd." Grace told Amelia about Charles's call.

Amelia tapped her finger against her temple. "Ah. I bet nothing happened. That's why Mike's been so closemouthed. His usual panache is gone and he's snappy and terse, all churned up, always in a hurry."

"We'll have to wait and see, then," Grace said.

From that time on, phone calls from Charles returned to their normal once a week. A lilt in his voice indicated that he was happy, and he chatted primarily about the business and his health, which had improved on new medication. With his increased vigor, he and

Roger were planning a Virgin Islands vacation in late February. When she spoke to Roger, he seemed consistently guarded, as if warning her to ask no questions. She didn't.

And then on that cold and frosty day in February, the day on which Amelia proposed to photograph Hannah's gardens, and Laura listened to Harold's tape, and after weeks of silent pouting and aggrieved behavior, Mike stopped by the house, and all hell broke loose.

35

Tangled Webs

Mike unraveled. Sitting on the floor of the ladies' living room, he wept and dragged his fingers through his hair, then stared, bewildered, at the long brown strands trapped between his fingers, as if to say, Where did these come from?

"What is it, Mike?" Grace asked, praying that Amelia or Hannah would walk through the door. Slipping from couch to floor, she eased her arm about his quaking shoulders. "What's upset you so?"

"Bastard, Roger." He wept softly in little gasps. "Forgive me, Grace. Roger's your son. I shouldn't have said that. Damn me."

"Roger's many things, good and bad. Tell me what happened." Grace longed to be up off the floor, for her legs, tucked beneath her, hurt—a residue of pain from her fall on the bridge. "Let's sit on the sofa," she said.

Mike pulled her to her feet, and a relieved Grace settled on the sofa and stretched her legs. Better. Much better. "Now," she said, "take your time. You haven't been yourself in weeks, not since New York. Maybe you'd feel better if you told me what happened and got it off your chest."

Attempting to remedy the toll that crying had inflicted on his face, Mike pulled a bandanna, one she had given him long ago, from the back pocket of his slacks, dabbed at his eyes and cheeks, and blew his nose. Then Mike untied his ponytail, smoothed back his hair, and rewound it. Red, swollen eyes brimming with melancholy peered at Grace over puffy lids. "Roger and I planned to meet in New York. I wanted it to be special, so I'd taken a room at the Plaza. Roger didn't show. I nearly lost my mind worrying maybe he'd been hurt, or killed." As Mike spoke, he yanked the bandanna taut. "By morning, I was totally a wreck, ready to call the police. When the knock came on the door, I was so confused I thought it *was* the police. In walked Roger, smiling. Can you imagine, Grace, smiling?" The bandanna became a tight wad in his clenched fist. He sniffled. "Smiling. My God in heaven, after the fright he gave me, the anguish he put me through."

"I'm so sorry," Grace said.

Mike buried his face in his hands, and when he lifted it, he whispered hoarsely, "Roger found someone else."

"What? He did what?" she blurted, leaning toward him, nearly toppling from the couch.

"He met someone on the train. Imagine. On the train. A pickup, a stranger." Bloodshot eyes spoke of disbelief, and then the sting of pain, a maimed, sick look settled into them.

"A stranger?" Grace recoiled.

"Sat right down in a chair and expounded in that cool, collected voice of his, as if he were a teacher and I were a fourth grader. I tell you, Grace, I froze. My whole body went cold." He wrapped his hands about his shoulders. "It's still cold. Roger said it was a foolish mistake for us to even have considered anything between us, what with Charles knowing and liking me and my closeness to all of you. Why didn't he think of that before raising my expectations? Bastard." He paused for a moment. " 'A tryst with a stranger,' he said, 'bore no significance.' Then he admonished me to silence. 'It'll be on your conscience, Mike,' he said, 'if Charles hears of this. The stress of it could push him right over into full-blown AIDS.' "

Mike's anger overwhelmed him, and he trembled uncontrollably. "*Me* responsible for Charles getting sick? Me? Roger's a damned fool. He'd assured me that Charles knew about our meeting, and they'd worked it out. Now, suddenly, if Charles gets sick it's *my* fault?" He shook his head vehemently. "I refuse to be the culprit."

The ache in Grace's knees subsided, and her head began to hurt. How convoluted this tale, how irresponsible the participants. Silently, Grace raged against Roger. What had he been thinking? A stranger? Dear God in heaven. Some stranger could have a disease, AIDS even. She studied Mike. A yellow stain, mustard perhaps, discolored his shirt. One of his shoelaces had come untied. Overall, he looked tattered, thin, too thin, and older than his fifty-plus years. One moment she pitied him; the next moment she disliked him intensely.

"I wasn't going to burden any of you with this. I shouldn't have told you, you of all people. He's your son. I'm sorry, Grace." Mike wiped his eye.

Grace refrained from touching or consoling him. Unwittingly, she edged away until she found herself jammed against the arm and back of the couch.

"I'm sorry about this whole thing." She heard the edge in her voice and regretted it. "Listen, Mike." Grace swung her feet to the floor and rose. "I need time to think about this, do you mind?"

Jumping to his feet, Mike tucked in his shirt, which bulged in disarray about his waist. He smoothed back his hair and stood there, his hands engaged in a seemingly unconscious game of tug-of-war with the bandanna.

Grace stifled the impulse to yank the bandanna from him. Instead, she moved toward the front door. "You go home, take a shower, and get some rest. If you have a tranquilizer, take it, but only after you get home. I'll talk to the others, and you and I will talk again."

"Must you tell Amelia? She'll loathe me."

"Amelia's worried about you." Grace swallowed hard. "She cares about you, Mike. She'd be hurt if she knew you told me and not her." She struggled not to repulse him when he hugged her at the door. Feeling meanspirited, recoiling from Mike was strange and alien to her. Why did she feel this way? He wasn't the one who had picked up a stranger. But Mike was the messenger, the bearer of potentially tragic news, and in that moment, Grace wished never

277

to see him again and felt relieved when his car disappeared around the corner.

✺

Morose and agitated, Grace reached into the freezer for ice cream. She brought the tin box, decorated with flowers and filled with cookies, to the kitchen table. How many points on her daily Weight Watchers chart would this cost her? Shrugging her shoulders, she reached for a cookie, then with a sharp movement threw the cookie back into the box. Slamming the cover shut, she returned it to its place on the shelf and shoved the ice cream back into the freezer. Grace ran from the kitchen. Frantic with worry, she had almost lost control. Damn her son and his irresponsible behavior, behavior anathema to the values she had sought to instill in him. All her married life, she had been a model of commitment and fidelity, never airing her frustrations or complaining about boredom and her disappointments with his father. She had adjusted, settled. That's what a decent person did.

Initially, his relationship with Charles had stunned her, but she'd adjusted and accepted them as a couple. She'd come to love Charles and believed that their commitment to one another was strong and reliable. How could Roger do this to Charles, to Mike, or worse yet, get involved with some stranger?

"What can I do?" she asked aloud. "What can I do?" and deep inside a voice said, "Nothing."

Nothing? Do nothing? When Charles shared every mood, every feeling? When the scar of rejection pained and marred Mike? When Roger walked a precipitous path? Do nothing? For the tenth time, Grace went to the kitchen window, hoping for the sight of Max's truck delivering Hannah home, or Amelia's car. It could be hours until they came. She could make herself sick with anxiety, eat herself into a sugar stupor, or she could bundle up and go find Hannah at Bella's Park.

Grace's car was in the shop. When she checked the thermometer on the porch, it registered thirty-seven degrees. Cold! But well layered with clothing, she could do it. Her mind resolved, Grace ran upstairs to change. Dying ladybugs snuggled together in a small V-shaped cluster in a corner where wall met ceiling. They came earlier and stayed longer every year, it seemed. Lifting her head to slip off her blouse, she pitied them huddled together, slowly starving to death. The warmth of the house had proved an illusion, offering false security to the tiny creatures. Soon they would tumble and scatter across her carpet to be vacuumed away.

Grace slipped on a silk undershirt. Over that she pulled on a short-sleeved cotton shirt and added a long-sleeved turtleneck. Downstairs, she shoved her arms into a cashmere sweater and then into her fleece-lined jacket, and slipped her feet with their merino wool socks into fur-lined boots. Soon she was walking briskly toward Bella's Park. The sky had turned bright, clear blue, and the fog had lifted. Walking proved invigorating. She appreciated the neatly painted fences and well-kept yards and homes. She appreciated that Cove Road boasted not a single broken-down car littering a yard, or a worn-out couch leaning on a porch, or crumbled barns and outbuildings as could be seen in spots along some country roads.

Velma Herrill's car passed, slowed, offered a ride. Grace shook her head and waved her on. Velma waved back. On Velma's rear bumper a sticker read STAND UP AND BE COUNTED. Grace pondered this and, seeking any excuse to interfere, wondered if the sticker was a sign sent as a reply to her question, What can I do? She could stand up and be counted by phoning Roger, being honest, expressing her fears, urging him to reconsider his behavior, making a pitch for fidelity. Or she could stop looking for signs, consider the bumper sticker coincidental and irrelevant, and mind her own business.

✺

Red cheeked from the cold and vigorously rubbing her hands together, Amelia sat in Hannah's office. Beside her on the floor her camera bag was unzipped, and her tripod, fully extended, leaned against a wall.

"Divine providence, both of you here," Grace said, pulling off her jacket.

"Must get a coat rack," Hannah muttered as Grace threw her jacket across the back of a chair. Then she saw the flustered, aggrieved look on Grace's face. "What's wrong?" Hannah asked.

"What isn't wrong?" Grace paced. Amelia, she thought, will be hurt and upset that Mike told me first, but here goes. "It's Mike."

Amelia's eyes flashed. "Mike? What's wrong? Is he hurt?"

"He's hurt, all right." And then Grace realized that Amelia meant physically hurt, as in a car accident. She raised her hand. "No, Amelia, not physically. He's fine." Then she blurted, "Roger wasn't with Mike in New York. He picked up some stranger on the train instead."

"Who picked up a stranger?" Amelia asked. "Mike?"

"No. Roger." Wearily, Grace sank into a chair by Hannah's desk, and her eyes appealed for comfort and for answers. "Why, why'd he do that?"

Hannah shrugged. "Cold feet, seeing as Mike's close to all of us?"

"But picking up a stranger."

"Really stupid," Amelia said.

Grace took a deep breath. "I've got to get hold of myself."

No one spoke for a time. Somewhere outside a door slammed. Heavy footsteps passed in the hall. Smoke from a pipe drifted in through the slightly open window behind Hannah's desk. She rose and shut it. "They smoke outside, and you never know when someone's lit up. Okay, now, Grace," Hannah said. "Take it from the beginning and tell us everything."

"Mike stopped in." She glanced at Amelia. "He was looking for you."

Amelia preened. Grace had stumbled on the right way to tell it. "He sobbed, couldn't wait, couldn't contain himself." Grace related his story in short, terse sentences as Mike had told it to her.

"I remember when I'd wait, and Lance wouldn't show up. I'd want to die, I was so miserable," Amelia said. "Poor, dear Mike."

"Juvenile, callow Roger," Hannah said.

Count on Hannah, Grace thought, to say it straight. "Exactly how I feel," she said.

Not to be outdone, Amelia said, "I agree with both of you completely. Stupid, stupid man."

"And Charles?" Hannah asked.

Loud voices and laughter came from the reception area. "Noisy office," Grace remarked.

"Never been this noisy before. Something's going on."

"Want to go find out what?" Grace asked, concerned to have intruded on Hannah's working day.

"No. This is more important."

Grace's heart warmed. Hannah put her first so often. Not too many people in life did that for you. "Thanks, Hannah," she said, reaching to touch her hand.

Amelia rose, came to where Grace sat, and hugged her. "I'm glad you were there when Mike came. I'll call him right away, poor dear. He must be crushed. He needs all the comfort he can get right now."

Relief washed over Grace. She could focus on Charles and Roger, and Amelia would take care of Mike.

From behind her desk, Hannah studied Amelia. "If anyone can help Mike now, it's you, Amelia. Don't think I haven't seen the way you've reached out to Laura, drawn her out of herself, helped her recover. You're been a good friend to her."

Amelia brightened. "She considers me a good friend?"

Hannah sat tall in her chair. She smiled. "Yes, Amelia, Laura considers you a very good friend, an important person in her life, and I do also. She's just upstairs if you'd like to step in and say hello before you leave."

"Upstairs? Yes, I'd like to see Laura's office. I'll go now. I'll leave my equipment here, okay?"

"Certainly. Turn left when you get off the elevator. Her office is at the end of the hallway."

The next moment, Amelia was on her way to see Laura.

Hannah swiveled her chair to face Grace. "And so, what are you intending to do? I know you. Your sense of righteous indignation's been aroused. You're not about to shuffle off quietly into the good night, are you?"

"How can I?"

"You risk the ire of your son, you know that?"

"I know that, but my sense of outrage is about to overwhelm me. It's odd, don't you think, that Charles says things are better than ever between himself and Roger. How can that be?"

"Maybe, Grace, he's come to terms with the situation. Isn't a casual fling better than a relationship with Mike? Mike isn't the kind for casual anything, you know that."

Grace nodded. "So you're saying I should cool it?"

"I'm suggesting you go slow, gather more information from Charles. Has Roger taken any more trips?"

"I don't think so, but what if the man he picked up lives near or even in Branston?"

"Don't let your imagination make you nuts, Grace. Listen, why don't you discuss this whole thing with Bob?"

Later that evening, Grace and Bob drove into Asheville for dinner. Traffic was light on Highway 19-23, but Bob kept to the speed limit, fifty-five. For once, she wanted to urge him to step on the gas, but didn't. It was five-fifteen when they reached the restaurant, early, but they wanted to avoid the rush with its attendant noise. Bob ordered steak. Grace chose salmon. The restaurant glowed in colors of rust and red. Bob told her that turnover of the tables was the main goal of color and he pointed to the maroon leather booths that he said mitigated against long, lazy dinners and encouraged folks to eat fast and leave.

Once seated, Grace said, "I need to discuss something with you."

He dipped a chunk of hot, crusty bead in herbed olive oil. "Shoot."

The waitress set a tall, frosted glass of beer on the table, and Bob settled back, sipped the beer, and gave Grace his undivided attention. "What's the problem, sweetheart?"

Grace told Bob everything she knew about her son and Charles's situation. When she finished, he uttered a short whistle. "Well, I'll be darned. A hell of a thing. You gotta feel sorry for Mike."

She did, and she didn't, but refrained from commenting. "What shall I do, mind my own business? I feel that I must talk to Roger. I'm terrified for him."

Bob grew philosophical. "Life's not easy. None of us gets through it unscathed, that's for sure. In a battle you expect bullets coming at you. In life you haven't a clue what's headed your way."

"I tried so hard to teach Roger, show him what was right and honorable and good."

"Relative terms, honey. Loyalty's big on your agenda. Someone else thinks it's a waste of time and isn't loyal because he or she doesn't expect it back. Maybe sometime or other they've been hurt."

"But infidelity hurts so many people. It can't be right," Grace said.

He sipped his beer again, then set the glass on the shiny wood surface. "What would you say if I told you I'd been unfaithful to my wife, rest her soul?"

She drew back. "I don't believe that. You're too good a man, too sensitive about other people's feelings."

"You know she wouldn't join me at any of my posts overseas. My wife bought a home in Atlanta and made a life for herself there. We had an understanding. We didn't ask each other questions."

Grace stared at Bob. Her mouth tasted bitter and tight as if she'd sucked a lemon. "What are you saying?"

"That there were other women."

"Women? Who? How many?"

"Does it matter? It was a long, long time ago, and we didn't have to worry about AIDS then."

"Please, tell me. Who? How many?"

He sighed. Just then, the waitress brought their salads.

Loud laughter rippled from what seemed a family group at the table nearby. Grace cringed. The wooden chair suddenly seemed hard and uncomfortable. "Tell me," she urged, wanting to know, yet afraid to know.

"Never prostitutes," Bob said scowling. "A nurse on the base, a colonel's secretary, once a blues singer in Paris. I was up-front with all of them. They knew I was married, had a kid, and had no intentions of changing my status. We kept it casual. These things happen in wartime. You look appalled, Grace. Close your mouth."

Grace closed her mouth. "I'm shocked, not appalled. Did you ever fall in love with anyone?"

"You really want to hear all this? I don't want you berating me about it some dark sexy night." He chuckled.

"Bob, be serious. I'm trying to understand what's going on with Roger."

"And I'm your case study?" He chuckled again and reached over to squeeze her hand. "I know, honey. You're essentially a tolerant person, live and let live. This thing with Roger's unnerved you. I've every faith you'll figure it out and come to terms with whatever's going on."

"You did fall in love, then?"

Bob sobered, finished his salad, and nodded. "Once. I flipped for a gal twenty years younger than I was. Good sense informed me I was hankering for my lost youth. It would never have worked. Hell, the woman wanted to ski and party every weekend. I couldn't keep up with her."

"Was it painful to break it off?"

"Painful as hell, even with my head telling me it was for the best. And then Russell got sick, meningitis, and I flew out of Munich posthaste. My connections got Russell the new drugs he needed and saved him. Notice how sometimes he thinks slowly? That's the residue he's been left with."

"Thank God. He could have died," Grace whispered.

"But he didn't. And I knew then that I'd never risk losing my son, especially not to another man, a stepfather. He had to know he had a dad, even if I wasn't home much of the time."

"Your wife didn't find someone else in all those years?"

"We had an agreement. She lived her life, did what she wanted. I asked only discretion where Russell was concerned. Actually she never had much of a sex drive. She was a career women and all wrapped up in work. Work became her lover."

Grace lifted both hands. "Don't tell me any more. That's enough to digest."

284

"People are just poor little creatures on a big, blue planet trying to be happy, trying to dodge and duck bits and pieces of the asteroids of life. Sometimes a big one hits them. You never know how you're going to react to a situation. Who'd have thought we'd end up like this, unwed and lovers?"

Grace's hand flew to her mouth, but her eyes twinkled. "Bob, stop that."

"It's going to be all right, honey. Roger may be going through a midlife crisis. From what I judge seeing them together, they're quite devoted to one another, like an old married couple. They'll work it out."

"But if Roger sleeps around, he could get AIDS."

"I guess he could." Their dinners sat before them. "Let's eat, then we'll go back to my place, and you can give Roger a call if it'll make you feel better." The restaurant was filling up now, and the noise level rose as a party of twelve entered and climbed the stairs to a private dining room above.

Later in Bob's apartment, the upbeat voice of Charles answered their phone. "Mother Singleton, how good to hear from you. We were going to call you. We've got a weekend coming up in April, and we're coming to Covington."

"What about your Caribbean trip?"

"Who's keeping the calendar in your household? We've gone and come back. Had a fantastic time. Oh, what glorious water, the colors amazing, and warm as a bathtub in February. I loved it. You'd love it. You and Bob should go down." He went on and on, telling Grace about renting a sailboat, about the islands stretching between St. Thomas and St. John, about Caneel Bay resort on St. John. "We had lunch there. Without a doubt the most scrumptious luncheon buffet ever."

Grace hesitated, then asked, "So things are good with you and Roger?"

285

"Better and better all the time. You know he changed his mind about Mike, don't you?"

She hesitated. To lie or not lie. "No, Mike's said nothing about anything." Grace crossed her fingers and said a silent prayer for forgiveness. What could she say? Her eyes lighted on a smudge on the wall, just under an Ansel Adams print of El Capitan, which she had bought and had framed for Bob for his last birthday. Phone in hand, she moved to the wall, and with the sleeve of her blouse rubbed the smudge.

"Roger said Mike took it pretty well, stiff upper lip thing, and they hadn't started anything anyway. I hope we can still all be friends."

Cockeyed optimist, Grace thought, turning from the photo. Ignorance *is* bliss. But then, she hadn't heard a lilt in his voice, or so much enthusiasm and zest in months, and she was glad for Charles and prayed for Roger to remain healthy.

"Oh, there goes the other phone," Charles said. "Business. Got to go. Talk to you soon. Love you." And Charles hung up.

"Why are you staring at the wall?" Bob asked. He stood in the doorway of the kitchen, holding a tray with two cups of tea. "Well, tell me, what'd they say?"

Grace took the tray, and they moved to the couch. "I only spoke to Charles. He said things are great. They had a wonderful vacation in the Virgin Islands and are coming for a weekend in April. Know what he said? That Roger told him that he did not have an affair with Mike."

"That's good, isn't it?"

"Nothing about picking up someone on a train. I'm so scared for him, Bob."

"They'll be here soon, and you can corner your son and have a good heart-to-heart." Bob sat back and drew one leg across the other. "Maybe baby Melissa Grace will have arrived by then."

Grace whirled about, her eyes dancing. "They've finally chosen a name?"

"Emily called just before we went for dinner."

"I must phone them. It's a beautiful name, Melissa."

"I said, Melissa Grace."

"Grace. For *me?*"

"Yes, they're going to name her after you."

Tears filled Grace's eyes, tears of a deep, sweet joy. "That's so good of them, but they don't have to do that. Won't Ginger be upset?"

"Well, they could name her Agnes for Emily's mother."

"Agnes? So that's Ginger's real name." Laughter came in ripples, and soon she and Bob laughed so hard they doubled over and held their stomachs. Tears smudged their cheeks.

36

By the Moon and the Planets

As winter puffed and huffed and blew its way along, Laura learned much from Harold's tapes: how the settlers cured ham, how they made toys and clothing and tools and musical instruments, and she came to admire their tenacity and ingenuity.

Harold spoke of home remedies, some of which amazed and set Laura to laughing. To bring down fever from pneumonia, it was recommended to soak a cloth in lard and quinine and lay it upon one's chest, and drink butterfly weed tea with whiskey.

She noted a smile in Harold's voice when he said, "For kidney trouble, red adder tea was the rule, and eat two pokeberries a day for several days."

Athlete's foot required that the afflicted person tie a wool string about his toe and walk in fresh cow dung. "It was widely known," Harold told his daughter, "that gunpowder and sulfur took away itching."

The only remedy familiar to Laura was the use of kerosene or turpentine for cuts and inflammation, and she knew of that only because Lurina had told Grace about her Aunt Emma, whose husband doused her open wound with kerosene. Aunt Emma had died of blood poisoning. I must tell Mother this one, Laura thought, as she listened to Harold explain to his daughter that chewed tobacco put on chigger bites relieves itching.

"Disgusting," Molly had exclaimed.

But it was the information about planting by the signs, and with the moon, that most interested Laura. She learned that with apples and pears, bruises won't rot if the fruit is picked in the old or waning of the moon. That was certainly worth trying. And crops harvested in the waning moon would keep longer.

"Preserves and vegetables should be canned in the last quarter of the moon," Harold said. "And crops planted in the earth sign Taurus or the water sign Cancer tolerate drought best. Tobacco or beans are best planted as the moon is growing, while underground things, like potatoes and peanuts, need to be planted as the moon decreases. Some of these old-time garden rules ought to be preserved." Harold coughed repeatedly before he was able to continue. Finally, he said, "I swear, if your corn makes flowers on bright nights of the moon, you'll get better pollination, 'cause insects can see better." He sighed then and coughed again. He paused, perhaps for a drink, and then his voice grew clearer as he spoke of miscellaneous things his grandparents did according to the signs and the moon.

"They'd never paint a house if it wasn't in a dry sign like Leo or Aries," he said, and Molly laughed.

"But who's got time these days to think about such things? You want to hear tell about all this stuff, Molly girl?"

"Yes, and about making soap, and keeping sheep for wool, and carding and dying and weaving cloth, and building looms, and about quilting bees and how they tanned hides."

"Lord be, Molly girl, you best go to the library and get you some of those *Foxfire* books. They tell all about life in the old days."

Laura wrote that name down.

After that, Harold related mainly personal stories about his family: siblings fighting and not speaking for years, stillborn babies, a cousin jailed for shooting a man over a rabbit, and other incidents meant for the ears of his daughter and grandchildren, and not strangers.

37

Russell, Emily, and Tyler Richardson
Announce the Arrival of...

✈ Emily delivered two weeks ahead of schedule. Shrieking, as if her life depended on it, Melissa Grace joined her family in this world on March 22 of the new millennium. Labor had been short, two hours, and mother and daughter were resting comfortably when Grace and Bob hurried into the hospital room, their arms brimming with flowers.

Russell had phoned his dad at home. Bob dashed to the house on Cove Road to pick up Grace. She'd been spring-cleaning closets, getting ready for a trip to the Salvation Army.

"Melissa Grace is here," Bob called from the bottom of the stairs.

Grace dumped shoes and boxes on the floor and ran downstairs. Bob grabbed her waist, whirled her about the foyer and into the living room until, out of breath, she begged to stop. And later, when they arrived at Emily's room in the maternity ward, Grace burst into tears at the sight of the baby's sweet, pink, puffy little rumpled face.

"Isn't she beautiful?" Emily held the infant toward her. "Hold her, Grandma Grace."

All of Grace's worry about not really being part of the Richardson family because of her unmarried status vanished. Grace snuggled six-pound Melissa Grace close to her heart, peered into the tiny, scrunched eyes, and fell immediately in love. "Little Melissa. Beautiful baby," she cooed. "You're the most beautiful baby I've ever seen."

A commotion in the hall, a loud, imperious voice demanding, "Where is my daughter?" announced the arrival of Ginger Hammer. Behind her Martin walked tentatively as if he were about to totter off a wall. "Why's her face so red and wrinkled?" Ginger studied the baby in Grace's arms, then pulled back. "You weren't wrinkled like that, Emily, when you were born."

"Melissa's a perfect, beautiful baby," Russell said, stepping between his wife and her mother.

"Not to worry," Bob said. "Week or so every last little wrinkle will be gone."

"Well, she certainly doesn't look like *our* side of the family," Ginger retorted.

Sunshine streaming into the room seemed to diminish. It takes no time at all, Grace thought, for Ginger to turn a bright day gray. The woman's a human vacuum cleaner sucking joy from the air as a vacuum sucks dust from a rug.

"When do you go home, Emily?" Grace asked, attempting to divert attention from Ginger's criticism.

"Tomorrow." Tears pooled in Emily's eyes. She cuddled the baby whom Grace had returned to her arms. Russell settled on the bed alongside his wife, and Emily's head dropped onto his chest. "We're thrilled she's a healthy little girl," she said.

Fiercely protective of mother and child, anger flared in Grace. She'd get Ginger out of here if it proved to be the last thing she did. Taking Ginger's arm, Grace propelled her toward the door. "Did you win your Scrabble tournament? Did you meet your old high school friend you located on the Internet? Such a busy lady. You must be exhausted just having gotten home. I'm sure you have a million things to do."

Martin's eyes found Bob's. A smile touched the corners of his mouth as he followed his wife out of the door.

"You're the only person, Grace," Ginger said with a whine, "who understands just how hectic my life really is."

292

"Well done, Grace, and thanks," Russell said when Grace reentered the room.

"How do you handle her like that?" Emily asked. "You saved us all."

"I divert her attention to things she's interested in," Grace said. "Now." Grace stretched out her arms. "Please, can I hold our baby again?"

The next day Amelia and then Hannah and Laura visited Emily and met Melissa Grace. They kept their visits short, for the baby was fussy, and Emily was struggling to breast-feed. After leaving the hospital, Hannah and Laura stopped for lunch at a Chinese restaurant in Asheville.

"I'll have good old-fashioned chicken chow mein." Hannah handed the menu back to the waiter.

"Cashew chicken for me," Laura said. At eleven-thirty the restaurant was quiet and uncrowded. Laura spread her napkin on her lap and leaned toward her mother. "I almost made a fool of myself and cried when I saw the baby," she said.

"You wanted to cry?"

Laura nodded. "Still want to. I'm over forty, and what have I to show for it? No husband, no children. What am I going to do with the rest of my life?" Her chin quivered. Pretending to wipe her mouth, she pressed the napkin hard against her jaw. Her distress lasted a moment, and then she regained control.

Laura's unhappiness devastated Hannah. She wanted to help, to offer her daughter hope. "You have time yet, Laura. Seems to me that we're constantly in the process of becoming. If we don't create change, it's foisted on us. Maybe we're intended to change, to reinvent ourselves. You're at a plateau . . ."

Laura bristled. "Why do you have to be so pedantic, Mother? Why can't you just listen and not try to fix things? I hate plateaus. They're barren wastelands. Too much empty time to think."

"That's one way to look at it." Hannah felt like a bumbling idiot.

293

She'd best keep her mouth shut. But then, she thought, what was the point of her lifetime of experience and hard-won insights if she didn't at least try to pass some modicum of them on to her daughter? Laura had been receptive to her when she'd shared her love and loss of Dan Britton. It had been the bridge, a narrow bridge, but one on which they'd met each other halfway.

At that moment, their lunches arrived, and they shifted in their chairs, sprinkled soy sauce, stirred rice and chicken and vegetables, and began to eat. Hannah's mind raced. She could tell Laura that having children was overrated. But that would refute all the enthusiasm following the birth of Melissa Grace. Truth was, you never stopped worrying about and hurting for your children, and their children. A great big circle of joy, yes, but a huge circle of pain and sleepless nights when you worried and wept for them. No, she'd best leave children out of this.

Suddenly, Hannah remembered a poster tacked above her desk when she worked for the chiropractor: HAPPINESS IS FOUND ALONG THE WAY, AND NOT AT THE END OF THE ROAD.

"It's all in the doing," Hannah said, setting down her fork. "Meaning comes from the living and doing."

"Work? Is that what you mean? What if you hate your work?" Laura demanded. In that moment, with her face set in tight lines and her eyes narrow, all her softness and beauty faded.

My daughter's dislike of me is just under the surface, Hannah thought, feeling pained. "Have you ever stayed at work you hated?" Hannah asked.

"Well, no. I haven't, actually."

"Do you like your work now?"

Laura's shoulders rose fell. "It's becoming interesting, as a matter of fact."

"So?"

Laura bristled. "It's all of my life I'm referring to, not just that one section. I don't want to be happy, to create a life without Marvin, don't you understand?"

"Yes, I think I do."

"Well, then. Let me wallow in self-pity."

Hannah's body tightened. With all the self-help, mother-daughter books she'd been reading lately, why couldn't she get it right? Why couldn't she not advise and only empathize. "I'm sorry, Laura. It hurts me to see you unhappy."

"We're all unhappy sometimes. You said so yourself."

"Yes, but a mother's unhappy for herself and unhappy when her children are."

"Don't be for me. I'll be all right."

They finished lunch in silence, and on the drive back to Covington, Laura said, "I was rude. I'm sorry. I didn't mean to upset you. Sometimes my tongue runs away in my mouth."

Hannah merely nodded. To the west, the sky glowed rose and gold. "The sunset's especially glorious this evening."

"Like sunsets out on the ocean," Laura said, "and it makes me want to cry for Marvin."

Several weeks later, in late April, the dogwood trees burst into bloom, followed closely by azaleas, and Charles and Roger arrived for their weekend in Covington. Grace had prepared chopped liver for Roger, and a toad-in-the hole casserole for Charles, and left both in the refrigerator in their apartment. After settling in, they phoned to thank her. Charles said he felt a cold coming on, and Roger asked if she were available and alone. "I'd like to talk to you," he said.

Icy fingers scurried along Grace's arms and neck. What in God's name would he tell her? "I'm here alone," she replied.

"I'll get Charles some tea and see that he's comfortable, and then I'll be over."

Fifteen minutes later, Grace watched with rising anxiety as her tall, handsome son parked the car and strode toward the farmhouse. Moments later, she opened the door for him and hugged him. Oddly, he did not pull away, as he was wont to do.

Roger declined tea and taking her arm, directed her to the living room, where they sat in two armchairs near the fireplace.

"I just hate what you've done to me," Roger began.

295

What now, dear God? Grace wondered. "What are you talking about?" she asked.

"I'm talking about loyalty and morality and all that crap."

Grace's heart shriveled. She pressed the soles of her shoes firmly on the carpeted floor. "Please explain that, Roger."

He smiled and shifted toward her. "You taught me that loyalty was a virtue to be desired. You modeled kindness and morality." He turned gruff. "Well, let me tell you, Mother, it doesn't apply to the world of work. It's damned tough out there, dog-eat-dog, that kind of thing." His voice grew softer. "It does, however, apply to relationships, especially long-term relationships."

She waited, hands clasped tight in her lap. The room grew warmer, too warm. A line of perspiration filmed her upper lip. "Why are you telling me this?" she asked.

"At first, on the train from Philadelphia to New York, I was filled with anticipation and excitement. Then, as the miles ticked by, I started thinking about Charles and our life together, the good years we've had, and I thought of you and Dad. I know life with Dad wasn't easy. He was a good man in the sense that he wasn't a drinker, he always provided for us, but he was taciturn and self-centered and not given to displays of affection.

"When he got sick, you rose to goddess stature the way you girded yourself with resolve, set aside the past, and cared for him. You moved past resentment, past his selfishness and indifference, to his humanity. Charles hasn't a selfish bone in his body. He's loved me, done for me, worried over me like a mother hen. I had to ask myself, Am I like Dad? Am I self-centered and callous? Can I hurt Charles so deeply? Suddenly I realized it was you, not Dad, I wanted to emulate."

Roger passed the sleeve of his shirt across his brow and smiled somewhat tremulously. "It was stupid of me to tell Mike I'd picked up someone on the train. I should have leveled with him. He'd probably have understood and not been so devastated. That was cruel of me, poorly thought out, but then I'd sat in a bar all night, and I was tipsy as hell. I feel terrible about it."

Grace listened with mixed emotions: surprise, confusion, wonder, joy, relief as she tried to make sense of what he was saying. "You didn't pick up a stranger?"

"You think I'm crazy? I'd never do that."

"My God, I worried so."

"You knew all this? Mike told you? You, my honest mother, said you didn't know anything." Roger laughed. "Good to know you're human like the rest of us."

Reaching over, she pounded her fist on his leg. "Roger, you scamp. I'm so relieved on every count, and happy for you and Charles." Her eyes clouded. "Mike. You must set it right with Mike. He's devastated. It was many weeks before he could even bring himself to tell us."

"I was an damned fool the way I handled the whole thing. Awful. How can I make it right with Mike?"

"Tell him the truth. He'll be able to handle the truth. Rejecting him for some stranger really crushed his ego."

"I can't do it with Charles around. He doesn't know I told Mike that story. Can you arrange for Mike and me to meet somewhere? Maybe you could visit with Charles while I do it, maybe take him over to see Hannah's gardens?"

"For this cause I'd lie, do whatever I have to."

"Thanks, Mother. I thought you'd know how to fix this. You always do."

I always do? She wondered at his words. She never knew he trusted her, respected her opinion or her values. Her life felt justified somehow and more meaningful. Thank God, she prayed silently, for letting me live long enough to hear these words of appreciation from the lips of my son.

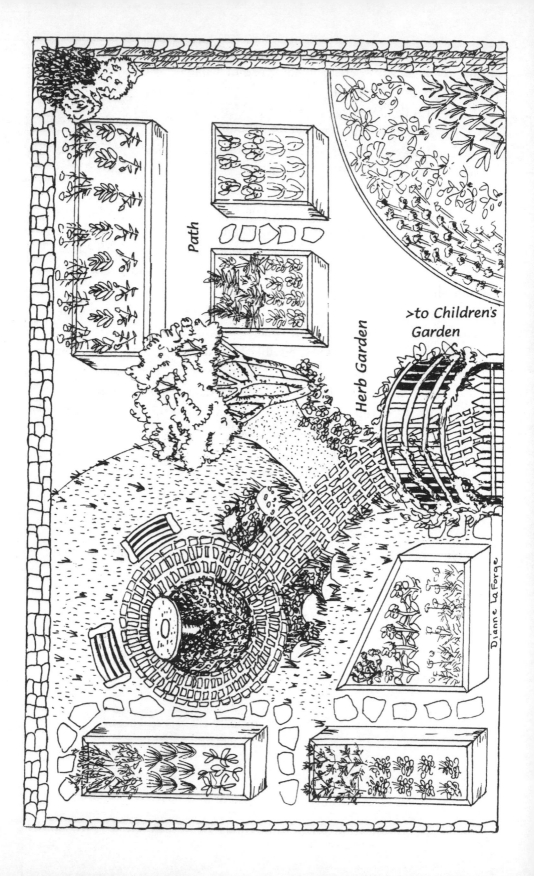

Path

Herb Garden

>to Children's
Garden

Dianne LaForge

38

A Walk in the Gardens of Covington

The moment Roger left, Grace phoned Mike. "Please, can you come by this afternoon?" Waiting for him to reply, she nibbled at a fingernail.

"Sure," he said, "you have a problem?"

"Yes," she lied. "I've decided to redo my bedroom. I wondered if you'd help me with it, you have such good taste."

His voice brightened. "Just what I need to divert my mind. I'll be there at two, that good?"

Grace's shoulders, neck, the muscles in her face relaxed. "Perfect. And thank you." Now to warn Amelia, Hannah, and Laura not to come home. A quick call to Hannah at the office took care of all three, for Amelia was shooting in the gardens. "So I'm going to bring Charles to see the gardens, okay?"

"I'd be delighted to see him. I'll have Cokes, and maybe Mary Ann can rustle up a dip and crackers for us. It'll stretch the time."

"Thanks, Hannah. That sounds great."

🌿

"How many gardens did you say Hannah's finished?" Charles asked as they drove down Cove Road. "Oh, do slow down, Mother Singleton." He twisted his head to look back at the yard about the church. "My Lord, look at those dogwoods and azaleas. They're gorgeous. We won't have them until next month."

"Spring is such a hopeful and promising time," Grace replied. Then she said, "Hannah has planted two of the gardens already, and the herb garden's in process, as is the children's garden. The kids from her class at Caster Elementary are helping plan that garden. In fact they're meeting about it this week."

"Smart idea. If they help create it, they'll appreciate it, talk it up with the other kids."

"It's exciting to see things transformed."

He chuckled. "It surely is."

Charles looked well. His cheeriness lifted Grace's spirits, which were in a tumult worrying about Mike, who had arrived to find her leaving and Roger in the house. Had she compounded the problem? Mike looked hurt and angry with her when he saw Roger there. But he had stayed. Oh, let Roger say the right things. Let Mike feel better. Let Mike understand her intention and forgive her.

They walked to the office, and Charles raved about the pink azaleas blooming alongside a variety of small, violet-flowered rhododendrons. "This is stunning," he declared. "Any fragrance?" He bent to smell them.

"No fragrance," Grace said. "Sorry."

Perched behind her tall desk, Mary Ann welcomed them with her bright smile. "Grace, don't you look lovely today. Rose is a such a becoming color for you."

Grace smoothed her blouse.

"Nice ponytail," she said to Charles.

"Nice smile," Charles replied.

"I found a cheese ball sprinkled with nuts in Mr. Maxwell's office fridge. Sometimes he has something like that for lunch. I'll replace it for him. I put this one in Miss Hannah's office. Enjoy." Mary Ann smiled her wide, happy smile.

Grace pointed out a large framed watercolor painting on the wall. The roof of the farmhouse in the painting glowed copper in the setting sun. "Recognize the building?" she asked Charles.

He shook his head.

"It's this office before Maxwell bought the place. Bella painted this just before she died."

"It's stunning," Charles said. Hands on hips, he studied the painting. "She had a lovely, light touch."

"She was a lovely woman. Hannah and I had the opportunity to spend some time with her the weeks prior to her death." They turned from the painting then and meandered out to the patio and through the arbor. A flush of green leaves had birthed along the stems of the wisteria vine. Soon lavender flowers would hang in clusters.

In the cottage garden, the smell of freshly turned soil rose to greet them. Already there was color, tall blue-purple hesperis dancing alongside mustard yellow Stella d'Ore daylilies. Delicate sprays of brilliant orange geum enhanced the blue-purple hesperis. Tiny green leaves dangled from the sprawling stems of pink roses, which climbed onto trellises positioned every eight feet along the brick walls of the garden. In the center of the garden, a bucket had been attached to a thick rope that was wound about a bar above the well.

"A wishing well?" Charles asked.

"Yes. It's got a false bottom and catches pennies through a grate. Got a penny?"

Charles fished in his pants pocked and brought out two pennies. "One for you," he said. He leaned over the well, shut his eyes tight, and threw his penny. "Now you," he said.

Grace closed her eyes. What did she want? A wish was important and must be considered and savored. Then she knew. She would wish that Tyler would love little Melissa Grace and not be too jealous. That the baby would grow into a beautiful child. That she would be a joy and a blessing to her family. Three wishes. Choose one. Tyler was, after all, her little love, and she wanted him to feel secure with all the attention a new baby was bound to receive. The coin rolled from Grace's fingers to plink and join Charles's coin. She smiled at Charles, took his hand, and led him through another arbor, past daylilies and irises to the canal garden.

This was a surprise, even to Grace, for the canal had been widened and the waterfall removed. Wrought-iron benches, secured at the edges of the walks, stood at intervals the length of the canal. Behind the benches, in deep loam-filled beds, miniature bamboo formed a backdrop for wide-leafed tropicals. Grace recognized calla lilies and colorful grasses. Palms, transported from a greenhouse in roomy clay pots, lined the planting bed and suggested a languorous, tropical scene. In the center of the canal, amid pots of papyrus and lilies also transferred from the greenhouse, sculptured metal fish leaped with wild abandon above the water.

For a time, they sat on one of the benches. "It's so quiet and peaceful," Charles said. "Hannah's gardens are wonderful, a haven for visitors. If I lived in Covington, I'd be here every few days." After a time, Charles rose. "Let's go to the right, over there, through that arch," he suggested.

They moved through a short arbor, which in June would explode with colorful clematis vines, and found themselves in a garden whose paths twisted and turned around planting beds built on stands thirty or so inches above the ground. These planter beds brimmed with tiny labeled plants. Charles leaned over to read a label.

"Rosemary, basil, parsley. It's an herb garden, Grace." He moved from raised bed to raised bed. "There are several varieties of basil in this bed, and also of rosemary. Here are chives." He held up a label, which he then reinserted behind the tiny leaves. "Garlic, chicory, mint, thyme, coriander. What doesn't Hannah have here?"

Hannah's voice sounded from the archway leading from the herb garden. "Put it over here. There's more sunlight."

"Hannah directing the men," Grace said. "I think she's come to love it. Max calls her the queen of Covington gardens. She protests, but I think she loves it."

"Marvelous," Charles said, "to be able to live out her gardening fantasies."

"And all because of her kindness to Bella in those last weeks of her life."

Charles drew close to Grace and slipped an arm about her shoulders. "You never know, do you, what door will open, or what small kindness might lead to something wonderful."

302

Grace wondered if Charles was leading up to talking about Roger's renewed commitment to their relationship, but this was not the time, for Hannah's voice grew louder, and moments later she stepped into the herb garden. Amelia trotted behind her, followed by a slim workman with sandy hair and dark sunglasses wrapped about his eyes. He toted her camera bag and tripod.

Perfect, Grace thought. A helper. It's actually just what Amelia needs, help with her gear when she climbs hills and shimmies down to streams.

"Well, hello," Amelia said, her voice warming when she spotted Charles. She hugged him. "Darling, you look well."

"Amelia, love, you're the picture of health yourself. I swear you look younger every time I see you."

A wide smile spread across Amelia's face. "I've been having such fun shooting Hannah's gardens. Imagine such lovely gardens in a little old place like Covington."

Somehow, Grace thought, when Charles and Amelia get together they both become a touch affected.

"Have you seen the cottage garden and the canal garden?" Hannah asked, slipping her arm through Charles's.

"Indeed I have, and I'm mighty impressed."

"They'll be in full color in summer. You must come back then. Now let's go to my office. Mary Ann has drinks and cheese and crackers for us. I could use a pick-me-upper."

🪶

It was cozy in Hannah's office. Max had had a small gas fireplace installed, and two love seats provided cozy seating. In fact, it was so delightful that many an afternoon, long after closing time, Hannah and Max could be found drinking tea or Coke, or Max having a gin and tonic while they hashed over the happenings of the day.

One day recently Amelia had asked Grace, "What on earth are they doing there for all those hours after work?"

"Talking. Going over plans. Hannah's become his partner in this venture. Max discusses everything with her."

"Is it romantic, do you think?" Amelia asked, her eyes dancing.

"That would be something, wouldn't it? Hannah and Max in love."

"Not love, a good friendship, that's all, and shared interest. Sometimes that's easier, more satisfying to live with."

Amelia shook her head. "It seems like more than work and friendship to me."

But it wasn't. Hannah and Max never shared the same love seat, never touched one another. Unspoken boundaries framed their relationship, a good working relationship, and a friendship, that neither chose to tamper with.

Now they settled onto the love seats: Charles and Amelia sharing one, Hannah and Grace on the other.

Charles turned to Amelia. "You still rocking babies at the hospital?"

"Yes, I am, and I love it. Only, last week we lost a baby, and that's sad. Everyone wants to cry, and we put on a brave front, or we'd flood the place with tears."

"Isn't it depressing, then?"

"No. Most of our babies thrive and go home. The parents' faces glow when they come to get them. I feel as if I'm doing something very special."

"You are," Charles said, and the others echoed his sentiment.

They were munching cheese and crackers when Max entered the room. He extended his hand to Charles. "Charles. Good to see you. Down for a visit? How long?"

He's starting to sound like Hannah, Grace thought.

"Just for the weekend. It's good to be here, to see everyone." His arm swept across both love seats.

"You've seen Hannah's beautiful gardens, I'm sure. Would you like to see the rest of the place?"

Charles started to rise. "Sit, sit," Max said. "First, I'll join you for a Coke and a cracker or two, if I may?" He pulled a straight chair from near Hannah's desk. "Great office, isn't it?"

"It certainly is. Done in the best of taste. I compliment you."

Max nodded, but his face said, I know all that and yes, I am terrific. Grace wondered that Hannah never spoke of Max's ego. Maybe she chose to overlook it, considering his ability to get things done almost magically. And his creativity and organizational skills had certainly benefited Hannah. They sat awhile. Max talked, as he often did these days, about the Indian settlement. They were putting on the roof of the main lodge inside the compound. Materials were slow in coming. "Always something when you're building," Max said. "You can never project a finish date when you begin."

After a time Max pulled in his long legs. A man in total control, he seemed to stir the air about him, to energize those around him as he rose to his feet. "Well, come on, Charles. Time for a tour."

Meanwhile, back at the farmhouse, Mike and Roger faced each other across the kitchen table. Both sat with their arms crossed, their chairs set back. After confessing his lie, Roger begged Mike's forgiveness, but Mike was not so easily bought off.

"You put me through a living hell," he said.

"You cannot imagine how sorry I am," Roger repeated for the seventh time.

"No, I cannot. You lied to me. You crushed me." Mike lowered his head into his hands for the seventh time. His shoulders shook.

"What can I do, say?" Roger threw up his hands. "I was a cad, a brute . . ."

"A damned liar."

"Yes, a damned liar. I was drunk, too, if you recall."

Mike's face grew redder, his bloodshot eyes bulged. "Recall? If I recall?" His voice was near hysteria. "The whole episode haunts me. I dream about you staggering in, saying cruel things, leaving, no, abandoning me."

"The truth would have hurt as much, think."

Mike half rose, then plopped back into the chair. "What do you know about hurt, you self-centered bastard? I hate you. I just hate you." His arms and chest and shoulders crumpled onto the table.

Roger sat silent, arms crossed, chair tipped back. Finally Mike lifted himself and sat straight. He rose and marched stiffly to the sink, where he wiped his face with a clean washcloth, and patted cold water on his eyes and forehead. "What I don't understand is why you encouraged me in the first place. Tell me that, why don't you?"

Roger coughed.

"Want some water?" Mike asked.

"Thanks, no. I was attracted to you, and I didn't think. I didn't consider consequences. As I told my mother, on the train I realized how her values and morals play a bigger role in my life than I realized. I've come to respect her and the way she's lived her life. Loyalty and commitment were, and are, guiding principles with her. I'm pretty disgusted with myself. That night, I didn't know what to do. I'm not proud that I took the easy way out for me."

"But not easy for me, unfortunately."

"I know, and again, I apologize."

"You could have spared me, told me the truth."

"Would you have understood?"

"Not at the time, probably. I was on the edge of hysteria picturing you hurt lying in some alley, robbed, heaven knows what." Mike glared at Roger. "That was cowardly, you know that? You could have come to the hotel and told me and gone back home."

"It was cowardly. I'm ashamed."

"What did you tell Charles?"

"That nothing happened between us. That I reviewed our life together and chose to honor my commitment to him."

"And have you?"

"I have, Mike, and I will."

"I can respect that, Roger. But I've hated you for all these months. I've tortured myself feeling utterly rejected and worthless. You want absolution, and I can't just switch off all those feelings."

Roger bowed his head. "I hate me too."

"You should. Well, then." Mike sat again. "I'm going to need time to work this out. I don't want to see either of you this trip and maybe not for several trips, if ever again. You've humiliated me. That's hard to get over. Right now I hate you. But I'll recover." He tipped his chin up. "I've survived worse, believe me. I've told the ladies. They've been supportive. I'm like a son in this house. That's important to me." He rose.

"Will you forgive me, Mike?

"Someday, because I love your mother and value her friendship, I'll forgive you, but not now, not today." Moments later Mike slammed the front door behind him.

Roger slumped. It had been harder, much harder than he anticipated. He felt like a heel. His fist came down hard on the table. He was a heel. It would take time for him to forgive himself, but, he sighed, confessing and asking for absolution were over.

39

Gratitude

In the April days that followed and into May, the world warmed. Coats and boots found new homes in closets. Light, fanciful breezes tickled the ladies' skins and danced among the grasses along the roadsides. The woods blushed with wildflowers. Grace spent several hours every week with Emily and Melissa Grace. The baby thrived and had put on weight. Her little cheeks rounded, her eyed turned golden brown like her father's, and the pale, blond fluff about her head increased. Grace adored her but spent time with her only during the hours when Tyler was in school. On weekends, she and Bob did things with Tyler.

Overcoming her dislike of cold water, Grace donned a hooded slicker, rolled up her slacks, and clambered into a rubber raft. Off they drifted down the French Broad River. Her anxiety vanished as she began to enjoy herself, enjoy the sky and clouds that skated across the tunnel of trees bounding the river. But then the river changed from glass smooth to churning and tumbling, and Tyler held to her arm as she screamed and cringed when they hit the first number-two rapids. White water slapped the raft and splashed against their slickers.

But at those times when they glided along, Grace pointed out to

Tyler how the river had sculpted the landscape, eroded the banks, carved cliffs, changed the shoreline. How happy she was. Her life had never been so full, so rich with love, so happy, and at every turn in the river, even when she clung to the side of the raft and held her breath, she thanked the universe for Bob and Tyler and her good fortune.

One morning as she rocked Melissa Grace, and Emily worked at her desk, Emily turned to her. "Grace, I never did make it to Lucy Banks's house, to check on things. Would you visit the family and be my eyes and ears? The social worker's pressuring them at the office."

Grace wanted to say no but heard herself saying yes, then wondered if she were qualified for such a mission. "I'm not trained to see things like that."

"Your instincts are better than any training, Grace. Whatever I'd have seen or felt, I'd have discussed with you. You love Lucy. You'll know if anything's amiss."

And so it was that on a balmy Friday afternoon, Grace turned her car off a paved road onto a one-lane, deeply rutted drive and plunged into thick woods. Grace slowed to a crawl. Brilliant scarlet and white wildflowers cloaked the feet and ankles of trees. Butterflies dove past. For a moment Grace lost herself in the green, cool comfort of the woods, until suddenly ahead of her, looking bleak and lonely in a small clearing, an unkempt, slightly off-kilter house trailer came into view. A dog of uncertain parentage and barking hugely rushed from beneath the trailer and ran with long lazy strides toward her car. Fast on its heels, Lucy and her sister, later introduced as Clara, raced after him.

Grace wound down her window. "Lucy," she called.

"Stop it, Bozoo. Stop it," Lucy grabbed the dog's shaggy mane. "Mrs. Grace. Mrs. Grace." She jumped up and down, then turned to face the trailer. "Pa. Pa, come quick like. It's Mrs. Grace a visitin'."

The door swung wide. Holding to the railing, a gray-haired man with a worn, sun-baked face and rounded shoulders descended the rickity wooden steps. Her grandfather? Grace wondered. But the next moment, Lucy was at his side, holding his arm, guiding him toward the car, and talking a mile a minute. "She's done come see us, Pa," Grace heard her say.

Grace sprang from her car. Bozoo wagged his tail and sniffed her legs as she moved across the yard, hastening to reduce the steps Pa would have to take, for every step seemed a great effort for him, and yet the child urged him on.

"Mr. Banks," Grace said, extending her hand.

"Howdy, ma'am." He grasped her hand with hard, bony fingers. "This here young un's been a talkin' 'bout you a long while now. We thank ye for givin' her that there book. All the young uns been a readin' from it."

Book? What book? And then Grace remembered the dictionary. "I'm glad it was useful for your family," she said.

A tall, skinny boy joined them, and two towheaded youngsters hung back in the doorway. "Randy, boy, get a chair for the lady. Set it there in the shade." Pa pointed to a tall pine that cast a slender shade across the trailer. "And get me a crate to set these old bones on."

"Oh, no," Grace said as Randy unfolded a tattered beach chair and positioned it in the shade. "I'll sit on the crate, sir. You take the chair."

"No, ma'am." Pa plunked down on the crate. "Wouldn't set a good example for the boy there now, would it?"

Grace couldn't argue with that.

"Lucy girl, you and Clara run fetch a Coke from that there cooler chest behind the house for Mrs. Grace here."

"Thank you," Grace said, not wanting to seem discourteous. She liked this worn-out old man. His eyes, set deep in his wrinkled face, were blue and kind, his smile quick and sweet.

"We're mighty pleased you came a callin'. Wife's workin'. Got her a new job days over in Weaverville at the Sony plant. Makin' more money too. And we're gonna be movin' closer in, so as the young uns won't be a walkin' three miles to catch a bus."

Lucy ran up with a can of Coke. Clara was taller, probably older, with a round, cheerful face, and for a moment Grace did not recognize that the girl had Down syndrome.

Soon, five of the seven children were running about the dirt yard, throwing a stick, which Bozoo delighted in retrieving. What was she to do now? How did you check for such a thing as sexual abuse? If a child did not act out or speak up, who would admit to such a crime?

Pa sat quietly, hands folded in his lap. With the toe of one of his badly scuffed black shoes, shoes that once might have been his Sunday best, he shoved the dirt about. Slowly, the line of shadow edged its way along the washed-out beige siding of the trailer. Lucy separated herself from her sisters and brother and walked over to them. Aware of their silence, she seemed to understand that Pa lacked the confidence or the words to converse with Grace. What she doesn't realize, Grace thought as she watched Lucy trot toward them, is that I'm quite comfortable with her pa and with the silence.

"Pa, Mrs. Grace is the best friend I got," the girl said, crouching at his feet.

His knurled hand found the top of her head and patted gently. "Well, you got you a mighty fine friend here, Lucy girl."

Taking the cue, Grace spoke of Lucy's progress in school, of the words they had worked on, and the fine sentences Lucy could now make. "And she draws real good too," Grace said.

"You seen a picture I made?" Lucy queried.

"Of cows, seven of them, and flowers."

"Wanna see more I drew?"

"I'd love to."

In a flash, Lucy dashed to the house, disappeared, and reappeared with a small sheaf of papers. She waved them high above her head.

"She'd draws good that girl," Pa said. "My ma used to draw some, way back when I was a boy over yonder in Tennessee." His eyes searched the sky as if seeking his mother. "Good woman, my mother. Passed too young." He shook his head. "Lucy's ma's a good woman too." Tears filled his eyes. "The palsey's got me young," he said. "Hands shakin' so bad some days. Couldn't work, couldn't feed my family."

Only then did Grace notice the tremor in his hands.

"Social worker lady . . ."

"Miss Francie," Lucy interjected.

"She brung me to the doctor fer some pills. Stopped the shakin' some."

Grace wanted to put her arms about Pa, to comfort him and assure him that he had nice children. She wondered how old he was. Then Lucy's drawings landed in her lap, and Grace turned her attention to them. The first sheet was colored blue, the sky with white fluffy clouds and angels with huge golden wings flying throughout. In another, the woods loomed, great patches of dark green and black, and along the bottom of the tree trunks a line of bright scarlet flowers. A re-creation of the scene that Grace had been so taken with as she drove through the woods. There were ten drawings, and in none of them were there dragons chasing children, or darkness, nothing to suggest suffering, anger, or pain. Again, Grace was struck by the optimism of this child, and she thanked the universe for giving her the opportunity to somehow, she did not yet know how, help Lucy Banks.

*

"I'd bet my life on it," Grace told Emily later. "I sensed nothing untoward going on at the Banks' home. Lucy's pa is sick with something like Parkinson's he calls 'the palsey.' The mother's gotten a daytime job in Weaverville now. The social worker did a good job. The family's moving out of that awful trailer. I hardly think you need to place those children in foster homes. They seem happy. I

313

doubt they even know how poor they are. They take care of Pa, and of each other."

"Pa?" Emily asked as she rocked the baby, who had just fallen asleep.

"I haven't a clue what his name is."

Emily chuckled. "Pa," she said again.

"Lucy's artwork's all about nature, sky, trees, flowers, animals, and angels. Nothing indicates sadness or anger."

"You like these people, don't you?" Emily laughed. "If you were younger you'd probably want to adopt Lucy, wouldn't you?"

"Probably, but I'd never separate her from her siblings. There's a Down syndrome child, a girl, sweet, innocent. Don't take my word for all this. I'll take care of Melissa if you want to go out there yourself."

"I might have to do that, for the office."

✸

A week later, Grace had a call from Emily. "I'm going to the Banks' place with the social worker, Francie Demillio. And by the way, Pa's name is Louis Banks."

"I prefer Pa."

"Can I bring Melissa Grace over there, or do you want to come here?"

"If you don't mind, bring her here. Everyone wants a chance to spoil her."

✸

Emily's opinion corroborated Grace's. Louis Banks had been flustered by company, she told Grace. They'd sat on crates, since the beach chair, the boy, Randy, explained, had fallen apart.

"Imagine, Lucy's mother brings home a bag of ice for the ice chest daily. That's how they keep food cold." Emily looked distressed. "I've never known or seen anyone so poor as those people. I had no idea, in this land of plenty, that people lived like that. All the girls sleep on pallets on the floor of one room. The chairs are wooden crates. The oldest boy, Randy, sleeps in a sleeping bag in the living room. Oh, by the way, Grace, 'Pa' is sixty-one."

"He looks eighty."

"He certainly does. How does that happen to someone?"

40

Renaissance

Standing at the window of her bedroom in the farmhouse, Laura realized that for the first time in months she had awakened not hating the sunrise. She counted the months: eleven, almost a year since the hurricane snatched Marvin from her and ravaged her life. How had she made it to this day? In those first months, pain and anger had led her to reject all overtures of help or comfort. She remembered that, but not the details, and was grateful that no one held her initial hostility against her.

Birdsong filled the air. Robins, Grace said, robins that sang so loudly and sweetly that they sounded as if they were on your windowsill when they were actually in a tree some distance away. She'd known nothing about birds when she'd first come here. Fish, yes. But not birds.

The wind, that potentially mighty and destructive force, was tame today and drifted not from the west but soft and balmy from the south. Below, in the vegetable garden, her mother, always an early riser, kneeled and weeded a bed of tomatoes. The bed was filled with marigolds. Companion plants, Hannah said. "Marigolds keep bugs off tomatoes."

Work had sustained her mother all her life. She had been right to urge Laura to accept Maxwell's job offer. Once made, that com-

317

mitment had forced Laura from bed, and filled the void in her mind, if not her heart. She thought of Hank, then blushed and felt ashamed. To consider Hank as anyone but a colleague was to dishonor the memory of her Marvin. But soon it would be a year. How, then, would she respond to Hank's obvious interest?

Below, Hannah raised her head, brushed hair from her forehead, and sat back. The long, narrow weeding tool dangled from her hand as she perused the sky, an arch of blue. She's truly happy, Laura thought, and for a moment she envied her mother.

Moving away from the window, Laura began to dress for work, even as her mind raced on. I used to love nature, until it hurt me so, she mused. Will I again? Perhaps. On the site of the log cabin the other day, above the noise of broadaxes chopping, mallets pounding wedges to split wood, and the tick of an adze squaring timber, she had found herself immersed in watching an industrious hummingbird, its wings whirring, skyrocket from flower to flower.

And another afternoon recently, she had walked away from the construction and into the woods, into a green world of verdant trees situated so close together that sunlight barely penetrated and moss pressed close about gnarled roots. She had stood there marveling. Used to the sea and the open horizon, she expected to feel claustrophobic. Instead, she felt comforted and safe. For a moment, a brief moment, her heart lifted, and then she thought of Marvin and how Amelia believed that souls soared. Thinking of Marvin had been her undoing, for she had crumpled against a tree trunk and cried.

Laura forced her mind to the day before her. She would be interviewing actors/interpreters to staff the log cabins and outbuildings. Max had urged flexible hours.

"There are actors who work part time, who'd be happy to pick up extra work if they have control of their hours," he'd said.

"There are locals who'd like to be involved," she'd said.

Max nodded. "I'm sure there are, and I imagine that a man who shoes a horse can plow a field or shuck corn. Professional actors could learn plenty from locals."

Harold's tapes were invaluable, as were the series of oral history

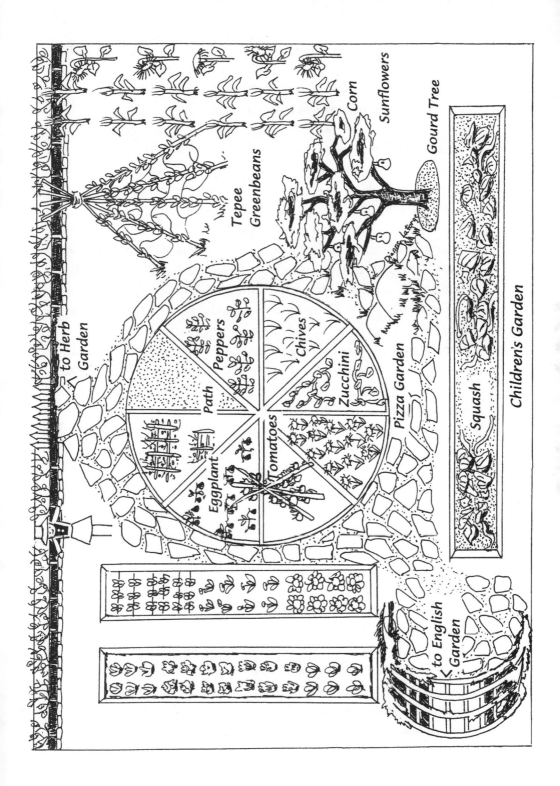

Foxfire books, which provided dialect and visual details. As she tracked down old-timers able to replicate a rope bed, a straw mattress, and other furnishings and clothing, the hollows and coves of Madison Country became increasingly familiar.

While visiting folks on their small wood porches, she came to appreciate the fierce manner in which they loved every inch of land, every tree, every creek, hill, and valley that they owned.

"Home," one elderly farmer told her, "was where folks worked, taught their kids, read the Bible, raised most of the food they ate."

Laura felt transported to another time.

Another old-timer said, "Family was everything. My own-born cousins were same to me as brothers. One time I went to Asheville. Worked there a week. I pined for home. I got me back soon as my feet would brung me. I'm a tellin' you, lady, what I was raised up with, time I was a little shirttail boy, don't go outta my head."

Irene Ramsey told Laura how families preserved food when she was a girl. "My sisters and I'd sit with a basket of beans. Ma'd thread a needle with strong thread, and we'd pushed that there needle through the center of the beans. We'd have a long strand and we'd hang it against the wall of the house outta the sun. When they dried, we'd store 'em in bags. As for potatoes, we'd dig us a hole below frost, put potatoes in, and cover it with straw. Then we'd pack dirt atop of that and set a piece of tin atop of that. They'd last all winter."

In time, Laura convinced Irene Ramsey and some of her friends to show the actors/interpreters the "right way" things were done.

※

And, always, in the background of her day, there was Hank. How could she possibly be interested in a man who paled in comparison to Marvin? Captain Marvin, larger than life and considered a character in every port, whose range of interests had left her speechless. What could she possibly see in a shy, quiet man like Hank?

Hank focused on work. If he dreamed big dreams, they were deeply private. Solid and steady, kind and caring, he had grown on her. His gentleness and sensitivity calmed her and helped ground

320

her. Where before she had raced toward adventure, now adventure and change frightened her. At Christmas, her mother had given her a jewelry box. Last month she had bought three silver bangles, and as she paid the saleswoman she worried about accumulating anything ever again.

Why couldn't she get her mind off Hank? He was a few years younger than she was. Yet lately, in the dark of night, snuggled under her covers in the cozy blue-and-white, guest room she had come to call her own, Laura sometimes wondered if maybe, just maybe, there was still time to marry, to have a child. One child of her own, she prayed, and her heart would lift with hope and joy, until her mind raced on and smacked into a wall and fell back into confusion.

Below, in the garden, Hannah pried the weeding tool deep into the earth, extracted a tenacious weed, and yanked it out. "Got you, invader," she said, tossing it into her trash bucket. Shoving herself to her feet, she brushed bits of grass and dirt from her slacks and hands. Time to change. At nine she would meet with her gardening class at Caster Elementary School.

With a deep sense of pride and satisfaction, Hannah could imagine them gathered around a big round table organizing their garden. Later, weeks later, she would have them bring in a small bag of soil from their own yards or gardens, and she would teach a lesson on soil and its amendments. But today they would work with concepts, and she would present them with books on children's gardens, magazines, and seeds packets, and demonstrate the need for planning. She would prod their minds with concepts of design, size, and shape—possibilities—then let their creative juices run wild.

Billows of perfume floated from the Chrysler Imperial roses that anchored the driveway. Hannah stopped and breathed deeply, then drew clippers from a pocket and snipped a half dozen roses for the kitchen table. Whistling, she went inside.

Laura came tripping down the stairs, also whistling. They stared at one another and burst into laughter. Moments later, Laura's secondhand Chevy headed down Cove Road, and Hannah, feeling content, poured herself a second cup of coffee and arranged the roses in a tall crystal vase.

Brenda looks awful. I hardly recognized her, Hannah thought when Brenda's sports car pulled alongside her station wagon in the school lot. "How are you doing, Brenda?" Hannah asked, as they got out and headed for the entrance.

"A little better," Brenda said. "But it's frightening living alone in that big old house." Tears flooded her eyes.

"I'm sorry, my friend." Hannah changed the subject. "The kids and I start planning the garden at Bella's Park today."

Brenda collected herself. "That's wonderful. You've done a great job teaching them about planting, Hannah. Thanks. You've given them something they can draw upon for the rest of their lives."

Relief flooded Hannah when they entered the building and moved in opposite directions. Brenda phoned Grace nearly every night, and Grace, bless her, patiently listened. That would drive Hannah crazy. She worried enough about Laura, who now, thank God, seemed to be on the road to recovery. Maybe later, Laura and Hank. Hannah smiled, and feeling lighthearted and young, quickened her gait.

A cluster of fifth-grade girls stopped jabbering and said good morning as she passed them. Samuel, a sweet boy from her class, ran by calling, "Be right back, Miss Hannah." She found herself humming.

The chatter in the room ceased when she entered. Expectant faces turned toward her. Hannah slung her canvas bag onto the table, and as the contents tumbled out, excited voices rose and hands reached for packets of seeds, seed catalogs, magazines, and books.

Samuel dashed in and claimed a chair close to Hannah.

"Teacher's pet," a girl teased.

Samuel shrugged.

"I want you all to see what our landscape designer, Mr. Hank, has prepared for us." Shoving aside the contents of the bag to make room for the drawing, she unrolled it and tacked it to the board, then passed a single sheet to each youngster. "Each of you has your own to work on. This is your garden. It's a replica of the one hanging there. I've made it clear to Mr. Hank that you'll have the last word. Do not, I repeat, do not put a line or a mark on your sheet until you've done some thinking and we've thrown around ideas. If you do, you'll have a mess on your hands." She strode to the blackboard.

"I'm going to draw the space." She sketched a rectangle with double lines around the edges. "These are the walls." She drew that she deemed to be an arch. "The exit from the garden. "We'll decide where the walkways go and what they'll be finished with: bark, tile, brick, flagstone."

"What's flagstone?" a red-haired girl asked.

"Look among the books, Susan. There's one on paving material. Look it up." The child began rummaging through the books.

"Here it is, Sue," Samuel said, handing her a long flat book with a shiny cover.

Hannah drew the walls. "Fifty-five feet wide. Thirty-five feet long."

"Is that big, Miss Hannah?" one of the boys asked as he pushed back glasses that had slipped halfway down the bridge of his nose.

She laughed. "Big enough for now, Dewayne." Hannah spoke a bit about dividing space. "How many of you want a large vegetable garden?"

Every hand shot into the air.

Hannah drew a large square in the center. "Is this where we want it to be?" Then she erased the square and redrew it to one side. "Or here? Or"—she erased again, put in a path and drew two smaller rectangles, one on either side of the path—"would it work better if the beds were long and narrow? After all, you'll have to weed them." She rejoined them at the table. "It's important to think about all the possibilities and plan ahead, or we'll be digging and digging, and making new beds, and leaving them for other beds."

"We'd end up with a hodgepodge," Samuel said.

Hannah nodded. "Planning is everything. Now, pass around the seeds. There are four of each kind, so there should be plenty for everyone to choose from. Take your time. Select those you think you'd like to plant. Doesn't matter if they're vegetables or flowers. Later, we'll consider the best placement for them in the garden."

"This is gonna be a lot of work," Susan said.

"But the results will be worth it, and you'll be real proud."

"You proud of your gardens, Miss Hannah?" This from a tall girl with long brown braids who reminded Hannah of herself as a child.

"Yes, Lily, I'm extremely proud of my gardens, both at home and at the park."

"Ma says you're gonna make a farmer outta me," a youngster with the odd nickname of Buckster said. "Ma says we done moved outta the fields, and I should go to school to be a teacher."

"Whatever career you choose, Buckster, gardening is a wonderful hobby you can have all of your life, even when you're as old as your grandpa."

"And he's old," Buckster said, grinning.

Hannah brought them back to the project. "Take home these books and magazines. Look through them for ideas. Exchange them, share them, those of you who live close to one another. When we meet again, we'll discuss your ideas and start to put something on paper."

The bell rang. In a flurry of excitement, they scrambled for books and seed packets, then raced from the room.

#

Bubbling voices and bright faces greeted Hannah the following week when she opened the classroom door. Within two minutes they were calling out ideas. With great attention to their words, she listed them on the board.

"Let's grow weird plants like bloodroot." Jackie made a ghoulish face. "It drips blooood!"

"I want to grow a pizza patch like the book shows. You divide a circle and plant different vegetables that you like on your pizza," Chuck said.

"Sure," Susan mocked, " 'cause you're a vegetarian."

"Meat's bad for you." Chuck smirked.

Billy leaned forward, hands clasped tight, eyes anxious. "My mom's gonna lemme have old boots, so I can plant inside them." Billy was shy. He hardly spoke, and now his eyes looked to Hannah for confirmation.

"Oh, what a good idea. Sounds like fun, Billy," Hannah said.

Billy relaxed, unclasped his hands, and sat back. One of the boys punched his arm in a sign of camaraderie.

"We gonna have a wall around our garden to keep the dogs and other critters out," Lily declared.

"Yes, but would you like a wooden fence, a brick wall, a concrete wall?"

"We gotta decide that too?" a chubby girl asked.

"If you won't, I will, Ellen May," Hannah replied.

Hands shot up. A chorus of "We want to" filled the room.

Ellen May pouted.

"Did you find seeds you like, Ellen May?" Hannah asked.

The child's face lit up. "Sunflowers," she said. "I want to grow sunflowers as tall as you, Miss Hannah."

"You can do that. Sunflowers are amazingly easy to grow, and some are very tall. There's a deep bronze one called Color Fashion. Look at the seed packets. Color Fashion grows five to six feet. There's a bright yellow one. Mammoth it's called, and it grows twelve feet, and there are small, two-foot-high sunflowers, so you have plenty of choice."

"Here it is, Mammoth." Ellen May waved a seed packet.

"I got Mammoth too," yelled Jackie.

"We gotta have a tepee big enough for kids to crawl inside and eat beans," Samuel said.

"And a cave of bushes you gotta crawl through to get into the garden."

"I want to grow teeny-weeny tomatoes."

"Wind chimes from painted Coke cans would be good. We'd be recycling them," Chuck the vegetarian said.

And so it went as they immersed themselves in the business of seed selection. The girls chose mainly flowers, yellows primarily and oranges. Billy held up a packet of purple verbena. Most of the boys selected beans, tomatoes, squash, and pumpkin. Lily wanted to plant zinnias and several varieties of lettuce.

"Write your names on these sticky tags, mark your packets, and put them in this box I brought," Hannah instructed. "Anyone think about the vegetable bed we talked about?"

Long and narrow was the consensus, but the location was hotly debated: off to one side, straight down the center. Then the bell rang. "On Saturday, how many of you can come over to the park?" Hannah asked.

Everyone's hand shot up.

Hannah wrote her office phone number on the board. "Anyone need a ride or have any problems, call me before six on Friday night. Off you go now." It's amazing, she thought as she gathered up her things, how patient I am with these children. Common interest, of course. That always helps.

Two weeks later, Hannah presented a rough sketch of the garden to Hank. The space had been neatly divided into sections: to one side ran a four-foot-wide by twelve-foot-long raised bed for vegetables. Within the bed, every four feet, a path of stepping-stones ran through the plants to provide easy access for weeding and picking. There was a circle for a pizza garden, and a triangular site for a large tepee. Meandering bark-mulched paths wandered past circular and crescent-shaped flower beds, which, like the vegetable beds, were raised a foot above the ground to allow for good drainage and easy working of the soil. For an entrance, everyone voted for a hole, half square, half circle, around which they would plant a thick vine. A spot to the north was assigned to tall sunflowers so that they would not shade sun-loving plants, and a place for exotica like bloodroot and soft, fuzzy lamb's ears was designated.

"I'm impressed," Hank said. "I'll transfer this to a larger than usual sheet so you can tack it up for easy reference."

"Reduce a dozen copies so each of the kids can have his or her own plan. The men will lay it out, set up the raised beds, and prepare soil," Hannah said. "We started the seeds in the greenhouse at school, and the kids will begin to work in their garden as soon as school's out the end of May."

"The kids are terrific," Hannah said to the ladies at dinner that night. "They're eager, funny, and quirky too. Designed their own garden."

"Really? And it's workable?" Amelia asked.

"Definitely."

41

Molly Lund's Plan

Several weeks prior to the end of the school year, Molly Lund sat at a table in the library pretending to read a book while she waited to talk to Grace. Finally, Lucy Banks skipped from behind the stacks, stopped, looked about her guiltily, and tiptoed from the library. Molly hastened to where Grace was gathering up her books and papers.

Seeing the strained look in Molly's eyes, Grace eased back into her chair. She was tired. She'd already shopped, prepared a tuna noodle casserole for dinner, spent two hours minding Melissa while her mother caught up on casework, and rushed to the school to work with Lucy. But Molly needed her, and for Grace, there was nothing to do but be there for the young woman.

"Grace," Molly began, "it's Mom. Have you taken a good look at her? She hardly sleeps. She say she hears noises all night long. I've told her that I remember creaks and groans in that old farmhouse, but she swears she's never heard them before. I'm afraid she's going to end up in the hospital."

"Is there something I can do to help?" Grace asked.

"Just hear me out and tell me if you think I'm nuts."

"Okay." Grace folded her hands on the edge of the table.

"I think we should all move into one house, probably ours. It's newer. We haven't a guest room, but until we build one for her, the boys can share a room."

Grace shuddered, thinking of Roger insisting she move out of her home. "Have you put this to your mother?"

"Not yet."

"Some women find it hard to live with their children," Grace said. "Perhaps Brenda would consider having a roommate, another woman, like Hannah, Amelia, and I have done."

"That would be great, but she's stubborn, and she's too proud and private for her own good, Grace. Remember how she wouldn't let anyone help us for months, until you intervened, bless you. I thought maybe she'd consider living with us." Molly hesitated, looked down at her hands. Her fingers slipped back and forth between each other. "I wondered if you'd broach the subject to her for me?"

Grace considered this. When she spoke, she looked directly into Molly's eyes. "No, Molly dear. This isn't for me to do. It's something *you* have to talk to your mom about. I suggest you do it in a neutral place, a restaurant perhaps. Expect her to resist. Don't argue or urge. Lay out your idea as an idea, not a plan. Give her time to digest it."

"I know she talks to you at night sometimes. After I've done as you suggest, if she calls you about it, will you help me?"

"I'll listen to your mother and try to help her sort out her feelings."

Molly lifted her hands, and they fell back into her lap. "Do you think it's a stupid idea?"

"Not necessarily, but you'd need rules and parameters."

"Parameters? Like what?"

"Like children's bedtimes, and privacy, and quiet times, and who's responsible for what," Grace said, thinking of the myriad details, the many occasions for misunderstanding until she and the ladies had found ways to communicate, to cooperate, to tolerate. "You can't snap your fingers and expect such a plan to run smoothly. It takes time and work."

Molly looked surprised and deflated. "I hadn't considered any of that."

330

"I'm certainly not suggesting it's not the best solution, merely that everyone must want to do it, the kids, your husband, Brenda, and that it takes planning."

"I'm glad I talked to you, Grace. I knew you'd have good advice for me."

"I don't know if it's good, but it's based on my experience. I appreciate what Brenda's going through. After Ted died, I heard noises. Even after I had an alarm system installed, I slept with a light on in the hall and in my bedroom. It takes time to adjust to living, to sleeping alone."

"Maybe Mom will adjust. I'll suggest an alarm system."

"Do what you think is best. But if you decide to go ahead with your original idea, be sure you talk it over carefully with your hubby, and involve the kids too."

Molly came around to her side of the table and hugged Grace. "Thank you so much for all you've done for our family."

"Life's about being there for those you care about, Molly."

Two nights later Brenda phoned Grace. "Molly's proposed something I'd like to run by you, my friend."

"Fine, go ahead."

"You know how I hate sleeping alone in this house. Her boys have offered to baby-sit Granny." She laughed. "Lord, what have I come to? Anyhow, this is what they've suggested. Rick would spend Friday nights, and Alex Saturday nights. Molly offered to sleep over one night during the week, and they suggested that I stay at their place two nights a week. That's five nights. I'd be on my own the other two nights. She suggested that I install an alarm system."

"How do you feel about these ideas?" Grace asked, pushing her toes high beneath her sheet, tenting her feet. How nice that the blankets and comforter were put away and she needed only a light-weight cover most nights.

"Mixed feelings. Foolish. It would be nice to be alone with each grandson. We haven't had many occasions for that. I feel guilt about Molly leaving her family to stay with me, and I really don't want to

331

sleep at their place. The boys would have to double up and they have twin beds in their rooms. Would you be comfortable in a twin bed?"

"Probably not."

"I know I'm not. We sleep in twins at Mother's place in South Carolina, and I toss all night."

"Would an alarm system make you feel more secure?" Grace asked.

"Who knows?" She could almost see Brenda shrug. "I've come to realize it's as much loneliness, and maybe even denial that Harold's gone, as it is fear."

"Brenda, did you ever consider having someone live with you? Share the house, like we do here?"

A long pause followed. Then Brenda said, "No, I haven't. It's an idea. You three women knew one another. Who would I ask, some stranger?"

Grace thought for a long time. How would her friend do this? "I think I'd start with a list of widows or unmarried women within a ten-year age range of yourself whom you know from school or church. Then walk about your house and decide what spaces you would want to share, which you need to retain for yourself. That's all I can think of now."

"It sounds so odd. What would people think or say if I took in someone to live with me?"

"If people's opinions are important, then don't do it."

Over the line, Grace heard Brenda crying. Finally she mumbled, "I don't know what to do, Grace. I'm so confused."

"Then don't do anything. Maybe it's a good idea to go with Brenda's plan. Offer to buy a double bed for one of the boys' rooms, so you'd be comfortable, and get an alarm system for those nights you stay alone. Try it for, say, four months."

Brenda sighed deeply. "Four months, or three even. I could manage that. Then I'd know better, wouldn't I?"

"You'll never know if you don't try it."

Brenda changed the subject. "By the way, I am so pleased that Ms. Dimillio and Emily concur with you about the Bankses. That family simply fell through the cracks, but now they'll get the assistance they need, housing allowance, food stamps to help them get on their feet. You know the mother's working days now?

"Emily told me."

"How's that new grandbaby of yours?"

Grace's heart swelled. How good that Brenda accepted her bond with the Richardsons. "She's a marvelous baby, good as gold," she told Brenda.

"She's an old soul, look at her eyes. You can tell by her eyes," Mike announced one day when baby Melissa was two months old. He had dropped in one evening on his way from the ladies' house, to deliver a framed photograph of Amelia's that Emily had purchased for her office.

"What makes you say that?" Emily asked.

"Can't you tell? She looks as if she's remembering important things."

"Probably got gas," Russell said and laughed.

"Oh, you people. It's not gas. When babies have gas they squirm and grunt and draw up their little legs and get red in the face."

"Since Melissa can't tell us, we'll never know, will we?" Russell replied and picked up the newspaper.

On the way to his car, Mike thought about the picture he had delivered, a pastoral scene of a meandering creek with cows lolling about in the shade of trees, a rather prosaic topic save for the exquisite light illuminating the scene, creating shadows and forms that conjured up fairies frolicking. He could see them. Amelia saw them. Could Emily have seen them?

Mike felt sad and disgruntled. Of all his friends in Covington, only Amelia was interested in his beliefs about the afterlife. Well, she had experienced not one but two out-of-body experiences. Maybe people required firsthand knowledge of paranormal phenomena before they could look beyond their original beliefs. He'd had a terrifying, yet amazing, experience when he was fifteen. He hadn't thought about it in eons.

They'd been a bunch of kids drinking beer, driving, and the car had plummeted off a bridge into a ravine. Looking up, he'd seen Ben, his friend and the driver, sitting in a tree smiling and waving at him. Mike tried to wave back, but his hand wouldn't rise. Something warm trickled down his cheek, and his shirt was wet. They said he was unconscious when they found him, but Mike would swear that he was awake and talking to a tall, fair-haired woman who spoke softly, comforting him and telling him to lie still, that help was on the way and he would be all right. Later, much later, his parents broke the news that Ben had been killed on impact.

"But I saw Ben. He smiled and waved at me," Mike had protested.

"You must have dreamed it," his mother said. She bent over his hospital bed with sad, red-rimmed eyes. "They were killed, all four boys, but you." And she had burst into tears.

After a time, after his broken ribs and arm and leg had mended, Mike came to believe that an angel had visited him, and that Ben had assured him that he was alive somewhere else and happy. The experience profoundly altered Mike's view of death and beyond. There were many folks in Asheville who shared his beliefs, but not in Covington. Well, at least Amelia had an open mind.

🌿

Back at the farmhouse, the ladies sat out on the porch watching the heavens explode with stars. "How clear it is," Grace said. "I love nights like this."

"Once," Amelia said, "when I was about nine, I sneaked out of bed very late, after my parents were asleep. It was a night like this, even more stars for we faced the ocean, and the only light I saw was a dim glow far out to sea. Our woods had filled with lightning bugs. When I saw the shape near the woods, I assumed it was a mix of fireflies and low-hanging mist from the sea."

"What shape?" Grace asked.

Hannah's eyes were closed and she rocked gently.

"I'm never sure, thinking back. First it seemed to be a woman with long hair, then it looked like a rugged old sea captain. Oh, it was probably nothing. But I felt light and happy. If the form had materialized and put out a hand, I'd have taken it and walked away into the mist. It's a silly story, anyway."

"Why are you telling it, then?" Hannah asked, not opening her eyes.

"I was relating it to Mike the other day. He believes in all kinds of things, angels, visions, who knows what all. He thinks my out-of-body experiences, you remember, in Pisgah Forest and then again after Lance, were God trying to get my attention. He may be right. During that last experience, I had the awareness that I was, for a moment, one with all creation. That's a special feeling. I never want to forget it."

"It's very special, then." Grace said. "And you needn't forget it."

"Just watch who you tell it to around here," Hannah admonished.

They were silent a long while. Orion climbed above Snowman's Cap and strode south across the sky. To the north, the Big Dipper was high in the heavens and clearly visible.

Grace said, "What would happen, do you think, if we had another lunch under the oak and invited everyone we know? Would our neighbors on Cove Road come?"

"Everyone would come," Hannah said emphatically.

"Why would you want to go to all that work?" Amelia asked.

"It's not work for me. I enjoy it," Grace replied. "Why do you exhaust yourself tromping all over Madison Country taking pictures?"

"Touché," Amelia replied.

42

The Gathering

Why do I want to go to the trouble of entertaining a large crowd? Grace mused as she lay in bed that night. Beyond her window, spring rains nudged the level of the stream almost to overflowing. The rains had been intermittent, however, allowing time to soak into the earth. Tonight the rush of water was clearly audible, pleasant if one didn't think of its potential to become a rampaging stream as it had two winters ago.

It was warm. Grace reached for the fan on the night table. The elaborate French Louis IV fan, with its ballroom scene painted on silk, had been a gift from Amelia, from her collection of antique fans purchased over many years during her travels. Collections. Frivolous, yes, but delightful. Collections warmed one's heart and made a room one's own.

From her bookcase, her recent collection of clowns with wide painted, upturned lips and helter-skelter clothing and poses set her thinking of Bob. He had given her all but three of the dozen porcelain clowns.

"Clowns bring happiness to people, like you do," he'd said when he presented her with the first one, a clown balancing a puppy on his head.

Bob would ask her why she wanted to have a party with all the work involved. Why did she?

She'd tried before, had invited all the families from Cove Road for lunch. Half of them never showed up, not even an RSVP. She'd invite them all again, of course, but there were other friends and acquaintances she wanted to include. Grace fanned her face. She'd ask the Amsterdams, the new owners of the Cottage Tearoom and residents of Loring Valley, and that nice Ellie Lerner, owner of the bridal shop. Mrs. Lerner had delivered the beautiful satin gown Lurina, and then Emily, had worn. She'd always meant to have lunch with her, get to know her, and Mrs. Lerner, a widow, had been so interested in the fact that she, Hannah, and Amelia shared a home. How had she let this go so long?

Must she ask the Hammers? How could she not. Grace grinned. Agnes, aka Ginger, was, after all, Emily's mother, and Bob liked Martin. Good heaven, now that she knew the woman's real name, she'd have to be careful not to slip up and call her Agnes.

Maxwell, of course, and Hank, and Mary Ann, the receptionist, and Hannah's foreman whom Mary Ann was dating. The list grew longer. Brenda and Molly's family, Mike, Jane, the librarian, and Millie, Brenda's mother, if she'd come up from South Carolina, and Lurina and Old Man, and Wayne, and Old Man's nieces, Wanda and Wilma, from Tennessee. And there were surely people Laura, Amelia, Hannah, and Bob would choose to include.

Excited now, Grace fanned vigorously. Sleep was banished. Returning the fan to its ebony stand, Grace hastened from bed to sit in her chair near the window and start a list.

🍂

The summer was whizzing by. Where had it gone to? Grace wondered as she chose the date, Sunday, July 9, at noon.

"July—I worry about Laura. She can be quite perverse sometimes, and it's coming on the anniversary of the hurricane. Who knows what feelings that'll evoke."

"You're right," Grace said. "I'll ask her before I get carried away."

338

"I don't care what day we have a pinic," Laura said when she was asked.

Billed as a picnic, the invitations had no sooner been addressed and mailed than Grace, Hannah, and Amelia began to plan the menu. Hannah suggested a presliced honey-baked ham.

"That sounds good," Grace replied, noting it on a yellow pad.

"Why not an all-salad meal?" Amelia asked.

"Why not?" Hannah seconded the motion. "Cold foods, salads of all kinds: chicken, fruit, and vegetable salads can be prepared ahead."

"Make one of your exotic chicken salads," Amelia said. "Chicken with pineapple and cashews, or chicken with grapes and celery."

"Or both," Hannah said. "Lots of tarragon on the grape and celery salad. Fruit and chicken go so well together."

Amelia said, "We'll cut and chop. Please make that great vegetable salad with the raspberry vinegar dressing."

"Let's rent tables and chairs, like we did for Emily and Russell's wedding," Amelia said.

"Paper tablecloths and plates and cups." To Hannah, simple was better.

Grace conceded that it would be much easier than trekking plates and glasses to and from the house.

*

Heaven smiled on them. July 9 dawned bright and sunny, with no threat of rain. Fluffy white clouds, like contented puppies, stopped to rub their bellies gently on mountaintops before drifting on. By eleven-thirty, cars lined the driveway and the roadsides along their and Maxwell's front yards.

Under the great oak, under swathes of blue-and-yellow tablecloths secured to tables with bowls of flowers from Hannah's garden, and yellow and lavender and orange balloons floating above them, the outdoor dining area was as festive as a carnival. Polka music issued from speakers strategically situated by Russell and Tyler on the front porch. Spontaneously, people danced, some barefoot on the grass. Laughter charged the air.

"It's going to be a great party," Grace said to Bob as he swept her in his arms and pranced about the yard.

Sybelle, the waitress from the tearoom, bustled about making certain that serving spoons and forks accompanied every platter and bowl, that ice filled the ice chests, that jugs of sun tea were placed on the drinks table, that bits and pieces of leaves and twigs, shed by the great oak, were ousted from dining tables.

Everyone on Cove Road came. Alma Craine handed Grace a jar of pickled watermelon rind, her specialty. "Thanks for helpin' Cousin Brenda," she whispered.

Flanked by Molly and her mother, Millie, Brenda walked solemnly up the driveway. Her grandsons trailed behind until they spotted Alma's granddaughter, Paulette, and Tyler. Then they galloped off like they'd been stung by ants. The four of them raced toward the stream.

Grace stopped dancing with Bob and headed toward Brenda. "I'm glad you came. I know how difficult this is."

"You're the best friend I have, Grace. I had to come. I won't stay long."

"Stay as long as you want to."

Bob offered Brenda his arm, and they moved somewhat protractedly across the fresh-cut lawn.

"Doing any traveling this summer, Brenda?" Bob asked, seeking an innocuous topic. Travel proved anything but benign. Brenda's grasp on his arm tightened.

"Harold and I planned to take a cruise through the Panama Canal. We had reservations. Harold hankered to see how those locks worked." Her voices cracked. "Now he'll never see them."

"I'm sorry," Bob said. The tables seemed leagues away, and he ventured no further conversation, allowing Brenda to collect herself.

Brenda's friends crowded about them, enfolding Brenda in caring energy. With relief, Bob felt Brenda loosen his arm. Soon she joined Emily and baby Melissa in high-back armchairs placed close to the great oak.

"You must know how proud Grace is you named the baby after her," Brenda said.

"We were happy to do so. We love Grace. And how are you doing, Brenda?"

"Well, I'd have to say a little better since my grandsons are baby-sitting me weekends." She laughed lightly. "Being alone nights is the hardest. Rick sleeps over Friday nights and Alex on Saturday nights. Thank heavens they're young and don't have girlfriends to run with."

"They seem devoted to Paulette, I must say." Emily turned her head toward the stream, where the four youngsters crouched with strainers and a big jug of water. "Grace insists they put their catch, minnows mainly, in water to be returned to the stream later. Tyler was telling me that his granny Grace says that each minnow must be returned to its family."

Brenda's mind was elsewhere. "I stay at their house two nights a week, and Molly spends a night with me. We talk. I never realized how much I missed that. After all these years, we have time alone and an intimacy we haven't experienced since she was maybe eight years old. May I offer you some advice?"

"Certainly." Melissa stirred, nuzzling Emily's chest. Pulling a light blanket over the baby, Emily began to nurse her.

"Make time alone with each child. Don't always lump them together, taking them to the same place. You probably won't take Tyler and the baby to the same places, but if you have other babies, closer in age to Melissa. I've come to know my grandsons in ways I never did before, even though we went to church and spent every Sunday together. Lord, Harold loved those boys." She dabbed at her eyes. "Well, I see my mother waving to me. Bye-bye, baby girl." She patted the round little rump under the blanket.

"À votre santé. To your health." Amelia lifted her cup of iced tea high in the air and turned in a half circle to include everyone gathered close to the buffet table preparing to fill their plates.

"And to your health." Mike saluted her.

Voices quieted as they ate. Grace had placed Ellie Lerner between herself and Lurina. "I'm impressed. You have so many friends," Ellie said.

Grace looked about her. Friends? Acquaintances, yes, but friends? After the many nights of exchanged confidences with Brenda, she considered her a friend in the deepest sense of the word, and her housemates, of course, and Mike and Max, and Lurina. She was about to say this, to make distinctions, then thought, why do that? She felt warmly toward everyone at this festive lunch and happy to see them all. There were, after all, layers of friends, some more intimate than others, yet they'd rally around in times of trouble, like folks did for Harold and Brenda.

Her eyes strayed down the table to Alma and Frank, and Billie, their eldest and the "son" of Frank Craine and Son's auto parts. Alma was smiling and poking Mike's arm. He laughed. A far cry from her attitude that first year they lived in Covington, when they'd all been to lunch in this very same spot under the great oak, and Alma had left in a snit when she realized that Mike was gay. What had happened to change Alma's attitude? Grace recalled finding them visiting Harold at the same time one day, then sitting out on the porch on the swing afterward. What had they talked about, she wondered? Amelia had told her just recently that Alma's daughter, Claudia, enrolled in Mike's beginners' photography class.

She didn't know the Amsterdams well, but she had urged Bob to sell the tearoom to them rather than to someone else whose bid was several thousand dollars higher, just because she liked them. They were warm and quiet people, and she saw the potential for a couples' friendship there.

"I feel quite at home," Grace said to Ellie.

Lurina heard that and leaned forward. "Good thing too. Just the other day I was sayin' to Joseph Elisha." She poked Old Man's arm. "I was sayin' we ought to be adoptin' Grace as our kin."

"She sure was, and I'm thinkin' it's a right fine idea." Old Man beamed. Sitting beside him, his grandson, Wayne, could not keep his eyes off Sybelle. "I agree. We ought to adopt Miss Grace, and Miss Hannah too."

"Amelia too," Lurina said, before her mind wandered. "The cousins, Wilma and Wanda, are sure missin' a good party."

"They're right good girls. They got them a sick aunt on their mother's side to look after," Old Man said.

Good "girls" of fifty and more, Grace thought, then she smiled at Lurina and Old Man. "I'd be proud as punch to be your kin."

Ellie said, "What a nice thing. I do appreciate you asking me to lunch, when you have so many friends."

Grace looked about her. "Yes, I have friends, but I'd like to know you better, to become your friend."

"I'd like that too," Ellie said.

Grace's eyes grazed the length of the table. At the other end, surrounded by Hank and Laura, Max, Mary Ann and her date, Hannah held court. Max made no effort to disguise the pride he felt when Hannah threw back her head and laughed heartily.

All smiles and dancing eyes, Amelia chatted enthusiastically with the Amsterdams and Mike, Alma, and Billie. Recently returned from the Army, Billie Craine was more self-assured than his relatives. He joked with Molly, whom he'd grown up with, and teased her. He teased Millie also. Millie returned his jibes in kind. Even Brenda seemed to have shed her sadness, for she talked animatedly for a time with Hank and Laura.

Only Ginger seemed distracted, sometimes staring up into the oak tree, sometimes studying her daughter and grandchild, speaking rarely, eating primly, as if she required a taster before she dared eat the food before her. Grace sensed the agitation, the lack of peace in the woman's soul. What would make her happy? she wondered, and decided it was not her job to provide the answer.

The children ate on their laps under the great oak, then rushed to continue populating the big glass jar with minnows. Grace's eyes rested on baby Melissa asleep in her cradle, which was propped on a chair between Russell and Emily. Love filled her heart and waxed large in her chest as if it were the biggest, brightest harvest moon.

Above in the great oak, squirrels leaped and played. A nut plunked onto the table, followed by bits of bark. Grace squinted against the glare as the sun slipped farther south and filtered through branches. What did I ever do that heaven so smiled on me, so blessed me with friends, with love, a new family, and a solid community? She looked at Hannah, smiling and chatting animatedly with Ellie Lerner, and Amelia engrossed in conversation with Mike.

Looking in the mirror recently, Grace could swear that she looked younger than when they had arrived in Covington. The light in Amelia's eyes, the spring in Hannah's step, the quiet calm she saw in her own face when she looked into her mirror—all were indications of contentment, and she thought of a quote from John Barrymore: "No one becomes old until regret takes the place of dreams."

At that instant, Bob's eyes found hers, and he grinned, a happy, slightly silly grin that made her want to be alone with him. Grace reached across their cups and plates for his hand, aware of how deeply she loved this man and how rich her life had become. In fact, she thought, as she looked again at Hannah and Amelia, Covington has given all of us a bounty beyond our wildest dreams.

THOMASTON PUBLIC LIBRARY
THOMASTON, MAINE